SHATTER

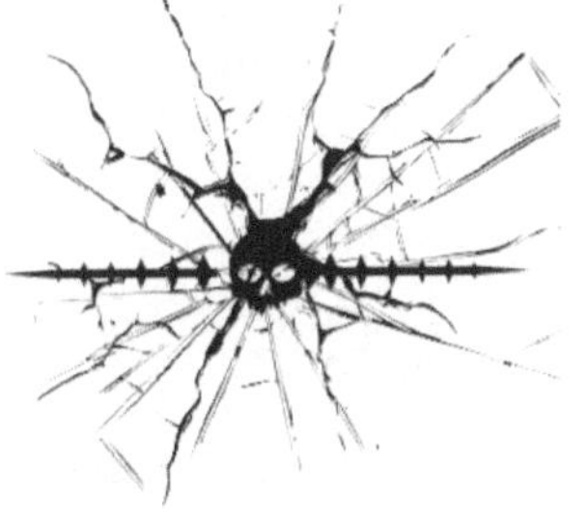

MELISSA SILVA

DEDICATION

To all the baddies out there, hold out for someone who will love you with all their heart, kill for you, and fuck you senseless.

TRIGGER WARNINGS

Violence
Physical Assault
Mention of Sexual Assault
Graphic Death Scenes
Sexually Explicit Scenes
Language
Torture
Death
Grief
Depression
Mention of Suicide
Anxiety
Verbal Abuse
Murder
PTSD
Child Death (Reese works at a children's hospital)
Mental Health
Graphic Violence
Emotional Warfare
Mental Breakdown
Edging
Exhibitionism
Voyeurism
Primal Play

PLAYLIST

FEAR- NF
Symmetry- SYML
Therapy- Voila
Serpent Kiss- drunken night
Petals- Voila
Devil in your eyes- Omido, Ex Habit
So Far So Fake- DarkLux, Xizt
Do I Wanna Know?- Dove Cameron
GhostFace- Drayce Music
STARVING FOR YOU- Cody Marrow
Power- Isak Danielson
Who Will Save You- Katie Garfield, Obeds
Save Your Soul- Lexxi Saal
COLD BLOODED- Chris Grey
Devil In Her Eyes- Bryce Savage
Sinner- Shaya Zamora
Ordinary Human- OneRepublic
Royalty- Egzod, Maestro Chives, Neoni
Rule the World- Zayde Wolf
You're Somebody Else- flora cash
A Storm Is Coming- Tommee Profitt, Liv Ash

COPYRIGHT

ISBN: 978-1-998500-31-4

PROLOGUE

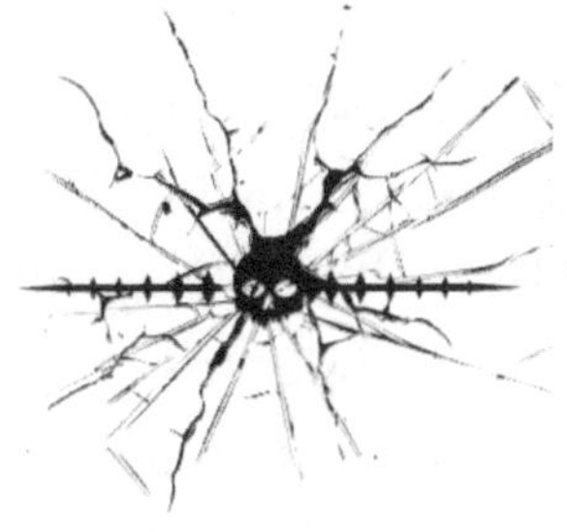

REESE

"I can't believe she killed herself."

"I wonder if there were problems at home. Jackson seems really kind, but we never know what's going on behind closed doors."

"That poor child. The fact he found her like that."

I look up when my mom squeezes my hand, her lips set into a sad smile. "Let's go, sweetie."

"But, mom—"

"We don't need to be here. The police will deal with this, and this isn't something a young boy should witness."

"But what about him?" I ask, pointing to the kid standing next to his dad while they wheel off his mother in a body bag. "He has to see."

She crouches down beside me and cups my cheeks, leaning in closer, like she doesn't want the others standing around gawking to hear her. "He has no choice, Reese. It's his mom, and unfortunately, he has to be a part of it. You don't."

"She's not coming back, is she?" She shakes her head. "Won't he be sad?" I look over towards the kid that looks to be about my age. His eyes are blank—unblinking. He doesn't even pay attention to his dad when he talks to him, only snapping out of it when he settles his hand on his shoulder and squeezes. "He's not crying."

"He's in shock. Losing someone you love is difficult and people handle it differently."

"Is he going to be okay?"

"I don't know, baby."

I can't take my eyes off of him. There's a nagging need to go up to him and hug him—to tell him it'll be okay. I've seen him at school, but I've never talked to him. He usually keeps to himself, only talking to a few people if they talk to him first. He doesn't try to make friends, and I've never felt like I should talk to him before, but now? Now I feel like I need to be in his life.

That nagging keeps pushing and pushing, like a voice in my head wanting—no, *needing* to make things right. This wasn't supposed to happen. His mom wasn't supposed to die. I don't know why I know that, but I can *feel* it. My mind feels a bit foggy and my body sways before everything becomes suddenly black.

I blink, confusion taking over.

How did I end up here?

My mom's eyes meet mine in the rearview mirror, that sad smile now bleeding into her eyes. Panic settles into me because I don't remember getting in the car. What just happened? How did I get in the car? Did I pass out? The last thing I remember was the kid staring blankly at his dad and the weird voice in my head wanting me to check on him.

"Mom?" I ask quietly. "What happened when we left?"

"What do you mean, baby?"

"Did I..." How do I even ask without sounding crazy? "Did I say or do anything weird?"

She frowns, tipping her head enough to glance at me quickly over her shoulder. "I wouldn't say it was weird; you were sweet. You went up to the boy and talked to him and gave him a hug."

Why would I do that?

Even though that voice in my head wanted me to check on him, I wasn't planning to go up to him. Especially not when his mother *just* died. He probably thought I was a weirdo for doing that, and now I'm cringing at the thought of running into him at school.

"I'm sure Kaine appreciated it, Reese. His dad didn't seem to know what to do or how to get him out of his own head. He didn't really react to anything or anyone until you went up to him."

Kaine. The kid's name is Kaine.

"You and Kaine Montgomery could become friends."

CHAPTER ONE

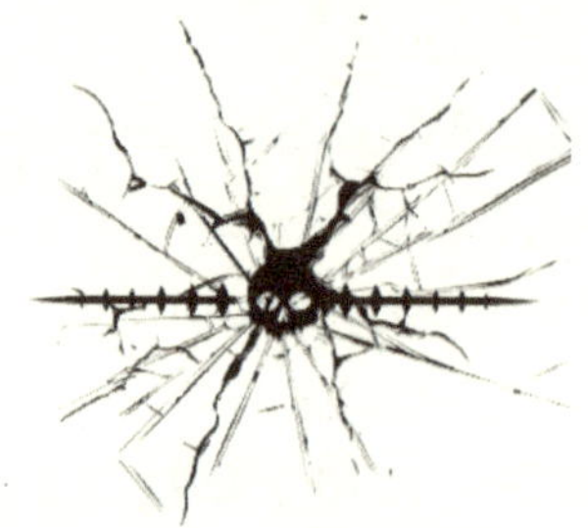

REESE

I hear him in my head.

"Let me in. Let me in if you want to save them."

I'm not aware and have no control over my body, but the words 'save them' have me agreeing to something I know nothing about.

I jolt upright in bed, sweat clinging to my skin while the sheet pools around my waist. I can't catch my breath and my eyes burn, trying to focus in the darkness of my bedroom. My head throbs and my ears ring, and I startle at the gentle touch against my arm.

"Reese?"

Air burns in my lungs as I try and fail to pull in a proper breath. It rattles out of me when I turn my attention to Ronnie lying next to me. Even in the darkness, I can see the worry creasing her brows. Her touch comes again, stroking up my arm to cup my cheek.

"I'm okay. I—I need to get ready for work."

She turns towards the clock on the nightstand when I shift myself to the edge of the bed. I can't get my body to stop shaking, my legs not wanting to stay stable under me and forcing me to sit longer than I want to. I need a shower. I need *something* to try and burn away the nightmare that's slowly playing in my head while awake.

"It's still really early. Your shift isn't for like three hours."

"I need to go in early," I lie, not wanting to worry her. It's not like I can tell her the truth about any of it. It's not just for the fact the events of the past are so far out of the normal world that she wouldn't believe it, but for the fact I don't need to drag her down into the dark void that's been swallowing me piece by piece.

I haven't felt normal for a long time, but after that day, things seem to have gotten worse. It's like there's a barrier erected within my mind. A massive obsidian wall that's hiding secrets and truths from me. No matter how much I pound against it—scrape and claw—I can't break through.

"Okay. I think my shift ends before yours. What do you want for dinner?"

"Whatever you want is fine."

I don't look back at her as I make my way to the bathroom. Ronnie has been amazing. The one good thing that came out of the shit show surrounding Kaine and Eden. I wasn't planning to date anyone, not with the way I've been living my life and the shady shit I'm still involved in. Slowly, I've been trying to pull myself away from that side of the family, but they know what I did. I thought I was careful about the cameras at the farmhouse, but the fuckers had more put in since I was last there.

They know I still have my hands dirty, covered in blood and gore, no matter how much I've tried to convince them that I'm out.

What a joke.

I was never getting out, and the last thing I want is to pull anyone else into my drama. Ronnie is too good and innocent to be involved with me, but I can't seem to find the strength to break it off with her.

I shudder against the burn of the water beating against my skin, but my breaths won't even out. Fragments of memories keep coming in like broken pieces trying to find their rightful place. My best friend bleeding out, the love of his life lying limp with that psycho Professor hovering over her, and then everything stops. Like time freezing with just a thought, and then my body is moving on its own.

The creature inside of me doing things that shouldn't be possible, but I'm no longer surprised by the idea of supernatural beings existing. It burns. This thing that took me over is trying to keep the pain down, but he's too strong to be in this body—a vessel not meant to be wielded in this way, but strong enough to withstand his soul. That's what it is. A pure, undiluted soul.

Shivers rake up my spine at the phantom sensations still lingering in my mind and body. It *still* burns, like the being inside of me left a permanent mark on me. I don't know if he's gone now, but I don't feel right. I wish I didn't remember. I wish I could tear and claw at the pieces flashing behind my eyes so that I could just forget what I went through.

I don't regret Kaine and Eden being saved, and I would do anything for my best friend, but is this too much of a price to have been paid?

Avery.

The fucking reaper that thought it was a good idea to ride me like a war horse into battle. The feeling of being used makes me sick to my stomach and I retch, fighting back the rising bile in my throat. I can barely keep myself standing, my arms shaking against the glass while my mind continues to play through everything. Another piece of myself breaks off, floating away in the current of my fucked-up life.

Kaine doesn't know the full truth of my life or my past or the future that's trying to be decided for me. I thought I could escape it or at least run away long enough to have some semblance of a life, but again, *at what cost*? I swear if anyone threatens my friends—my *chosen* family—I'll fucking end them all. I have enough blood on my hands that the skin has been permanently inked in red, but not on the surface. No. That truth lies deep beneath the surface. A secret I still fighting to keep.

The shower does me no favours. It doesn't ease the tension in my body or chase the chill that's settled deep into my bones. Ronnie is fast asleep again and guilt settles into me at how short I was towards her when I first got up. My limbs tremble as I pull on my clothes, the scrubs beginning to fit a bit looser than they did a few months ago.

I haven't been feeling well. Between slowly becoming more and more mentally unstable, and the fact that I keep replaying scenes from my past in my head which are making me physically ill, I've lost a bit of weight. Ronnie has mentioned it already, but I just brushed it off, telling her that I've just been stressed with the new placement. Don't get me wrong, I love my job, but it does tend to take a toll on me.

Working with kids has been my dream, mainly because I don't expect to have any of my own. I would love to, but I wouldn't want to bring a child into my fucked-up world. My own life wasn't the worst, but it wasn't normal either. Up until my mother finally pulled away from the family, escaping from that fucked-up life and my fucked-up dad. I didn't even keep his name, taking on my mother's maiden name once we left the life behind us.

The kids I've been working with lately have been amazing though. No matter what's been thrown at them, they keep such a positive outlook on life. I'll admit, I second-guessed taking on the position in the pediatric ward, having originally wanted to just be a general practitioner specializing in children, but seeing their smiles when they look at me has brought me more joy than I expected.

I haven't been working there long, but there are a few already that I'm not looking forward to seeing their end. Between autoimmune diseases and cancer treatments, they're strong little things, fighting for their lives. I haven't lost any of them yet, but it's only a matter of time.

CHAPTER TWO

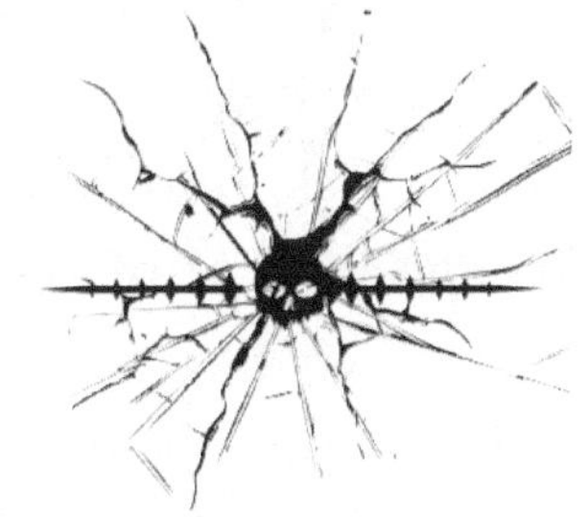

REESE

"Dr. Reese!"

I smile at the wide, toothy grin greeting me. "How's the best princess doing today?"

Julia giggles, brushing her blonde locks behind her ear. I frown when I see a chunk of it come out, tangling in her fingers. She notices it, too, her mouth popping open in shock. Her eyes glisten, tears welling along her pale lashes as she hiccups out a sob.

"It's okay," I say quietly, carefully taking the strands from her. She rubs her eyes, but the tears won't stop coming. I tuck the chunk of hair into my scrub pocket and sit down on the edge of her bed, brushing my hand gently over her head. "Breathe, Julia. It's okay. You look beautiful today."

"Really?" She sniffles, peeking at me through her fingers.

"Really. You're always beautiful, but today you look extra radiant."

"Why are you so nice to me?"

"Do you want me to be mean?" She shakes her head. "You deserve someone who is nice to you. You're a sweet princess who deserves to be pampered." I brush my fingers lightly against her ear and she breaks out into a fit of giggles. "Where's your mom and dad?"

Her face falls and she fidgets with the edge of her blanket, not wanting to look at me. "Mommy and daddy were yelling earlier. Daddy left and mommy came in to say she would be back after my tests."

I frown. Her tests were completed over an hour ago. It's not like them to leave her here like this, without at least one of them present for moral support. "Okay. I'm sure she'll be back soon." I pull her into my side, my heart breaking when her little fingers dig into my back, clinging to me and any form of affection she can absorb. "Try and get some sleep."

She nods, shifting down into the bed and closing her eyes. I grab her clipboard, hating the results that came back from the latest labs. The cancer has spread further through her system, and at this point, I think the chemotherapy treatments are doing more harm than good. I'll have to talk to her oncologist and see what the next steps will be, but they're not looking good.

The thought that this sweet girl could be gone tomorrow sits like a boulder in my stomach. My steps are slow as I make my way towards the door, glancing back at her as I dim down the overhead lights. It's the least I can do for her; a small comfort in this cold medical building which she's now bound to.

"Can we get a couple more blankets in Julia's room?"

Nurse Kyla looks up at me, blinks, then glances past me to the door. "Is she cold?"

"Just get the blankets," I snap.

This is one thing I hate about this place. The staff is great for the most part, but there are a few who really don't give a shit. They're here to earn their paycheck, bragging about their title, but not putting the effort into actually doing their damn job. Plenty of them are overworked, the hospital being short staffed, even with the number of graduates that came out of Cameron this past year. A few of my classmates ended up moving or picking hospitals that were more privatized.

I can't blame them. Places like this expect long hours for shitty pay, but I stayed. I didn't want to abandon the kids here. I had my placement here, and I grew attached to some of the patients, Julia being one of them. She was the first official case I took on, and I plan to stay with her until the bitter end.

Kaine went the general practitioner route, preferring the stable hours and less heavy cases, but I can't blame him for wanting something simple after his entire life has been a giant complication. Eden isn't even practicing officially. She dove headfirst into the research aspect of the field and hasn't looked back. She's thinking about teaching at some point, once she gets what she wants out of her deep dive into medical phenomenon. She's still looking into Lazarus, wanting a more in-depth, formal take on the syndrome.

I turn away from the nurse, grabbing the next file for the next patient, but I pause when I notice a dark shadow creeping across Julia's door. Panic settles into me and my feet are moving before I register it. Ripping the door open, I freeze, watching the shadow shifting towards the girl's sleeping form.

"Hey!" The shadow stops and wavers. "Get away from her," I growl, my body coiling with anger.

"What's going on?"

I startle when Kyla comes up beside me, peeking into the room. "You don't see it?"

"See what?" She frowns, sliding the dimmer up to wash the room in light again.

The shadow is gone, leaving a sleeping Julia in its wake. "Never mind, I think—I think I need some sleep. I'm going to take my break."

Pushing past her and tossing the file back onto the desk, I head to one of the break rooms, turning off the lights the second I step through the door. The light burns my eyes, and the persistent pounding in my skull isn't helping the situation any.

Was I imagining it? I know I haven't been sleeping well, but I didn't expect myself to start hallucinating. I'm not exactly sleep deprived so none of it makes any sense to me. What was that? The shadow sent goosebumps rippling across my skin, but at the same time, I felt a sense of...familiarity. The thought is right there, just behind the veil in my mind, but the moment I reach out and try to grab it, it floats away on a phantom wind.

CHAPTER THREE

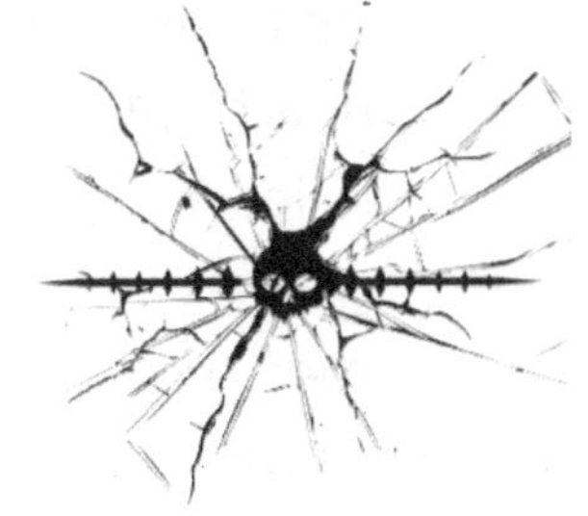

REESE

I'm exhausted by the time I get home. It's not even physical at this point, my mind just seems so fragmented and chaotic. The day itself wasn't the best for me, and after my short-lived break, I ran into problem after problem. It's like the floor was cursed, finding everything possible to go wrong. Multiple patients coded and Julia's parents never came back the entire time I was there. What could have possibly happened for them to abandon their child when she needed them the most?

I couldn't handle calling them to tell them the news, leaving that problem to her other doctor to deal with. If I spoke to either of them, I would have lost my shit, and I know I can't let my personal feelings interfere with my work.

Soft music greets my ears and the subtle scent of cinnamon wafts through the apartment. I drag my hand down my face, trying to lock down my stupid thoughts so I don't upset Ronnie in the process. She's been great, supporting me and talking to me when she notices me slipping. I haven't fully lost it in front of her, but I worry that it's only a matter of time.

She's at the stove in only a long T-shirt—one of mine more than likely. Her body sways to the music, the cute messy bun on the top of her hair shifting around loosely. She hums softly to the tune, stirring whatever the contents are in the massive pot in front of her. Her body stiffens for a second when I wrap my arms around her from behind and bury my face in her neck. She smells like lilacs and vanilla, and I pull her scent into me, loving the way it settles my nerves and relaxes my body.

"Smells good," I murmur, kissing her neck.

She shivers and leans back into my, lifting her free hand to grip into my forearm. "I made chili."

"Hmm, I was talking about you, but the chili is nice, too."

"You're ridiculous," she says breathlessly.

I got really lucky with her. After Kaine threw me under the bus and made it public knowledge that I was available to the majority of the girls in our classes, I had an annoying influx of interest in me. I didn't want any of them, and I wanted to pummel Kaine for doing that to me. I don't date. I haven't since high school, and that was for a very good reason. It's dangerous being around me.

Hanging out with Eden was the small joy that I allowed myself. I never got close to women and never entertained any of their advances. Admittedly, I was a bit jealous of Kaine. Not for having Eden because I wasn't interested in her in that way and she wasn't interested in me either. I think that's why I enjoyed her company so much. Being able to be around someone of the opposite sex without the expectations and awkwardness that comes from it. There's always an ulterior motive, at least with all the girls I had come in contact with. All of them...except Veronica.

Now, Kaine was extreme in his psychotic, overprotective behaviour, but with his level of trauma, I couldn't exactly expect anything less. It still irritated me how mad he would get just for me touching her, but everything with her was innocent. I was starving for some form of friendship from her—a friendship other than Kaine's. Little did I know she had just as much trauma as Kaine, something I seem to be attracting like I'm some sort of emotionally damaged magnet that draws in the mentally unstable and unhinged.

I'm no better. Like calls to like, and my own unhinged side—even if it was hidden—was obviously pulling in others like me in. At least they're both controlled versions of unhinged, unlike Conrad and Stephen. I would have done the same thing in Kaine's shoes in that situation, and I wouldn't have had a single issue in dealing with Stephen myself without Kaine watching.

It felt good. It felt *right*. I haven't let that side of myself out for a long time, and feeling the collar loosen was something I didn't think I would get to experience again.

That was the point of all this. Changing my name to officially cut ties with the dark side of my family and carve my own path. I wanted more for myself, and they've left me alone for the most part. They still try to ask me for favours, trying to draw me back into that lifestyle and depravity, but I can't do it. If I have any chance in surviving and living a normal life, I need to keep the darkness within me contained. I can't cut or maim or kill whenever I please.

Kaine thought *he* was the psychotic one, but he's only seen what's above the surface. If he knew what I was really like and what I was capable of with no remorse, he would end our friendship in a heartbeat. He wouldn't want someone like me around Eden. He might not care about his own safety, but his motives and life mission have changed. Everything revolves around her now.

I'm thankful he hasn't pushed me out of his life because he's so focused on her and his job, but he might feel as though it's an obligation at this point. I know too much. In my line of work, someone like me would be killed. Maybe not in the most obvious of ways, but in a discreet sense so no one would be suspicious of ulterior motives.

Ronnie tips her head to the side, trying to look at me, but I bury my face into the crook of her neck again, kissing her shoulder where the shirt has dropped away. She's a small thing, barely reaching my chest in height, but her personality makes up for it.

She's kind and sweet but has a savage tenacity that I adore. She didn't exactly show interest in me, but we hit it off pretty quickly. She reminded me of Eden in a lot of ways with her awkward social skills and quiet tendencies until she was provoked. We happened to sit next to each other in one of the classes, my usual seat being taken by one of Stephen's stupid friends. She was kind, introduced herself and asked me a few questions about my ambitions and plans after graduation. She didn't throw herself at me or make sexual advances, and that was what I needed.

Knowing how happy Kaine was with Eden made me want that for myself, even if it was only for a short while. I know she likes me; enough so that she moved in when I asked her to, but I don't know if she *loves* me. I hope she doesn't. I don't want to end up breaking her heart when shit hits the fan.

"Did you have a good day at work?" She asks, brushing her fingers through my hair and turning in my grip to face me.

I step to the side and press into her, pinning her against the counter. "It was okay. How about your day?"

She shrugs. "A normal day. It was pretty busy and Kaine seemed distracted. I ended up having to pick up some of his slack with the walk-in shift."

"Did he say what was wrong?"

"I think he's just stressing over the wedding."

"I thought they hired a wedding planner. What the fuck is he stressing over?"

She shrugs again and stares at me with those big, beautiful hazel eyes. She's gorgeous—timeless. Nothing about her screams out bombshell, but everything about her adds up in a way that's almost too perfect to exist. She's definitely too good for my sorry ass. I have no idea what she sees in me except for my looks.

"What is it that you like about me?" Fuck, I'm an idiot. The struggle to keep my inside thoughts inside is getting harder with each passing day.

She frowns, reaching her hand up to my jaw. My eyes flutter closed at the gentle touch, her fingers trailing gently against the stubble I've let grow in over the last week.

"Are you sure you're okay?"

"You don't have to answer that," I sigh. "I'm sorry. I'm just...I feel a bit trapped in my own head."

"Look at me." I open my eyes slowly, hating the way her gaze takes on a pitying tone. "I like everything about you. You're sweet, kind, gentle, easy to talk to, and just all around an amazing person." The fact she just named off things about my character and personality says a lot about her. Not one word gets mentioned about my looks. "You're smart, too, and that was one of the things that attracted me to you. You don't take any shit from anyone, but you would do anything for the people you care about."

She grips my jaw and props on her toes as she drags me down to her, pressing her lips softly against mine. The briefest contact possible, but that phantom sensation shoots heat right through my body.

"What's this about?" She asks, her breath ghosting over my lips.

I shake my head, fighting with the need to pull away from her so I don't taint her with my dark thoughts. "So, it's not my looks that drew you in?"

She smiles and kisses me a bit more firmly, tugging my bottom lip between her teeth. "I'm not complaining about your looks, but that wasn't what I liked about you from the start. Do you think I'm superficial like that?"

"No, not at all. I'm just trying to figure you out."

"There's nothing to figure out, Reese. I'm just...me."

CHAPTER FOUR

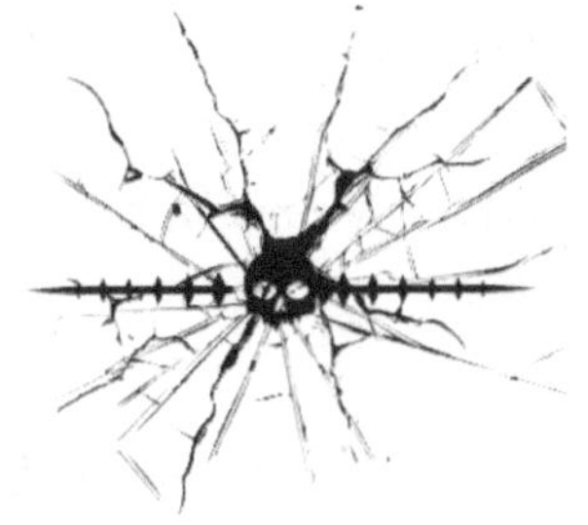

REESE

“Dinner was amazing.” Ronnie sits back in her chair, a smile tugging at her lips while she swirls one of her fingers over the rim of her wine glass. A soft hum begins to resonate, drawing my attention to it in a hypnotic way. “What time do you work until tomorrow?”

“Around the same time as today, but I’m supposed to be meeting up with Eden for drinks after work.” I drop my eyes to the bowl in front of me, swirling the spoon around absentmindedly. “I can cancel if you’d rather I stay home.”

“No. No, you should go. You deserve a night out.”

“What time do you work until?”

"I—I picked up another shift, so I won't be home until later in the night." It's a lie, but I can find work to do if I need to. I feel needy as fuck, not wanting to be left alone longer than I need to with my own thoughts. The lingering thoughts from my dream last night are still swirling around in my head, and no matter what I do to distract myself, they just won't go away.

"You seem off," she murmurs, her chair dragging back against the tile loud enough that I wince. "Sorry."

"It's fine. I'm just tired and I have a bit of a headache. I think I just need to get some sleep."

"Okay. If you're sure..."

She's too observant, noticing the subtle changes in my behaviour like she's naturally gifted in psychoanalyzing me. She's quiet as she washes the dishes but doesn't flinch away when I step in behind her, pressing my body against her back. I love pinning her like this, completely encompassing her body with the subconscious need to protect her, but who can protect her from *me*?

"Thank you for making dinner, Ronnie," I whisper, kissing her cheek and trailing my lips down the side of her neck. She lets out a cute little hum, tipping her head to the side in invitation. It doesn't go unnoticed, and she shudders when I sink my teeth playfully into the tendon on her neck. "I'll have to make it up to you for taking care of me."

"I didn't do it expecting a reward."

"I know you didn't, baby. I know you do these things because you care." Of course she cares. We've been together for almost a year now, even if we only moved in together a few months ago. Kaine ripped into me about that one. Constantly chirping me and calling me a pussy for not taking the leap. He can see how good she is for me, and he thinks I deserve to be happy. He's wrong, but it's the thought that counts.

Her soft whimper when I nip at her again has my body tingling, but I pull away from her. She grips into the edge of the counter, glancing back at me over her shoulder. "I—I should finish cleaning up," she says breathlessly.

"I—do you want me to help you?"

She shakes her head. "It's fine. I'll be in there in a minute."

My heart thumps wildly in my chest as I walk down the hall to the bedroom. We haven't been intimate as much as I think she's hoped we would, but with our fucked-up work schedules barely lining up, we've sort of fallen into a strange dynamic. We're more roommates at this point, going about our day and getting frisky at random. It's not that there's no passion in our relationship, but I'll admit, I haven't been at the top of my game.

I've never been that sex focused to begin with, only having a few hookups when I was younger, and only one relationship that I would consider serious. If you can call dating for three months serious. The girl said she loved me way too soon and I ended up panicking and breaking up with her the next day. Of course, that made me look like an absolute dick since it looked like I just fucked her and left her.

Fuck, I'm seriously an idiot. I don't know if I would have reacted the same way with Ronnie if she ended up dropping the bomb with that one, but I would hope I've matured enough not to freak out over a simple word. It shouldn't hold as much meaning as it does, but everyone always wants that for themselves. Everyone, except me. I don't want that word to be thrown around like it's the most natural thing in the world. Kaine's said it to me before, but he's like a brother to me and that kind of love is different. He's my ride or die, quite literally.

I head for the shower again, once again hoping that the heat of the water burning into my skin will give me some relief from the tension I'm feeling. It's useless, just like it was earlier because this tension is created from my mind. I think back to the shadow that sneaked into Julia's room today. The way it flickered and faded like it was a trick of the mind; something that didn't exist outside my exhausted and delirious brain. I can't believe I'm starting to see things that aren't there.

I should have known that it would happen eventually. The thought that I'm going crazy on top of the issues that I already have, graciously passed down to me from my father, is a horrifying thought. My self-assessments have come back clear; no signs of me breaking the way my father did. That's something I never told Kaine either, but it wasn't a story he needed to know. Not after what he experienced with his mother. He and I are similar in many ways, but none of them are the good kind. I've just done better than he has to keep my issues locked away, neatly tucked into the recesses of my mind where no one can rip them to the surface.

I crank the heat up higher, feeling it burn into my flesh painfully, but I rather the physical pain versus the mental strain I've been feeling all day. *'Save them'*. That voice still echoes in my mind, quickly becoming one that I would recognize if I heard it again.

Fucking Avery.

Why me? Why was I the one chosen to be a reaper's bitch; a fucking vessel for him to do what he wanted. I can't rid myself of the feeling of being used and manipulated. Kaine said that he used me when I was younger as well, but the friendship I formed with him was my own making. How can I be sure? What if my entire life here has been a lie. One that's been chosen for me with a path paved for me to follow without question.

CHAPTER FIVE

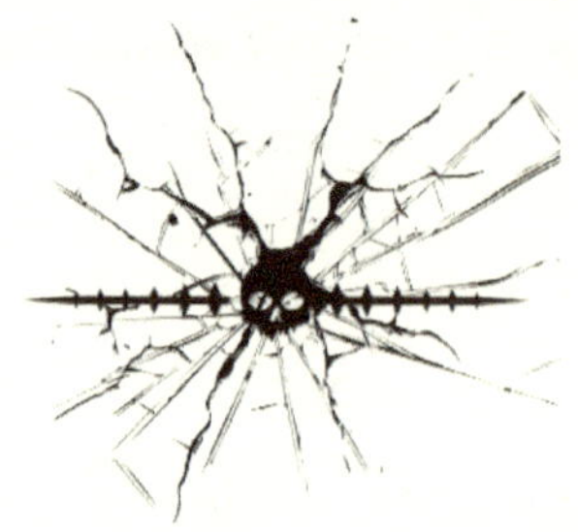

REESE

I freeze in the doorway, my hand gripping the towel tighter around my waist as my eyes fall on the sight in front of me. I swallow thickly, watching Ronnie slowly drag one of her bare legs up against the other in a sensual sweep of skin on skin. The black lace lingerie set leaves barely anything to the imagination, and my cock agrees. The material hugs her curves, merging with her skin in a tantalizing dance of beauty.

"Ronnie, I—"

"Do you not want me anymore?" She asks. I snap my mouth closed, hating the sadness bowing her eyes. I make no move towards her, and I don't say anything because I don't know what to say. Of course, I still want her, but how do I explain to her that I'm not right in the head and she'd be better off leaving my ass behind for someone better. "I see," she murmurs, dropping her eyes and shifting off the bed. She moves quietly towards the closet, pulling out a long white robe to cover herself. Her ass stretches the material, the soft, buttery skin peeking through the lace.

My feet move on their own, everything in my brain screaming at me to just let her go, but my heart is crying out a different tune. I don't want to be alone. I don't want to keep cutting people out of my life because I'm afraid they'll get too close and see just how fucked I am.

"Ronnie, I *do* want you. I'm sorry if I've acted in a way that makes you think I don't."

"You barely look at me, Reese. You can't even handle touching me for longer than a few seconds and you pulled away from me earlier. I thought it was because of me. I thought I was the problem, and you thought I was boring. I'm sorry if I'm not as exciting as your other conquests, but this is all new to me."

"You're not a conquest," I say quickly, gripping her arm and turning her to face me. She keeps her eyes locked on the floor between us, her chest heaving lightly with each panicked breath. "Please, look at me." My heart breaks at the tears pooling along her lashes. In my desperate attempt to not push her and hurt her, I've done it anyways without meaning to. "I promise it's not you. I'm just—I'm fucked in the head right now. I'm struggling and I'm not sleeping right."

"You're still having nightmares?" I nod. "Why won't you talk to me? Why can't you just trust me and tell me what's going on?"

"Because even *I* don't know what's going on!" She flinches, and I realize too late that my grip on her has tightened in my frustration. "Fuck, I'm sorry," I choke out, ripping my hand away from her. She steps towards me and presses her hands to my chest. "Ronnie—"

"Stop. Stop pushing me away, Reese. You say you want me, but you're acting like I'm a roommate." Fuck, she noticed it, too. "Do you...not find me attractive anymore?"

"Of course I do."

"Then why? Even if you're going through shit, you know I'm here for you. I—I lo—"

I slam my mouth against hers, stopping her from saying the words. This is what I was afraid of, but I don't want her to acknowledge those feelings towards me. I can't handle it. Not now and probably not in the future either. Is what I'm doing manipulative? Absolutely, but I don't know what else to do. I don't know how else I can convince her that I *do* want her, even if my mind is fighting against my heart.

"Reese," she pants, lacing her fingers through my hair and tugging on the strands. The sensation radiates up my spine, sending a wave of goosebumps rippling across my skin. I grip into her ass, lifting her up onto my hips and spinning her around. She gasps when I toss her on the bed, her pupils blowing wide and overtaking the golden-green hue of her irises with need. I rip the towel away from my body and climb over her, loving the feel of her soft, cool skin against my heated flesh.

She swallows hard, her eyes drifting down between my legs. At least my body still responds to her the way that it should. I *do* like her and care for her, and she's been an amazing partner who sticks by me and has helped me through some of my lesser rough moments.

"Is this what you wanted?" I murmur, brushing my lips against hers and pressing my body down into her.

"I want you to *want* me, not do this because you feel you have to."

"Do you think I would be able to get this hard if I didn't want you?" I drag my cock against her, the thin material of the silky lace rubbing against me with blissful friction. She tips her head back, her eyes fluttering closed. "Do you think anyone could force me to fuck them?" I grip into the edge of the underwear, ripping it from her body hard enough that she snaps her eyes open at the force. "Do you honestly think that if I didn't want this, I would willing do any of these things." I grip the bra next, tugging down one of the cups to expose her perfect tit.

My breath hums out as I slowly drag my tongue against the swell of her breast, latching onto the quickly hardening nipple. Her tit is soft and warm, perfectly plump and enticing with its soft skin. I swirl my tongue and nip my teeth against it, pulling a small cry from her lips. She tugs at my hair, pulling me up to her mouth to claim me. I can't resist her, quickly giving in and allowing her to guide me to her. I smile against her lips, diving my tongue into her mouth, stroking and devouring every whimper and moan that falls from her lips. She tries to follow me when I pull away, and I smirk, wiping my lips with my tongue as I stare down at her.

She really is beautiful and so fucking willing. I'm sure I could do whatever I wanted to her, and she wouldn't complain about any of it. Her eyes widen when I shift myself back, lowering myself down between her supple thighs. My lips skim the soft skin of her inner thighs, slowly drifting to the heated perfection between them. Her body trembles at the light touch, barely-there grazes that pebble her skin in the wake of my mouth. My eyes roll back when my tongue touches her, the pure bliss of her taste exploding on my tongue. I lick and suck and lap at her clit, nipping at it until she cries out and digs her fingers through my hair. She rips at the strands, her legs curling against my shoulders.

I could drown myself in her taste—completely suffocating myself—and I would love every second of it. My mind is quiet now, my only focus on her. The eerie stillness of my thoughts sends a shiver up my spine, every chaotic thought that has been nagging me all day, getting obliterated because of her. Maybe I'm wrong. Maybe she's the key to stilling my internal storm. For this alone, she deserves to be rewarded.

Two of my fingers glide into her and her hips jerk, her back bowing off the bed. I settle my other hand onto her stomach, pinning her down and forcing her to take what I'm giving her.

"Oh, fuck!" She cries out, and her walls tighten around my fingers, making it difficult to pull them back out.

She's soaked, her legs trembling and falling back down to the bed while her chest heaves with each breath. Her eyes are hooded as she watches me slip my fingers into my mouth, licking each one and swirling my tongue around until I've cleaned every drop of her off them.

"You taste fucking delicious." She squeaks in surprise when I grip into her hips suddenly and yank her towards me. Her eyes follow my hand firmly stroking my cock before pressing the head of it against her. I'm barely inside her but her walls pulse as though begging me to sink into her. So, I do. I thrust into her, muffling her garbled cry with my mouth. The heat of her cradling around me is a welcoming embrace. It feels like it's been so long—too fucking long since I've been buried deep inside her. "You're so tight. You take my cock so well, don't you?"

She whimpers into my mouth, diving her tongue in against mine. My breath shudders out of me as I slowly drag my cock back, thrusting into her again, deeper than before. The bed creaks beneath us, the headboard smacking against the wall with each thrust of my hips. Her voice rings out, soft moans and quiet whimpering mewls that spiral me higher, tightening the band of pleasure building inside of me until I can barely contain myself.

"Such a good girl," I moan, nipping at her lip and jaw, trailing my mouth down the front of her throat and inhaling her deep into my soul. Her nails drag against my back, scraping the skin hard enough that my breath hisses out of me. I bite down on her collar bone, drawing a high cry from her.

Fuck, I love the way she makes me feel. Everything about our encounters is feral and passionate. We started off tentative with our relationship, with chaste kisses and stolen touches, but we both quickly found out what we liked.

I grip into her throat, my fingers tightening until she moans and her eyes roll back. I pound into her again and again, and each scrape of her nails against my skin has the darkness shrouding me receding back. I hate the thought of using her, but she's my anchor in the turbulent storm battering around in my mind. The waves of thought don't crash against the barrier as viciously, her touches and sounds creating a safe haven for me. Ronnie is my peace, and she doesn't even know it.

"Fuck, Reese," she gasps, curling her legs around me and drawing me in deeper. I groan, slamming my mouth against hers and stifling her cry of pleasure. She comes so hard around me that I struggle to keep rutting her. She's panting now, each breath puffing against my lips while I come undone in her hold. "I love you."

My body stiffens, but I'm too spent and my limbs are trembling too hard for me to pull away from her. Why did she have to go and say that? She couldn't possibly feel that way. She's just caught up in her emotions after I fucked her into oblivion. But if that were the case, why does she seem to be in control? Why does she stroke her fingers gently up and down my back soothingly?

"Reese?" She whispers.

"Let me clean you up." My words slur together, and I struggle to pull away from her, but it's all I *can* do. The bed creaks, but I don't look back, making my way towards the bathroom while I try to tame my rapidly beating heart. A small sob filters through the room and that one sound breaks me. Fuck. I know I'm fucking everything up with her. I don't know what the fuck I'm doing. I don't *want* to hurt her, but no matter what I do, I'll end up hurting her one way or another.

I take a minute in the bathroom, staring at myself in the mirror and no longer recognizing the man that stares back at me. I splash water on my face over and over, hoping the frigid liquid can bring some sense of reason back into my brain, but it feels useless. I *can't* say those words back to her. I'm not like Kaine. I can't admit to my feelings that easily because I was brought up in a way that made feelings feel like a weakness. They're useless and easily used against you. Admitting that I love her will just put a target on her back. I mean, look at what happened to Eden.

Kaine showing interest in her and claiming her so publicly basically turned her into a beacon for the dark and depraved fucks that thought it was a good idea to go after her. I know I'm capable of defending myself as well as Ronnie, but I don't want to risk it. I don't want even that fraction of doubt to exist. The stupid what-ifs that pound away in my brain over and over, mixing in with the vehement thoughts consistently telling me I'm fucking useless in the end.

I mean, they're right. I *am* useless. I was useless when it mattered—when Kaine and Eden needed me the most. If it weren't for that reaper fuck taking hold of my body, they would both be officially dead right now. I would have lost my best friend and the only person who gave a shit about me in my darkest days. He gave a piece of shit like me attention and friendship without question. He was broken, too, and I figured, why can't we just be broken together?

My head snaps up at the sound of the front door clicking shut and I bolt out of the bathroom, my breaths sawing in and out of my lungs when I see Ronnie is no longer in bed.

"Ronnie?" I call out, grabbing a pair of sweats off the back of the chair and heading into the main area of the apartment. "Ronnie?"

Nothing.

Silence greets me as well as the darkness. She fucking left me. I really fucked this up.

CHAPTER SIX

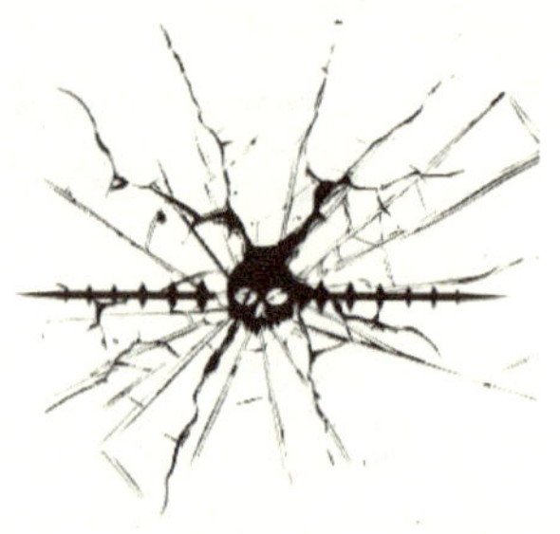

REESE

I feel like ass, and no matter how much coffee I chug back, I can't get rid of the brain fog that's settled into me. I stayed up way too late last night, calling Ronnie over and over again, even when she turned off her phone and forced my calls to go to voicemail. That didn't stop me from leaving message after message of useless and stupid rambling until her mailbox was full. Even then, I still kept calling, hoping that I could catch her before she went into work.

Needless to say, I didn't sleep a wink last night, but it's just as well. I live in hell in my dreams already, so what difference does it make now since I'm experiencing hell in the waking world, too.

Every chance I get at work, my phone is in my hand, mindlessly dialing her number again and again to no avail. She must have known I have an aversion to the words since she's stuck around this long, moved in with me, and has been there for me. I knew it would only be a matter of time, but that was probably the worst timing. What with the way my brain has been fried and trying to process these fucked up memories.

Our relationship isn't *normal*. I wish it were. I wish *I* was normal. I should take this as I sign that I can't actually have anything good in my life because any time I even think that I might have something normal, it gets ripped away from me. Like Kaine. I knew he was fucked up because of everything that happened with his mom, but even with his trauma and the struggles he went through, our friendship was tame in comparison to what it could have been. He saved my ass a few times, and I've done the same for him. He's like a brother to me, and I would never question helping him...even if it meant killing someone and disposing of a body. I would do it again without question because he's all I have left of that life.

With my mother's passing when I started college, he was the only person there to hold me together. I didn't *want* to reach out to my family, and my dad died when I was thirteen, something that didn't really register in my brain. My mother mourned as much as her broken heart would allow, but he wasn't good to her—to either of us. That's why she ran and stayed hidden as long as she did, trying to protect me from the horrors of the family.

It didn't help in the end though, did it? I still got involved with them. Maybe not directly in the heart of it all, but my hands are no longer clean, and I send up a heartfelt apology to my mother for failing her and the life she tried to provide me.

I think if anyone knew my secrets or how fucked I really am, they wouldn't even entertain speaking to me. That's one of the main reasons I keep that shit locked down as much as possible, and the one person I can't afford to lose is Kaine. He's the last tie I have to my old life—the life I lived and the happiness at having a friend care about me. I don't think I would be able to survive it if he decided to no longer be my friend.

It was bad enough when he shunned everyone after the Conrad incident at his house, but I was thankful he didn't lump me in with those assholes. If I had known Stephen and Conrad were like that, I would have ended their lives before they got their hooks in Kaine. It would have been easy, too. Kidnapping them and disposing of their bodies where no one would ever find them.

They're still looking for Stephen, but halfheartedly. By this point, they should just give up. I get it though. They don't want someone accused of drugging girls out in the wild, but I can't exactly tell them that he'll never hurt anyone else without admitting guilt to his untimely demise and removal from this mortal plane.

"Julia's new testing results just came in, if you wanted to take a look at them." My head snaps up, my eyes blinking slowly as I try to focus on Kyla in front of me. She frowns, tipping her head curiously. "Is everything alright?"

"Fine. I just didn't sleep well last night."

Or at all, but I don't need to go around gossiping about the fact my girlfriend left my ass in the middle of the night because I couldn't get out of my head and accept the fact that she loves me.

Fuck.

I'm still pissed about my behaviour, and her even speaking is making me focus on that knowledge once again. I take the clipboard from her, scanning over each test and the results, but each page has my unease growing.

Fuck, these results are worse than the ones that I went through yesterday. It's not looking good for the girl, and I honestly don't know how much time she has left at this point. It'll rely mainly on her and her will to fight, but in the end, she's not going to make it. The cancer has spread through her entire body, and the chemo and radiation has done nothing to slow down the process. My heart tightens at the thought of losing such a young soul. She'll be the first, and she's the one I've grown the most attached to.

"Has the doctor spoken to her parents yet?"

"Her mother is here right now. Her father hasn't been in since yesterday."

The stupid prick. Even if he and his wife are having issues of their own, they should both be here for their kid. He shouldn't be making her suffer, especially now knowing that she doesn't have a lot of time.

"Her birthday is tomorrow," Kyla says quietly. "A few of the nurses were thinking about getting her a cake to celebrate."

"I think that's a wonderful idea." It's the least any of us can do for her. She's been here for six months, and she's had moments where she's done well and seemed lively, only to crash even harder days later. She deserves to have this—a day to celebrate her life. "I'm going to go check on her."

Her smile is sad, her eyes turning pitying, knowing full well that my emotions are on the brink of tipping the scales. She pats me gently on the arm before heading back to her station, leaving me once again with my rampant thoughts.

I'm trying to steady my breathing and clear my mind of the fog as I make my way to her room. The doctor comes out when I reach it, eyes widening when he sees me. "Dr. Mitchel," he murmurs, nodding his head.

"How is she?"

"As good as she can be. We've moved into the quality-of-life phase, so I've stopped the treatments for now. Her mother agreed that it was the best course of action for her final days."

My eyes widen. *Days?* She only has days to live at this point. I thought she would have a bit more time than that, even if the results showed a complete takeover in her body. "Thank you, doctor." I don't know what else to say at this point. I know he can't do anything else for her, but it's still not fair. This is one of the worst diseases to plague the human body. A fucking mutation that knows nothing else than to take over like a parasite and destroy everything good until there's nothing left but a broken soul and a husk of a body.

My hand is shaking by the time I work up the courage to grip into the door handle, and I'm instantly met with the sound of quiet sobs. Julia isn't the one crying, but even in her young body, she smiles, the expression sad, but resolved as she comforts her mother. Diana is curled over her child, sobs shaking her entire body as she clings to her daughter desperately. Julia's eyes drift up to meet mine, so clear now in the wake of her ending life.

"Hi," she says quietly. Her mother jerks upright, quickly wiping away her tears before turning her reddened face towards me. She can't quite meet my gaze, but I can't blame her for that.

"How's my princess doing today?" I smile at Julia, giving Diana a reprieve to compose herself.

"I'm okay."

"You sure?" Her chin wobbles and she drops her eyes down to her lap. She curls her fingers over and over again, her nervous tick I'm realizing. "Julia?"

She pulls in a sharp, unsteady breath, and quickly wipes at her eyes. "It is what it is." The absolute defeat and devastation in those few words have my heart breaking for her. I don't know what to say to her. What *can* I say in a situation like this? The kid is dying and has mere days to live, and anything she could have hoped to do in her life has just been ripped away from her.

"It'll be okay." I cringe at the fact I just said that because how could anything about this possibly be okay?

A dark laugh bubbles out of her, a sound that is so far from a child's it sends a shiver skittering up my spine. "It won't," she says bluntly. "But I'm glad I met you, Dr. Reese."

I move to the other side of the bed and brush my hand down her hair, hating the fact that even more chunks are coming out. I want to hug her to me and protect her from the inevitable, but I can't. I'm weak and useless as a human. I may have been possessed by a reaper, but I don't have the powers of one. I can't decide who lives or dies with the snap of my fingers, but my past mimics that of the supernatural beings hovering in the in-between. I've ended plenty of lives, their souls destroyed in the palm of my hands, but this girl...this girl is someone I want to save.

She's so young and should have years before her end, but life isn't fair. "Try and get some rest." Diana looks up at me then, fresh tears streaking down her cheeks. "Can I speak to you for a moment?" She nods, kissing Julia's forehead before following me out of the room. Now that she's standing, I take in her features, not liking the amount of weight she seems to have lost over the last week. Her cheeks are sunken, her eyes hollow, and her hair is a tangled, oily mess. "Where's Peter?"

"He—I think he's at work."

"You think?"

She shakes her head. "He hasn't been home much the last week, and last night he said he was staying late at work for a while." She chokes back a sob, covering her mouth with her hand. "I think he's cheating on me, but I hate that he can't just be here for her. I don't care about myself, but Julia needs her dad."

I do something I probably shouldn't and wrap my arms around her, squeezing her close to my body. Hugs are so underrated, and Eden showed me that. I know how much they can affect your mental state, allowing you a small fraction of acceptance for whatever you're going through at that moment.

"You're here and that's all that matters. When everything is said and done, you're the one who was strong and stood by your daughter when she needed you. Don't let some useless man control you or your life."

"You really are kind. Julia speaks so highly of you and what you've done for her while she's been here. I'm glad you were able to bring a small bit of joy and happiness into her life."

"I'm so sorry that you couldn't receive better news, Diana."

"I'm struggling to accept it. I don't know what I'm going to do. How do I go on knowing that my baby is going to—she's going to die." She sobs again, burying her face into my chest and I squeeze her harder. "I don't know if I can survive it. A parent shouldn't outlive her child at any age, but she's so young. What did I do in the past for this to happen to her? She's innocent. She doesn't deserve to die. If I could take her place, I would."

Just another reason I don't want children of my own. I don't think I could handle this type of grief or the responsibility of caring for something so small and innocent. I never had any pets growing up either, though, I was quite fond of cats. I would feed the strays in my neighborhood, but that was as much as I would allow myself.

"You should go be with her." She pulls back from me, wiping her eyes again and finally tipping her head up to look at me. She smiles. It's genuine and kind, even if it's filled with sadness. She doesn't say anything else, but she doesn't need to. I know what she's feeling, and I wish I could change the outcome of Julia's fate.

My phone vibrates in my pocket, and I look like an idiot scrambling to grab it. My small hope is quickly crushed when I notice Kaine's number on the screen and not the person I was hoping for. I push the call to voicemail, not feeling up to talking to him at the moment. It buzzes again seconds later though, and now I'm wondering if something has happened.

"I'm at work," I say quickly, walking down the hall, away from prying eyes and dumbo ears.

"I figured as much, but I also thought I should call you anyways. Did something happen last night?"

"What do you mean?"

"Between you and Ronnie. She's been weird all day, and I caught her crying in the break room. When I asked her what was wrong, she just gave me a dirty look and left. I know she's supposed to be hanging out with Eden tonight, but I wanted to make sure everything was okay."

For someone who pretends not to give a shit about anyone, Kaine's heart is way too big for his own good. "She walked out last night," I admit. The line is silent for a few beats, long enough that I pull the phone away from my ear to check if the call is still connected. "Kaine?"

"What the fuck happened?"

I *really* don't want to talk about it, but his obsessive ass will just hound me until I spill the details. He's a bit of a gossip whore, more now than he was before since we're not in the drama like we used to be.

"I'm at work, Kaine. I really don't want to talk about this right now."

"Do you want to grab a drink later? I get it if you don't, but I'll be all alone, wondering what Eden is doing, and if there are any guys I need to pummel once she gets home for even looking at her funny."

"You're ridiculous," I snort. His sense of humor always seems to pull me out of my slumps.

"What? She's hot, and you know how guys are. I mean *you're* a guy."

"True, but I don't think of your fiancé in that way."

"You better not," he grumbles, and I roll my eyes.

"Seriously, dude, when are you going to get over the fact Eden and I are friends? You're getting married for fuck's sake, and you were basically told that you're soulmates. I don't think a mere human like me can come between that."

"Yeah, but your tall, and buff, and really smart, and you're funny, and—"

"You're spiraling." He sighs on the other end, and I can just picture him, losing his cool because of his obsession with his girl. "Fine, I'll meet you for drinks."

"Really?" He asks, failing miserably at hiding the happiness in his voice. He may have won this battle, but the war is just starting.

"Yes, really. I'll go home and change and meet you somewhere. Is there a specific place you want to go?"

"Hmm, why don't we go to Night Owl. The drinks are cheap there and they have great appetizers."

"Alright. I'm off at seven."

He hangs up the phone, and for the first time today, I feel a bit lighter. That ever-present darkness that has been trying to swallow me up has receded back into the corners of my mind, even if it's only for a short while. I still try to call Ronnie again, but my calls are still being pushed to the already full voicemail, and now I'm wondering if she blocked my sorry ass.

CHAPTER SEVEN

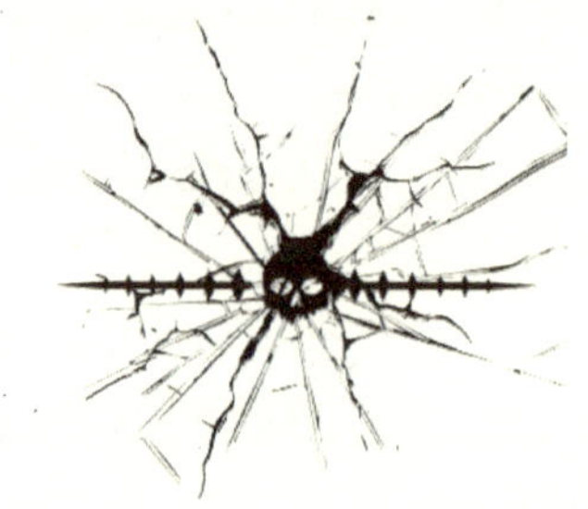

REESE

Kaine flops down into the seat across from me, startling me out of my thoughts. He smiles when he notices the beer waiting for him and grabs it, chugging half of it before setting it down and leaning back into the booth.

"So..."

"So..." I mimic, quirking a brow.

"Your girlfriend is currently at my apartment with Eden, and let's just say, I couldn't get out of there fast enough. I think if I hung around any longer, I would be getting yelled at on your behalf."

My shoulders slump and I drop my eyes, picking at the label on my own beer. "She was upset?"

"If you can call it that. What the fuck did you do?" I open my mouth to finally tell him, but the waitress pops up out of nowhere with her little pad in hand. Kaine doesn't even look at the poor girl, his eyes locked on me while my attention shifts between him and her. "Can we just get an order of nachos and the wings. We'll take honey garlic on them."

"Oh...okay," she says carefully, glancing down at me. I just roll my eyes and nod my head, letting go of the fact he just ordered for me like I don't get a choice in the food.

"Spill it."

"She said she loved me." He leans forward and frowns, his lips pressing into a thin line. "I...didn't say it back. If anything, I made it worse because I didn't even acknowledge the fact she said it."

"You guys have been dating for almost a year, and you've never said you love each other?" I shake my head. "Why the fuck not? Do you *not* love her?"

"I *care* about her."

"That's not what I asked. Why are you together then? You moved in together and I thought everything was going great with you guys. You seem perfect for each other, too. Obviously not as perfect as me and Eden, but we're like, God-tier relationship goals."

His ego somehow still astounds me. He's not wrong though. To actually be soulmates, their relationship *was* blessed by the gods to some degree. I couldn't imagine having that type of relationship or unabashed devotion from someone else.

"I don't know, dude. I feel like that's just what was expected at that point."

"If your relationship is based on expectations and not feelings, you shouldn't be in it. It's not fair to you *or* her at this point."

"I know it's fucked up to say, but I can't picture my days without her there though. Last night was rough and I didn't get a wink of sleep because of it. I've called her so many times but she's ignoring my calls."

"This isn't easy for her, at least from what I witnessed. She was really upset today."

"Did she mention where she stayed?"

"I heard her telling Eden she went to her dad's. She didn't seem too happy about it, and I'm a bit worried if Eden extends her an invitation to stay at our place. I can't exactly fuck Eden where I want if she's there."

"Her dad's? She hasn't even talked to him in ages." He shrugs, sipping on his beer. "Come to think of it, I haven't met her dad."

"She hasn't met your family either, though."

"You *know* why. If I can avoid interacting with them, I will, and my mom is dead. As far as I'm concerned, I don't have any family." He frowns and I roll my eyes. "Except for you," I add, pulling a wide grin from him.

"I'm the best and only family you need."

"Coming from someone who *has* family and doesn't speak to them."

"Pot. Kettle," he says, jabbing his finger into his chest and then at me. "Your family hasn't done anything to you directly, while mine has been nothing but a problem and secretly hating the relationship I have with Eden."

If he only knew what my family had done to me. I mean, not directly for a long time, not since we lived with my dad, but the extended family was no better after the fact. They've pulled me into their world, giving me a bit of freedom, but the leash hasn't come off, it's only been extended until they decide to recall me. I wish I could escape them, but it's too late now. I've established myself and my life here, and I have no desire to uproot everything to go on the run. It's not like I can hide though, not unless I give up my career completely. Having to use my name would give them an easy way to find me, and I don't want to tap into my connections to change my identity...not for this.

I just have to suck it up and grin and bear it until I can figure out another way out of what is expected of me when they decide it's time to collect.

Seriously, if Kaine knew who I was—who I *really* was—he wouldn't be my friend. The Brennan family isn't as well-known as some, but we keep to the darker parts of that society, so people don't anticipate the things we end up doing in the shadows. Fuck me. I hate that even in my head I'm still associating with them and their ways, but I want *out*. I want to escape that world and the clash of titans.

The family has enemies, most of them do anyways. We're technically part of the mafia, but not directly. My uncle is more involved than my father was, but he was the younger of the two males in the family and wasn't straddled with that responsibility.

Uncle Declan took the reins with a smile on his face and a dream in his mind, pushing his territory further and further until they finally clapped back. It's been quiet enough for the last couple of years, and they've left me alone for the most part while

I finished my program, only asking for favours here and there that were still terrible in the moral sense, but nothing compared to what I've done in the past.

"My family doesn't give a shit about me, Kaine. They never have and never will." We go quiet when the waitress shows back up with our food, setting the plates down in the middle for us to share. She stands there, expectantly, but when Kaine glares at her, she just pulls in a sharp breath and scurries off. "I see your real personality is in full force today."

He shoves a chip into his mouth, crunching it loudly between his teeth. "There's no one here I need to impress. If these people don't like the real me, they can fuck off."

"I'm surprised Eden likes the real you if this is how you act."

"She happens to adore me, actually. I also don't act like a total dick in front of her much since we both know how that turns out."

The memory of what happened to her the last time Kaine lost his shit shoves itself into the forefront of my mind. "Has she...slipped again?"

He shakes his head, twisting a random jalapeño between his fingers. "She's been pretty good. She seems happy, and I plan to keep her that way. She's excited about the wedding, even if certain things tip her over on the emotional scale."

"It'll get easier once it's over. Weddings are a big deal to girls, and they just want everything to be perfect."

"If it's not perfect, I'm going to snap. I swear to fucking god I will murder someone if something happens." I quirk a brow, pausing my chewing. "Too soon?"

I laugh, the first genuine laugh in a while it seems. "You're sense of humour is a bit fucked."

"Yet you're still my friend," he grins.

"It would take a lot more than that for me to stop being your friend."

His smile falters and his eyes drop down to the table. It's interesting to see how quickly his mood changes with the smallest comment, but I didn't say it for him to shut down.

"I really appreciate you. I don't know what I would do if I didn't have you in my life, Reese. I wouldn't have survived last year if you weren't there, and Eden would be dead, too."

"That wasn't me, it was Avery. If I could have done something myself, I would have, even if it meant going up against a psychotic rogue reaper to save you."

He shakes his head. "But you were there. You were there through all the hard shit, and you didn't freak out when you learned the truth about me and what I did, and about Eden."

"Trust me when I say this, Kaine, nothing you could ever say or do would push me away."

Fuck me, his cheeks actually redden and a goofy grin tugs at his lips when he looks up at me. "I love you, man."

"I love you, too."

He blinks, tipping his head curiously. "You didn't even hesitate."

"What?"

"You said you love me, but with Ronnie, you haven't said it."

Fuck, he's right. I didn't even think about it when I said it back to him, but when Ronnie said the words, I wanted to run away and hide in a corner. When she said it, it felt like she was trying to strip me bare. Like she was trying to tear down the carefully crafted walls I've put up around myself. With Kaine, it's easy because he's familiar and my brother. Maybe not in blood but chosen family ends up having a stronger tie than those forced to acknowledge you.

"You know that it's different with you, Kaine. You know way more about me than I'll ever consider telling Ronnie. You've been with me since we were kids and we grew up together, eventually experiencing similar heartbreak in losing our moms. With you it's easy to say because I consider you a brother, and the love I have for you is different than the one expected of me when being said to someone like Ronnie."

"You don't trust her." He doesn't bother to word it like a question, clearly sensing where my mind has headed and is now firmly lodging itself within the boulder of this fucked up thought process.

"Maybe eventually, but not right now—not like that. Would I do what I need so I can protect her? Absolutely. I care about her and that won't change. I've spent almost an entire year with her, where I talked to her or saw her one way or another. This isn't something I can just lose feelings over or cut out of my existence."

I say that, but if I was thrown into a choice of choosing her over Kaine, I don't know what I would do. The right choice *should* be her. That's the standard and the expectation of the white knight I'm meant to be, but if Kaine died, it wouldn't just be the loss of him, it would be the loss of Eden as well. They won't survive without the other, and the thought of losing two souls instead of one should push my decision correctly.

"That's pretty fucked up." I glare at his bluntness, but the fucker just shrugs his shoulders and shoves another loaded chip in his mouth. "Being with someone every day like that, you should trust her. Now, I'm not saying you need to divulge all your deepest, darkest secrets because that takes time, but there should be trust there, Reese. Are you scared?"

"Of what?"

"Of the relationship. Of your feelings for her and the lack of empathy you seem to be showing. This isn't like you, man. You're not cold, far from it, but you're distancing yourself *within* your relationship."

"I didn't realize you went on to specialize as a psychiatrist. You shouldn't be psychoanalyzing me when you've got enough problems on your own that you barely deal with."

"First off, I give great advice, and I don't need a medical license to prove that. Second, I've dealt with my problems, and I don't hide shit from Eden. My temper has gotten better, and I've been patient with her."

"Yet your psychotic obsessive tendencies seem worse than before."

"Hardly. I haven't actually *hurt* anyone because of her. I've done my ten steps and I'm on my road to recovery."

"Ten steps?" What the fuck kind of program could he possibly be on that supposedly cures him from his weird ass behaviour.

He grins, nodding his head excitedly and leaning on the table towards me before lowering his voice. "Yup. Step one: acknowledge you're a psychopath." I snort, quickly covering it with a cough at the feral glare he pins me with. He clears his throat, jutting his chin out. "Step two: when in doubt, fuck that doubt out of them."

I can't help it, I cackle, earning some glares from the other patrons. "That's not part of any ten-step program I know."

"It's loosely based and taken from different sources. Obviously, I modified it so that I was more likely to stick to it, and it's working perfectly."

"Let me guess, the other steps involve sex or the like."

His eyes widen in mock horror. "Who shared my trade secrets before I had a chance to tell you?"

"Lucky guess," I muse. I'm glad his humor stayed intact through all the shit he went through—something that took a hard hit when Eden tried to kill herself, but little by little, he's gone back to his goofy self. This is the Kaine I remember when he was a kid, but as he got older and kept getting picked on, his defense mechanism to make jokes of everything turned into a shutdown Kaine and someone that became more violent and vindictive.

His phone buzzes on the table, and through the pang of jealously at the smile on his face, I smile as well. That smile quickly turns into a frown while his thumbs move rapidly over the screen.

"What's wrong?"

"Eden is going to a club."

"Okay, and that's a bad thing, why?"

He glares up at me through his lashes before rolling his eyes. "Guys get handsy at clubs."

"You're being controlling."

"No, I'm being a protective fiancé. You should be worried, too. Ronnie is with her."

"She's free to do what she wants."

"Oh, yeah? So, she's free to *do* some random dude she sees at the club?"

His brow slowly lifts the longer the silence stretches between us. I can't help the quickening of my heartbeat or the flicker of anger coursing through my chest. His eyes drift to my hand, where the subtle squeak then crack of glass draws his attention.

"Uh..." He points to the bottle shattering in my hand, the liquid spreading across the table. "Fucking hell, Reese. You just crushed a fucking bottle. You on steroids?"

I shudder, the pain barely registering as I glance down. Small shards of glass are imbedded in my palm, but it barely hurts. The sting of the alcohol does nothing to tamper down the picture Kaine painted in my head.

"It's not like there's anything I can do about it." My words are harsh and clipped, and the sting on my palm is starting to get to me. I grab a napkin, quickly picking out the small shards before gripping it in my hand to stem the bleeding.

Kaine lifts his hand to the waitress, barely giving her a glance when she comes over to our table. "Can we get the bill and some to-go boxes?"

"Is everything okay?"

"Yes, we just have somewhere else we need to be." She tugs the bill from her apron and sets it on the table before heading back to the kitchen to get some boxes and a towel for the spill. "I got it," he says when I reach to grab it.

"I can pay for my own shit."

"Sure, but I'm the one who invited you out. It's my treat since you're going through some shit and I feel bad." He grins widely. "See? I'm a great friend, aren't I?"

"The best," I chuckle.

The waitress comes back with the boxes and grabs the money Kaine left for her. "Keep the change," he says, which seems to surprise her. She blinks, looking down at the bills in confusion. I get *why* she's confused; he left her a pretty hefty tip, even though she didn't really do much or even talk to us. To be fair, Kaine didn't really give her the chance *to* talk.

She stumbles back when he steps out of the booth, stretching his arms above his head. His shirt rides up, the new tattoo he got a few months ago peeking through. A fox with Eden's name scrawled through the tail.

"Let's go." He bows his head towards the girl, shoving his hands into his pockets, and walking off like he just *expects* me to follow him.

I just sigh and give the waitress an apologetic look, grabbing my takeout containers and widening my steps to catch up with Kaine. "What club are they at?"

"Apollo."

I glance at our clothes, frowning. "We're never getting in dressed like this. They're high-end, especially when it comes to guys. The girls can pretty much wear anything as long as it's not sweatpants."

"It's fine. I bought shares in the place last month; that's the reason Eden picked the place."

"You what?"

He shrugs. "Just a small side hustle. The extra income is great, especially since I plan to retire young so I can enjoy my life with Eden."

"Fine. I'll follow you there."

CHAPTER EIGHT

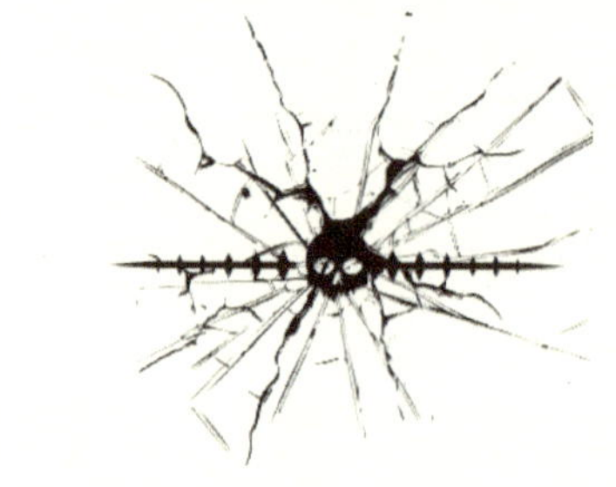

RONNIE

"Maybe you should slow down!"

Eden's voice barely gets through the sound of the pounding music around us, and the fog from the drinks I've already had are quickly affecting my brain, but I just don't care. I'm glad we came. At least here, I can try to forget about Reese and the fact he ignored me when I told him I love him.

I've been putting it off, sensing that something was wrong with him. I've loved him for a while now, but I could tell he had something against those words. I'm the idiot for springing it on him like that, but we never had a proper conversation about it.

It should be normal to feel that way—at least, I think so. We've dated for a while, and we live together for fuck's sake. If he doesn't feel that way towards me, what's the point? What the fuck is the point in any of it?

My panic and sadness made me do something I never planned to do. I went to my father's house, which now I realize was a huge mistake. I've avoided him and the family for a while, but in my moment of weakness, I went with what's familiar. I should have just called Eden to see if I could stay with her and Kaine or gone to a hotel until I could figure everything out, but my dumb ass just showed up at my family estate.

He was welcoming, albeit a bit suspicious. He knows nothing about me outside the fact I went off to school to get a career in medicine. I lived on campus and made no effort to go home, not even for holidays.

Home.

It hasn't been a home for a long time, not since mom passed away. She was my guardian—my protector. With her gone, things got a lot worse. His expectations of me were ridiculous and overbearing, and there was no way in hell I was letting him control my life the way he wanted to.

I shoot back another shot, flagging down the bartender again while I feel Eden glaring at me. She's being good, babying the drink she has in front of her, but I'm not here to sight-see, I'm here to get smashed so I can forget the events of the last two days. My hope was to drink myself into oblivion and get Reese out of my head, but it's not working. Shot after shot, drink after drink, but every time my eyes drift closed for a fraction of a second, all I see is him.

"Seriously, Ronnie. If I knew you planned to come here so you could self-destruct, I never would have agreed to it."

"Stop it. You wanted to come out and party just as much as I did. Soon you'll be completely locked down to Kaine, and you won't get another chance to have fun."

She frowns, stepping closer to me. "Kaine isn't like that. Just because we're getting married doesn't mean he's planning to lock me away from the world."

"Really? He's pretty overbearing and overprotective. I highly doubt he'd be happy if he knew you were here instead of at home."

"He knows and he's fine with it. He just wants to keep me safe and—" I turn when she stops talking suddenly and pulls her bottom lip between her teeth. "Trust me when I say this, Kaine has my best interest at heart."

Her sudden change in demeanor has me leaning closer to her, checking her eyes and noticing the slight shimmer forming. "Did something happen?" I haven't been close friends with her for very long, and the way she's acting is making me think that something huge happened that she hasn't told me about.

"I—" She swallows thickly, dropping her gaze to the floor. "I tried to kill myself last year. Kaine found me and he...he got to me in time."

My eyes widen, the conversation sobering me up quicker than I thought possible. "Eden, I—"

"It's fine. Only Reese and Kaine know what happened, and I just haven't felt comfortable enough to share it. I went through a lot last year, and it all just caught up to me. Kaine's been working really hard and been really gentle with me, making sure I don't get pushed over mentally. So, if he seems really overprotective, that's why. He almost lost me, and he never wants to experience that again. Fuck, *I* don't want him to ever experience that again. If I have to let him know how I am and where I am at all times to make him feel better, then that's what I'll do."

"How do you do it?" She tips her head in question, furrowing her brows. "How do you love someone to that level and earn their love in return. I thought things were great between me and Reese, but the more time that's passed, the more distant he seems. I just want to know if it's me, but when I asked him, I couldn't even tell if he was being honest or just saying the things he says to keep me with him because he's lonely. I get it, I really do, but if he's only keeping me around for company, then I don't know if I can stay with him. I'm not some pet, but our relationship has felt more like we're just roommates now and not lovers."

"Reese has been through a lot in his life as well, and last year was hard on him, too. Kaine is his best friend, and seeing him suffering the way he did because of me took a toll on him, too. I think you need to give him a break and look at it from his perspective."

"I've given him a year, Eden! An entire fucking year to open up to me, but he still hasn't told me a single thing about himself except for the fact his mom and dad are dead. I know how hard it is to lose someone you care about—someone who holds your world together—but he's made no effort in telling me anything of value about his past."

"Maybe he doesn't want to burden you with it. Kaine was the same way. It took a lot of effort to get him to open up to me."

"Are you saying I'm not putting any effort in?" Irritation starts to bubble inside me at the fact she even thought of saying that.

I've tried. I've tried so fucking hard to get him to talk to me about *anything*, but he's like a vault when it comes to his life before going to school.

She sighs, setting her drink down on the bar-top. "That's not what I'm saying at all, but maybe it takes a different way of doing things with Reese. I'm just trying to help you, Ronnie."

"Hey, gorgeous. Can I buy you a drink?"

I startle at the voice behind me and sudden heat of a hand on my lower back. Eden's glare pins the guy behind me, and I slowly turn to take him in. He's definitely good looking, with his blond strands pushed back and dark blue eyes shimmering in the strobing lights of the club. Those eyes are hooded and slightly bloodshot, the alcohol he's consumed apparent in the way he sways slightly towards me. A goofy grin spreads across his lips, and he leans down towards me, but Eden steps towards him, placing her hand on his shoulder.

"Back off," she snaps, her glare turning more threatening than I've ever seen before.

"I'm just asking if the pretty lady wants a drink." His words slur as he shifts his gaze to her, swaying once again. He squints at her, the grin returning. "You're pretty, too. Do you want a drink?"

My back stiffens when he drapes his arm across my shoulders, tugging me closer to him and making me slam into the stool in front of me. Eden looks about ready to kill him at this point, but I just settle my hand on his chest, pulling his attention back to me.

"Sure, I'll take a drink."

"Ronnie," she hisses, reaching out and gripping my arm to try and pull me away from the drunken idiot.

"It's fine. It's just one drink."

"Yeah, Bambi. Back the fuck off," he spits out, pulling me even harder against his side.

Her eyes widen, drifting to the space behind me. "Kaine." It's barely a whisper, but her lips form the name, trembling with a hint of fear.

The next second, the guy hanging off me gets ripped away from me, pulling shocked gasps and screams around me. I turn, and fear grips my chest at the scene playing out.

Reese.

He doesn't even look like himself. His hold on the guy's throat is vicious, his eyes blazing with fury. His arms bulge, pressing into the fabric of his shirt in a way that I think he might actually rip it.

The drunk guy scrambles against the bar-top, his hands gripping into Reese's forearm to try and pry him away, but it's useless. His fingers tighten and spittle starts to form at the edges of the guy's mouth while his droopy eyes bulge out of his head. His legs flail, trying and failing to kick Reese. The poor bartender stares in open-mouthed shock, but the security has already caught wind of what's happening and starts heading towards us.

"What the fuck were you thinking?" I hear Kaine say harshly. I look back over to see her tipping her head up at him in defiance, even if her eyes still show an edge of fear.

"I was trying to get him to leave us alone," she claps back, putting herself in a glaring match with Kaine.

"Don't touch my fucking girlfriend," Reese snarls, ripping my attention back towards him. "I should break your hands and rip out your tongue for even *thinking* it was appropriate to speak to her and place your filthy hands on her."

"Reese." He ignores me, pressing further into his throat to the point I think he might actually kill him. The security guards show up beside him, trying to pull him away, but Reese is like an unmovable wall, snarling in their direction. "Reese!" I say again, but he still doesn't turn to look at me.

"Reese. That's enough," Kaine snaps, and this time, he listens. The fact he ignored me but listened to Kaine just pisses me off further, and when he finally turns to me, registering my presence, I don't even want to look at him.

"Are you okay?"

I balk at the question, stepping back when he reaches towards me. "No one asked you to step in!"

He frowns, his hand dropping to his side limply. The security guys help the drunkard down from the bar and turns to grab Reese again, but Kaine steps between them. "He's fine."

"Sir?"

"I said he's fine."

Sir? What the fuck? My jaw drops when they step away, leading the man out towards the exit. Does Kaine know the owner?

"What are you doing here, Ronnie?"

"I could be asking *you* that. I don't think I need to tell you what I do or where I go. You ruined my fun, Reese. I liked him and you just had to be a macho man and step in."

"Ronnie, let's just go home so we can talk." I hate the way he lowers his voice and softens his face when he looks at me. He plays the part of liking me well, but after what happened yesterday, I just don't know what to believe anymore.

"I'm not going anywhere with you. I'm staying at Eden's."

"The fuck you are," Kaine snaps. "I like you, but I'm not getting involved with whatever the fuck is going on between the two of you."

"It's not just your apartment, it's Eden's, too."

"Kaine," Eden sighs. "Don't be a dick."

"You can call me whatever you want but you're not helping the situation any by allowing her to avoid him. They need to talk this shit out, vixen."

I'm not going to get anywhere with Kaine because I can already see Eden caving to his demands. "Fine. I don't need any of you."

Reese grips my elbow, but I rip away from him, stumbling back on unsteady legs. "Don't fucking touch me."

"Ronnie—"

I don't wait to hear whatever other excuses he's planning to come up with, quickly making my way through the club and out the door. I don't bother to hail a cab, not wanting to give him any time to catch up to me, and instead make my way down the street, looking for the closest motel for the night. All my shit is in my car that's parked at Eden's apartment complex, but I'll just get a ride out there in the morning and get changed at work. I don't need them—I don't need anyone.

CHAPTER NINE

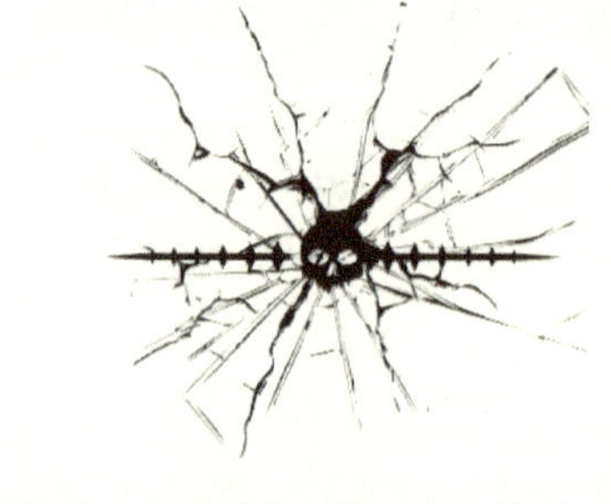

REESE

"You should have just let her go to your place!" I can't help but yell at Kaine at this point because what the actual fuck. She's gone. I thought she would call a cab and that would have given me time to catch up to her, but the second I stepped out of the club, my heart plummeted.

"She needs to be going back to your place. Our home isn't a halfway house for girls who can't talk through their feelings. Ow! What the fuck?"

I turn at his cry of pain, watching him rubbing at his arm while he glares at Eden. "If our home isn't a halfway house for girls who can't talk through their feelings then I shouldn't be there either!

Get your head out of your ass. This isn't like you. You don't push people away when they need help."

He looks like she just slapped him across the face, his jaw dropping and his face paling. "You can't compare yourself to Ronnie. I love you, and I'm sorry to say this, but I don't fucking care what she does with her life. She's fucking all of this up and tearing my best friend apart, so how do you expect me to react to all of this?"

"It's not just Reese! Ronnie is fucking gutted by all of this, too, Kaine."

"I'm literally standing right here," I sigh. I hate when they do this shit. The fact they can talk about me so easily while I'm within earshot is fucking traumatizing to say the least. Admittedly, I hate hearing Eden saying that Ronnie feels that way, but if she was that broken up, why did she react the way she did earlier?

They don't even react to me speaking, going on with their own argument like I don't exist. I sigh, turning on my heel and heading to my car. They can deal with their own insecurities at this point because I don't want to be involved or be the cause if they end up in a fight tonight. Mind you, they'll probably fuck it out later when it's all said and done, which I know is the main reason Kaine reacted the way he did. He said as much; not that I can blame him.

I dial Ronnie again, listening to the line ring and ring and ring. I'm about to end the call since her voicemail was full the last time I called, but I pause when it actually goes through. The beep cue sounds in my ear, and I pull in a shuddering breath, hating the dead silence on the line.

"Ronnie," I whisper. "Please come home. Please. I just want to talk to you and try to explain. Please."

I sound pathetic but I don't know what else to do. I don't really have hope that she'll call me back or show up at the apartment. Why would I? Nothing good ever comes my way out of sheer luck or chance. Everything I have, I've had to fight for tooth and nail, fighting my way through this fucked up world and the life that's slowly catching up to me and threatening everything I've known or care about.

Is it too much to ask to have some semblance of a normal life?

Is it too much to ask to just be allowed to *live*?

I keep hoping that I'll see her on my way to my car, but she's nowhere to be found. Did she go to her dad's again? Fuck me, I don't know what to do with myself. This night ended horribly, and the small hope that things were going to go right and I would get the chance to talk to her were completely ripped away from me.

I can't get that small flicker of fear in her eyes out of my head when she looked at me. It didn't last long, quickly overtaken by anger instead. Would she have gone home with that sack of shit drunk bastard if I hadn't shown up? I couldn't think straight. The second I saw her and saw *him* with his arm around her, I fucking lost it. Kaine tried to stop me, but that's as useless as trying to stop a freight train with your bare hands. My sights were set on one thing, and if he hadn't have snapped me back to myself, I think I would have killed the guy.

He touched her. He fucking *touched* her and all I saw was red. All I wanted was to expend the anger that's been coursing through me for the last few months. I wanted to feel something else, even if it was the pain of my hand slamming into his skull over and over again until his warm blood oozed out over my knuckles. Maybe then the chill that's been permanently residing inside of me would be tampered down. No. I don't think even that would have satiated me or tamed the rage burning through my veins.

My family history is bad enough, but Avery keeps popping into every thought running through my head. I feel tainted and used, and that's a feeling I never want to experience again. Even now, I still can't shake the feeling of him taking over my body. The pure terror and rage that burned through his own hold into me. I feel like he's changed me in some way—something fundamental within me being moulded and converted to the point I don't feel *normal* anymore. It's like I can *still* feel him beneath the surface, leaching into my system.

My soul was already tainted, but it feels so much worse now. These hands of mine were never born to do good or to help people, but that was also one of the reasons I wanted to go into the medical field. It's the biggest reason why I chose to work with children, too. I wanted to change my fate and help the innocent in this world. If I die tomorrow, I want the people who know me as I am to know I did something *good* while I was here. It's why I picked up so many shifts when I first started my career.

I feel drained by the time I get back to my truck, falling into the seat with a heavy thud. I can't even get my body to move to start the fucking thing, my hands shaking around the smooth leather of the steering wheel, my palms clammy and sticking to the surface.

I need to get home. I need to try and get some sleep tonight so that I can be present in the mind for Julia's birthday tomorrow. I need to focus on her right now for the simple fact she doesn't have much time left, and I want to make this a special day for her.

Thinking about her makes my heart hurt, the organ clenching painfully in my chest. I've gotten attached, something a doctor shouldn't do with a patient. It's the way of the industry, especially in wards like the one I'm working in. People die. I knew that going in, but I wanted to be a small light for these children in the hopes I could brighten their day in the wake of the darkness trying to shroud them through their sickness and fatal diseases.

"You're good," I whisper, my eyes flicking up to the rearview mirror. I look awful, dark circles starting to form under my slowly darkening eyes.

Little by little, the light inside of me is fading, turning me into the void of a being my family wanted me to become. I hate it. I never wanted this, but I'm struggling more and more to get off the path that's set before me.

I need to get home. I need to fucking get *home*. My chest feels tight with each staggering breath, but I get my body to function, finally starting the truck and pulling onto the road at a snail's pace. I can't help looking for her, peeking into every darkened alley and every hotel entrance that I come across on my way back to the apartment. It just makes me feel worse, knowing that she ran from me that quickly. She looked wasted, and I hate knowing she's out there with her inhibitions skewed while feeling betrayal from me.

By the time I reach the apartment, I feel exhausted beyond belief, and it takes everything in me to drag myself out of the car and into the building. My nose crinkles at the musky smell of stale sweat lingering in the cabin of the elevator, the tang seeping deep into my nostrils. This place is high-end, so I never expected it to get to this point. I'll have to contact management to have it dealt with because there's no way in hell I'll be able to handle it, especially if it gets worse. It sort of reminds me of the scent of death. Like the obnoxious odor that would waft up from the pits at the farm. It's not quite that pungent, but it's pretty fucking close.

The lights flicker in the box, the elevator shuddering enough to have my heartrate spiking before the door opens to my floor. I have no idea what the fuck that just was, but the creepy sensation rolling up my spine has the hairs on the back of my neck standing on end. A wicked chill settles over my skin, sinking down right into my bones. A sudden need to run grips at my chest but I fight it back, not understanding why I suddenly feel like I'm in danger. My entire body is shaking by the time I reach my door, my hand slipping each time I try to shove the key into the lock.

Go. I need to go. Open, you stupid fucking door. I swear I see my breath puff out in front of me seconds before the door finally swings open. I slam it closed, leaning my back against it as my legs give out from under me, forcing me to crumple to the floor in a heap.

Sweat beads along my brow, the slight fear I felt moments ago, turning into something heavy and thick in my chest. My breathing turns heavier and ragged, each inhale feeling like needles pricking my lungs over and over until I'm gripping my chest to try and make it stop. Darkness flickers across my vision, creeping in further and further until my body sways, hitting the floor.

I can't breathe. I can't fucking move. I try to blink away the black spots crowding my vision, my hand clawing at the floor, but it's useless. My limbs feel numb at this point, no longer functioning the way I want them to. I can't even reach for my phone to attempt to call for help, but I don't know what the fuck is wrong with me. Am I having a panic attack? It has to be, right? I need to breathe. I need to get up off this floor and calm myself down, but I can't. I let my eyes close, letting the darkness take over and swallow me whole.

CHAPTER TEN

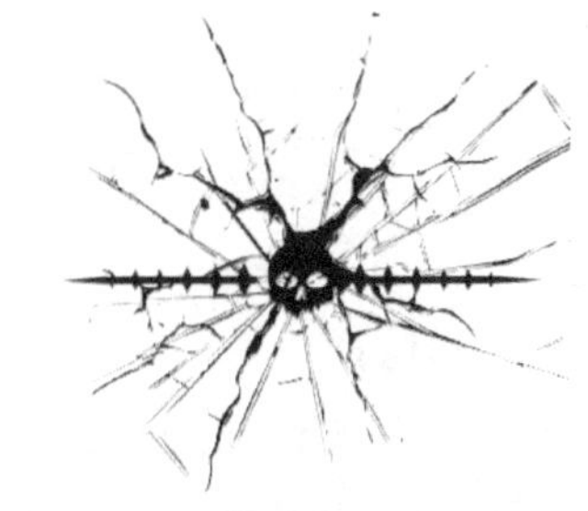

REESE

My eyes feel heavy, but the incessantly obnoxious sound blaring around me forces me to pry them open. Fuck, I'm still on the floor, my body sore and stiff from the unforgiving bed I claimed last night. Palming my pocket to rip the phone out has my back screaming in pain, but I sit up, blinking rapidly to clear my vision of the haze still settled there.

At least my heartrate feels more stable than it did last night, but I still feel like shit. I wish I could blame this horrible morning on drinking, but I only had that single beer at dinner. Fuck. I left the food in the car. The nachos should still be good to eat at work today, but the chicken has got to go. No way in hell am I risking food poisoning. The *last* thing I need to add to the list of my already shitty shortcomings is shitting myself or throwing up, or worse, both at the same time.

I shudder at the thought, crawling myself up the door until I can get my legs under me. They tremble under my weight, but I need to get my ass in gear if I have any hope of making it to work on time. At least I slept through the night, unlike the last few with the lack of sleep and the nightmares that have been plaguing me at the worst possible moments. Who would have thought that I would get a proper night's rest while in the fetal position on the floor. The aches and pains are a small price to pay for a slightly clearer head going into the day.

I stumble my way towards the bedroom, hanging onto the wall with every step because I'm seriously scared I'm going to fucking keel over. I just need to get through today. I have the next two days off and today is too important to skip out on my shift.

The sigh of relief I let out once I reach the bathroom almost pushes me to weep. A grown man that portrays himself as strong and unmovable, nearly being brought to tears for the simple task of getting into the bathroom. It's fucking pathetic, but at least no one is around to see how fucking weak I am.

Well, that was a stupid train of thought because now I'm focusing on the fact I'm alone. I'm fucking alone, and once again Ronnie never called me back. Yes, I checked the second I turned off my alarm like a pathetic simpering idiot, but what else can I do?

"You're such a fuck up," I murmur, staring at myself in the mirror. "You're fucking useless and you always fuck everything up." My fingers curl around the edge of the sink, the porcelain squeaking under the pressure. Deep, heavy breaths rip through my chest, but I force myself to calm down, slowly uncurling my hands. The cuts from last night burn and rip open, blood now dripping down onto the stark white material. I'm going to have to deal with that before I go into work, too, but I welcome the sting. It's a cruel reminder of the mistakes I've made.

Ripping off my shirt, I wince at the pops radiating through my body with such a simple movement. Seriously, everything fucking hurts. It feels like I've gone ten rounds with a grizzly bear and it sure as fuck doesn't feel like I've won.

I'm thankful the shower begins to steam quickly enough, but even with this level of heat, I can't seem to shake the chill that's settled into my bones. The water beats against my back, seeping into the muscles and feeling useless all the same. I flex my throbbing hand under the cascading stream, hissing against the burn spreading across the cuts. I still have no idea how I even managed to break the bottle the way I did. I've never done anything like that before, and that was the worst time for something like that to happen.

Kaine seemed a bit spooked by the whole thing, but no more than I felt myself. It didn't register right away—the pain. None of it even crossed my mind until he pointed it out. I didn't think I was gripping the stupid thing that hard, but maybe the glass was already compromised. Yeah, that's it. That makes the most sense.

I wish I could stay under the water longer, letting it flow over me and pound into me until the heat runs out, but I need to get moving. I sigh, turning it off and stepping out of the shower, giving it a longing look while I wipe myself down and wrap a towel around my waist.

A pang shoots through my chest when I walk out the door, remembering the last time I did it. Flashes of last night cycle through my mind. The way Ronnie was laid out on the bed, ready and waiting for me. The way her eyes darkened when she saw me and the hopeful desire that radiated out of her until I took control. It's beyond lonely now, looking at the empty and untouched bed. Will it ever hold the both of us again? Will I get to curl myself around her small frame, cradling her in my arm ever again?

With the way things are going and with how quickly she cut me off, I don't have high hopes for that to happen, but I need to keep trying. I know I need to give her at least something to satisfy her in the sense of what's going on with me, but how do I bring up a conversation that I never had any intention of covering?

I pause when I open the closet, my eyes landing on one of my Halloween costumes from a few years ago folded up on the shelf above the rack. I think Julia would be happy if I dressed up for her birthday, and all I want to do for that girl is bring her a little joy into her life. I quickly change, rubbing the towel through my hair to dry it a bit better before grabbing the teddy bear I picked up for her on the way home yesterday.

I hate the silence in the apartment, my natural reaction being to say *'have a good day'* to Ronnie before leaving. There's no point in it, but I still look over at the bed again, picturing her lying there with a smile on her face as she cuddles into the pillows. "Have a good day at work," I whisper, feeling even more pathetic as I walk out of the room, grabbing my keys from the floor where I dropped them last night.

I need to find some way to distract myself so I can stop obsessively thinking about her. For my stupid claims of not loving her, I'm sure as fucking acting like a lovesick pup desperately waiting for his master to come home and shower him with affection.

Pathetic.

Useless.

No one truly loves you.

I shake the thoughts from my head, but they've already wormed their way into my psyche, slowly eating away and destroying every good thought I've had of myself and my accomplishments. It's not like she's ever said those things to me herself, but I've heard similar words from my father. Those memories have slowly been resurfacing, and I know they're taking a toll on me mentally. It's obvious I'm not as strong as I thought I was, but I've done well to play the part to those around me.

I don't struggle as much when I need to be strong for someone else—it's natural really. My mother and I never had anyone wanting to protect us, and I took it upon myself—even from a young age—to do everything I could to keep her safe. It was useless in the end, being taken too soon by a disease that ravaged her body and transformed her into a shell—a fucking husk of her former self. At least she didn't suffer for long, a small kindness that the reapers who haunted her granted her fragile soul.

She's another reason I got into medicine. My own dissertation covered the devastating effects of her condition and my own theories on medical advancements that needed to be funded to try and slow the degenerative process. There has to be a way to still the chaotic nature of the disease, and my hope is reliant on the future. I don't have the funding or the backing of medical professionals to attempt the research on my own, though, it was never my intention to get involved in the testing aspects of it, but if my own research and findings can help future victims, at least I can feel like I did something good in this world.

Something needs to happen. Something needs to come of the work and effort I put in. In the end, I felt like it was a curse thrust upon her. For what other reason would she develop such a rare disease with barely a glimmer of medical aid? RPDs have multiple causes, none of which can be isolated fast enough to slow or stop the progression completely. Weeks or months. My mother got two weeks before all cognitive functions ceased.

By the time we clocked the first symptoms, it had already progressed. Her personality changed quickly and she had small bouts of hallucinations, thankfully none of them led to full on psychotic breaks or violent delusions, but it was still difficult to watch, especially at a younger age where I wasn't able to process or understand what was happening to her. I dove headfirst into research though, trying anything I could to help her because the doctors were doing fuck all, but there *was* nothing they could do.

Clinical trials were scarce and showed no results, and that was after contacting my uncle to push her into legitimate testing and not the placebo trials. I was desperate, and because of favours like that, I was pushed into owing him for the things he did for her. It was worse when she started to lose her speech and when her body suffered from myoclonic jerks. Those were terrifying to witness when they got severe, and I hated seeing her having to be strapped down so she wouldn't end up hurting herself or those trying to aid her.

I'm a terrible person. I hated that some of the trial patients saw some results, pushing their life expectancy to a year or two, but their conditions were more than likely a bit different, taking well to the procedures and drugs being administered. My mother wasn't so lucky. She clearly had a prion disease like Creutzfedlt-Jakob disease, but hers was more aggressive. The tests ruled out that specific one, and she was progressing too quickly for it to be a temporal course.

That's the thing with neurodegenerative diseases; every case is different, with different effects and symptoms, but they all have the same result in the end—death.

I couldn't do anything for her except being there with her until the end, but it was beyond difficult. I'll never forget her face or the rattle of her lungs as her system began to shut down. Her own body was fighting against her, claiming every last shred of self and dignity until there *was* nothing left of her. She didn't remember me in the end, but I hope she does in the afterlife. I hope she thinks of me as much as I think of her and remembers me as I was when I was happy and smiling and living the best life she could have given me.

I loved her.

Of course I loved her.

She loved me, too. She gave up so much in order to give me a good life and a proper upbringing away from the fucked-up mafia-style life.

Someday, I'll thank her again, and this time, she'll remember my words as I speak them to her. She'll look at me and I'll see the light in her eyes and the recognition sparking in their depth as I tell her how much I miss her and love her and how grateful I am to be able to call her my mother. Rory Mitchel was and is an amazing woman. One who didn't deserve to die at such a young age but was taken none the less.

She was the light in my bleak life and pushed me to befriend Kaine. If she hadn't pushed me out of my comfort zone and wiped away the doubt I felt in getting involved with someone as broken as him, I wouldn't have the best friend I have today. He's all I have left of that life, and I know I was meant to find him.

The fact Avery was keeping an eye on Kaine at such a young age and used me even then is terrifying. I hated hearing that from Kaine, no matter how much he reassured me that Avery didn't manipulate our friendship.

It's like I can't trust myself or my actions because I don't know if my actions are my own. How can I really know that I wasn't being manipulated the entire time I was with Kaine? How can I be certain that Avery wasn't pulling the strings and forcing my words and actions behind the scenes? I want to believe that he didn't and that he wouldn't, but that doubt is still in my mind.

CHAPTER ELEVEN

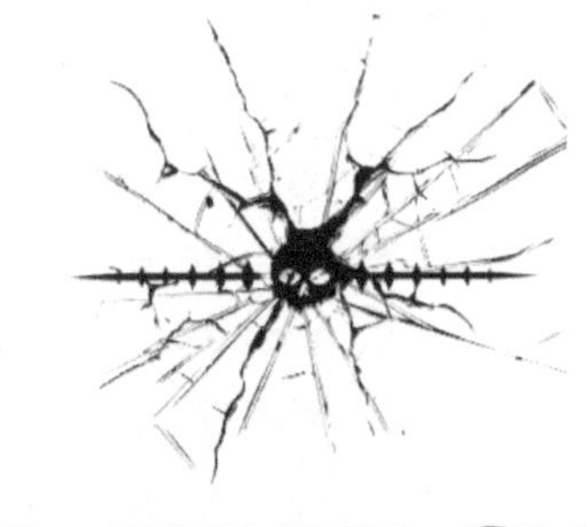

REESE

I put on a fake smile walking through the halls of the hospital amid the wide eyes and giggles from the nurses. Some of the male staff give me appreciative smiles and fist bumps, even if they don't know the reason for my sudden uniform change. I probably should have run it by the head doctor, but I just don't give a shit what he thinks or says. I only care about making Julia happy.

"Nice outfit," Kyla snorts, giving me a once over and letting her eyes linger a bit too long on my abs and just below.

"What's a birthday celebration without a costume for the kid. Do you think she'll like it?"

Her gaze meets mine, softening while a sad smile pulls at her lips. "I think she'll love it."

"How did she do over night?" She shakes her head. "Are her parents with her?" She hesitates long enough that I narrow my eyes at her.

"Her mom is here."

What the fuck? Her dad's not here? On her fucking birthday? He should have been here the moment visiting hours started so he could spend as much time with his daughter as possible. I couldn't imagine not wanting to make each day special for her until the end, even if I were in a petty argument with my wife. Why can't people put aside their differences and hold it together for the sake of their dying kid. Anger pulses through me and I wiggle my fingers at her.

"Give me Julia's entire medical file including contact information for the parents."

"Reese, you can't contact family for no reason."

"You think *this* is no reason? She's got *days*, Kyla. Fucking days, and he can't be bothered to be here for his daughter, on her birthday no less."

"It's against hospital rules."

"Fuck the rules!" My anger shouldn't be directed at her, but her mentality is still pissing me off. How does she not see how wrong it is for that dickhead to not be here? She tries to argue again, snapping her mouth shut at the murderous glare I shoot her way.

I pull my phone out of my pocket as I make my way down the hall, punching in the phone number on file for the douche while I slip into the breakroom. It rings and rings, getting pushed to voicemail, but I call again and again until a very irritated voice screams out from the other end.

"What?" He snaps.

"Mr. Kent. This is Dr. Mitchel calling. I'm sure your wife has informed you of Julia's medical findings, but I wanted to reach out to you and make sure you were okay since you haven't been by in a few days."

I struggle to keep my voice calm, but it's nearly impossible to keep the slight bite out of my words. This prick has the audacity to laugh. *Laugh*. What could possibly be funny about any of this?

"Did she put you up to this?"

"Excuse me?"

"Did Diana put you up to this?"

"I don't know what you mean."

"Oh, so she hasn't told you that Julia might not even be mine? She's lied to me all these years. She never expected me to find out about her affair and when I confronted her about it, she had the audacity to argue that Julia was mine. The kid doesn't even look like me!"

It's true, Julia doesn't have many characteristics that mimic his own, having mainly taken after her mother, but how can he not see the smaller details? I've only known them for a few months and even I can see that Julia is in fact his daughter. The breath I take feels strained, crushed by the anger slowly building within my chest.

"Even if that were the case—which I'm not confirming or denying since I don't know the situation—Julia is your daughter. You've raised her since she was born, she loves you and calls you dad. How can you question the fact she's your daughter?"

“I don’t give a fuck.”

I gape, my eyes blinking slowly at the sudden silence on the other end of the line. I pull the phone away to see that he’s hung up on me. The mother fucker had the nerve to say that to me and then hang up the fucking phone. He doesn’t give a shit about Julia, even though he’s raised the child her entire life. How can he be so cruel? How can he not *feel* anything towards her? She’s lying in a hospital bed dying and her own father wants nothing to do with her.

My breath rattles out of me, and it takes everything in me to uncurl my quickly whitening finger from around my phone. My hand trembles as I push the call button to Ronnie again, not expecting her to answer, but still feeling disappointment when it goes to voicemail again.

“I miss you,” I whisper, my voice hitching on the words. My eyes burn with the need to cry crawling up my chest painfully. I hate this. I also hate the need battling in my chest. The need to go home but hating the idea of it because I know how dark and empty it is now.

A knock at the breakroom door has me wiping at my eyes just in case and shoving my phone back into the pocket of the suit. “Reese?” Kyla’s voice is timid on the other side, and when I open the door, she quickly takes a few steps back from me. “We’re going to do the cake shortly if you want to go in and surprise her now, you can. Or if you want to be the one to carry in the cake, you can do that instead.”

I hold up the bear I got Julia. “I rather just go in with this. You guys can go in a little bit after me to surprise her with the cake.”

"Okay." She fidgets with the hem of her scrub top, no longer meeting my eyes. "Did you get a hold of Mr. Kent?"

"I did."

"And?"

"He's not coming." My tone is clipped and she steps out of the way when I breeze past her, making my way down the corridor towards Julia's room. I knock, giving them a few seconds to compose themselves before I barge in on them. I peek around the door, seeing Diana right away, wiping at her eyes while once again Julia is left comforting her. "I hear a princess has a special birthday today," I say with as much happiness as I can muster within my quickly deflating heart.

Her eyes widen when I step into the room and the wide grin she gives me makes all of this effort worth it. "Captain America!" She squeals happily, her mouth popping open in surprise when I hold up a bear dressed the same way I am. "Dr. Reese! It's so cute. Is it for me?"

"Of course it is, sweetheart," I smile, setting the plush bear on her lap. Something so simple brings her so much joy. I'm enamored as I watch her study every detail of the outfit and how she runs her fingers gently through the stuffed animal's fur. "Do you like it?"

"I love it," she sniffles, and the sound breaks my heart. "You didn't need to get me anything."

"I know I didn't, but I wanted to."

"Why? It's not like I get to enjoy it," she says bitterly, and that's the first time I've heard true heartbreak in her voice. She's given up the small shred of hope she's clung to all this time. I wish I could tell her it would be okay, but we both know it won't be.

"Julia," Diana snaps.

"It's alright." I shake my head, sitting myself on the bed next to Julia. "I don't know what to say in these situations, princess. I'm not good at any of this."

"I know, I'm sorry."

I brush her hair behind her ear, what's left of it anyways. It looks like it's continued to fall out more and more since yesterday, and the thin wispy strands look dull in the light of the room. I don't acknowledge it, just touch her cheek with as much care as I can.

"You never need to apologize for anything. I'm sorry if you don't like the gift and I'll be sure to get you something better next time."

"Next time," she snorts, wiping at her eyes.

"Yep, next time. Do you want a bigger bear? Maybe one that talks and moves around for you? I could get one that you can teach swear words to." She laughs at that, bringing a bit of light back into her eyes. "Whatever you want from me, I can give it to you."

"I've never been kissed before," she whispers. Her mother clears her throat, pulling my attention towards her where her expression shows a mixture of horror and amusement. "I know that's too much to ask, though."

This poor kid won't get to experience any of the joys in life. Not her teenage years and rebellious phase, not her first kiss, first crush, first true love. She'll never have a future to look forward to or ambitions of what she wants to be when she grows up, and thinking about all of that breaks my heart into a million pieces.

I lean closer to her but keep my eyes on her mother. "I'll let you have one kiss, but don't get too frisky." She laughs, nodding her head excitedly. "Close your eyes." She does what I ask without question, her eyes fluttering closed as she tips her chin up towards me. I give her mother another glance and she smiles, nodding her head.

I press my lips gently to her cheek, barely lasting a second before pulling away. Slowly, she opens her eyes again, wide and glistening with interest. "Thank you," she whispers while placing her hand to her reddening cheek, like she's trying to hang onto that sensation for as long as possible.

A knock comes from the door, and I shift myself off the bed, patting Julia's head as the nurses all walk in with the lit cake and smiles on their faces. I join in on their singing, loving the way Julia's face lights up, but hating the tears that form along her lashes. Her mom claps along, her own tears streaming freely down her cheeks while she smiles at the happiness on her daughter's face.

She blows out the candles, her chest heaving like that took the last bit of energy out of her. I stand quietly off to the side, taking one of the plates from Kyla when she hands it to me. Julia keeps stealing glances at me while she talks with the nurses, each time her cheeks heating and pinking adorably. Diana comes over to me, gently bumping into my side.

"You're very sweet," she says quietly.

"Anyone with a heart would have done the same thing."

She shakes her head. "You went above and beyond for her today. The fact you remembered that Captain America is her favourite Avenger and then gave her that small kindness of the kiss on the cheek. It's all very sweet and not expected of you."

"She's a good kid and deserves as much happiness as possible."

"She does. I just wish her father could be here."

That piece of shit doesn't deserve a kid like this one. I'm not condoning the fact Diana cheated on him, but his behaviour is disgusting and downright cruel. Julia is his kid, whether that's by blood or not, it shouldn't matter. He witnessed her growing up and then suffering through this terrible disease, and somehow, he's just able to turn off all his emotions.

Maybe he's been faking it the whole time. Maybe he's a sociopath and has been masking the emotions that are expected of him. I can't bring any of this up because Diana hasn't spoken to me about any of it, making excuses for him, even now.

Movement at the door catches my eye and my body stiffens when dark shadows seep from under the crack, crawling across the white tile floor in stark contrast. "Do you see that?" I whisper harshly.

"Hmm?" I point towards the dark tendrils and they stop, flattening down against the floor. "The tile?"

"No. The weird black smoke crawling across it." When she doesn't respond I rip my gaze away from them to look at her. Her brows knit together and her head tips to the side. I know that look. I've seen that look countless times and not once has it meant anything good. "You don't see it?"

"Have you been sleeping well? There's nothing there, doctor."

I haven't been sleeping well, but it's not a hallucination. At least, I don't *think* it is. "It's been a rough week." The pitying look on her face just makes me feel worse at this point. "I'm heading out to do my rounds." She nods, but I can feel her eyes burning into me as I make my way over to Julia again. The nurses give me room to crouch down next to her. "Enjoy your cake and I'll check up on you later, okay?"

"Okay. Thank you for the teddy." She grins, leaning closer to me. "And the kiss," she whispers.

I chuckle, pushing myself back to my feet and patting her head. It's sweet how her eyes close at the touch and how she leans into it like she's starving for attention. I know her mom has showered her with as much love as she can over the last few months, but these few days without a father figure have taken a toll on her mental state.

The darkness is no longer lingering over the white tile when I walk back towards the door, but a slithering sensation crawls up my spine when I cross the threshold. A sudden cold settles into my bones, nothing new as of late, but jarring none the less. I would love nothing more than to head into the breakroom and crash for like twenty minutes, but I really do need to make my rounds. Julia isn't the only patient under my care, but admittedly, she's my favourite.

CHAPTER TWELVE

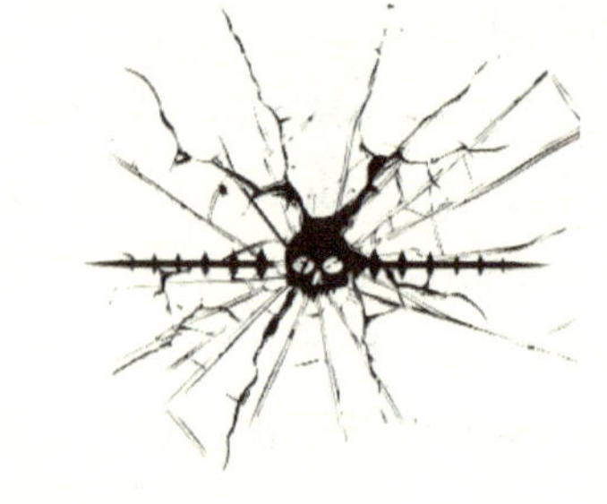

REESE

The rest of my day goes well enough, but my mind keeps drifting to Julia. I want to check on her again, this nagging feeling in the pit of my stomach burning through me and pushing me to speed through my daily check-ins.

I catch one of the nurses at the South station, tapping on the counter with a smile to get her attention. "Can you do me a favour and check in with North Wing and see how Julia Kent is doing?"

"Sure," Nicki grins.

Ah, the benefits of being good looking. All it takes is a warm smile and laying on the charm to get them to do what I need them to. Thankfully, I'm not a creep who takes advantage of that fact. I'm not looking for anything from them other than these small favours I ask of them.

I watch anxiously as she makes the call, talking animatedly to who I assume is Kyla on the other end. I roll my eyes at the obnoxious hyena laugh she lets out, composing myself within the second she glances up at me.

"Can you tell me how Julia Kent is doing?" She smirks, her eyes drifting to my own lips pulling up into a smile. "Yes, Dr. Mitchel is here." She nods, twirling her hair in the most exaggerated way. "Thanks, Kyla." She hangs up the phone, props her elbow on the table and settles her chin against her hand. "So, what do I get in exchange for this favour?"

My temple pulses with irritation. "Excuse me?"

"How about a date?"

"How about you tell me how she's doing before I contact H.R.?"

That shuts her up, her mouth popping open in shock and her face paling. "I—I just thought I'd ask. You're not dating anyone right now, right?"

Bile rises in my throat, and I struggle to keep it down. "I am, actually."

She sighs. "She's fine. Kyla said she was a bit worn out after her little birthday party and she's sleeping at the moment. Her mother took the opportunity to run home and take a quick shower."

Of course she did. As much as she may not want to leave her side, she still needs to take care of herself. Between the sobbing, the knowledge her daughter is dying, and the clear lack of proper sleep, she's not doing well mentally or physically.

"Thank you," I murmur, turning away from her.

"If you ever find yourself to be single—"

"No chance in hell. I don't date co-workers."

Was that cruel? Probably. It's not the fact that I don't or *won't* date co-workers, it's the fact that I don't *want* anyone else. I'm not too keen on letting Ronnie go, but if I make a move now and crowd her worse than the slight stalking and obsessive tendencies of calling her consistently, she'll end up lost to me for good.

That's how she is. She might be shy, but she's independent, and I'm lucky to have warranted her attention. Would I have pursued her on my own? No. Absolutely the fuck not, but she won me over with her nerdy tendencies and meek personality. She wants nothing, and because of that, I've given her everything she needs. Well, except love, but that's beside the point.

Me being the pathetic idiot that I am, I try calling her again as I walk down the hall to my next patient. "Fucking damn it," I grumble when once again it goes to voicemail. "Just answer your fucking phone." Grinding my teeth I slip the phone back into my pocket and muster up a decent smile as I open the door. "How are you feeling today, Ryan?"

"I'm okay," he says quietly, eyes darting to his dad standing at the corner of the room. Odd behaviour, but I've seen weirder, so I brush it off for now.

Taking the clipboard from the end of his bed, I quickly scan over his test results, feeling satisfied with the prognosis. "Things are looking good for you. I think you'll be able to go home at the end of the week if these results hold."

"Really?" His father says, finally perking up and stepping out of the shadows. He looks like shit, but he's been here almost every night since Ryan was brought in. He's on his own, having lost his wife last year in a car accident from what I overheard the nurses saying. The poor guy definitely has it rough, and I'm sure it hasn't been easy for him with the fear that he would end up losing his son as well.

"Yes. The antibiotics are working as they should and the infection is being managed well. I think with a few more treatments and some testing we'll be able to discharge Ryan." I turn my attention back to the boy, smiling down at him. "You'll be back to playing hockey in no time."

He grins, turning to his dad. "I'll be able to make tryouts for the travel team!"

"I'll leave you to it," I say quietly, glancing back at them as I step towards the door. A twinge of sadness and jealousy hit me at seeing the care and love in the father's eyes. The way he brushes his son's hair back with such gentleness. It's something I never had from my father, and it's too late now to even attempt a relationship because he's dead.

My day is almost done now, but I want to check in on Julia before finishing my final rounds. I wonder if she's still sleeping and if her mother is back yet or not as well. My steps slow when I notice a figure dressed in black trousers and a long sleeve shirt that looks like a tunic stepping into Julia's room. I've never seen him before, but it could be a family member—someone Diana decided to call to get their final goodbyes in.

An alarm sounds and chaos breaks loose. The nurses go running and the scream of anguish that tears through the air has me running flat out towards the room.

No. This can't be happening. My eyes dart frantically around the room, taking in the insane frantic movements of everyone in here. I catch a glimpse of the man I saw earlier in the corner only because of the stream of light traveling from Julia's limp body towards his now shadowy form.

No. It can't be. There's no way in hell this is happening. Diana is refusing to let go of her daughter while she screams and cries for her, the nurses trying desperately to pull her away so they can get to her and work on her. The flat sound of the heart monitor rips through my brain, no fluctuation in the noise, just a steady screaming that mixes and merges with Diana's desperate cries.

The creature absorbs the light just as his eyes pulse like liquid silver. Those eyes lock on mine, narrowing when I don't turn away from him. I can't. I can't stop staring at him while pain and anger builds in my chest. A deep ache settles into my bones, followed by a cold resonance streaming through my veins. The chill is so vicious it feels like fire lancing through my blood stream and my head begins to throb. I can hear my heart beating in my ears, drowning out the rising staccato of the screams in the room.

Diana calling out Juilia's name tears my attention for a moment, but that's enough time that when I look back again, he's gone. I rush towards the bed, looping my arm around her torso to tear her away from her daughter.

"No! Let me go! Julia! Julia!" She screams clawing at my arms and wriggling in my grip, but I hold her firmly against my chest. I want to go to her and help her, but the nurses aren't strong enough to hold back a desperate mother trying to reach her child. Her chest heaves on each inhale, the sound of her choked sobs and moans of anguish burying deep into my chest. "Please!" She wails. "Please save her!"

There is no saving her. No matter what they do for her now, I know she's gone. I know what I saw. I know what that man was because his presence has been burned right into my soul. I don't think it was Avery, but it was a reaper. Why could I see him? I've seen death plenty of times and not once have I ever seen the shadows or felt the devastating presence near me.

The doctor comes running in, rushing to aid the nurses in a desperate attempt to bring her back, even if it's only for a little while longer. They have no choice but to attempt saving her, the futility of it not registering amid their panic. Some of the nurses cry along with Diana, having grown attached to Julia during her stay as well. Try as they might to hide and quell the tears, I see them glistening in their eyes while trying everything they can to bring the innocent girl back.

There is no breath, no heartbeat, no *life* left here. She's a shell now, a mortal husk while her immortal soul was taken to whatever afterlife the reaper who took it sees fit.

"Call it," the doctor says shakily.

Kyla sniffles, glancing up at the clock. The ticking of its hands sounding like a gong beating loudly in my head. "Time of death, 18:45."

Diana sobs, lifting her head shakily as he walks over to us. "I'm sorry for your loss."

Sorry. That's all he says. Fucking sorry is all he *can* say. Diana's weight shifts in my hold, her legs giving out from under her through a shuddering breath. The low moan she lets out is haunting and pained, resonating through my body and sinking deep into my bones. My skin feels itchy with prickling heat as my own breaths turn ragged and laboured. My hold on her tightens through the shaking in my arms. I'm the only one here for her. Her husband never came to see their daughter, and she has no one to comfort her or hold her through this devastating ordeal.

I walk her over towards Julia's bedside and sit her down in the chair, crouching down beside her. "I'm so sorry, Diana," I whisper.

"She—she can't be gone. She can't be. She's all I have left." Her eyes scrunch together and more tears cascade down her cheeks. "My husband left me and now my daughter. I have no one."

Lurching to my feet, I pat her shoulder before turning to face Julia for the last time. She passed in her sleep; the teddy bear I gifted her nestled against her side. In the end, she was happy, having experienced some joy, even if it was only for a few short hours. It could have been worse. She could have suffered and felt pain, so this was the biggest kindness granted to her. I didn't even get to say goodbye.

"Rest easy, sweet girl," I murmur, brushing back what's left of her hair. My own emotions are taking hold, colliding within my heart and mind, pushing me to move.

"Where are you going?" Kyla asks when I reach the door.

"I'm done. I have something I need to take care of."

My mind focuses on one thing—one task that might quell some of this rage brewing inside me. I pay no attention to anyone

I walk by, ignoring the questions and concerns streaming from their stupid mouths. Grabbing my keys from my locker in the breakroom, I rush out of the hospital towards my car, my phone pressed to my ear.

"Holland. I need a location. Track down Jeremy Kent."

CHAPTER THIRTEEN

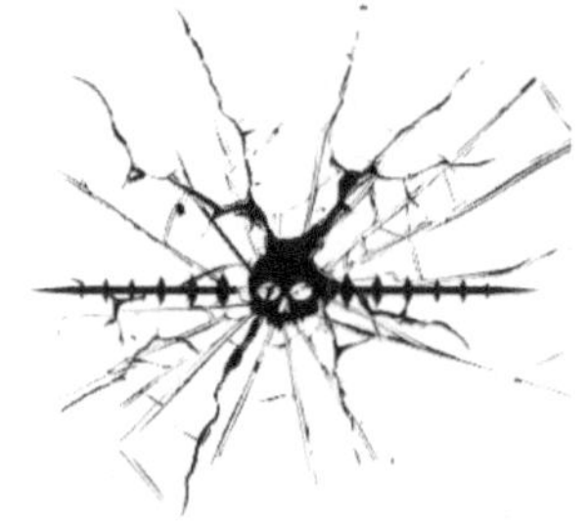

REESE

My eyes are locked on the small home in front of me, a shadow crossing in front of the window with the drawn back curtains. The mother fucker has a second house. According to Holland, Jeremy bought it about three years ago when he decided to move in with his mistress. The sorry twat doesn't even know he's married and has been living a lie with a man that had the audacity to punish his wife for cheating. It wasn't even cheating. I had my guy dig into that, too, and at the time, they weren't together.

Diana felt guilty for having been with another man while they were separated, but that isn't cheating in my books. They weren't fucking together, and guess what? Julia is his. *Was* his.

Holland pulled medical records and somehow found DNA files archived for me, running it through the system against Julia's own DNA sequencing. The bastard works fast, but he's got connections far deeper than me in the medical field. He would have to, what with working for the mafia.

Is it stupid of me to rely on someone who works under my uncle? Yes. Yes, it is, but a guy has to do what he has to in situations that require knowledge and a bit of finesse.

The front door opens, forcing me to press further into my seat to stay hidden. The woman—Lena—steps out onto the porch, turning back to a grinning Jeremy. She's dressed formally, on her way to a charity event being held by the company she works for. I'm surprised the asshole isn't going with her, but people like him are smart. He's not *that* smart since he decided to bed another girl that's in the same city as his wife. The risk of being seen out in public and getting recognized doubles in this situation, but he *is* clever for not going to an event like that where the media will more than likely be present and covering it.

I watch as she hops into her overpriced car, revving the engine before pulling away. He stays in the doorway, watching her driving away for a moment longer, a look of longing on his face.

Fucking asshole. If he didn't want to be with Diana, why didn't he just divorce her? How is this better for anyone? How can he love someone else while pretending with the one he *claimed* to love for as long as he did?

I hate him. I can't even say I don't hate him for myself because I do. He's an insult to men, and dicks like him are what give good, genuine men, a bad reputation. This kind of shit is the stuff women expect of us because the ego and privilege are so extraordinary, there's no point in trying to pretend to be anything else.

I would never do that. I could never act the way he did or treat his loved ones the way he has. His daughter is dead and he's off galivanting with some random woman. I'm glad he has a home and not an apartment since an apartment complex has built in security systems to monitor who comes in and out of the building. This fuck still has trust issues though.

"I'm dealing with the security feed now." Holland's voice crackles through the bud in my ear. "Do you need me to kill the lights while I'm at it?"

"Sure. Let's put a bit of fear into his sorry ass."

He chuckles. "You're a sick fuck, you know that?"

I grin, but a twinge of regret settles into my chest. I don't want to be this person, but I was born to be. No matter what I do or how I try to change things, my anger and actions have been ingrained in me since birth. I will say, I won't regret what I'm planning to do tonight.

This is justice. This is vengeance for a little girl who deserved a father who was present through the worst time of her life. She deserved to be surrounded by the people who love her, and she died knowing her father didn't because he couldn't be bothered to show up on her birthday. Now, she's dead. Now she's *fucking* dead and this waste of space is living a life of happiness and luxury while his daughter is going to be put into a box and lowered into the ground to desiccate and be eaten by the creatures beneath.

That thought fuels me further, pushing my body into autopilot, and stepping out of the truck. I lock down every emotion except for the one that matters. Fury. I don't even need to be discreet about any of this. I want him to see me coming. I want him to know it was me when the light finally leaves his eyes.

The house gets plunged into darkness. Scratch that. The entire block loses power one by one, settling an eerie silence through the area. "Holland," I sigh.

"My bad," he snorts. "It's fine. The power will come back on in five minutes, so do what you need to do."

I'm trying to decide what the best course of action is. I could kill him here and leave him to be found by his mistress. It'll get out that he's a cheating fuck since Diana will see that he's dead and the truth will come out, but will it hurt her further to know that he died the same day as her daughter? I could whisk him away and dispose of him myself, something I've done countless times before and have no issue or reservation in doing, but then it'll just look like he left her and there will be no closure on her end.

Decisions, decisions. The end result will be the same, it's just what comes after that will depend. I want justice for Julia, and the only way for that to happen is for me to let my anger take hold.

I rap my knuckles against the door, honing my senses until I hear the quiet shuffling of feet from the other side. He opens it, eyes widening in surprise. "Dr. Mitchel, I—" He grunts when my palm slams against his face, completely covering his mouth and nose as I shove him back through the door, slamming it behind me.

His back hits the entry wall hard enough that the picture frames clatter on their hooks. My eyes drift to each photo. Photo upon photo of him and his mistress in settings I doubt he ever went to with his actual wife. Vacation spots on beaches and scenic cliffs, cozied up at what seems like a ski resort, both their wide grins telling me he does well living in a lie.

He claws at my hand, and I give him a slight reprieve, shifting my fingers enough to allow partial air through his nostrils. "Nice place you got here," I muse, taking in what I can see of the home. "How does it feel living a second life while your wife is grieving the loss of your daughter?" His eyes widen, darting around frantically. They gleam in the small bit of light from the moon coming through the bare window, but it's enough for me to see fear in them. No sadness or regret, just fear for his own life.

He must know how bad this situation is and how dangerous I am. I'm not attempting to hide my true nature because what's the point? I get off on the stench of fear coming off of him, the way his skin turns clammy and the frantic beating of his heart. His pulse thuds heavily in the vein at his neck, and the urge to strangle it until it stops overwhelms me.

"Her birthday was today. She got news yesterday that she only had days before her illness completely overwhelmed her tiny system, but she didn't have days, and you couldn't be bothered." My fist collides with his ribcage, and my hand shifts from his face to his throat. The gurgled scream that chokes out of him sends a thrill racing up my spine. "I had tests run. You *are* her father by blood, and you left her." Another punch. "On her fucking birthday." My hand tightens around his throat, and I lift him up the wall, loving the way his breaths turn harsh while his legs flail under him. "On her fucking death bed."

The lights in the home flare to life and his eyes bulge in their sockets. I know what he sees. I may not be a true reaper, but to him, I'm death. I can see it in his face, the realization of what me being here means. If the small beating I've gifted him wasn't enough of a clue, the rage pulsing out of me with each passing second is.

I'm an omen of death to most. That was my role within the sub-section of the mafia, and within those circles I was feared. I didn't even have to do anything, I just needed to show up. The moment any of my uncle's enemies saw me, they knew. They knew what awaited them and had no chance of changing the outcome. Once the order is made, there's no going back.

These hands are caked in blood, marked red beneath the surface. They're not meant to be gentle or kind, aching to maim and torture those who deserve it and some that probably don't. I never looked into half the people that were marked to be taken care of, but my mental well-being wouldn't have been able to handle it if the truth was, they were innocent. They could have done nothing wrong in their life except owing money to the wrong people. It lets me sleep better at night, living in my own delusional world where I believe I'm doing good in this world.

Thinking about all of it is just pushing my anger further, making it burn and bubble over until I want nothing more than to release it. I throw the stupid fuck, watching him skid across the ground just to slam into the opposite wall. He coughs and sputters and tries to scramble away, glancing back at me while I take easy, leisurely steps towards him.

He has nowhere to run and nowhere to hide, and I plan to make him suffer for the despair he's made his family feel. "That's it, Jeremy. I want to witness your panic before I end your miserable life," I chuckle, the sound anything but amused and filled with mirth.

"You're—you're a doctor. What the fuck is wrong with you?" He spits out.

I grab his ankle when he fails to kick out at me and drag him back across the floor. He grunts in pain, crying out when I grip it between my hands and twist. The sickening sound of the bone snapping fills me with joy, and I dump his body at the base of the stairs. He writhes, curling in on himself while cradling the now broken limb. He screams when I rip one of his arms up, pulling hard enough for the shoulder to pop out of the socket. I don't stop there, flexing against his forearm until that bone snaps under the pressure as well.

He's a blubbering mess, whimpering and crying like a fucking coward. He should have thought about the consequences of his actions before he made the mistake of fucking with someone I held dear. I may not have known Julia for long, but I knew her long enough to see the shining bright light within her. I witnessed that light slowly dimming day after day, test after fucking test, until there was barely a flicker remaining. Now that light is gone. The one thing I looked forward to while at work has been snuffed out of existence and this asshole couldn't give her an hour of his time.

"She asked for you. Your daughter wanted you there with her and you couldn't even set your ego aside to give her one thing. Thankfully, her dying wish had nothing to do with you and she still got to experience some happiness on her birthday. No thanks to you."

I grip his jaw, dragging his limp, shaking body up so I can stare into those soulless eyes. “Please,” he whimpers. “Please let me go. I promise to do better. I promise to be there.”

“Don’t you get it? You’re too fucking late!”

Snap.

Those soulless eyes turn truly lifeless now, his neck bent at a horrible angle. His death wasn’t satisfying enough, but if I have any hope in making this look like an accident, this is the way it needs to be done. Once they find him, they’ll think he fell down the stairs. There won’t be any evidence to prove otherwise once I’m done. This is all I can do for them. This is my final gift to the sweet angel and her broken mother.

My feet move on their own, pushing my body towards the kitchen where my natural instincts kick in. Glancing around for the best way to go about this, I smirk at the fact they have a gas stove. He’s made this way too easy.

I flick on every burner, listening to the hiss emanating from the appliance until it’s all I hear. I should feel guilt for leaving the woman with nothing. Not a home, not clothes or any of her personal belongings. She’s innocent in this, having fallen for Jeremy’s lies, but she can rebuild and move on.

I tap the earpiece, flinching at the crackling static. “I need a distraction.”

“Did you do it?”

“Yeah, just need to cover my tracks, but walking out the front door with all the lights back on might draw a bit of attention.”

“The cameras are all off in the area so you should be good though.”

“Just fucking do it, Holland.”

I end the connection before he can argue further and start making my way towards the door, smelling the quickly spreading scent of gas through the house. Car alarms wail in the distance and I roll my eyes, but at least he did something. Snagging the box of matches by the fireplace, I jog the rest of the way to the entrance, glancing back at Jeremy's broken body one last time. I swear I see the shadows in the corridor darken further and move, but I shake my head, locking my eyes on the dead body.

"Burn in hell," I murmur, striking a match and tossing it into the heavy air beginning to creep into every room. The match catches on the runner along the hallway, quickly lighting up along its path towards the gas, and I bolt out the door just as it catches. An explosion erupts, sending me flying and crashing into the front lawn. "Fuck me," I croak. I thought I got far enough away, but I underestimated the blast. I struggle to my feet, limping towards my truck before the neighbours notice me.

It's beautiful. A funeral pyre and an offering to Julia and Diana. They deserved better. Hell, the mistress deserves better, and now, the two women can move on and hopefully find someone who is worthy of their time.

The drive back to my apartment feels slower than usual, giving me way too much time to overthink everything. So much for me wanting out. I had vowed that the Stephen thing would be the last time, but of course I fell back into my old ways. I'm a killer at heart and the life comes easily to me.

My entire body is shaking by the time I pull up to the building, my heart thudding rapidly and threatening to beat right out of my chest. I just need to hear her voice. With trembling hands, I grab my phone, dialing Ronnie again. No surprise she doesn't answer, but her voice on the answering machine has my throat burning with the need to cry.

"Hey, it's Ronnie, leave a message."

It's barely a taste of her. It's not enough—not *nearly* enough. I found comfort in her company, a small blessing while Kaine slowly slipped away. Eden makes it a point to force him to call me, but she shouldn't have to do that. His attention has been so focused on her that my own sanity is slowly slipping away, and he doesn't even realize it.

I call him next, staggering out of my truck on unsteady legs. "Hey, man. What's up?"

I let out a shaky breath, trying to find the words—any words that can help bring me back from the edge. "I—I just needed to talk to someone," I whisper.

I hear shuffling from the other side and the sound of a door closing. "Reese, what's going on?"

I can't tell him what I did. He wouldn't be able to handle that level of insane, and it's not right to burden him with it anyways. I go with the biggest thing that's bothering me, feeling the prick of tears against my eyes. "I lost a patient today. She was just a kid, and it was her birthday."

"Fuck, dude. I'm so sorry. Do you need anything? Do you want me to come over?"

"No," I choke out, unable to stop the sobs now shaking my chest. I can barely get the key into the door to the building at this point, but I need to get upstairs before I completely breakdown.

"Where are you? You don't sound right."

My voice goes empty, just like my heart. "Goodbye, Kaine." With that, I hang up, feeling like I already burdened him enough.

It was a mistake to call him and unload my problems on him, and the hope that talking to someone—anyone—would ease this numbing pain spreading through my body was a failure.

It's like I black out, not even remembering the elevator ride up or how I actually got into my apartment, but the silence and darkness snap me back to the present. Alone. Pathetic and completely alone. I rip off my clothes, now covered in soot and debris while I stare at the costume on the couch that I changed out of just hours before. Looking at it just brings forth a flood of emotions, ones that I wish I could burn out of my mind like the fire eating away at the home I just torched.

A wave of sorrow hits me and the tears burning my eyes finally break through, cascading down my cheeks in hot waves. I stumble towards the bedroom, slamming into the wall while my lungs seize, cutting off my air. I need to clean myself off. I need to wash away the dirt and debris and the fucking sins caking my body. Not like it matters though, the water alone, no matter how hot I get it, won't be able to absolve me.

Once again, I find myself in front of the mirror, my slowly bruising hands gripped around the edge of the sink. The man I see looking back barely looks like me. The dark circles under my eyes, the disheveled hair, the crazed expression. The man staring back at me looks broken and deranged through the blur of my tears.

My mind is playing tricks on me. I swear my image changes, morphing into someone else—someone darker than my own reflection. His expression looks nothing like the one I feel right now, his eyes shifting from my brown to a silver blue that seems to glow internally. His expression darkens as he takes me in, eyes narrowing and brows furrowing. Tattoos form and crawl up his neck until they completely circle his throat. My own hand moves to my neck, clawing at the skin. I freeze. The reflection doesn't move, not a single twitch to mimic my movement.

"Reese." A deep voice resonates in my mind.

"No." My fist flies, slamming into the mirror and shattering it, but I don't stop. I keep punching it over and over again until it splinters and falls to the sink and floor. My knuckles throb in pain, shards embedding under my skin and splitting my flesh until deep crimson runs in rivulets down my arm.

I'm hallucinating. It's not real. He's not real. It's not *fucking* real. I can no longer see any of my reflection in the mirror, but I can't escape the lingering sound of his voice in my mind. My name wasn't spoken aloud, sinking deep into my psyche and burying itself right into my mind.

Am I going crazy? Have I finally snapped mentally with no way of coming back from it? I was a danger to others already, but now I no longer know if I have control over myself or my actions. I think I'm a danger to myself, too. I can feel myself slipping, little by little, and no matter what I do, I can't get a hold of those fragments of my soul that are blasting away.

CHAPTER FOURTEEN

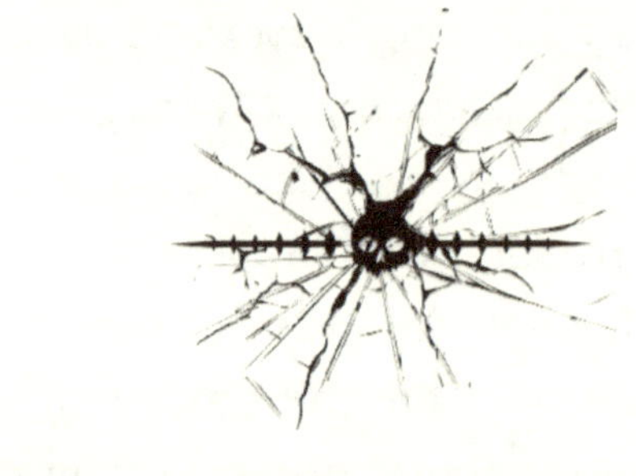

RONNIE

"Can I settle up my tab?"

"Sure, Hun." The bartender walks away from me, grabbing my bill before she settles it in front of me.

I place some bills on top of it and slide it back over to her, giving her a small smile. "Keep the change."

"Thank you."

My life has turned into a pathetic series of events. Kaine practically ignored me at work today, giving me strange looks every time he caught me staring at him. I texted Eden a few times throughout the day and ignored Reese's calls once again. I wish he would just give up and let me move on with my life, but he's persistent, I'll give him that. I didn't even listen to the last string of voicemails he left me, but I have another two sitting in my inbox plus a slew of text messages. I gave up reading them, leaving him on read.

I just can't deal with him. No. It's not even him, but my own feelings as well. I could have picked a better time to tell him I loved him, but I wanted him to know. In the moment it felt right, but looking back, I think he felt trapped and put on the spot. I thought he would hesitate, but he just ignored the words like I never even spoke them.

In my avoidance of everything and my hesitation to go back to my dad's, this is where I ended up. Not my best choice in bars, but I was worried that if I went to one I frequented before, Reese would find me. It's a seedier part of town, a couple of blocks away from the motel I've currently made my home. I thought about going back to the apartment to grab the rest of my things or at least some of the more important ones, but I'm avoiding it like the plague.

It's not even the fact of possibly running into Reese, though that is a concern, but because I don't think my emotions can handle going back there quite yet. It's my home—*our* home—and seeing it again is going to bring up a heavy dose of emotions that I'm currently not prepared to deal with.

Tonight seems to be a bit chillier than usual for this time of year. The temperature is dropping enough that I'm thankful I put on one of my favourite sweaters. I mean, it's not *my* sweater, it's Reese's. I pull the collar up to my nose, breathing in the subtle scent of him still lingering on the fabric. He smells like comfort and strength. He smells like home. Cedar and vanilla with a hint of mint and cinnamon, all smells I liked before, but grew to love more because they remind me of him.

Tears prick my eyes, pressure building in my throat as I make my way down the quiet street. My phone buzzes and rings in my purse, forcing me to frantically paw through it and wondering if it's Reese calling again. I frown when I see the caller I.D. answering it and bringing it to my ear.

"Kaine? Is everything okay?"

"Have you talked to Reese today?"

"Uh, no. You know I haven't been taking his calls."

"I think you need to call him. He called me a few minutes ago and he didn't sound right. He said one of his patients died today, and when I offered to go over..." He trails off, pulling in a stuttering breath. "Never mind. I'll go check on him myself."

"Tell me what happened." Panic claws at my inside, pushing my feet to move faster towards the motel where my car is now parked.

"All he said was goodbye, but he just sounded so...empty. I'm worried he's going to do something. I need to pick Eden up from her shift, but I'll head over to the apartment after that, so forget I called you."

"I'll go."

Silence greets me for a few long seconds. "Are you sure? I know you two aren't really talking right now, and you were pretty pissed off at him last night."

Pulling in a slow breath, I swallow down the anxiety building inside of me and grip the phone a bit tighter. "I'll go."

"Okay. Keep me posted and I'll head over there if you need me to."

"Okay. Thank you for letting me know."

"I'm sorry he hasn't been the best to you, but he's going through some shit, so please don't shut him out, Ronnie."

"I'll try." I end the call, my thumb hovering over the voicemail button. I need to listen to them just to get an idea of where his headspace is at.

"Ronnie, please come home. Please. I just want to talk to you and try to explain. Please." He sounds broken, the words barely heard through the tiny speaker. The next voicemail comes through, just as broken as the last. *"I miss you."* The timestamp between this one and the first one is a few hours, same as the next one he leaves me. *"It's Julia..."* A quiet sob slips out before he clears his throat. He says nothing more, but I can hear his ragged breathing on the other end. Long seconds tick by, and just when I think that's all there is, he speaks again. *"I'm not okay."* Click. The line goes dead and I pull the phone away, staring at the screen as new panic claws through me.

Kaine is right, he doesn't sound right. Reese is good at keeping himself composed most of the time with the odd slip up here and there, but he's pretty normal in his reactions to things. I've only seen him truly angry a few times, and the number of times he's been upset enough to bring himself to tears has been even less. He's not good at expressing his emotions, keeping them locked up and well hidden behind the wall he's created.

I quickly grab my things from the motel, jogging back out to my car and throwing the bag into the back seat. I'm kicking myself for picking a place so far from the apartment, but once again, I didn't want to risk running into him. At least the drive gives me time to think. I run through every possible scenario I might be walking into, my upbringing kicking into autopilot to try and create plausible interactions and reactions from him when I walk through the door.

I don't want to upset him further by showing up unannounced, but when I try to call him, the phone doesn't even ring, going straight to voicemail. That's weird for him. He always has his phone turned on in case he's needed at the hospital, but for him to have it completely off, something *must* be wrong with him. That thought has me pushing the accelerator while I weave in and out of traffic to make up some time.

By the time I pull up to the apartment, I feel lightheaded and out of breath. Reese's car is park haphazardly in his space, another sign that something is wrong. I run up to the building, quickly unlocking the door before darting towards the elevator.

"Come on, you stupid thing," I snarl, smashing the button to close the doors over and over again. This fucking thing seems to be fucking with me, ticking up as slow as molasses. I stare at the numbers as they slowly climb, finally stopping on our floor. The lights flicker in the hallway the second I step out of the box, the sudden drop in temperature making me shiver involuntarily. What is up with this building?

I pause at the apartment, staring at the slightly open door before mustering up the courage to push it open the rest of the way. He would never leave the door open like that, and I'm greeted by utter darkness when I step inside. Quietly shutting the door behind me, I turn on the tableside lamp, which illuminates a bit of the living space while my eyes adjust to the dimness. The first thing I notice are his keys on the ground, then his clothes. I pick them up carefully, noting the faint smell of smoke wafting off of them and the dirt caked into the material. One of his Halloween costumes sits draped on the back of the couch, a strange place to put something so random.

"Reese?" I call out, my voice breaking and barely cutting through the deafening silence in the room. Slowly, I head towards the bedroom, where no light fills the room either. "Reese?"

Still no response, but I hear the faint sound of running water coming from the bathroom. I shouldn't go in there. I shouldn't just barge in there while he's naked and wet, but something urges me forward. I don't know if it's my anxiety or just the strange pull I have towards him, but my feet move carefully across the floor until I'm pushing the slightly open door further.

My eyes widen in horror as I take in the room. Pieces of mirror are scattered all over the floor, the sink in ruins, and the vanity light flickering with only one bulb remaining out of the four. The shower *is* running, with Reese inside it, but seeing him tears my heart in two.

He's on the floor, his legs drawn up with his arms wrapped around them and his face buried into his knees while he slowly rocks back and forth. The glass of the shower is clear of steam, the door open for water to splash out against the tiles, soaking the bathmat at its entrance. I shiver as I step closer, quickly realizing that he's shivering and his skin has long since pruned.

How long has he been sitting here with cold water pelting down on his body. He doesn't even react to my presence and doesn't flinch at the icy cold droplets raining down on him.

"Reese?" No reaction. Not a twitch of muscle breaking from the metronome rhythm of his rocking. He doesn't glance up, not even when I finally get close enough to turn off the shower. I thought that he only had the cold water running, but I realize he's been sitting in here long enough for the hot water to run cold. He didn't even turn the cold water on to regulate the temperature, and he must have burned himself with how scalding I know the water can get.

His skin is angry red along his shoulder and upper back where he took the brunt of the hot water when it ran. His skin pebbles, rippling wildly when I turn off the water and the cold air settles against his skin.

"Reese, please get up. You're going to make yourself sick."

His rocking stills and he slowly lifts his head enough for his eyes to settle on me. They look bleak—hollow. Not looking at me but looking *through* me. "You're not real," he croaks out, his head lifting further, enough for me to notice his bluish lips and the way his bottom jaw trembles. His teeth clench together, squeaking viciously as they chatter. "You're not real," he says again, slamming his eyes closed before burying his face into his knees again.

This is bad. I've never seen him like this, and I don't know what to do. Do I call Kaine now and tell him I need help with him? What would he do in this situation? Maybe Reese needs to see someone, but I think it'll piss him off if we haul him away to some institute to check him over, but he's not right mentally. I can't figure out why he thinks I'm not really here, unless my ignoring him has broken him to the point where the thought of me showing up would be nothing more than a figment of his imagination.

My actions towards him might not have been the final nail in his mental coffin but they sure as fuck were the catalyst to his downward spiral. If he lost Julia, he would be devastated, so the way he's acting now just confirms it. The girl was so young, and I know he was worried about her and the prognosis of her condition. It's not healthy for him to react like this though, and maybe his line of work isn't the best thing for him. Not mentally anyways. He's forming attachments with the patients, probably a side-effect of not having parents of his own that cared for him the way they should have.

I know his mother passed away from a degenerative disease as well and that was one of the main reasons he went into medicine to begin with. He never went into detail as to why he chose to work with kids, so everything is based on assumption and observation.

I grab a towel off the rack, crouching down next to him to drape it over his shoulder and around his body. "Hey, look at me."

I brush my hand through his hair, pushing back the wet strands as he slowly lifts his head once more. He doesn't look at me though, staring blankly at a spot in front of him. His eyes are rimmed red, the tissue underneath them darkened like he hasn't gotten proper sleep in a few days.

I know he was struggling with nightmares, more so lately in comparison to when we first moved in, but I chalked it up to stress at work and nothing more. The mind has a funny way of trying to figure out your actions in the waking world by throwing you into situations in the subconscious mind, but this is beyond anything I've seen from him.

This exhaustion I'm seeing isn't just physical, but mental. He's drained himself to the point he no longer realizes what's real and what's imagined, and I'm hoping that some proper rest will at least give him a small reprieve from the turmoil within his mind.

"Let's get you to bed and warm you up. I'll make you a hot cup of tea, and you can sleep, okay?"

He blinks, tipping his head enough that he finally glances at me from the corner of his eye. "Ronnie?"

"I'm here. Come on."

A small sob gets trapped in his lungs, but he nods his head, letting me help him to his feet. I carefully guide him around the broken glass still strewn across the floor, halting him to stand still while I wipe down his body, drying him off as much as possible before leading him back out into the bedroom.

He stands like a statue where I leave him, not moving a single muscle outside of the small sway his body does, as though fighting with itself not to collapse. Seeing him like this is difficult. He's always been strong and put together and funny at the perfect moments but seeing him broken like this shatters my heart.

I rummage through his drawer, pulling out a warm pair of flannel pants and a t-shirt before heading back over to him. His head is tipped down, allowing his still damp hair to fall chaotically over his dark eyes. Seeing him like this already makes me miss the light in his eyes, but there's nothing there but shadows and shattered thoughts.

"I'm going to get you dressed. Is that okay?"

He says nothing. Not a flicker of emotion across his face or a nod in acknowledgment, but I pull the towel away from his hips and toss it off to the side. I'll never get used to his body, honed to perfection. He's beyond muscular, every curve and bulge prominent like it's been cut from marble. He has a few scars, ones he's refused to tell me how he got, which now makes me realize I don't know all that much about him.

"Lift your leg for me." He hesitates long enough that I wonder if my words are registering in his brain, but eventually, he reaches out a shaky hand to brace against the wall, lifting one of his legs and then the other for me to get his pants on. I slide them up his thighs, sucking in a sharp breath as I reach his hips, settling the material there. My fingers trace along the lines of his obliques, his skin cold to the touch. Goosebumps rise in the wake of my touch, scattering across the surface and making him visibly shudder.

"What are you doing?" He whispers, his voice low and so fucking broken.

I clear my throat, grabbing the T-shirt from the floor before standing up in front of him. I pull it on over his head, helping him slip his arms through the holes and settling the material down over his torso. I don't like the fact that he looks so pale and that his lips still look blue in the flickering light still coming from the bathroom.

"Come on." I hold out my hand to him, reaching towards his when he makes no effort to take the offering. His steps are sluggish as I lead him over to the bed and pull back the covers. "Get in." I help ease him down, his shuddering breath tightening my chest. He crawls under the covers, letting me pull them over him and tuck them around him.

He's still too cold, so I head over to the closet and dig through one of the storage containers to pull out my heated blanket. I barely used the thing since he always ran warm, not needing a heater when I had him lying next to me. Now, it might be the only thing available to get his temperature back up to a safer level. I plug it in quickly, tossing it over his lumpy form.

"I'm going to make you some tea."

He doesn't respond; not like I expected him to. He's almost reaching a catatonic state, going through the motions while only reacting to outside stimuli on a primal, base-species level. It's like the human side of him has taken a nap, leaving room for his lesser self—his lizard brain—to take over. It's survival instinct, but it's doing a shitty job if it allowed him to freeze to the point he did.

He basically tortured himself, waterboarding his own body to the point of borderline hyperthermia. It's a fact I shouldn't know much about, but I've witnessed far worse in my younger years, memories I wish I could lock away and forget. Cacophonies of screams still echo in my mind, no matter how much I try to overwrite them.

His body still trembles, whether it's just from the chill that's seeped into his bones or from the trauma of the events of today or quite possibly a combination of both, I'm not sure. I settle my hand on his hip, feeling the blanket slowly warming against my palm, and hopefully warming his frigid body. Quietly making my way out of the room gives me time to think—time to process what I can from what I've witnessed and experienced in these short minutes I've been here. Home. This *was* my home and I miss being here.

His smell lingers over every surface, mixed in with my own scents, things I've placed around the place to make it feel like *our* home. Other than the bathroom, the apartment looks untouched. Has he not eaten since I left? The thought has guilt rearing in my system, and no matter how hard I try to squash it down, it still claws and scrapes at me.

I didn't do this to him, but I made it worse. I wasn't there for him when he needed me. I wasn't there when he went through something as traumatic as losing his first patient. He tried to call me, and I ignored him once again—my own hardheadedness pushing me to cut him out like I've done with countless others in my life.

I set the kettle down on the stove to heat, moving to my special cabinet with my assortment of specialties teas. I can't help smiling at seeing them, my little collection of bliss. Reese has helped add to them over the last few months, enjoying my happiness every time he gave me a new one he claimed to have found at random. I don't think it was random, not even close. I've tried to find some of them in stores, but they're only available online, and at a hefty price. I appreciate his efforts though, even if he's spent too much money on me for something as useless as tea.

I pick one of my favourite ones—one that helps with sleep and relaxation. Opening the tin, my eyes flutter closed at the sweet and heady aroma seeping into my sinuses. Hopefully he likes it. He supports my tea obsession, but from what I could tell, he was never a fan of drinking them himself. The kettle begins to whistle, so I quickly grab one of my favourite mugs—another small obsession of mine for collecting—and set the bag into it, pouring the hot water over top. I smile at my cute, little tea timer, pressing the kitty's head and watching the time tick by.

Once it's finished, I add a little bit of milk and carefully carry it back to the bedroom. Reese is exactly where I left him, in the same position under the covers. I set the mug down on the nightstand and gently tug the blanket down to touch his shoulder. His body is slowly warming, but I hate how he still doesn't react to my touch.

"Reese? I brought you tea. Can you sit up for me." I peek over him, seeing that his eyes are open—unblinking. "Reese?"

He tips his head to the side, one of his eyes settling on me for a second before he finally sighs and carefully rolls himself over. He winces in pain while he attempts to sit himself up, and I help him by pushing his pillows under his shoulders against the headboard.

"Here. It's nice and warm so it should heat you up from the inside out."

He lets out a humourless huff but doesn't say anything as he takes the mug from my hands. He avoids touching me, grabbing it gingerly and bringing it to his lips. The sip is tentative, but his shoulders relax. He glances at me through his lashes, his eyes finally focusing on me like he's seeing me for the first time. He stares, taking another sip and letting out a small hum.

"Dreamweaver," he murmurs, licking his lips. I gape at him, surprised he knows the name of the tea when he's never had it before. "It's one of your favourites," he says, as though reading my thoughts. My expression must show my surprise, enough that he was able to figure out what my train of thought was.

His eyes follow me as I make my way over to the plush chair in the corner of the room, and I swear I see a flicker of disappointment. He doesn't voice it though, sipping the tea until he tips back the mug, draining the rest of the contents. He shifts himself back down in bed, rolling over so his back is to me once more.

I want to talk to him. I want to ask him if he's okay and what else is going on with him. I want to tell him I love him and that I wish he would just accept that or admit to me that he doesn't want me. Round and round my mind goes—chaotic and unfiltered—but I don't ask any of those things. He's already going through enough and I don't want my bombardment of questions to overwhelm him further.

So, I sit and watch him. Watching over him until his breathing steadies and I know he's asleep. Quietly, I lift from the chair, moving to the heated blanket to turn it off. I'd love to leave it on for him, but I don't want to overheat him once his body gets back to its normal state. He still needs to warm up more though, my fingers brushing along the back of his neck and still noticing he's quite cold to the touch.

I do the only other thing I can think of and strip out of my clothes, grabbing one of my baggy T-shirts from the drawer, and climbing into bed beside him. I stare at his sleeping face. The way his hair curls as it dries, falling loosely across his brows and over his lashes. He's been talking about getting a haircut for a while now but hasn't found the motivation to go get one.

I'm not complaining. I quite like the way he looks when it's longer like this, the desire to run my fingers through the soft strands, a nagging voice in my head. Carefully, I do just that, pushing his hair away from his eyes. My fingers linger on his skin, running over the bridge of his nose and the ridge of his cheekbone. His lips part slightly on an exhale, drawing my eyes down to the plump pillows.

Colour is beginning to come back into them, turning them back into their luscious pink hue that I love kissing. I run my thumb over the bottom one, tugging it gently down and smiling when it snaps back up once I release it. I've always loved his lips. Scratch that. I've always loved everything about him. He's beautiful in a mysterious way, exuding an edge of danger and darkness that lingers beneath the surface of his perfectly sculpted body. His eyes have always held such warmth, whether towards me or his friends, a deep chocolate brown that I get lost in every time I stare into them.

Tonight, they weren't the same, not even close. Tonight, they seemed distant and void of any hope or kindness within their depths. Tonight, they seemed darker, as though possessed by the ghosts of his past and the traumas of the present.

Tomorrow, we need to talk, something I've been avoiding when I knew I couldn't avoid it for long. We both need to deal with what is going on between us, whether that's to get closure on the end of our relationship, or a possible path for our future. I've waited a long time, but after seeing how broken he is, I know I need to be patient with him. I just wish he would really talk to me. Not just about us or mundane things, but about what makes Reese, Reese.

CHAPTER FIFTEEN

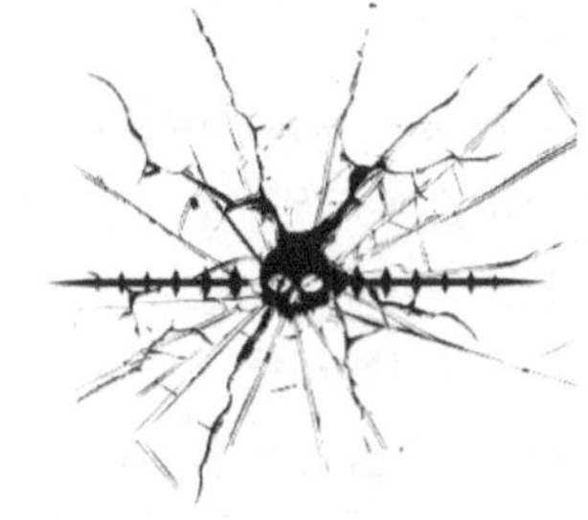

REESE

I'm frozen. Physically frozen. Okay, so maybe not *physically*, but it sure as fuck feels like it. I blink a few times, trying to process whether or not this is a dream or a reality. The wiggling toes between my calves sure as fuck feel real, but I still reach out my hand towards the girl in front of me, lacing my fingers through her hair and letting the soft strands sift through my fingers.

She nuzzles her head into the pillow, letting out a soft sigh as her eyes slowly open. They stay hooded, but they're clear and locked on mine. "Is—is this real?" I whisper.

Her brows dip and her lips press into a thin line. I don't want to upset her, but the question seems to have done just that. I can't handle it if she pulls away from me now, not when I can feel the soft skin of her cheek against my knuckles as I tuck her hair behind her ear.

"Are you okay?" She asks, and I don't know whether to be thankful or disappointed in the fact she didn't respond to my question.

"I don't know."

"What happened last night?"

Memories come flooding in, pushing bile to rise in my throat. Julia. Killing Jeremy. Seeing someone else staring back at me in the mirror. After that, everything is a blur of thoughts, sensations, and sounds. I start with the easiest thing to explain, but the hardest and heaviest on my heart.

"Julia passed away yesterday. She only had a few days to live after the test results came back the day before, but she didn't make it. It was her birthday."

Her eyes bow and she reaches her hand up to touch my cheek. I can't help the small gasp that slips out at her touch, my eyes closing of their own volition. "I'm so sorry. I know how much you cared about her."

"It's not fair."

"It never is. We can't control who gets taken and when, all we can do is be there for them and do the best we can to make the people we care about feel loved." Her thumb moves rhythmically across my cheek, soothing and kind. "Even when they don't want to accept the fact that someone does love them," she whispers.

This is a dangerous subject to be throwing at me in my moment of mental instability. I've not been well since she left me, and the source of that discourse is because she said three words, I wasn't ready or capable of hearing. "I can't do this right now."

She frowns, her eyes focusing on her hand as she shifts it down to settle at the side of my neck. She tries to be subtle, but I know she's checking my pulse point. Whether it's to make sure I'm okay or to test if I'm lying to her, I'm not sure. Either way, she keeps her fingers pressed to the area, glancing up at me through her lashes.

"Do you want me here?" She whispers.

"Of course I do."

"Will you ever feel the same way about me that I feel towards you?"

I swallow around the lump forming in my throat. "I hope so."

She stays quiet, studying my face for a few long breaths. I'm not lying. I *do* hope I can feel that way about her. I think I already do, but I can't let myself feel those emotions. I'm too fucked up—too broken. Love is a weakness that can be used against you. Love gets the people you care about hurt. Love hurts you in return because once that love is ripped away from you, there's nothing left of you. No soul, no emotion, no fucking life. The will to live becomes a battle. A fight that feels all-consuming and futile.

"Did you destroy the bathroom because of Julia?"

No.

"Yes."

Her gaze softens at the lie. I wish I could tell her. I wish I could talk to her about everything that's going on inside my head, but I don't even understand it myself. I need to talk to Kaine. I wanted to avoid it for as long as possible, but now I'm seeing things that shouldn't be there. Is it a trick of the mind, or is Avery haunting me. My hand twitches at the urge to slam my palm against my temple in a desperate attempt to dislodge the images of him staring back at me. It had to have been him. He's still here. He's still inside my fucking head.

"I should clean up the mess."

"I already did last night. Once I knew your body temperature was back to normal, I cleaned up the glass and everything." She turns, shifting herself until she's lying on her back, staring up at the ceiling. "I called Kaine, too. He's the one that called me, worried."

"He asked you to come here?" Disappointment settles into me at the fact she didn't want to come here on her own but was coerced by my best friend out of guilt and nothing more.

"He was going to come himself. He called to see if I had spoken to you and showed concern about your behaviour when you called him." She tips her head to look at me, a sad smile pulling at her lips. "I told him I would check on you and then update him, so I did."

"You didn't have to."

"I know, but I *was* worried about you, Reese. I know you don't want to hear it, and you would rather pretend like it didn't happen, but I do love you. You don't have to say it back because I rather it comes from feeling it yourself sincerely and not out of obligation or expectation. If you never feel that way towards me, well..." She pulls in a long breath, closing her eyes. "We'll deal with that when it comes to that point, but for now, I don't want you to push me away. When will you realize that you can trust me and talk to me? I don't need you to spill all your secrets or your life story at once, but I hope that eventually, I'll be able to understand you properly."

"You don't tell me much about yourself either," I snap back, feeling my defensive wall going up, brick by brick. "You've never told me anything about your parents other than you don't speak to your father anymore. Pretty funny considering you ran off to him the night you left here."

Her mouth pops open in surprise before she huffs out a breath and rolls her eyes. "Fuck's sake, Eden has a big mouth."

"Did you seriously think she wouldn't tell Kaine?"

"He didn't need to tell you!"

"He's my best friend."

"Right, and that's why he knows more about you than I do."

I balk at that. "We've known each other since we were kids. We grew up together and he's like my fucking brother. You can't compare my relationship with him to ours."

"And what about Eden? She's known Kaine for a little over a year. They're getting married and they know everything about each other and they fucking talk to each other."

"How do you know they tell each other everything?"

She lifts a brow, a rueful smile tugging the corner of her mouth. "They're basically the same person. One of them jumps and the other one follows. You can't tell me that people who act like that—who practically move as one being—don't know everything about each other. If soulmates actually existed, they would be the ones to represent that."

If she only knew how right she was on all counts, but once again, it's something I can't talk to her about. It's not my secret to tell, and at this point, it would be dangerous for her to know.

What's to say the reaper douchebags don't decide that her knowing all the information of their inner workings and manipulation would be grounds for her removal. I couldn't live with myself if she were taken from this world because she found out the truth about everything. It's bad enough she's at risk for even being in my presence, not just because of Avery still lingering about, but because of my family.

"What do you want to know? I can't guarantee I can tell you everything about myself because there are things about me that are better off being left in the dark."

She props herself up in bed, hovering half over me with wide eyes. The way her hair curtains over her shoulder to drape slightly across my chest is enticing to say the least. It makes me want to run my fingers through it, grip into it and tighten against her strands until she lets out a blissful moan. I want to do it, but I don't, too enamored by the curiosity in her gaze.

"You're serious?" I nod. "Tell me about your mom."

I blink, surprised that's the first thing she asks. She already knows a little bit about her, at least what happened in my later years right up until she passed away.

"What exactly do you want to know about her? I've told you about her before."

"What was she like when you were younger? I don't really remember a lot about my mom, but the small bits I do remember...I think they're good memories. She would take me and my sister for ice cream every Friday." A sad smile spreads across her face, her eyes slightly glazing over as the memory settles into her.

"You have a sister?" This is news to me. I thought she grew up as an only child like I did.

"I do. I still talk to her, but we don't hang out very much. She's apparently moving to Cameron in a few months and she's getting married, so I might get to hang out with her more then. Dad likes her more than me, but she doesn't give a shit about him either."

"What's her name?"

Theresa, but I just call her Tessa."

"It's nice that you still have family that you can talk to."

She settles her hand on my chest, slowly drawing her fingers across my pecs before placing it over my heart. She flattens her palm, staying silent for a few chaotic heartbeats. My body stiffens when she lowers herself, moving her hand out of the way and replacing it with her ear, her cheek nuzzling into my muscles.

"Is this okay?"

Hesitantly, I curl my arms around her, letting the warmth of her small body seep into me. "More than okay."

She hums out an adorable breath, wrapping her arm around my torso and pulling herself further onto my body. "I missed you."

"I missed you, too, Ronnie."

"So, your mom..."

The little stink. I took advantage of her distraction and hoped that she was letting me off the hook, but that was clearly too much to ask for. I need to at least give her something because I don't want her to feel like I'm hiding things from her for the sake of hiding them. I'm not. At least, I think I'm not.

"My mother was the sweetest woman you could ever meet. She was kind and gentle, and an extremely loving parent. She did everything she could for me while we still lived with my dad, and even more once we left him. We moved to a small town just outside of Cameron when I was eight years old with nothing more than what we could carry."

"Did your mom divorce your dad?"

I shake my head. "Our family doesn't *do* divorce. My father wasn't a good man. He never loved my mother, it was..." I'm bordering on dangerous territory here, but I don't think she'll let it go since I've already breached the subject. "It was an arranged marriage. It was a stupid one in my opinion; nothing gained on my father's side, to my knowledge. He had nothing to lose though, while my mother gave up everything she ever knew for him. I think...now that I think about it, I wonder if it was just some sort of deal to pay of a debt on her parents' side."

She stiffens against me, pushing me to glance down at her, but her face is turned away from me so I can't see her expression. Is this topic difficult for her? I know it's unconventional in this day and age and I don't agree with it myself, but unfortunately, it's part of the history of how I came into existence.

"What was her name?"

"Rory. Rory Mitchel."

She pushes herself up to look at me, her brows dipping in confusion. "Wait. Why did you just say your last name? Isn't it a given?"

"I—I have my mother's maiden name. She had everything legally changed for both of us when we left him."

"What's his name?"

My throat dries at the question. I need to tread carefully, or I'll risk exposing who and what I am to her. The Brennan family isn't extremely well known, but any bit of research on her part will show her what that side of the family consists of.

"I can't answer that."

"Can't or won't."

"Can't and shouldn't. It's...a safety concern."

"Is he famous or something? Are you some rich kid with a massive trust fund?" She snorts.

"Something like that." I rather she thinks that, than to know the truth.

She folds her arms on my chest to rest her chin on them, keeping her eyes locked on mine. My gaze shifts to her mouth when her tongue darts out to wet her lips, making them glisten in invitation. "Thank you for telling me."

"Is it satisfactory?"

A wry grin. "For now," she chirps. "But I hope you'll keep answering my questions to the best of your abilities. It's okay if you can't or don't feel like sharing certain things about yourself or your life, Reese, but even small bits at least give me a small window into the person you used to be."

"The person I used to be doesn't matter. I don't *want* to be that version of myself ever again."

I say that, but the words feel like acid on my tongue. I may not want to be him, but the past never truly goes away. It lies dormant until it decides to activate once more, festering and spreading until the new life that has been attempting to grow is completely snuffed out by the haunting ghosts.

"Hmm, well I'm not complaining. I like this you. You're sweet and kind and pretty and really good in bed."

"Is that all?" I laugh. Fuck, it feels weird to laugh and actually mean it. These last few days have felt like a piece of myself has been missing, and it has. I didn't realize how much Ronnie had ingrained herself into me, but having her back here, lying in my arms, feels like the final piece of the puzzle sliding into place.

CHAPTER SIXTEEN

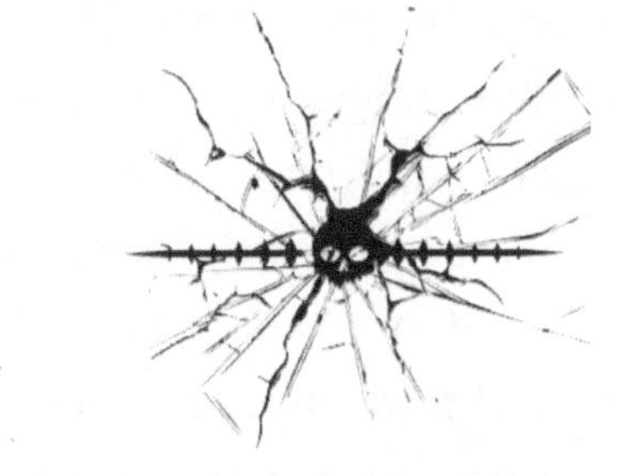

RONNIE

I can't stop staring at him. I'm in so much trouble, seriously. It's like his body has a hypnotic hold on me, drawing me in and melting away the reality trying to press in around me. I consider myself lucky to be with him. Reese was the unattainable. He barely entertained any of the girls at college, only dating a few his first year in the program and brushing off everyone as the years went on.

There was a rumor that went around that he was gay, but I didn't believe it. He's quiet and keeps to himself, only really socializing with Kaine. Kaine had parties all the time. I got invited to a few of them, but I kept saying no since it was never really my scene, until eventually, I stopped being asked. I kept to myself, too. It was nice; being able to observe people around me and learning all their tells and mannerisms. It was something my father taught me from a young age. It's easier to get into people's heads if you stay under the radar and watch for their mistakes and habits. It gives you leverage in situations you might not be able to get out of otherwise.

I've spent plenty of time observing Reese, but I was too shy to speak to him. He was intimidating, and the way he never gave girls a second look just made my self-confidence plummet further. When Kaine put out that little notice that Reese was single, it gave me hope. If he hadn't paid attention to the bombshells that attempted to throw themselves at him, maybe they weren't his type. He never made it obvious that he was into Kaine, and then Kaine made it public that he was with Eden.

I hated the rumours that started about them and the way people talked because they were—are—stepsiblings. They met that year, so how can anyone be against a relationship like that? It was inspiring and motivational. Seeing someone like Eden, who was shy and not the typical girl Kaine hung out with, bagging one of the biggest hotties in the program, gave me the courage to speak to Reese.

I talked to Eden a few times and Kaine was nice enough in classes, but my small obsession turned into a bigger one the more time passed. The tipping point for him was probably when he saw me slap one of the girls across the face for talking shit about Eden, calling her fat and ugly. I begged him not to tell her, and he just smiled, leaning down towards me to whisper in my ear. *"Your secret's safe with me."*

I still remember his voice so clearly that day and the heat of his body. Everything about his presence in that moment had my skin pebbling and the hairs on the back of my neck standing on end. It was like he siphoned all the air from my lungs, causing my chest to tighten and my heart to beat at a rhythm that should have killed me. His smell was a welcoming embrace then, and now it makes me feel at peace—like I'm home.

Watching him now while he moves around the kitchen making breakfast—something he insisted on doing, and when I tried to argue, he threw me over his shoulder and slammed me down in the stool at the island—I can see myself being with him. Like *really* being with him. I can see our future forming right in front of me and it's something I want so desperately to become a reality.

Finding out my sister was getting married sent a wave of emotions through me. I'm happy for her, but I'm a bit jealous as well. She's always been sociable and easy to talk to. She had a ton of friends growing up and got along with pretty much everyone. She's got a bit of a mean streak though, and if you risk crossing her, she has no issues fighting back, and that's what I love about her. She was my protector once mom died, filling in the maternal void and keeping our dad's attention away from me.

It worked for a time, but there's only so much someone can handle. Once she went off to school, she couldn't protect me anymore. She tried. She's the one that encouraged me to move out and live on campus so I could get away from dad. I learned a lot from him, but I also learned what I didn't want in a man. Each day I stayed in that house while Tessa was gone, was another piece of my soul slowly getting carved away.

I shake my head, trying to break the hold my memories continue to have on me. "Do you have to work today?" He asks, glancing at me over his shoulder.

"No. You?"

"I took a few days off, but I'm planning to go to Julia's funeral once Diana gets everything arranged."

I hate the way his shoulders slump and how his voice lowers in sadness. I've lost people in my life and so has he, but I have no experience losing someone so young. I don't know how he does it—working with kids and knowing that they might not leave the confines of that hospital.

"If you want company, I'll go with you."

He turns, a plate loaded with an egg white omelet, sausages, and rye toast in one hand, and a steaming cup of tea in the other. He sets it down in front of me, propping his forearms on the island to lean towards me. I take in the spread, warmth spreading through me at how good he is to me.

"You would do that?"

I blink, prying my eyes away from the food in front of me to look at him. I lick my lips, covering up the fact I was just drooling over food. Fuck, these last few days have been rough. I can't cook for myself in a hotel or at work, so I've had to live off takeout, and those options are pretty limited around here.

"Of course I would. I'll do whatever you need me to do."

He quirks a brow, his lip twitching as he fights back a smile. "Will you now?" I shudder at the drop in his voice and bite my lip, giving my head a small nod. "Hmm, eat your breakfast."

"Yes, Sir."

He snorts, rolling his eyes and pushing off the counter to get to work on his own breakfast. I can't keep the stupid grin off my face because why is he so fucking adorable? I miss the playful side of him. I don't know what darkness has been plaguing him, but the nightmares that were few and far between became more frequent, and since then, his mood has shifted and his personality has shut down. He used to joke all the time, easily making me laugh and doing the stupidest things with me. Even with Kaine, he's been different, his eyes seeming empty and his mind wandering, even when he's being spoken to directly.

I don't want to push him, but I want to find a way to bring him back. He hasn't kicked me out or pushed me away for asking about his mother, and I could tell that subject was a touchy one. I'm sure it helps that I didn't put pressure on him to express himself and profess his love for me in return, but I wasn't going to hold back in telling him the truth or try to play it off that I didn't actually mean it. Of course I meant it. How could I *not* love him when he's been amazing and everything I could ever ask for.

It's like he expects me to want more; like he wants me to find someone better because he's undeserving of the affection and love I have to offer him. I don't *want* anyone else, and the sooner he realizes it, the happier he'll be. He's still hiding things from me with his quick wit and easy evasion. It's as though he's been trained in what to say and how to speak, lying in a way that doesn't feel like lying but borders on deception and manipulation. I studied a bit on psychological disorders and mental health, but I haven't found any signs in him that would point to a personality disorder or psychopathic tendencies.

Could Reese be a dangerous person? Absolutely. I think everyone is capable of doing bad things and have probably done something questionable at some point in their lives. Do I think Reese could or would ever hurt me? No. There isn't a doubt in my mind that Reese would never be capable of causing me real harm. Emotionally, yes, but I know he didn't do it on purpose.

He lifts a brow when he turns again, tilting his head in question when his eyes drift to the still full plate in front of me and the quickly cooling tea. "Is something wrong?" I shake my head. "You haven't touched your food or your tea."

"I was just lost in thought...and I wanted to wait for you," I add, kicking myself for having been so distracted with my mental analysis that I didn't realize I'd just been staring off into the abyss.

"What were you thinking about?" He asks, sliding into the stool next to me and shoving a healthy helping of scrambled eggs into his mouth. The man can eat, but with a body like that, it's no surprise he needs the energy. *So* much fucking energy. He has the stamina of a fucking cheetah and can go for hours and—"Ronnie?"

I shake my head again.

Fucking hell, get your fucking mind out of the gutter, Ronnie.

"Lots of things, but mainly us."

"Oh?"

"Are you happy?"

"What do you mean?"

"Are you happy...with *me*?"

I squeak out in surprise at the sudden jolt of my seat towards him, the legs of the stool scraping against the tile as he drags me closer to him. I can feel his eyes burning a hole into the side of my face, and heat quickly scatters up my neck into my cheeks. I risk a glance at him from the corner of my eye, looking away quickly when that penetrating gaze catches me.

"I'm sorry if I've made you feel like you don't make me happy."

"No, that's not it. I just—if there's anything I can say or do to make you more comfortable because I've made you *uncomfortable*, I would hope you would tell me. I can't fix something if I don't know what's wrong."

"You've done nothing wrong."

"But in your eyes, saying that I love you, *was* wrong." I close my eyes in horror; at the fucking word vomit that I can't seem to keep under control when I'm being torn apart by his eyes.

He sighs, leaning slightly away from me. Panic settles into my chest at the thought of him pulling away again, like he did the last time because I can't seem to keep my fucking mouth shut. Why can't I let this go? Why can't my brain just file this stupid argument away for later when we're both in a better headspace than the fucked up one we're both clearly experiencing right now?

"I'm sorry," I whisper, finally picking up my fork to dig into my meal. "It's really good, Reese. Thank you." I'm trying anything I can to move away from the stupid topic that I can't let go of, but the longer he sits there without speaking, the more my anxiety spikes. I hold back a sigh of relief when I hear his own fork clinking against the plate.

We eat in silence after that. I'm too scared to bring anything up because I don't want him to think I'm trying to just evade the subject, even though I am. I settle into drinking my tea once I'm done, sighing happily at the taste of the creamy earl grey. The mug pauses against my lips when he slips the plate out from in front of me and walks over to the sink with the dishes.

"I can clean up, you cooked."

"It's fine."

"Reese—"

"I said it's fine, Ronnie." I snap my mouth closed, slowly setting the mug back down on the counter. He sighs, shoulders hunching once more as he curls his hands around the edge of the sink.

"I'm sorry."

"Stop apologizing!" He snaps. "Just...stop." The edge to his words turns into a plea. It's so hard to see him like this. He's always so put together, so seeing him snapping so easily and getting rattled by the smallest things is difficult to deal with.

His back stiffens at the sound of my stool being dragged back but he doesn't turn to look at me. The way he holds his body freakishly still and rigid makes me wonder what he could possibly be thinking. Does he think I'll walk away from him again? It was cruel of me to leave him the way I did that day, without a word or any sign that I was pushed to that point, but I couldn't handle my own emotions. I hated the feeling of rejection, and I was afraid that if I had stuck around, I would have broken in front of him completely.

I don't want to seem weak in his eyes. He's surrounded himself with people who can hold their own and stand up for themselves, and I don't want to be considered a weak link—a chink in his armor. I want to be someone he deserves; someone who can stand by his side and not someone who just slinks along in his shadow. I want to be there for him and show him that I'm ready for whatever gets thrown at us because we're stronger together than when we're apart.

All these wants are just that—wants. I can't make them come true unless he wants that, too. I can't make him see that I'm strong unless I actually put in the effort to prove that to him.

I settle my hand on his back, rubbing gently between his shoulder blades and feeling the tight bands of muscle flexing under my palm. "Reese—"

"I didn't mean to snap at you, I'm just—I'm having a hard time right now."

"It's okay to be vulnerable, especially with me. You don't have to hide from me. You don't need to pretend like you're okay when you're not."

He lets out a humourless laugh, bowing his head. "I'm definitely not okay."

I wrap my arms around him and press my lips to his back before nuzzling my cheek into him. I can't help but taking a deep inhale of him, letting his scent settle into my system. His abs tense under my wandering hands, the ripple of muscle flexing harder the further down I go.

"What can I do to make you feel a little better?"

CHAPTER SEVENTEEN

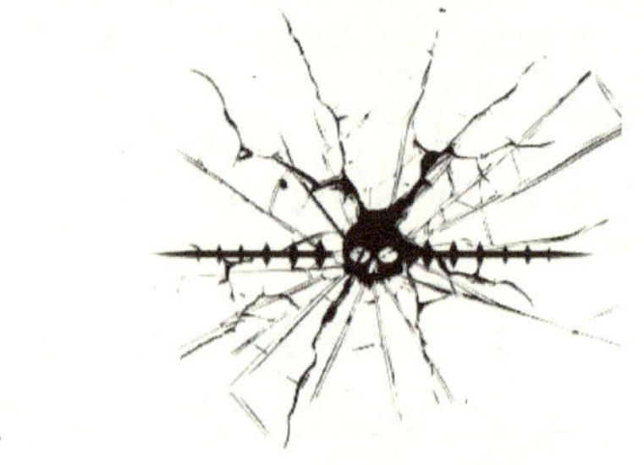

RONNIE

I expect him to pull away or grumble that there's nothing I can do for him. What I don't expect is for him to rip my arms away from him and turn quickly to face me. I stare up at him, eyes burning into mine with a spark I haven't seen in a long time. The flecks of gold and amber seem brighter—more prominent.

He settles my hands on his chest and slowly drags his own down my sides. They trail heat across my body, curling around to my back to grip into my ass. His fingers knead and grip into me, sending a wave of warmth and pleasure pulsing through my body. Heat builds in my stomach, shifting lower when he pulls me closer to him, holding me firmly against his own body.

I shudder at the feel of his fingers trailing down to the edge of the shirt, slowly lifting the material up enough to expose my naked flesh to the suddenly chill air.

"Hmm, you're not wearing any underwear," he muses. I shake my head. "Is there a reason for that?" I swallow, my eyes fluttering closed when those rough hands dig into my bare flesh. He palms me, gripping into each ass cheek to spread me. "Tell me, Ronnie. Were you expecting something from me when you decided to dress like this?" He slides a leg between mine and shoves my knees apart. My stomach clenches, the need to close my legs to hide what he's doing to me making my entire body tremble.

"I—I didn't expect anything."

"No?" He whispers, leaning closer to my ear and pulling the lobe into his mouth. His tongue swirls and licks before his teeth clamp down. The sensation courses through me and my hands curl into his t-shirt in an attempt to steady myself. My blood roars in my ears, my heart beating so frantically I'm sure he can hear it over the deafening silence between us. "Hmm."

He dips his head into the crook of my neck, and my breath shudders out of me, panting and chaotic as he slowly and lightly drags his nose up the tendon, inhaling deeply. "Reese," I say breathlessly.

"I want to forget. Even if it's just for a little while. Can I get lost in you, Ronnie? Will you let me drown myself in your smell?" A kiss to my throat. "Your heat?" He whispers, sliding his fingers down between my legs. "Your taste." A tentative press of his lips to mine before pulling back enough to look down at me once more.

I barely manage a nod through the hazy fog curling around my brain. I can't think straight, getting lost in the feel and smell of him all around me. It's all-consuming, but I don't want to be anywhere else. I want him. I want him so fucking badly that I would do anything for him at this point. I don't want to give him up because if I do, I have nothing—no one. I can't handle being on my own anymore with the looming threat of my father finally calling me back home.

He threatened it already when at my weakest moment I went to him. He has plans for me, but I don't want that life for myself. He couldn't control Tessa, so he's trying to flex his power and control over me now, claiming that I've had my fun but it's time to grow up and do what's expected of me. Reese is my only option. He can save me or break me, but I can't tell him what's waiting for me if we end up breaking up.

I gasp when he hikes me up onto his hips, crushing me against his body as he turns us around and settles me onto the edge of the counter. "Reese, what are—" My eyes widen when he locks his eyes on mine and slowly lowers himself down onto his knees, spreading my legs wide. Goosebumps break out against my skin as he slowly kisses my inner thigh and drags his hot tongue up and up until... "Oh, god," I moan, tipping my head back at the pure bliss of his mouth on me.

My fingers curl around the edge of the counter, my legs tensing and tightening against his shoulders with each lick of his tongue. He swirls against my pussy, lapping and delving it deep inside me. The feel of his mouth on me is mind-numbing and my body practically buckles when he sucks my clit into his mouth and then nips on it.

"Fuck," I whimper, thick heat spreading through my body and making my limbs go numb. He hums against me, and the vibration sends me floating higher. My hands launch out, gripping into his soft strands while he continues to eat me like he's a starving man.

"Fuck, you taste so good," he groans, lapping at my pussy with enough pressure to tip me over the edge. "That's it. Fucking drown me. Fuck, I love how wet you are."

For being so quiet in public, he's got a filthy mouth behind closed doors. Whether he's talking dirty or praising me, it gets me riled up and hot for him. I've had one boyfriend in my life, and it was the biggest mistake I made in my younger years. He didn't care if I came or not, only worried about his own pleasure and satisfaction. I thought there was something wrong with me, like I was broken or fundamentally wrong.

My first time with Reese wasn't what I expected. In my panic, I opened up to him, telling him how I felt and what had happened in the past. He didn't judge me, but he sure as fuck made it his mission to test everything he could think of to make me come. We didn't even have sex. He was perfectly content focusing his attention on me, tasting every inch of me and burying himself between my legs until I felt like I would pass out from the ecstasy.

My chest heaves with every breath and I struggle to look at him as he slowly lifts to his feet, pressing into my knees to slide his body between mine. His arms flex as he reaches behind him, pulling the t-shirt off his body. Fuck, he's ripped. Every muscle on his torso ripples and flexes with the movement and I can't pull my eyes away from them.

I gasp when he slides his fingers against my wet pussy, slipping his fingers in and curling them deliciously. He pulls them out too soon, leaving me aching and wanting.

"Open your mouth. I want you to taste yourself. I want you to lick these fingers clean of what I do to you."

I swallow, slowly opening my mouth for him to shove those fingers in. He slides them against my tongue, pressing up to his knuckles. He quirks a brow, smirking when I close my lips around them and swirl my tongue, licking up my own taste.

"Such a good girl," he purrs, pulling them out of my mouth and replacing them with his tongue. He moves so quickly that his mouth on mine steals my breath. I whimper into his mouth at the feel of his straining cock pressing against me through his sweatpants. The friction is amazing, but I want so much more.

"Fuck me," I breathe, tugging his bottom lip between my teeth and gripping into his ass with my legs to draw him closer. I fumble with the string on his pants, frantically trying to shove them down off his hips.

He growls against my mouth, diving his tongue in deep while his hands move to his pants to shove them down the rest of the way. He breaks the kiss long enough to grip the collar of my shirt, literally tearing it down the middle to pool uselessly over my body.

"Damn it. I liked that shirt," I grumble.

"I'll buy you a new one."

I giggle when he tears it off the rest of the way and tugs me closer to the edge of the counter, pressing his cock into me in the same motion. He groans into my mouth, the sound feral in the way it vibrates through my entire body. His fingers dig into my back, and I feel like I can't breathe. He's suffocating me with his kisses, lighting up my entire body with each deep thrust.

His fingers thread through my hair, yanking hard to expose my neck to him. He trails his tongue along the expanse, my mouth gaping open on a low moan. He nips and sucks at the skin, ramming into me hard enough my ass skids across the counter.

"Fuck," he growls, biting down hard on my jaw and lifting me up off the edge to seat me against him completely. His muscles bunch and bulge under my weight, but he moves me easily against his length, bouncing me up and down on his cock like he's trying to impale me.

His fingers tighten in my hair, forcing my mouth back on his, and then we're moving. His steps are sure and unbothered as he moves us to the wall, slamming my back against it. "Reese!" I cry out, pinned completely between his steel body and the unforgiving wall behind me.

Rolling his hips into me, he grabs my hands, lacing his fingers through mine, and pinning them to the wall above me. There's no escaping him. His grip is tight, his body is like fire, and his kisses are devastating. Each thrust of his hips is savage and punishing, sending ripples of pleasure through my entire body. My nerves are electrified, sparking against every nip and lick of his mouth and every slam of his hips against mine. I could die like this and I wouldn't care. Being surrounded by him—consumed by him—is a good way to go.

CHAPTER EIGHTEEN

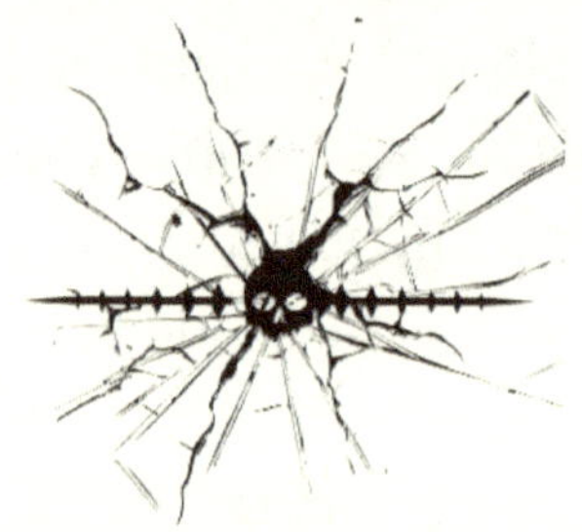

REESE

My mind is quiet, filled only by the sound of our mingled breaths and chaotic hearts. Her body trembles in my grip, arms weakly draped over my shoulders while I grip into her thighs to keep her pinned against me. I wanted to use her as a distraction and ended up getting lost in the feel of her and her willingness to let me do whatever I please. She's argumentative on the best of days, but when it comes to sex, she's been more than happy to do as I ask and take what I give her.

That's what happens when you *actually* take care of a woman. Her previous boyfriend was a prick, nearly ruining the girl and making her believe that there's something wrong with her. She wasn't the problem, *he* was. With her eyes finally open to the pleasure that could be given to her, she's done everything I could ever want. I've never pushed it too far though, not wanting to scare her with my deep need for control and desire to completely overtake my lovers.

This is the first time I've been this thoroughly aggressive with her, pinning her to the wall and nailing her like a god damn butterfly. She was completely at my mercy, unable to do anything but allow me to rut into her like a wild beast.

Her neck and jaw show signs of how aggressive I got, biting and sucking on her skin until I marked her. I'm sure she'll end up having bruises on her hips and ass too by tomorrow, but that's a problem to deal with at a later date.

I pull my face out of the crook of her neck, checking her over again. Her eyes are closed, lashes fluttering against her cheeks while harsh breaths puff out of her parted lips.

I tuck one arm under her ass, curling my other one around her back as I pull her away from the wall. She nuzzles her face into my neck, gently brushing her fingers into the hair at the nape of my neck over and over again in soothing strokes. I can't stop the shiver that skitters up my spine at the feel of her nails gently scraping against my skin, so gentle and lovingly.

No. I can't let my mind wander to that topic again. Not now, and probably not for a while. I'll let her feel what she needs to feel, and I have no intention of making her feel or believe that what she's experiencing is a mistake. It's not, and I do feel happy at the fact she cares about me that much. I care about her, too, I may even love her, but that's not an emotion I can allow myself to feel until I get control over all my thoughts and the other emotions running rampant through my head.

"Let me run you a bath," I murmur, carrying her towards the bedroom.

"Will you get in with me?"

"Hmm, you might be able to convince me."

I laugh at the way she clings to me like a koala, even though her limbs still shake, she's trying her little heart out at trying to stay attached to me while I run her bath. She doesn't release me until I slowly lower her into the tub, but just when I think about getting in, there's a knock at the door.

"Let me see who that is. It could be the landlord since I put in a complaint about the elevator." She frowns, biting her lower lip as she stares at me, but she doesn't say anything, just nods her head and lowers herself further into the water.

I quickly pull on a pair of sweatpants before heading back out, where the knocking has turned into full blown banging now. I rip it open, ready to beat whoever it is to a pulp, and stop short at the sight of a very angry Kaine.

"About time," he huffs, breezing past me without invitation. He pauses, turning slowly to look at me. He takes in my attire, or lack there of, and quirks a brow. "Did you and Ronnie make up?"

"Why do you ask?"

His grin widens. "It smells like sex in here." I roll my eyes, shoving him hard enough that he stumbles. "You seem to be in a better mood than you were when I talked to you last night," he laughs, following me into the kitchen.

"I *was* in a better mood until you showed up at my door unannounced."

He flops down on one of the stools, pointing towards the coffee pot with some of the leftovers from my breakfast. I sigh, pouring him a mug and sliding it over to him. "Ah. You make the best coffee."

"Why are you here, Kaine?"

"You don't look happy to see me."

"It's too early to be dealing with your obnoxious, overbearing personality."

"Well, maybe if your phone wasn't off, I wouldn't have had to come over to make sure you were still breathing. Ronnie never responded to my messages this morning either, so sue me for wanting to check on my best friend."

"Why did you call Ronnie last night? I didn't call you for you to go and do that."

"Don't fucking start. I was worried, and the way you just hung up on me, I didn't want you doing something stupid. Sorry for actually caring, Reese, but I don't exactly have the best luck when it comes to people I care about doing stupid shit."

"Low blow."

He shrugs. "Eden has rewired my brain chemistry, so I can't help but think of the what ifs anymore. Call it a defense mechanism."

"I'm fine."

"Are you?"

"No, I'm not, but I'm better than I was last night. I wasn't in the best headspace after everything that happened with my patient, and I called you out of habit."

"Why are you lying to me?"

"Excuse me?"

"I've known you for years, man. I know when you're lying."

Thankfully, I know that's not true. I hate to admit it, but I've lied to him plenty of times, the only time he's able to catch me in those lies is when I'm not thinking clearly, which is apparently right now. I haven't had enough time to process everything that happened last night, with Julia dying while I was on shift, me going off and killing her piece of shit father and then coming home to an apparition staring back at me in the mirror. I shudder at the memory of those grey eyes glowing through the darkness within the glass, hating the way he seemed to be judging me, like *I'm* the issue here.

"What do you want me to say, Kaine? Do you want me to tell you that I was so fucked up in the head that I went off and did something stupid?"

"Did you? Do something stupid I mean."

"No. I didn't go off and do something stupid." Not a lie because killing Jermey wasn't stupid, it was the right thing to do, and I would do it again if that fucker ever came back to life. I didn't exactly regret my actions last night, but it was just one more thing to add to my already fragile state. Another bullet against the slowly cracking glass protecting my psyche.

"Reese, is everything...oh...Kaine." I turn to see Ronnie walking down the hall in nothing but a towel wrapped around her frame. Her eyes are wide, fingers curling tightly around the material to keep it snug against her. "I didn't know you were coming over."

"If you bothered to check your phone, I wouldn't have had to."

"Oh, uh...I got a bit distracted this morning and didn't check it." A blush creeps across her cheeks when her eyes land on me.

I just smirk, turning my attention back to Kaine whose eyes are drifting back and forth between us.

"You mean, distracted by a big dick."

Her mouth pops open in surprise. "Reese made me breakfast."

"Oh, I'm sure he ate," he laughs.

"I'm going to punch you," I grumble.

"No wonder you're in a better mood," he grins. "If you were still all depressed after having sex, I'd be a bit more concerned." He props his elbow on the island and settles his chin on his palm, smiling like an idiot. "What's he like in bed, Ronnie?"

"Uh." She's floundering. Kaine's always been pretty open about *his* sex life, but he's never delved into mine. I'm not sure if I like it, and my hand twitches with the urge to throttle his ass. Is this how he felt when I was hanging out with Eden? Our interactions were innocent enough. I liked the girl, but I would have never crossed that line because of Kaine. She takes a step back, her eyes pleading with me.

"Will you leave her alone?"

"Is there a problem with me talking to your girlfriend about your sex life? I vividly remember you having these sorts of conversations with Eden."

He's got me there. What was I supposed to do, let the girl panic because she didn't know what she was doing? It's not like she was open about it to begin with because it took some coaxing to get her to speak up, but I think having someone to talk to about it was helpful. She didn't have any friends—definitely no girlfriends to gossip about—and sometimes it's nice getting that sort of info from a guy. I mean, if I like something I rather the girl knows it, and she was way too shy to straight up ask Kaine what he did and didn't like. He was also too lovestruck to be honest with her if she did something wrong. Except for that first time when she used teeth, but I would have panicked, too. Self-preservation and all that.

"That was different."

"How was that different?"

"Because *she* didn't know what she was doing and she wanted advice. It wasn't like we were just randomly talking about the two of you boning for shits and giggles."

"Wait. You gave her advice?" His eyes widen as he sits up straighter to stare at me.

"I mean, yeah. She didn't have any friends, dude. Who else was she going to ask?"

"Me! She could have asked me!" I don't even say anything, I just glare at him because he should know *why* she wouldn't.

"I'm going to put some clothes on," Ronnie says quietly.

"Why?" I smack him for that one, nearly knocking him off the stool. "What? She doesn't need to get dressed just because I'm here. I'm not going to look at her."

"Fucking hell, you're an asshole."

"Do you *want* me to look at her?"

"I honestly don't care. I'm not a sociopath like you who tries to maim anyone who even *looks* at Eden."

A sharp intake of breath has me glancing over towards Ronnie. She frowns, turning quickly and heading back down the hall. "Nice going," Kaine murmurs.

"Fuck." I'm wracking my brain, playing what I just said over and over again because I know I just fucked up. "I'll be back." He waves me off, sipping on his coffee like he's the Queen and can't be bothered with my panic. By the time I get to the room, Ronnie is tugging on a sports bra and already has underwear on. "Ronnie, I'm sorry."

"For what exactly?" She says, not bothering to look at me as she paws through her clothes until she finds a tank top and some yoga pants. She moves to the closet next, grabbing one of the sweaters hanging there before finally looking at me, lifting a brow in question. "Well?"

I have no idea *what* I'm apologizing for, but I know I should be doing it. What the fuck do I say? Fuck it. "I don't actually know. Clearly, I said something that upset you, but I can't figure out what it was."

She huffs out a derisive laugh. "You know," she starts, setting down the clothes on the bed to pull on her pants. "For someone who is *so* smart, you're sort of a dumbass." I balk at that, the words like a physical blow that jerks my body into taking a step back. "What you said out there...do you think that would make me feel good, Reese?"

"What part exactly?"

"The fact you don't care if others look at me. The fact you're shaming Kaine for giving a shit and *wanting* to protect Eden from guys."

"He literally threatened me on multiple occasions, and I wasn't even looking at her in a way that would ever show I was interested in her."

"You're missing the point here."

"As are you. I don't care if Kaine looks at you because I know he doesn't see you in that way. I know he won't try to take advantage of you or touch you inappropriately."

"That's not what you said though."

"Did you forget the part where I physically assaulted a guy the other night because he was fucking close to you!" I scream, my anger taking hold of every rational sense within me, fighting for its life. "Ronnie, obviously I give a shit, but not in this situation."

"So, if I walked out there right now and hung myself all over Kaine, you wouldn't care?"

My eye twitches, jaw clenching as I rush her and grab her arms to spin her around. "You will do no such thing."

"Who's going to stop me? You?" She snorts, squirming in my grip and frowning when my hold on her tightens. "Let me go, Reese."

"Where are you going?"

She tips her chin up defiantly, like she's contemplating telling me off or snapping at me. Thankfully, she does neither. "I'm going to the gym and then I'm meeting up with Eden to taste test some cakes." When I don't let her go, she lets out a heavy sigh. "Is that alright with you?" Her tone implies that she doesn't give a shit whether I agree or not, but I slowly release her, my arms falling limply at my sides.

She brushes past me, and the void that I thought was getting smaller opens up again. "What do you want from me, Ronnie? Do you *want* me to be possessive and controlling? Do you want me to be more like Kaine?" The question shouldn't hurt me as much as it does, but I thought I was doing right by her in giving her freedom and not letting my true nature take hold.

"Sometimes. At least Kaine shows how much he cares, Reese."

Her words are like a sword through my back as she walks away, leaving me swaying and struggling to pull in a proper breath. Kaine's always been the first pick on everyone's list. I mean, it's not like I've made it easy for people. I'm nice enough, but I don't usually give anyone the time or means to get to know me, and anyone in the past who has shown interest in me has just been boring and a hassle in my eyes. Ronnie was different—*is* different—but here she is, wanting me to be more like *him*.

A knock at the door rips me out of my head and I slowly turn to see Kaine standing in the doorway, eating one of my protein bars. "You good?"

"No," I grumble, finally moving out of my stupefied state to grab myself a shirt and a sweater.

"She seemed pissed when she left. Did she leave, or did she *leave*?"

"She's going to the gym and then meeting up with Eden for cakes."

"Oh, right. That's today."

"Don't you have to work?"

He shifts out of the way for me to slip through the door but quickly catches up to me. "I took a few days off. I figured my friend would appreciate some company."

"You figured wrong."

"Hey." I ignore him, grabbing my keys off the side table. "Reese," he huffs, grabbing my forearm just as I reach out for the doorknob. "What is going on with you? You're not usually this...cold, or short-tempered."

"You try losing a fucking kid on her fucking birthday and then tell me you wouldn't be feeling like shit," I snap.

He shakes his head. "I know you, man. There's something else going on with you. Do you not trust me enough to talk about it?"

I hate the way his face falls when he says that. He's trusted me with some of his deepest and darkest secrets, admitting to me the fact he can't die under normal circumstances, and the fact he killed someone to save Eden. Fuck, I helped him kill Stephen and I wasn't even sorry about it. That prick had it coming for a long time. I never liked him, but I tolerated him because Kaine did.

"It's not that I don't trust you, there's just some things I'm not ready to share. Ronnie is already pissed about that fact, too, so I really don't want to deal with it from you. Mentally, I'm trying to work through some shit, but when I feel ready, I'll talk to you, okay?"

I could talk to him about the Avery shit and the fact I saw a reaper hovering in the hospital and then in Julia's room when she died, but I'm still trying to figure out why I can see them now when I couldn't before. With all the number of people I've seen die in the past, I should have been seeing them if Avery already had his hooks in me since I was a kid.

"Fine," he sighs, shoving the last bit of the bar into his mouth and shoving the wrapper in his pocket. "Where are we going?"

CHAPTER NINETEEN

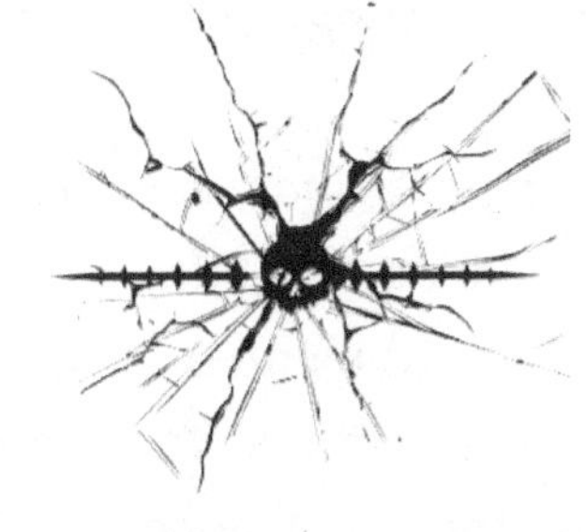

REESE

"I didn't realize you had stalker tendencies."

I pull my gaze away from the building to glare at Kaine. The fucker is eating, *again*. He insisted on picking up snacks and he's already gone through more than half of them in the hour we've been sitting outside the gym.

"It's not stalking it's...observing."

"It's the same thing."

"It's not. Stalking would be watching someone that I don't know personally."

He pulls out his phone, typing something out before a grin spreads across his face. "Well, according to my search, stalking involves unwanted surveillance and obsessive attention."

I smack the phone out of his hands, satisfied when it slams onto the floor. "It's only stalking if it happens more than once. I'm not planning to make this a habit." Not yet anyways.

"Fine. Is there a reason why you're watching her now? She hasn't done anything to warrant it."

"She made a comment before she left that was pretty harsh."

"Do you think she's cheating on you?" I shake my head. "I don't get it then."

"Just eat your fucking pork rinds, you weirdo."

I don't think she's cheating, but I don't like the way she made that comment, like she was trying to be vindictive. That would be one way to get back at me, and I don't fucking like it. There's no one to blame but me at this point since I've done a stellar job at shutting her out and pushing her away. The fact she even came for me last night was a miracle, but she wouldn't have done it if Kaine hadn't called her.

I sigh, settling back into my seat and wondering what the fuck she's doing in there for so long. By the time we got here, she should have been in there for at least forty minutes, and we've been out here for an hour. My own workouts aren't nearly that long because I don't dawdle. I get my shit done and get the fuck out of there. I'm not there to socialize or flex in the mirror like some of the twat meatheads that frequent the place. I'm kicking myself for not having a membership at the same gym as her, but if I would have walked in there and she saw me, I wouldn't exactly be subtle about what I'm doing.

"Oh, there she is." I sit up straighter, following Kaine's line of sight. I let out a sigh of relief when I see her walking out alone, but I hate the fact she's wearing her damn headphones. She knows better than not to listen to her surroundings, something I've told her time and time again because of how easily Stephen got the drop on Eden. "That's weird."

I see it, too, but Ronnie doesn't. There's a black SUV with dark tinted windows following her the second she pulls out of her parking space. It was sitting there the entire time we've been here and I didn't see anyone leaving the vehicle or coming back to it. Who the fuck could possibly be following her?

"You're following her?"

"I'm following whoever is following *her*. Whoever it is, sat in their car the entire time she was in there."

"...like *you* did?"

"Again, not the same. I don't have any ill-intentions towards her, while they probably do." My hands tighten around the steering wheel when they make the next turn behind Ronnie. "Plus, if they're following her, they'll be where Eden is soon."

That gets his attention enough that he sits up straighter, curling his hand into a fist on his thigh. The easiest way to get Kaine to go along with your crazy ideas is to make sure Eden is involved in some way. I don't like the fact that this might put her in danger as well, but there isn't much I can do while we're driving unless I ram into the SUV to stop them. As tempting as that is, it'll draw too much attention to us, and it'll risk Ronnie knowing that I was following her.

She pulls over, parking along the sidewalk, and so does the SUV a few spots behind her. "Fuck, what do we do?" Kaine murmurs, knee bouncing chaotically.

"Nothing yet. If we do anything now, it'll just look like we're the psychopaths."

"Eden is in there," he says through gritted teeth. "I'm not risking her getting caught up in whatever the fuck this is."

"At least she can't die," I shrug.

"Not the point. You know her Lazarus has slowed down, dude."

"Sure, but Avery said you guys still had a long time to live. That has to count for something."

"So, what? You're willing to risk Eden getting hurt, or worse, just because you don't want to deal with this *before* something happens?"

"What do you expect me to do, Kaine? I don't know who the fuck these people are. I have no information on them or ways of knowing if they're dangerous, and if they are, what they're capable of. Yes, they're following her, but I need to figure out *why* before I do anything."

I say that, but my instincts and rational brain are at war with each other. Part of me knows I'm right and need to take my time with this to not make it worse, while the other part of me—the darker part of me—wants nothing more than to stroll over there, rip the fucker through his window, and bash his head in for even *looking* at Ronnie. Welp, Ronnie was right. I'm more like Kaine than I realized.

"Fine. You can stay here. *I'm* going in there and supporting my fiancé while she tastes cake. Plus, I need to make sure she's actually tasting them and not just making Ronnie do it. She's gotten weird about eating again and her weight, complaining that her dress won't fit her if I keep force-feeding her goodies."

"You're leaving me here?"

"You're more than welcome to come."

"Right. That's going to be *so* easy to explain to the both of them."

He shrugs, opening the passenger door. "You have the day off and we're hanging out. Is it really that weird?"

"It is because I wouldn't fucking hang out with you doing this shit. Ronnie *told* me where she was going. She's going to think I'm following her around."

"Which you are," he grins.

I roll my eyes. "The whole point of this was to *not* draw attention to myself."

"Suit yourself." He bolts out of the truck and slams the door, leaving me staring at his form running across the street while I just sit here and gape like an idiot.

"Fucking dick," I grumble, grabbing my phone and turning off the truck to run after his stupid ass. I risk a glance at the SUV as I run past it, barely making out one guy sitting in the driver's seat with sunglasses on. I wish I could get a better look, but anything more than this will definitely draw more attention to me than I need at the moment. Kaine grins when he sees me, holding the door open with a lavish bow. "Not a fucking word."

The moment I step inside I'm assaulted by the sickly-sweet smell of vanilla and sugar. Fucking hell. I would actually die working in a place like this because some of the desserts on display look so fucking good. I would devour them, getting my ass fired while I'm comatose in the corner of the bakery, dying a slow, sugary death. I don't indulge often because admittedly, I have a wicked sweet tooth.

Eden spots me right away, eyes darting from me to Kaine stepping up beside me. Her back stiffens and those eyes shift to

Ronnie sitting in front of her. I can't hear what's being said, but I see Eden's lips moving seconds before Ronnie's head whips around to look at me. Yeah, she's pissed. Her brows are furrowed, plump lips pressed into a hard line, and eyes narrowed so viciously I'm surprised there aren't physical daggers being shot at me like lasers.

She launches out of her seat, her fork clattering onto the plate as she storms over to me. "What the *fuck* are you doing here?" I just point at Kaine, who just grins at her. "You're both idiots," she huffs, throwing her hands up in frustration.

Kaine leaves me to deal with the little firecracker, making his way over to Eden, who smiles up at him lovingly. She's adorable and deserves all the good this world has to offer. I love the way her eyes flutter closed when he bends down to kiss her forehead gently, and the soft smile that pulls at her lips while a blush of pink creeps across her cheeks. He drags over a chair from another table, flopping down into it backwards to stare at Eden like there's no one else in the room.

Me? I can feel the flames of Ronnie's laser eyes burning into me until I turn my attention back to her. "What?"

"Are you following me?"

"No," I lie, shoving my hands in my pockets.

"I feel like you are. I don't need you supervising me, least of all when I'm with Eden."

"Seems like Eden doesn't mind us crashing your little get together," I say, jerking my chin towards her and Kaine. She turns to look, letting out a heavy sigh. "Great. We're never going to get anything done now."

"Pretty sure you weren't getting anything done anyways. Eden doesn't even have cake in front of her, Ronnie. Why the fuck are you letting her act like that?"

"What?"

I quirk a brow. "Wait. Do you not know about her eating?" The look of confusion on her face confirms it, and I have to give it to Eden, she does well to hide her idiosyncrasies from people.

"She tried a piece already."

"Let me guess. She took a tiny ass bite then pushed her plate towards you to finish it." She hesitates for a second but then nods. "She has issues with her weight. That's her discreet way of not showing people how much it bothers her. More now because she's trying to make sure she fits into her dress."

"Well, that's stupid. You shouldn't change yourself for a dress, you change the dress to fit you."

"I agree, but Eden has always had issues with her self-image."

The way we treated her those first few days of living here didn't help the situation either. I wasn't directly involved in making fun of her, but I didn't do anything to stop it either. Kaine never made direct jabs at her weight, but he still implied it with some snide remarks; moments he regrets and probably will for the rest of his life. He hates that he ever did anything to hurt Eden, and when she was ignoring him, he was losing his fucking mind. He just about sent himself off the deep end when she started talking to Conrad and hanging out with him.

"Thanks for letting me know. You can go now."

"No."

"Excuse me?"

"Pretty sure I'm free to be here. There are no rules stating this is a private event, and guess what, love? *You* can't tell *me* what to do."

"Fine. Then enjoy your fucking day tasting cakes with *your* friends."

She turns, stomping her way towards the table to grab her purse. "Where are you going?" Eden asks, frowning at Ronnie.

"Reese insists on staying and Kaine is here, so you don't need me."

The poor girl looks like she just got slapped across the face, her mouth popping open in surprise. "Ronnie, I *want* you here. You're my maid of honor."

Ronnie doesn't say anything else, turning away from a shocked Eden. Kaine's expression darkens, bordering on that murderous rage I know so well. He doesn't take well to people hurting his girl, whether that's physically or emotionally like Ronnie is doing to her now. The bell on the door rings as Ronnie heads outside.

"Sorry," I say quickly, darting out after her. She's already halfway to her car, but my eyes drift to the SUV parked further behind. I lengthen my strides, gripping into her arm before she gets the chance to attempt opening her car door.

"Hey!" She screams, but I drag her quickly into the alley between the bakery and the sub shop next door. "Let me go." She squeaks out a breath when I slam her against the brick wall, caging her in with my arms braced on either side of her.

"Stop *fucking* running," I snarl. "Do you have any idea what you just did back there? Do you have any fucking idea how much you just hurt that girl?"

"Of course you care about *her* feelings, but you're treating mine like they don't matter."

I step into her, pressing my body completely against hers. Her warm breath fans across my neck as she stares up at me, eyes wide and lips parted. "If you honestly think I don't care about your feelings you're a fucking idiot. I wouldn't be here if I didn't care. I wouldn't be going out of my fucking mind trying to fix our relationship if I didn't care. I wouldn't be fucking stalking you if I didn't fucking care, Ronnie."

"You're—you're stalking me?"

"Isn't it obvious? That's twice now I show up where you are."

"I thought Kaine was dragging you around."

"Do I look like the type of person that could be dragged around?" She shakes her head. "I want to see you. I *want* to be with you, even if you're starting to feel like you shouldn't be with me. Please don't hurt Eden just to hurt me. She doesn't deserve that. You're her best friend, Ronnie, and she asked you to be her maid of honor."

Guilt settles into her features, and she drops her eyes to stare at my chest. "I don't want to hurt her," she whispers.

"Then don't. I'm sorry if I made you uncomfortable, but I'm losing my fucking head when you push me away like this. If you want me to leave, I'll leave."

I hate it. I hate the idea of giving into her stupid request, but I'll do it for Eden and Kaine's sake. He'll probably rip into her anyways for that outburst and for making Eden feel like shit on a special day, but there's only so much I can do to defend her when her actions are unwarranted. I'll leave her in the shop to hang out with them, but I won't leave her unsupervised. Not when that SUV is still following her. I need to get the plates and put a call into Holland to try and get as much information as I can on whoever it is.

"I just...I wanted one day to just feel *normal*. It's been a rough couple of days, and I just wanted to hang out with my friend."

I cup her cheeks in my palms, forcing her to look at me. "I'm sorry I've been so shitty." I hate the way her eyes begin to glisten, like she's trying to fight back tears that I've created.

She lifts her hands to cup the back of mine, slowly closing her eyes. "You've been through a lot, too, and I haven't been very understanding."

"You have every reason to be angry with me. I'm sorry I can't give you what you want right now. I just ask that you be patient with me if you want to still give this a chance—give *us* a chance."

"I do. I don't want to be with anyone else, Reese."

I kiss her. It's desperate and needy and the only way I can show her how much she means to me right now. She doesn't resist, easily melting into me and greedily sucking on my tongue before diving hers into my mouth. Fuck, I love kissing her. I love the way she bends and gives into me. The way she touches me with gentle fingers that turn needy, clinging to me and drawing me closer.

She digs those fingers into my hair, scraping my scalp and tugging at the strands with each swipe of my tongue against hers. I nip and suck on her bottom lip, pressing into her further and wrapping one of my arms around her back. My other hand dives into her hair, tugging the band tying her soft locks off her to let her hair cascade down her back in sensual waves.

She surprises me, sliding her leg and hip between my legs, grinding against my quickly hardening cock. "Ronnie," I pant out, groaning when she rocks harder, rolling her body into mine. "Fuck, baby." My mouth moves down along her jaw, her scent blasting into my senses like a heady drug. She smells amazing and tastes divine, a combination I can't get enough of.

I just want to mark her; bite into her flesh in a way that stays permanent for everyone to see and know she belongs to me. Such a savage thought—primal and beast-like, but that's what she does to me. I didn't even realize how crazy I was for the girl until the threat of her leaving me loomed over my head. That thought alone makes my chest ache and my heart stutter chaotically. I should have been better for her and more present, but I haven't been able to pull myself out of the dark void threatening to swallow me whole.

She shoves me hard enough that in my surprise I stumble back, but the next second, she's grabbing me by the waist of my pants and pulling me until my own back hits the wall. She glances up at me, a wicked grin spreading across her face as she tucks her fingers into the waist of my pants.

"What are you doing?" I say breathlessly. Slowly, she lowers herself down to the ground, drawing my pants down with her as she settles onto her knees in front of me. "Ronnie, I—" I groan when she glances at me through her lashes and takes my cock into her mouth. "Fuck."

My fingers thread through her hair, gripping into it and following her head as she bobs along my length. My stomach tightens at the feel of her tongue swirling around my tip before taking me in completely. Fuck, the way her throat tightens around the head is bliss, causing heat to build in my body and shivers to creep along my spine.

This is definitely unexpected. I would have been perfectly happy kissing her until her face flushed and her lips swelled from our fervor, but this...this is bold. We're not exactly out in the open, but it's daylight and anyone could walk by the alley, especially this time of day with the food shops only a few feet away. Why does this excite me so much? I've never done anything like this before. No show of public affection beyond hand holding and chaste kisses. I fucking like it.

This is waking up something inside of me that is going to be difficult to shove back into the box. I'm not new to kinks, but after looking through Eden's little voucher book, I realized I was pretty vanilla in comparison to some people. I like sex, don't get me wrong, but I've never been as obsessed with it as Kaine. He used it as an outlet for his fucked-up head and aggression, while I tend to keep things internalized. A side effect of my upbringing in my younger years, where once again, emotions could be viewed as a weakness. The only emotion my father pushed on me was anger and violence while my mother encouraged kindness and love. It fucks with your head when you have two completely opposing sides pushing different objectives for who I need to grow up into.

I'm ripped from my thought when Ronnie hums against my dick, licking and swirling her tongue while her hand grips my shaft. I still can't figure out *why* she decided to this this, especially now of all times.

Weren't we in a fight? I figured the mini make out session was enough to tamper down at least a small fraction of her anger and disappointment in me, but fuck me, I never expected her to want to suck me off in public. My head smacks off the brick wall in pure ecstasy when she pops me out of her mouth, sucks on my balls, and then drags her tongue up my length before diving back down on me and sucking, *hard*.

"Fuck," I grunt, curling my fingers harder into her hair and shoving her down on me. "Fuck, Ronnie. God fucking damn it, I'm coming." My balls tighten, stomach flexing, entire fucking body coiling as she hums again, moaning around me as I unload into her mouth. "Such a good fucking girl," I croon, watching her as she swallows everything down, licking up every drop of cum.

She swipes her thumb across her bottom lip, pulling it into her mouth to suck on it, and that sight just about does me in. Helping her to her feet, I grip her arms, steadying her while her legs tremble under her.

"Are you okay?" I ask, bending down to rub the dirt off her knees for her. That couldn't have been comfortable, but she didn't even hesitate to drop down for me.

"Yeah," she says breathlessly, chest heaving while she tries to fix her disheveled hair.

"Why did you do that?" She tips her head in question, and the adorable gesture makes me want to bundle her up like a burrito to protect her. "You didn't have to do that. Not at all, but especially not here."

"Did you not enjoy yourself?"

"Of course I did, but you know I don't expect that of you."

She smiles at that, shaking her head through a soft laugh. "You're always taking care of me, Reese. I wanted to show you that I'm in this and that I'll wait until you're ready. I'm sorry I overreacted this morning."

I pull her into me, wrapping my arms around her. The way she melts into me and sighs against my chest sends my heart fluttering. This is what it's like to have someone who loves you, no matter how shutdown and broken you are. Seriously, I don't deserve this girl in the slightest, but I can't seem to let her go, even if that's the right thing to do.

"Come on," I murmur, pressing my lips to her hair. She slides her hand into mine and lets me pull her along behind me, back towards the bakery. We walk in on an interesting scene to say the least. Eden's eyes dart to me, the only part of her that Kaine is allowing her to move. He has his fingers pressing into her cheeks, prying her mouth open while he slides a forkful of cake into her mouth. "Let's go," I sigh, releasing Ronnie's hand.

He finally looks at me after giving Eden a peck on the lips while she scowls at him, chewing the cake angrily. "Can't you see I'm busy?" He grumbles.

"Let's leave the girls to enjoy their day."

He frowns, looking back towards Eden. "Do you want me to go?"

She gnaws on her lip, eyes dropping to her lap. "I want to spend time with Ronnie," she whispers.

"Fine. Text me when you leave here." She nods. Lurching to his feet, he drags the chair back over to the other table dramatically, glaring at Ronnie when she retakes her seat across from Eden. "You better be nice to her," he snaps.

"Kaine," I grit out, hands flexing at my sides, and the urge to physically drag him out of here ripping through my system. He gives her one final glare, doing that stupid fingers to the eyes move and then pointing at her like a fucking psychopath. "You're a dick," I hiss out, clocking him around the neck when he's within reach to lead him out of the shop.

"No, your *girlfriend* was being a dick first. What the fuck is her problem?"

"She's mad at me and took it out on Eden. Though, your behaviour didn't fucking help."

"What the fuck did *I* do?"

"Other than existing?"

"Asshole."

"Prick." I poke him in the ribs, snorting when he squeals like a little girl, shying away and almost toppling over. He's so fucking ticklish and so easy to rile up. He tries to shove me as hard as he can, but I'm ready for it, snapping my hand out to palm his face. "Don't do it," I laugh.

"Let go!" He huffs, his voice muffled through my hand. I don't; laughing harder when he grips my wrist in a feeble attempt to pry me off him. I jerk back suddenly, gagging as I shake out my hand. "Gross!" This mother fucker just licked me. "What are you, a dog?"

"Woof." He grins, skipping away as he cackles, now trying to avoid me lunging for him. He ends up in the middle of the road, taunting me, and then my eyes widen.

I run full tilt, tackling him out of the way just as the fucking SUV I've been watching screeches past us. "Fuck," I groan, my head thudding against the concrete as Kaine props himself up on my chest. His eyes are wide, mouth gaped open in horror. "Are you okay?"

"Are *you*?"

"I'll be fine." He reaches out, touching my cheek with his fingertips. I hiss out at the sudden sting burning through my skin and shy away, but he grips my jaw, holding my head still.

"Maybe you should go to the hospital."

"Fuck that." I wince when I try to sit up and he quickly scrambles off of me, reaching his hand down for me to take. "Thanks."

"I almost just died," he laughs awkwardly. "I mean, I would have come back, so you didn't need to risk yourself like that."

"You're an idiot if you think I would just stand by and watch you get turned into a pancake, Kaine. I don't give a fuck if you're immortal or not, I'm going to fucking protect you either way."

His chin trembles and he turns away quickly, clearing his throat. I didn't expect him to get emotional over that, but maybe he hasn't leveled out mentally as well as I thought he had. "You got hurt," he mumbles.

"I'll be fine. Nothing a few band-aids and pain killers can't fix." My pants are torn from taking the brunt of the fall, my momentum shredding the material enough to still cause some damage to my skin. My left wrist aches, the skin on my hand raw and cut up, but I took both of our body weight on it to try and break our fall a bit more. I protected him though, and that's all that matters. "I was hoping they would have stuck around long enough for me to grab their plates."

"AV4F37."

"What?"

"The plate. While my life was flashing before my eyes, I got a damn good look at it."

I grab his shoulders and spin him around. “Fuck, I could kiss you,” I laugh.

He looks horrified. “Please don’t.”

I quirk a brow. “Just a peck on the lips?” I tease. He shakes his head vehemently. “Fine,” I snort. “Let’s go.”

CHAPTER TWENTY

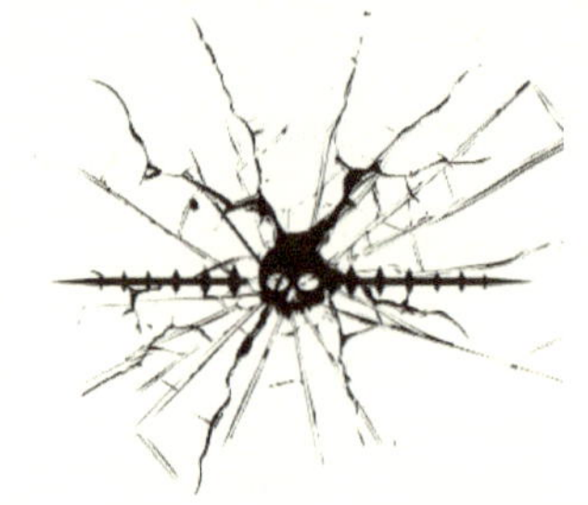

RONNIE

"Which one do you like better?" I blink, focusing on Eden while my fork hovers over the fifth piece of cake in front of me. "I don't know if I should go with a vanilla base or chocolate, or maybe both."

I can't figure out what's more overwhelming; the urge to vomit, or the need to pass the fuck out. Why the hell are the portions so big when it's supposed to be a tasting?

"Ronnie?"

I blink again. "Sorry," I murmur, setting my fork down on the table. "I'm so full."

"Yeah, they're not shy about their samples."

"Which one do *you* like?" I ask.

She glances over all the plates covering the table between us, her lip slipping into her mouth in her horrible habit of chewing on it when she's anxious. "I don't know. I don't know which one Kaine will like more."

"Eden, forget about Kaine for two fucking seconds. You know if he were here, he would tell you to pick whichever one you like the best. He's not picky, and he's not going to get mad at your choice."

"I just—I want this day to be perfect. We've both been through a lot and we both deserve something special."

"Anything you choose will be perfect for him. I see the way he is with you. He loves you so much and would do anything for you."

"Yeah, you're right. I think I like the vanilla the best, with the coffee butter cream méringue. It's not as sweet."

"It's a great choice."

She pushes her plate away and starts fidgeting with the napkin, tearing small chunks off and rolling it between her thumb and finger. "Are you and Reese okay?"

"I don't know. I think so."

"He's a really great guy, Ronnie. He's been through some things over the years, and I think he's just having a hard time with everything. Kaine told me about his patient dying, too."

A seed of irritation hits me at the fact she knows more about him than I do. She's only known him personally for a few months longer than me, but it still hurts. What's the difference between us? Why is he comfortable sharing his past with her but not me? Maybe I can get some information out of her. It feels like an invasion of privacy, but I'm fucking desperate.

"Reese doesn't really talk to me," I say bluntly.

She stiffens at that. "What do you mean?"

"He doesn't talk about his past. I don't know anything about his family or his life growing up aside from the small bits and pieces I've dragged out of him. He's not...open with me. Not like he is with you and Kaine."

"I think it's just because we went through a lot *together* last year. He's not doing it to piss you off, Ronnie."

"Am I not cool enough to be a part of your special little club? You all seem to be hiding something, and I can't figure out what it is." Her face falls at that, and once again, I'm being an asshole. This isn't me. I'm not normally so short tempered, at least, not anymore. I've learned to regulate my temper over the years after being conditioned into embracing the anger that's always bubbling beneath the surface. "I'm sorry." I say quickly.

"I'm sorry if you feel like you're being left out, but trust me, Ronnie, it's better if you don't know half the shit that me and Kaine have been through, and Reese just because he's friends with us. Maybe someday I can tell you what's going on with me, but for now, it's better if I don't."

What could possibly have happened to have them all on guard like this? The way she's talking makes it sound like the major issue is between Eden and Kaine, while Reese just happened upon their secrets, but I know Reese. There's something going on with him, too.

"I just feel like I'm being kept at arm's length."

"We don't mean to make you feel that way."

"Do you think Reese will ever love me?"

She sits quietly for a minute, mulling over what to say. I'm sort of putting her on the spot with that question, but the thought that he doesn't and never will keeps nagging at me, gnawing and eating away at the little bit of self-esteem I have left.

"Honestly? I think he already does. Reese is complicated. He may seem like he's stable and well put together, but he still has a hard time talking about things, especially his feelings. He was pretty open with me, but I think it's because I was at the brink of breaking and he was trying whatever he could to make me feel like I wasn't alone. He wouldn't be doing what he does and acting the way he does if he didn't care about you, Ronnie."

"I don't know what to do."

"Can you see your life without him in it?" I shake my head. "Then there's your answer. Give him time. In the meantime, just keep being who you've always been. You've supported him and been there for him. If he didn't see himself being with you, he wouldn't have entertained the idea of dating you."

"Did you know there was a rumour that went around school that he's gay?" Her eyes widen and I smile. "I never believed it; I just figured that he was selective with who he talked to. Plenty of girls threw themselves at him but he never gave them any real attention."

"I mean, I knew he wasn't interested in anyone. Not until you came along. You're good for him." I snort, rolling my eyes. "What?" She laughs. "You are."

That's where she's wrong. I might actually be the worst thing that could have happened to him, but I can't let him go.

CHAPTER TWENTY-ONE

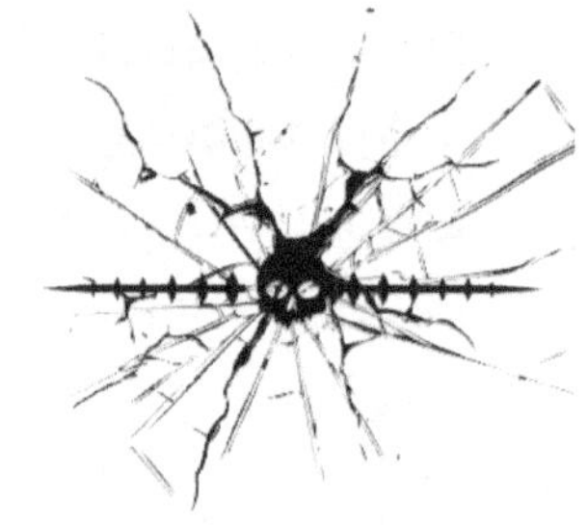

REESE

My skin prickles at the feel of Kaine watching me while I pace back and forth in my apartment. I keep glancing over at him, catching his gaze shifting from me to the laptop propped open on the dining table.

"Hurry up, Holland," I grumble, running my hand through my hair in frustration.

"You seem to be asking a lot of me lately."

"Hardly. It's not like you're that busy anyways, so what the fuck is taking you so long to find info on one fucking vehicle?"

"You're in a shitty mood. Did murder not tame your beast?"

"Holland," I grit out, my eyes flicking to Kaine's, but he's now busy rummaging through my snack cupboard to eavesdrop on my conversation. "If you keep this up, you'll be next on my list," I whisper yell, moving myself into the living room.

"Sheesh. So violent. Keep your pretty little head on, I'm sending you the information now."

"Finally."

"You're welcome!"

I don't respond, hanging up on him before he gets lippier with me and tempts me to follow through with my threat. I settle into the chair, scrolling over to my email, where sure enough, Holland came through.

"Who was that you were talking to?"

I jolt in my seat, whipping my head around to see Kaine hovering behind me, folded over me so he can see over my shoulder to the computer. His loud chewing makes me want to punch him in the face, but I refrain.

You can't kill your best friend. You can't kill your best friend. You can't fucking kill your best friend.

"Do you mind?" He quirks a brow when I make a shooing motion for him to back the fuck off. "Dude, seriously."

"But I want to see. Is this some spy shit? Do you have some dude that acts like your Robin?" His eyes widen. "Are you Batman?" He grunts, wheezing a breath and stumbling back from the elbow I just jerked into his chest. "I'm telling mom!"

"Mom?"

"Eden."

"So, she's your mother now? Stepsister and mother. Who knew you were so fucked up?"

"That's not...dude, what the fuck?"

"You started it."

"You have to admit, she's pretty mommy."

"I'm not going to justify that with a response for one. Second, you'll beat my ass if I *do* agree with you. Well, you'll try to anyways. We both know you don't stand a chance against me."

His mouth pops open in shock, hand going to his chest in mock horror. "I would definitely put up a valiant effort."

"Don't make me manhandle you again."

"That was one time!"

"Do you want me to make it two?" I quirk a brow. "I promise you a good time," I grin.

"No, thank you."

"Then sit your pretty ass down like a good boy." He sputters, cheeks flaming red as he gawks at me. "You have a praise kink, don't you?"

"None of your business!" He chokes out, but his voice goes up to an abnormally high pitch.

"Want to sit on my lap?"

"I hate you," he grumbles, flopping down in the chair next to me and pouting like a child.

I shake my head, thankful for his lighthearted nature since he always seems to pull me back to the present. I scroll to the email, clicking on the zip file Holland sent me. Damn, he's good at his job. Not only did he get the basic information on the vehicle and the owner, he did a full background check and also pulled CCTV footage of the SUV up until about thirty minutes ago when it pulled into a warehouse off Cassidy Drive.

Dimitry Sokolov works for Misha Petrov. My eyes widen. Why the fuck is someone from the Russian mob following Ronnie? It makes sense why he tried to run Kaine over since they have no issues killing people, especially those they feel are in their way, but none of this makes sense.

"Why are you frowning like that?" Kaine asks, leaning towards me to try once again to look at my computer.

"This...isn't good."

"What?"

"The guy following Ronnie today is part of the mafia."

"What the fuck. For what reason?"

"If I knew that, I wouldn't be as confused as I am. He's tied to Misha Petrov according to the information my source got for me."

"I have no idea who that is."

"Of course you don't." I sigh, dragging my hand down my face before diving back into the photos of him, Misha, and the camera footage of the SUV. It looks like the fucker followed her from here to the gym which means he knows where she lives. The building has its own security cameras and shit, but it's definitely not equipped to handle a mobster if he decides to get in here.

If Dimitry is working for Misha, the bigger question is why the head of the Russian mafia in this city is watching my fucking girlfriend. Did she piss someone off? What the fuck could she have done to draw the attention of someone so dangerous?

"Have you gotten any seedy people into the clinic lately?" I murmur, glancing up when Kaine doesn't respond. "Dude."

"Oh, uh, not really. We get some weirdos in on occasion and the ones just looking to score drugs, but no one that screams mafia. How do you even know who the fuck that is?"

"Remember what I told you last year at the farmhouse?"

His eyes widen. "Are you Russian mafia?"

I shake my head. "No."

"Oh, thank fuck. Don't scare me like that, man."

"Irish."

His teeth physically clink together, making me wonder if he shattered a molar at the force of it. He frowns, tilting his head from side to side while his eyes roam over my features. "Are you sure?"

"Of what exactly?"

"That your part of the Irish mob."

"I'm not a part of it. I just have ties to it."

"Are you adopted?"

"What? No. Why the fuck would you think that?"

He waves his hand, motioning to my body. "You're not a redhead."

"Seriously? *That's* what you're getting at?"

"Irish people have red hair."

"Not all of us, you twit. I look like my mom."

"Who's your dad then?"

I should have just kept my mouth shut and kept him in the dark about all of this. He already knows how dangerous and deranged I can be because I didn't hesitate to torture Stephen. It was more difficult to stop than it was to actually rip his fucking teeth out. I would have finished him off myself, but Kaine needed the closure, even if that meant his hands got tainted red.

"My dad is dead, Kaine. It doesn't matter who he is. He's not the one in charge and he never was."

"But you just said—"

"I know what I said. It's bad enough I've even mentioned the fact that my family is tied to the fucking mafia, I don't need you getting involved."

He frowns, settling back in his seat. "When I helped you out of that situation when we were teens, where did you go for those two weeks after?"

For being a dumbass at times, he's oddly observant of details. My uncle got word of my rebellious streak and wanted to have a chat with me. He made promises to keep me out of jail if I did him favours on the side, but I still refused. Those two weeks weren't the best, and my mother was worried sick about me.

When she died, I didn't have many options on where to stay. I was too young to legally live on my own and I didn't want to go into the foster system, so of course my uncle stepped up. I might have been better off being put into the system, but at least he didn't keep me locked up and let me continue my life as long as I held up my original end of the deal. Kaine only knows about those two weeks because I was absent from school, barely keeping in contact with him to check in, and that was only because my aunt took pity on me and let me have access to the phone he confiscated from me. He didn't even want me to contact my mom, but he quickly realized she wasn't someone to mess with. She threatened calling the cops and exposing his entire operation if he tried to keep me from her. He has connections within the police system, but he knew better than to underestimate a mother hellbent on destroying his life for her only son.

"I was with my uncle," I murmur.

"Is he mafia, too?" I don't need to say anything; my blank face is enough for him to put the pieces together. "Why didn't you just tell me?"

"Maybe because I wanted to keep you safe, Kaine. Maybe because I didn't want you looking at me differently or treating me differently if you knew. Sometimes things are better kept to yourself for the protection of peace of mind."

His face softens, his hand reaching out to grip my forearm. "You're my best friend, Reese. It wouldn't have changed anything, but at least then I could have been there for you. I dumped all my fucked-up shit on you and dragged you into an insane situation, so why would you think that now you wouldn't be able to be honest with me?" I shrug, not really having an excuse when he puts it that way. "Is this what you're keeping from Ronnie?"

"Who said I was keeping anything from her?" I laugh at the incredulous look he shoots my way. "Fine, it's part of it. It's better if she doesn't know that part of my life. I'm trying to get out, but I always seem to keep getting dragged back in, favour after favour."

"What's the other part?"

"Just...life catching up to me. I love my job, but there are days where I question if I made the right choice in career paths." I can't tell him about Avery or the reapers that seem to be haunting my hospital. Not yet anyways. I need to get a better handle on everything first before I even attempt to explain anything to him. How can I explain what's going on with me when I don't understand it myself?

Kaine's phone buzzes on the table, and I can tell by the way his eyes light up and the stupid grin on his face that it's from Eden. "They just left the bakery so I should go."

"Okay."

"Unless you want me to hang out longer. I can message Eden and tell her I'll be a little while."

I shake my head. "No, you should go. I'm fine."

He gets up and ruffles my hair playfully. "I know you're not, but I'm here when you're ready to talk about it."

My own phone buzzes, and I'm expecting it to be Holland with more info, but it's not.

Ronnie: I'll be home soon. Xo

I'm grinning like an idiot. How can something so simple as a text message ease the weight that's been pressing down into my shoulders, threatening to crush me?

"Hmm, I think you'll be okay without me," Kaine chuckles. "Assuming that's Ronnie?"

"Yeah, she says she's on her way home."

"That's a good thing, right? It means you guys have worked through your shit?"

"I hope so. I know she's upset and worries that I don't feel the same way about her, but I just don't want to put her at risk with everything still going on in my life."

"Maybe you should give her a bit more credit. She seems strong and capable, so don't assume she can't handle you or whatever dark shit you're going through."

If he only knew what I was going through. I think it would worry him. I think it might actually send him off the deep end if he thinks the reapers are back to finally claim him and Eden. They've still been doing more research on the side in regard to Lazarus syndrome, trying to find anyone else that might be experiencing what they have, but from what Kaine said, Avery made it pretty obvious that split souls are rare.

There was one person they found out about in Canada who went through a Lazarus with smaller near-death incidents after the fact, but when they finally reached out and decided to go check him out for themselves, they were dead. Choked on a god damn piece of gum, if you can believe it.

"I know how strong she is. She's put up with my ass for this long and somehow is still here."

"Because she loves you. I wish you would just accept it and open your own heart to her."

"I'm trying."

He stares at me, blinks slowly, and then smacks the back of my head. "You're not. You were never as distant with Eden as you are towards your own girlfriend. I'll be honest, it made me think you actually liked Eden more than a friend." He laughs awkwardly, shaking his head. "There were plenty of mixed emotions going through me that whole time you guys were hanging out, and even now, you would jump the moment Eden asked anything of you. Would you do the same for Ronnie?"

"Of course I would. I fucking care about her, Kaine, but Eden is different. She's been through so much in her life and I feel for her."

"How do you know Ronnie hasn't been through similar things? I feel like you guys are strangers who live together and fuck at random, but do you know *anything* about her personal life or her past?"

"I know what she's shared. I've asked her things before, and she tells me stuff but evades any details."

"So, she's like you then. Man, you two really are perfect for each other. Both secretly fucked up and closed off."

"I'm not closed off with you."

"That's a lie. You hid your entire past from me up until ten minutes ago, and even now, I feel like you're still hiding shit from me."

This little fuck. I miss the Kaine who gave a shit but didn't push me to *express myself*. I get it, he cares, but sometimes I wish he didn't and would just let me wallow in my own self-hatred and pity. Fuck me, how I am supposed to deal with this version of him on top of Ronnie trying to get me to share my feelings, too? So, what do I do? I get defensive.

"Like you've shared everything with me?"

He blinks. "Actually, I have. I've told you everything that's happened to me because you're my best friend. My biggest secret is out in the open, Reese. What more could I possibly hide from you that would make you look at me any differently? You know about my mom and what she did to me, you know that I've killed people and you helped me with one, you know about Eden, and that wasn't even my secret to tell. I've told you everything, Reese. You've seen me at my worst moments, and you've been there for me through it all. Please, let me be here for you."

Fuck. How am I supposed to keep pushing him away when he's being so open and honest with me? My secrets feel like a burden—a fucking death sentence. Clearly Avery knows I can see him if my reaction to his reflection in the mirror is any indication, but how would he react if I told Kaine? Would he go back on his word to leave him and Eden alone? No. I can't risk it. I couldn't live with myself if I'm the reason they end up truly dying.

"I'll talk to you tomorrow, Kaine." The way I'm brushing off his words is harsh and I know it, but it's the only thing I can do right now.

His face falls, shoulders slumping in defeat. "Okay. Let me know when the funeral is for Julia."

"Why?"

"Because I want to support you."

"You didn't know her. You have no reason to go."

"I might not have known her, but you did and you cared. That's reason enough for me to go."

We stare at each other, neither of us speaking, but he nods his head before turning away from me and heading for the door. His kindness keeps cracking my defenses, tearing down my walls piece by piece. No matter how hard I try to keep everyone around me from knowing the real me, I can't seem to stop them from trying to tear down everything I've built.

He doesn't say anything as he slips out the door, but he gives me one final look. Like he's waiting for *me* to say something. I won't. I *can't*. So, I don't, letting him walk away from me, knowing a bit more about myself but having more questions than answers as he heads home.

CHAPTER TWENTY-TWO

RONNIE

Kaine is coming out of the apartment complex when I pull in, looking like a puppy that just got kicked. What the fuck happened up there?

"Hey!" I call out, quickly getting out of my car. He stops at his door, head down and shoulders slumped. "Kaine, are you okay?"

He doesn't turn to face me, but the rattling breath he lets out is enough to know that something is wrong. "I'm fine. It's just been a long day, so I'll talk to you later, Ronnie."

"Did Reese say something to upset you? He hasn't been himself for a few weeks now, but I know that his patient dying has sort of pushed him over on the mental scale."

He lets out a humourless laugh. "Reese is just being Reese." He glances at me over his shoulder, but his eyes quickly look past me for a second before meeting my own. "You should get inside," he murmurs, pulling out his phone as he opens his car door. "It's not safe out here."

I gawk at him, flinching when he slams the door closed between us. What the fuck does he mean by that? This is one of the safer parts of the city and I've been out here more times than I can count at later times than tonight. Something about the way he said that though, has the hair at my nape standing on end, skin prickling with a sudden anxiety.

I back up, giving him room to back up out of the space, but he doesn't pull away. He glares at me through the windshield, pointing to the entrance and mouthing *'go'* before glancing down at his lap. It's dark enough in his car that I see the glow of his phone screen radiating against his face. I bolt for the door, not liking the sudden edge he had to him. The second the door clicks behind me, I turn around, watching Kaine as his eyes drift from his phone, then to the street, then to me. I follow his line of sight, noticing a black SUV parked in the street parking, lights off, but I swear I see someone moving inside through the tinted windows.

That's not creepy at all.

Has that truck been following me? I thought I saw the same one parked outside my gym, but admittedly, I wasn't really paying attention. Reese's continuous warnings about always paying attention to my surroundings rings through my mind, and I'm kicking myself for not listening to him.

Kaine gives me one final look, his hand coming up in a half-ass wave before finally pulling away. I stand and watch until his taillights disappear and then shift my attention back to the SUV.

"Get away from the door." I startle, spinning around to see Reese storming out of the elevator towards me.

"What?"

"Now, Ronnie. Get upstairs."

He blows through the door and heads straight for the SUV. There's no way in hell I'm going upstairs when he clearly knows about the vehicle parked outside. Did Kaine message him? What the actual fuck is going on right now?

Just as he gets close to the SUV, the headlights flare to life and the engine roars as the vehicle peels out of the parking space. I squint through the window, seeing Reese pull something out of the waistband of his pants and pointing it at the retreating vehicle. No fucking way.

"Reese!" I scream as I open the door. His arm wavers, his attention snapping to me long enough for the SUV to make the turn at the next street over. I don't even recognize him. Fury covers his features, jaw clenched together and a heavy crease between his brows.

He lowers the gun. His face softens, but only a fraction as he makes his way back over to me. "I thought I told you to go upstairs," he says, his tone harsher than it was earlier.

"Who was that? Why do you have a gun?" I glance back into the lobby, clocking the cameras there and shifting myself in front of him to cover the weapon from view. When the fuck did he get a gun? Has that been in the apartment the whole time? He grips my hand, the safety clicking back on before he tucks it back into the waistband of his pants. “Reese,” I huff, trying and failing to stop him from dragging me towards the elevator. “Will you tell me what the fuck is going on?”

“Did you piss someone off?”

“What?” He doesn’t answer, his eyes trained on the elevator until the door finally opens and he drags me inside. “Will you talk to me?”

“That car has been following you since you left the apartment earlier, Ronnie. It followed you to the gym, and then it followed you to the bakery. The fucker tried to run Kaine over when we left you.”

My eyes widen in horror at the bombardment of information. “What? Wait...how do you know how long they’ve been following me for? Did you fucking stalk me all day?”

“Not *all* day, but long enough to know most of it. Do you know who that is?” I shake my head. “Does the name Dimitry Sokolov mean anything to you?”

The blood drains from my body and it’s taking everything in me to stay standing and keep myself composed. “No,” I whisper, shaking my head.

“No?”

“I—I don’t know who that is.”

But I *do* know, and now my brain is frantically trying to figure out what my father’s guard is doing surveilling me. How the hell did he figure out where I live? I didn’t tell him any of that, and as far as he knows, I’m living on my own closer to the college campus. Not once did I mention Reese in my stay at his home, and for good reason. The last thing I need is my father finding out about Reese and starting a scene. It’s none of his business who I date anyways. Not anymore. I relinquished my ties to him and the family when I went off on my own, the same as Tessa.

Is this some sort of revenge plot he's trying to scheme behind my back? Daughters are nothing but a bargaining chip to mafia men, and no matter how much he tries to claim that he's different from the typical Bratva leaders, he's still the same. They're *all* the same. At least a male would become an heir, but a female is only good for one thing; making deals with other houses to strengthen their alliances and expand their territory.

The fact that Reese knows who's following me has me looking at him in a new light. How would he find out that information anyways? When the fuck did he get that good of a look at him? It's not like Dimitry is well known outside of the familial ties or to people that are owned by or owe the mafia.

"How do you know who it is? Do you recognize him from somewhere?"

Reese's jaw clenches hard enough for the muscles to flutter aggressively. "I was worried when I noticed the guy following you, so I had someone look into the vehicle for me."

The answer is blunt, but I can tell he's hiding something vital from me. I can't just let this go because it's a big fucking deal. The last thing I want is Reese getting involved with my family, and pissing off the Russian mob is never a good thing. Plus, there's still the fact he has a gun and apparently knows how to use it. There was no hesitation in his movements, and he was ready to shoot that car down in the middle of the fucking street.

The elevator pings and Reese wastes no time exiting it, his long strides making his shirt rise up enough for me to see the butt of the gun poking out of his back. I hesitate to follow, and that is enough to have him pause and turn back to look at me.

"Are you coming?"

"Why do you have a gun, Reese."

He frowns, but I don't see anger on his face, I see worry. "Don't be scared of me," he whispers pleadingly. He steps towards me, hands outstretched but pauses when he notices my body shift back slightly. I didn't mean to do it, but my defenses have gone up now and I'm struggling to control the sudden overwhelming emotions trying to rule over me. His hands fall limply back at his sides. "I—I'm not going to hurt you, Ronnie."

"Tell me why you have a gun. How could you hide that from me? You kept a weapon in our home and didn't think I should know about it? Who the fuck are you?"

"I got it to protect us—to protect *you*. I've had it for years and I'm sorry I didn't tell you about it. I'm still me, Ronnie. I'm still the person you fell in love with."

Those words wrap around my heart, tightening it to the point I can barely breathe. "That's not fair," I grit out, fighting back the urge to punch him in the face. He's using my feelings for him against me—to manipulate me. He knows I love him and he's doing everything he can to sway my thoughts and feelings.

"What do you want me to do, Ronnie? I won't get rid of it. I can't, especially now. Not with that guy out there following you for God knows what reason."

He's doing this to protect me. I let that thought overrule every other one running rampant in my head, clinging to it like a life raft trying to drift away from my outstretched hand.

"It needs to stay locked up."

"It has been. I haven't touched it outside of maintenance once a month."

"Have you shot it before?"

"Yes."

"Have you shot someone with it before?"

I think he might not answer, but silence would just confirm my suspicions. I thought I knew Reese, but apparently, I was very wrong. "Yes," he says quietly, almost regretfully.

"Have you killed anyone before, Reese?"

"Please don't do this."

"Answer the question."

"What if I say yes? What then, Ronnie? Are you going to leave me? Are you going to be so afraid of me that you can't handle being in the same room as me? Maybe I don't want to tell you because I don't want to risk losing you. Why can't you just accept the fact that I'll never hurt you and I would do anything to protect you?"

"Maybe because all you're doing is giving me pretty lines and claims of devotion! Maybe because you've tried to prove how much you care except in the way it fucking matters to me. I love you. I fucking *love* you, but I don't even know who the fuck you are!"

"Ronnie—"

"You've lied to me. This isn't even an omission or trying to hide shit about yourself, this is a full-blown *lie*, Reese. Who are you?"

"Reese Mitchel. I'm the same person I was when you first met me."

"Meaning you were always this person, this *stranger*."

"You know the me that matters," he whispers, voice cracking as his body sways in exhaustion or defeat, I'm not sure.

"You don't get it. *All* of you matters. Every secret, whether painful or dark, is a part of you and I want to know those parts, Reese. How can I love someone that makes me believe a lie?"

"Because the truth is never a pretty thing, and all I wanted was to give you all the beauty in the world, Ronnie, even if that meant creating the illusion for you to live in."

"Maybe it's better if I leave. We clearly need some time apart because this relationship is turning fucking toxic."

"No. Wait!" He chokes out when I step back towards the elevator. "Please don't go. Please don't leave right now. I can't handle it if something ends up happening to you because Dimitry is still out there. I want to figure out why he's here and what he wants, Ronnie, but I can't do that if the risk of you getting hurt or worse is looming over me."

"I can take care of myself." He drops to his knees in front of me, head bowing and shoulders slumping. "Get up," I hiss out.

"Tell me what I need to do to get you to stay."

"Tell me the truth."

"The truth is too dangerous. Just come home, Ronnie. I won't bother you and I'll sleep on the couch, but I would sleep better if I knew you were safe."

The fact he's willing to do that says a lot about him. I understand his worry. I would be worried too if it weren't for the fact I *know* Dimitry. He won't hurt me because my father would have his head if he did, but without knowing the reason he's watching me, I can't trust that he won't do something stupid. I need to message my dad and find out what the fuck he's up to.

"Fine." He lifts his head at that. "I don't want to be bothered."

He shakes his head. "I promise to leave you alone, but the apartment is small so we can't exactly avoid each other."

I nod and he slowly lifts to his feet. I walk past him, making sure to leave room between us as I do so he's not tempted to reach out to me. I can't handle it if he touches me right now because it would end up breaking my mental resolve. This is going to be nearly impossible when all I want to do is crawl into his lap and snuggle him while I beg him to just tell me everything. I don't understand why he's insisting on hiding things from me, but I guess I can't really talk.

I've been hiding things from him, too, but my secrets are probably far more dangerous than his. I can't let him get involved in that part of my life because I know my father. He's let me be on my own for this long, much to his dismay, but I have no idea how he would react if he knew I was with someone—living with a man that I've fallen in love with. It goes against everything he stands for because he still held out hope for me to fall in line and do my duty to our family. You'd think he would get the hint when I legally changed my name to my mother's, completely disowning the Petrov family name.

He follows quietly behind me, keeping his distance from me. "Did you want some lunch?" He asks when I step into the apartment. I turn and glare at him, giving him a very obvious '*are you fucking kidding me*' look. "Never mind," he murmurs. "Can I grab some things from the bedroom before you lock yourself in there?"

"Of course."

He heads off down the hall while I stand awkwardly in the living room, trying not to let myself panic at this whole situation. He comes back quickly enough, a duffel bag packed with some of his things, which he tosses next to the couch. He sets some pillows and blankets down on the cushions, pulling the gun from his waistband before going over to his stereo system in the corner. I watch as he pops the side off one of the massive speakers and punches in a code on a secret panel. Seriously, who the fuck is he? A door pops open and he quickly unclips the magazine, putting everything into the secret compartment. He's not even trying to hide it, a small sign of trust from him.

"You should eat something."

"I had a ton of cake. I'm good for now."

He doesn't argue with me, slowly getting back up to his feet and making his way over to the dining table to grab his laptop. I take that as a sign that I can leave now and make my way down the hall. "I'm sorry." His quiet voice drifts through the apartment, not slowing my steps, but breaking my heart none the less.

By the time I get into the bedroom and close the door, tears are streaming down my cheeks. My head thuds against the wood before I allow my body to slide down its length until my ass hits the floor. I curl my legs up and bury my face in my knees, sobbing like my heart just got broken. It did though. Knowing that he doesn't trust me enough to be honest with me hurts just as much as him not loving me back.

It's stupid of me to feel this way because I know I'm doing the same thing to him, but I'm not the one bringing a gun into this home with no hesitation in using it. With the way his mind has slowly been breaking, what's to say he doesn't snap and threaten me with it? No, he would never do that, but now my thoughts drift to the horrible thought that he might use it on himself.

I don't think Reese is suicidal, but how can anyone be sure? I didn't think Eden was either, but she tried to kill herself and would have died if Kaine hadn't shown up and gotten her the help she needed. I hope he doesn't feel that way or resorts to that, and the thought that I'm contributing to his mental issues doesn't sit well with me.

It takes all my mental willpower to drag myself up from the floor, but my body feels numb as I make my way to the bathroom. I need a shower, where hopefully the heat will ease some of the tension settling between my shoulder blades. I took extra time off work so I could spend it with Reese while he grieves the loss of his patient, but now it's turned into a tricky situation where we're both prisoners of our secrets and lies.

The shower does nothing. There's no relief or ease on my sore muscles because I can't get my mind to relax. It keeps drifting out to the main area where Reese is, wondering what he's doing and if he's panicking about the situation we've found ourselves in.

I throw on some comfortable clothes, and being the pathetic girlfriend that I am, I grab one of his sweaters instead of my own, getting lost in its warmth and the lingering scent of him on the fabric. I'm drowning in it, but it's cozy and welcoming as I settle onto the bed and turn on the TV.

My next mistake is putting on a sappy movie, where I just cry the whole time, wishing that the love I see on the screen could be my life. So far, the only thing I'm getting out of that fantasy is the heartbreak before the happily ever after, where in my life, I don't know if I'll get one. At least not with Reese. I want it to be with Reese, and I can't help the jealousy I feel towards Eden, that she was able to find someone who could love her the way Kaine does, even with all the flaws she believes she has.

By the time I finish the second movie and my eyes are practically swollen shut, my stomach growls. I have no choice but to go out there. I want to see him even though I shouldn't. I need to be strong and stand my ground if I have any hope in getting him to finally let me in.

I try to be as quiet as possible as I sneak out of the room, and I'm instantly assaulted by the smell of garlic bread. My mouth waters, my steps short and stealthy as I peek around the corner of the hall. Reese is sitting on the couch with his laptop settled on his knees. He's in heavy concentration; brows furrowed with the soft glow of the screen casting deep shadows. He has the living room almost completely dark, the only light coming from his screen and the sink light in the kitchen.

The floorboards creek and his head comes up, turning to look at me right away. His eyes widen slightly, but he doesn't say anything to me, watching me as I make my way to the kitchen. There's a plate on the stove, covered with tinfoil, which I risk a peek under.

"It's for you if you're hungry," Reese says quietly.

Even after all of that he still made me dinner. A healthy helping of chicken alfredo and three pieces of garlic bread stacked on top. It smells amazing and it's still warm, which means he figured what time my stomach would be protesting to be fed.

I turn with the plate in my hand, freezing when I notice him still watching me with those eyes. Eyes filled with sadness and regret. I clear my throat, lowering my gaze as I walk towards the bedroom. I risk a small glance at him as I pass the living room and notice the way his face falls. Did he expect me to sit in the kitchen and eat? Or maybe he thought I would go sit with him. It hurts my heart seeing him like that and takes everything in me to turn away from him.

I swear I hear a small sob as I reach the bedroom and it's enough to make me shatter all over again. There's no wall left to hold back my emotions, not at hearing him break like that. Tears fall down my cheeks as I fight back my own sobs. It makes me not want to eat, but I can't let the food he made me go to waste. He's trying. He's putting in effort to try and ease my worries, but I'm just not ready to deal with the conversation that is waiting for us at the end of this.

I'm shaking as I climb up into bed, covering myself with the blankets which let off a waft of Reese's scent. My eyes flutter closed, nostril flaring in a desperate attempt to cling to that part of him. I sigh, opening my eyes slowly and getting to work on eating my meal. It's delicious. Of course it is. Reese is an amazing cook, something I haven't quite mastered myself. I smile at the memories of him trying to teach me new recipes, how we would laugh so hard I would snort because of the mess I would make. He's a great teacher and patient, even when I made big enough mistakes that we would end up having to order food.

In my depressive state, I put on another sad movie. Clearly, I'm a glutton for punishment, but I'm crying anyways so what difference does it make? Soon I finish the meal, settling the plate onto the nightstand before tucking myself into bed and letting the movie continue to play out in the background. My body feels exhausted, my eyes growing heavier with each passing second. I wish I could sleep for a few days and wake up in the past, taking back everything I've said to him. If I could change things, I would. I don't want to hurt him, but can I really say that I would take back my feelings for him?

I love him. I love him so fucking much and I can't just ignore these feelings for him. I love him enough that I can't walk away from him no matter how much my mind is telling me to run.

CHAPTER TWENTY-THREE

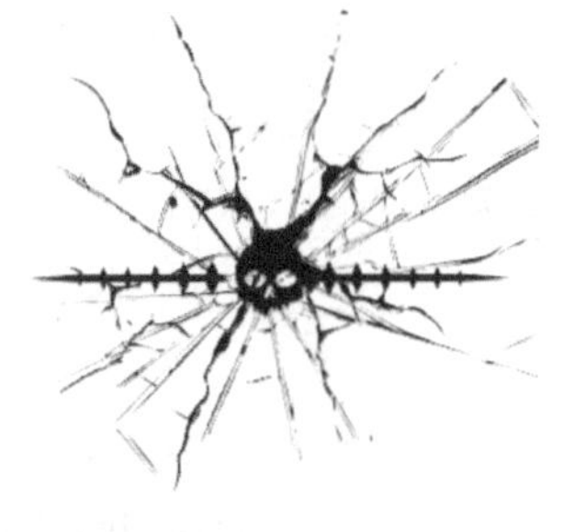

REESE

She fucking hates me. I wasn't thinking straight when Kaine called me, my body moving on its own like the machine it was trained to be. I only had one goal, get to Ronnie, keep her safe, and neutralize the threat.

The girl never listens. For once in her fucking life, I wish she would just do what I asked without questioning everything. If she had done what I told her to do, she wouldn't have seen me pulling the gun. She wouldn't have seen the *real* me.

I fucked up. I fucked up so fucking bad and I have no idea how to fix this. Telling her the truth won't fix shit at this point; it'll only make it worse. I didn't admit to killing anyone, but I didn't have to. My silence was enough. It's just as well. I knew all along that this was too good to be true because my life is a tragedy. Everyone who gets close to me dies. The only lucky thing about Eden and Kaine is the fact they can come back from it. If they couldn't, I would be alone again.

I can't let that happen to Ronnie, and I know that if I finally tell her about my family, it'll end up putting a target on her back. I've done well to keep our relationship under the radar, but my uncle isn't exactly keeping that close of an eye on me. He has no reason to. I've done nothing to warrant his attention, and he's been pretty good about leaving me alone now that I have a respectable job.

The last time I heard from him was after graduation when he sent me his congratulations and made it a point to let me know he knew about my little rendezvous at the farm. I should have known he has the place under surveillance, but he's never pointed out my times there before. Of course, he wouldn't need to call me out since every other time I was there before was to deal with *his* issues. He didn't say anything about Kaine and that's another reason I haven't been as adamant about refusing his requests. My luck, he would look into him and use him against me, but for now, he's safe. Kaine would lose his shit if he knew the mafia knew about him and what he did in that building, they might even try to recruit him.

I've gone over everything Holland sent me again and again, going as far as to message him for him to get me all the information he can on the Petrov family and all their ties and dealings. We try to stay out of each other's way, keeping to our own territory and going about our business in peace. The last thing I need is to be dragged into a fucking mafia war, but if this keeps up, I might have to contact my uncle to help me deal with this. Holland hasn't gotten back to me, but I'm not surprised. He's been good and I can't keep hounding him with all my issues.

I close down the files, opening up the one I hid on my computer in case Ronnie ever tried to snoop. Photo upon photo comes up, each thumbnail a harsh reminder of what I've had. Photos of my mom and me flicker past, and then photos of me and Kaine as kids, then teens. All good memories I try to use to remind myself that it's not as bad as I think it is. I settle on the latest pictures—the ones of me and Ronnie—and my throat burns with restrained emotion.

We were happy. The first few months of our relationship were some of the happiest moments I've had. Small things we did together, carnivals, dinner dates, me giving her a key to my apartment. Each one stabs at my heart until the screen begins to blur in front of me. I close the laptop, a shuddering breath rattling my lungs.

I know everything in life happens for a reason. People come into your life to teach you something, and whether they stay or they go is already set in the path created by fate. That's a fear that continues to grip at my heart though. The people I have in my life at the moment are the people I wish to have forever. I don't want to let them go, and I'll fight with all I have to keep them, Ronnie included. I wish I could change myself to be what she wants—what she deserves—but this is who I am. I don't know what I can do to make her see that I'm here for her, even if I don't tell her everything.

Can I bring myself to tell her how I feel about her? Can I risk it? Those I love get hurt and die, so the natural reaction is to keep them close, but not close enough to be tainted by my darkness.

It doesn't help that I have a new darkness haunting me. Today has been okay; no weird shadows, feelings of unease, or flickers of light, but it doesn't mean they're not there. I'm sure they've become wise to the fact I can see them, even though I'm not a part of their world. The reaper in the hospital looked right at me. He didn't react, but I could tell. No. I could *feel* that he wasn't happy about it. Not like it mattered. There was nothing I could do to stop him from taking Julia's soul.

I hope that where she ends up is somewhere she can enjoy and be happy, free from the pain and fear she felt in the mortal world. If reincarnation is a thing, I hope her next life is filled with all the good this world has to offer. She deserves it. She wholeheartedly deserves the best life possible after suffering through one that was cut short.

I shake my head, closing down the file and opening a search engine to see if Mr. Kent has officially made the news. Sure enough, it's on The Cameron Local, a photo of him plastered on the article. I feel awful for Diana finding out about everything like this, but she needed to know that her husband was not a good person and that it wasn't her fault that he was behaving the way he was. That's what cheaters do. They try to change the narrative and shift the blame to cover their own misdeeds.

'An explosion occurred at a local residence today and an investigation is underway. One of the homeowners was within the home, Jeremy Kent, at the time of the fire. The coroner report states that Mr. Kent had multiple broken bones and was located

at the base of the stairs when his body was extracted. There is currently no evidence of foul play. The other homeowner, Lena Sawyer, was at an event at the time of the explosion but has been taken in for questioning for any leads that may shed some light on what happened.

As the information comes through, we will keep everyone informed with updates.'

Nothing is mentioned in the fact he's married, but I'm sure that will all come out eventually. Fucking asshole. He still got off easy in my opinion, but I needed to make it look as much like an accident as possible for this to work out properly for Diana. Lena will get nothing from him or his life insurance, and the knowledge that Diana should be set for a little while is a small consolation. At least the financial burden can be eased enough for her to bury her daughter properly without worrying about being left in ruins.

I pause my hands on the keyboard, a sudden chill creeping across my skin and pulling goosebumps along the surface of my forearms. Glancing around in the dim lighting, there's nothing out of the ordinary, but a sense of being watch prickles the back of my neck. Fuck, I just had to go and jynx it.

"Leave me alone," I hiss out through gritted teeth, slamming the laptop closed and setting it down on the coffee table.

I need to get some sleep and just be done with today. Ronnie hasn't come back out after getting her dinner and I doubt she will at this point. I push myself off from the couch, crouching down to grab my toothbrush from my bag before heading down the hall to the spare bathroom. I could really use a shower right now just to warm up my body, but the only one we have is in the bedroom and I'm not planning to bother her when she's pissed at me.

The lights in the bathroom flare to life and I avoid looking at the mirror as I stand in front of the sink. The fear of seeing Avery there again is ripe in my mind, and the fact it feels even colder here is a massive warning sign. What could he possibly want with me? He got what he came here for, taking his little psychotic reaper friend to whatever pit of hell existed.

I can feel him under my skin, a constant thrum that just won't go away. "Please," I whisper, risking a glance up at the mirror but only finding my own reflection looking back at me. I don't know whether to feel relief or disappointment at that, but even still, I don't let my eyes linger for long. I could barely look at myself before, knowing who and what I am, but now? Now there's a new fear that threatens that last shred of sanity I'm trying to cling to.

There's no response or acknowledgement that he's here or that he's heard me, pushing my frustration to the maximum level. If only it were easy to talk to him, or any reaper for that matter. Kaine and Eden should have asked more questions when they had the chance, the secrets to the normal Lazarus were right there. They could have gotten their full discovery of the phenomenon, the reason why these people get touched by death, just to be spit back out again for a time. They can't escape true death, and I can't imagine what they feel at having cheated it only to be taken later on.

My joints feel stiff as I walk back to my temporary bed, the cold having settled right into the marrow of my bones. I'm glad I grabbed as many spare blankets as I did, cocooning myself in the pile to try and warm up and get some sleep. The exhaustion is there, but the dream world still feels out of reach when my mind is still running circles and going over everything that's happened and possible scenarios that might happen. I need to get a handle on everything, my life itself being the most pressing one.

Tomorrow is a new day. One that I hope holds solutions to the shit I'm fucking dealing with and not more problems. There's too much that's happening at the moment and so much that needs to be done. Why can't my life just be simple? What I wouldn't fucking give to just have that small peace for myself. A life where I can actually enjoy my job, hang out with my friends, and spend every spare moment that I can with the woman I've fallen for.

Instead, I'm waiting for a funeral date, trying to navigate the issue of a mafia henchman stalking my girl, and the drama that is my friends' wedding, plus the fucking reaper that won't leave me alone.

CHAPTER TWENTY-FOUR

RONNIE

I startle awake, blinking away the sleep and confusion coursing through me. My heart is thumping loud enough that I can hear it beating in my ears. A visceral scream ripples through the apartment, pushing me out of bed. My feet slap against the floor, coming to a screeching halt at the sight in front of me.

"Reese?" It's him. He's the one screaming at the top of his lungs, body thrashing and getting tangled in the pile of blankets covering him. His body arches off the couch, a pained cry tearing through his lung. "Reese!"

I run to him, not sure what I can do to help him, but he doesn't hear me. His eyes are closed, the light of the slowly rising sun barely shining through the windows. His jaw is clenched, teeth gritted so hard I hear them squeak against each other. His entire body is tensed so tightly that his muscles bulge and ripple, like he's seizing. A thin sheen of sweat covers his bare chest, which is moving rapidly with each harsh breath.

The air around him seems to ripple with energy, making it difficult to breathe. What the fuck is happening? He's had nightmares before and he's woken up completely shaken, but I've never seen anything like this. I crouch down beside him, gently touching his shoulder and wincing at the sudden sharp pain that shoots through my arm, taking my breath away. His body stills, coiled painfully before his muscle twitch and convulse. His fingers curl around the edge of the blanket, knuckles white and cracking at the force behind it.

"Reese?" His eyes launch open, mouth gaping on a silent scream. Something is wrong, even in the dim light I can see it. His eyes are completely black, his pupils blown and overtaking the colour trying to burn through. Bigger and bigger, flaring out to cover the whites of his eyes. It must be a trick of the light, or my brain is still fogged up from waking up the way I did because there's no way I'm seeing this right. He looks...off. He looks fucking demonic.

His mouth snaps closed again, chest heaving while his breath wheezes out of him. "A...ver...y," he rasps.

Who the fuck is Avery?

His head jerks, neck bending at an awful angle. "Reese," he whispers.

Okay, this is *beyond* weird. Is he just randomly saying names now? I swear if he says my name while he's in this state I'm going to fucking shit myself. This is some exorcist bullshit and every instinct in me is telling me to run, but my heart is telling me to help him, to save him, to do *something*.

I throw myself over him, wrapping my arms around his still trembling body. He's freezing even though he's sweating and his muscles feel like stone beneath me.

"Shhh. I'm here."

The minutes tick by excruciatingly slowly, but eventually, his body relaxes under me. His breathing is still harsh and stutters randomly, but he's slowly coming out of the nightmare that just destroyed his body.

"Ronnie?" He croaks.

I pull away from him carefully and stare down at him. His eyes are back to their normal hue, although the exhaustion in his is glaringly obvious. He looks like he just went ten rounds with a sociopath, bags under his eyes, thin red veins spreading through the white parts. Even though they look the same in colour, they're not as vibrant and lively as they usually are. To be fair, I haven't seen true light in them for a while now.

His eyes flutter closed when I gently brush back the sweaty strands of hair sticking to his forehead, and my heart breaks at the small whimper that sneaks through his lips.

"Are you okay?" I ask, cupping his cheek. He shakes his head, brows furrowing on a wince as he leans into my touch. "Do you want to talk about it?" He opens his eyes slowly and shakes his head again. "Okay."

"Is it?"

"Yes. I can't imagine what you're going through right now or what you're feeling, Reese, but these nightmares are destroying you."

"I'm sorry I woke you."

"Stop. We might not be seeing eye to eye on things right now, but it doesn't mean I don't care about you and that I'll stop worrying about you. I hate seeing you like this."

I shiver at the feel of his hand sliding up my side, the touch too gentle and cold. "I don't know what's wrong with me."

His hand pauses on my hip when I climb on top of him, laying myself along the length of his body. I will my own body heat into him, wishing that he would warm up and relax enough to get some proper rest. I smile into his neck when I feel him trying to tug the blankets over the both of us. He rubs at my back in soothing circles, and a small hum of pleasure vibrates deep in my throat. My own body relaxes into his like a puzzle piece falling into place.

I can't stay mad at him. I don't even think I was really mad at him to begin with, I was mad at myself. It's not like I really fell for the lies, I just believed everything was okay when it really wasn't. I'm just as much to blame as he is.

We lay like this for what feels like hours, but the sun hasn't risen fully outside the window yet. Eventually his hand on my back stills and his breathing evens out. I risk a peek up at him, smiling at the peaceful look on his face, the way his lashes spread against his cheeks, and the soft parting of his lips on each exhale. Poor guys is exhausted beyond measure, and each night he spends locked in these vicious nightmares, is another crack within his soul. I don't know what else I can do to help him other than being here for him. If I had allowed him to stay with me last night, he may not have had the nightmare, and that's something I'll have to live with.

I feel like I'm losing him little by little to whatever is going on with him. I don't know if talking about it will end up being enough at this point either. Maybe I need to suggest he talk to a psychiatrist or something just to have someone to listen to him that won't affect him on a personal level. That could very well be the reason why he's so guarded about everything, he doesn't want to risk pushing away his friends with whatever is bothering him.

I hate the idea that I'm not enough for him. It hurts, and I wish it weren't true, but I'll do what I have to in order to get him through this rough part. As long as it takes and whatever it takes. In the meantime, I need to speak to my father and find out why he's sent Dimitry after me. I'll also have to have words with him at the fact he almost killed Kaine. I don't know what they're fucking doing but I can't have them trying to kill my friends.

I settle my cheek on his chest, feeling the warmth finally coming back into his body. I can't help running my fingers across his bare skin, loving the feel of the tight muscles underneath. Each passing second draws my eyes closed and my body sinks deeper into him until my own exhaustion pulls me under.

CHAPTER TWENTY-FIVE

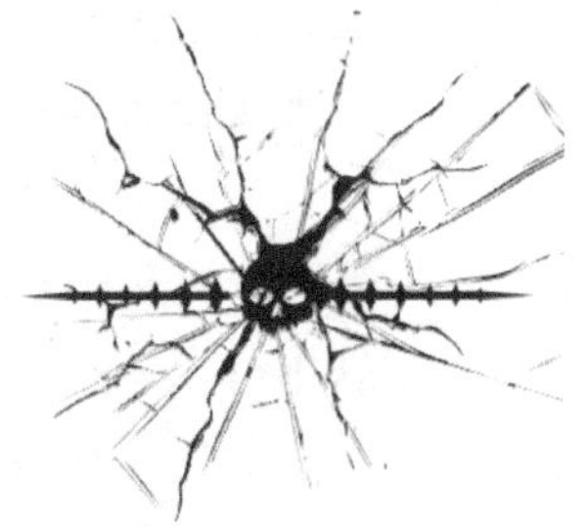

REESE

Everything hurts. From my muscles to my bones, nerve endings right down to my skin, everything screams in pain. The only comfort I feel is the warm body draped over me. There's no way the position is comfortable, but she stayed the rest of the night and well into the morning in this position. I don't actually know what time it is, but the sun is high in the sky now, streaming in through the glass in broken waves that glitter and reflect in prismatic tones across the ceiling.

My hands are still wrapped around her body, tucked under her shirt where I can feel the softness and warmth of her skin radiating into me. I run my fingers up her spine, gently scratching my nails along her shoulder blades. She shudders against me, pulling a smile across my lips. She's big into the back scratches, but so am I. I love when she digs her little demon fingers into my skin, scraping and clawing at me, but more when I'm fucking her into oblivion. That's pure bliss. Just the thought of being buried inside of her has my semi-hard cock thickening in my pants.

I slam my eyes closed when she wiggles her hips into me, pressing into my cock. My breathing shallows when she does it again, and that's when I realize she's awake and doing it on purpose.

She props herself up on my chest suddenly, eyes hooded and a wicked grin spreading across her face. The way she tugs her bottom lip between her teeth, slowly letting it slide back out to pop back into its plump form, makes me grip into her hips to grind her down against me.

"Morning," she says with amusement in her voice. "Did you sleep better?"

"I did, thanks to you."

"Hmm. Am I the cure to your nightmares then?" She asks, rocking her pelvis against me.

"You're a cure to a lot of things, Ronnie, and the nightmares seem to be one of them."

She leans closer to me, hovering a breath away from my lips. "That's a good answer," she purrs, finally closing the distance.

It's definitely unexpected after everything that happened yesterday. She's being very hot and cold with her emotions, but I'm not helping any with the way I keep fucking with her mentally. I love the way she presses her body against mine, like she's trying to merge us into one being. The way she slides her tongue between my lips, diving it into my mouth to claim me in that possessive way of hers. She acts sweet and she is, don't get me wrong, but I'm also thankful that I'm the only one who gets to see this feral side of her.

It's addictive. Everything about her is, but this obsession she seems to have with me is mirrored by my own. I don't even know when my compass shifted to point towards her instead of the norm of moral acuity. I would do very bad things for this girl with no hesitation. Plus, I would do bad things *to* her, but I know she would like them. Hell, she'd probably beg for them.

Begging. I practically begged her yesterday to stay. I literally got down on my knees for her, something I've never done for anyone, but for her...for her I would crawl. I would stay down on my knees if it meant keeping her.

"Want me to make you feel even better?" She gasps, nipping at my bottom lip.

I would love nothing more than to drown myself in her taste and smell, revel in the feel of her body wrapped around me, but a nagging voice at the back of my mind is telling me we need to stop. I get it, I really do. The way we keep trying to fix things with sex is probably not the healthiest way of doing things, but if it's so wrong, why does it feel so fucking good?

It's like we're both using it as a way of avoiding what we're trying to hide. I know she's hiding something from me, something darker than I care to believe. Her reaction to my mention of Dimitry's name wasn't the reaction of someone who didn't know who I was talking about. She stiffened and her breathing quickened for a fraction of a second, giving away the fact that she *does* know who he is. She locked it down fast enough that anyone else wouldn't think twice about it, but I know better. I've been trained to know better.

She rolls her hips again, and fuck me, I *want* to give in. My body reacts on its own, fingers digging in harshly, pulling her closer to me. I moan into her mouth, savouring every whimper she lets loose because this damn girl is grinding herself against me, chasing her own pleasure while she uses me.

Fuck it.

I claw at her clothes, hearing the distinct rip of material as I tear it from her body. She huffs, pulling away to pout down at me in the most adorable way. I can't help it, I grin.

"What?" I muse, fighting back the laugh threatening to bubble up my throat.

"You know exactly what."

"I'll buy you new ones."

"You keep saying that!"

I laugh, sliding my hand down her ass to dip my fingers into her pussy. She shudders, eyes fluttering closed while her mouth pops open. "Anything you want, I'll buy it for you as long as you keep letting me rip them from your body."

"You're playing dirty," she pants.

"Oh, baby, I'm fucking filthy." My cock strains against my sweats, begging for release to slide into her. "Can I fuck you?" I huff, curling myself up enough to lick and suck on her neck. I love the delicate expanse of flesh. So creamy and soft and untainted.

She whimpers, biting her lip when I nip at her collarbone. "Yes," she says breathlessly, reaching down between us to finally free my cock. I groan when she sits herself into me, taking me completely.

"You know," she whispers, rocking her hips and drawing herself up my length. "We seem to be using sex as an excuse."

"You think so?" Obviously, I agree, since I came to that conclusion myself.

She nods, closing her eyes and tipping her head back when she settles back down, taking me in deeper than before. "Mmhmm. It's probably not the best plan."

"It feels pretty fucking good to me though." She snorts and slowly opens her eyes. "If you think it's a mistake, you know what to do." She frowns. "You're the one in control right now. I'm not pinning you down and fucking you. You're the one sitting on me and riding that cock like you want to."

"But it's such a good cock."

"Fuck," I moan, digging my fingers into her ass and spreading her wider. "Don't stroke my ego like that."

"Hmm, maybe you're right." She stops moving. My dick pulses inside of her and it's taking everything in me to lay perfectly still instead of gripping into her and forcing her to move again. Her walls are slowly pulsing around me, making the task way harder than it needs to be. "So, you agree then?"

"With what?" I grit out, silently begging for her to move, to shift, to fucking do anything but just sit here and torture me.

"That what we're doing is evading, Reese."

"If I say yes, will you at least let me finish."

She huffs, rolling her eyes before smacking my chest. "I'm being serious."

"So am I! I'm fucking dying here. Blue is not my fucking colour." She tips her head in question. "Please, don't leave me hanging." The last thing I want is for her to stop and either leave me to suffer or fend for myself. I have no issue with jerking off, but why would I want to when she's right here, sitting on it with the delicious warmth of her cunt wrapped around it. I felt bad for Kaine when I found out Eden did that to him, but here I am, about to experience it for myself. I don't like being edged; never have and never will.

"Fine, but only because it feels good."

"So, you're using me?"

"Yup."

Sassy little shit. She boosted my ego just to tear it down right at the knees. It crumples under her words, but I refuse to say anything because fuck me, I need her to ride it. She grips into my hair, tearing my head to the side to expose my neck where she trails her hot tongue along the front of it. My throat bobs at the sensation, the wet heat of it sending a flurry of sparks rippling through my body. My cock throbs inside her, relishing in the pulsing heat and slick grip she has on me.

"You like that?" She murmurs, biting my jaw before moving her mouth to hover over mine again. She increases her rhythm, bouncing on me until all I hear is the sound of our panting breaths and the slap of skin on skin. My heartbeat is loud, too, thrumming in my eardrums as she pushes me higher and higher. My stomach tenses with each drop of her hips against me until my entire body heats with the need to spill into her. "Answer me," she growls, biting my lip and tugging hard enough to feel the sting.

"Yes. Fuck yes, I love it."

"You love it?"

"Yes."

"Do you love *me*?"

I come. My brain short-circuits on the natural reply that is hanging at the tip of my tongue. I choke it down, hating that she's picking now, of all moments, to fucking do this again. For fuck's sake, what am I supposed to do?

"Ronnie."

Her jaw trembles, and just when I think she's going to break down and cry, she locks it down. Her face goes blank, eyes darkening like my lack of response just killed a piece of her inside. I can see it. The normal light in her eyes slowly fades until they look hollow.

"Sorry," she murmurs, shifting off of me and grabbing one of the blankets to wrap around herself. I reach out to stop her from walking away, and I half expect her to rip herself from my hold, but she doesn't. "I shouldn't have done that, I just—is it me?"

"No, it's not you. It's me, Ronnie. I—" I can't keep doing this to her. I didn't want to take the risk in telling her how I feel because I'm trying to protect her, but maybe my thoughts are wrong. Maybe I'm not cursed to be alone. Maybe it was just bad luck and unfortunate events that took everything I care about from me. Even if it's true, I'll do whatever I can to keep her safe in this world, even if she needs protection from *me*.

"I'm fine, Reese," she says quietly.

"I love you."

The words spill out of me, and some of the weight that has been pressing into me eases. The worry is still there, but it's manageable, especially when she turns to look at me with wide eyes.

"I love you, Ronnie. I have for a while now, but I didn't want things to get...ruined. I'm sorry if you ever felt like I didn't, it's just hard for me to express myself because—" I swallow around the lump forming in my throat—on one of the thoughts I've been keeping to myself. "The last person I loved, died. I'm scared. I'm afraid that acknowledging how I feel about you will put a target on your back."

"You love me?" She whispers.

I nod, my heart clenching at the well of tears forming along her lashes. "I do." She throws herself back on top of me, sobbing into my neck while her hands claw at my body in desperation. "Shhh, it's okay."

"I won't leave you," she hiccups. "Thank you for being honest with me."

"I don't want to see you broken anymore."

She lifts herself up and wipes her eyes, laughing through another sob. "You just made me so happy, Reese."

I cup her cheek, rubbing my thumb under her eye to clear away the tears that are still freefalling uninhibited. "You've made me happy for a while. I knew you were special right from the beginning, and I don't want to give you up. I'll fight for you, Ronnie. I'll fight for *us*."

There it is. The light that was dimming in her eyes flares to life, making her entire face glow with new life. Three simple words spoken in earnest were enough to completely change her. There's joy chasing away the sadness that was threatening to consume her and completely destroy her from the inside out. I never meant to hurt her, and the fear is still there in my heart. I don't know if there's anything I can do to chase it away when locking it down seems useless. This isn't a mistake, and if I let myself feel regret for speaking the truth to her—the truth that's been clawing and screaming its way out of my heart—I'll end up hating myself.

"I love you," I whisper.

"I love you, too. I love you so much, Reese."

Her words sink into me. They act like a salve against my blistered heart; against the damage that has been done to it over and over again until I thought there was no way to heal it. She's doing it now and doesn't even know it. With her here, with me, I can feel free. I can live in the little dream world we've created for ourselves—the bubble of lies we tell ourselves because that's what it is. Until we speak our truths and shatter the illusion, how can we know our reality is real?

We're two fucked up souls, hiding things from each other while blaming the other for doing just that. I haven't confronted her to the same level she has to me, but she's got better defenses than I do. My walls have been blown apart, devastated to the point I don't think I can rebuild them quickly enough to stop the darkness lying dormant there from waking and seeping over the edges and through the cracks in the foundation.

My phone buzzes on the table, forcing me to rip my gaze from her face to look over at it. *'Unknown Number'* flashes across the screen. Who the fuck could that be?

"Are you going to answer it?"

"I don't know who it is. Let it go to voicemail." I cradle her head, coaxing her down to settle on my chest. It rings again. "For fuck's sake."

"It could be important."

She giggles when I grip into her and stretch out as far as I can to grab the stupid thing off the table without letting her go. "Hello?"

"Dr. Mitchel." My body stiffens and my fingers grip into Ronnie's back, a defense mechanism to try and ground myself. "It's Diana Kent."

"How are you doing?"

She pulls in a rattling breath, letting out a barely there laugh that holds no joy or amusement. "I'm hanging in there. Um, have you heard about Jeremy?"

"I saw the article last night."

"I don't know what to do," she whispers. "Finding out that he was living another life while our daughter—" Her voice breaks off on a sob and Ronnie lifts her head enough to look at me, a frown forming on her face.

"Diana, it's your decision on what you wish to do about his passing, but if I were you, I'd leave it for his mistress to deal with. You owe him nothing, but he owes you everything. You'll get the life insurance and everything else will be transferred to you because you were still married."

"She didn't know though."

"It doesn't matter. She'll grieve in her own way, just as you will, but you have more important things to focus on."

"The funeral is tomorrow for Julia."

"Where?"

"St. Paul's, and she'll be buried at The Hollows Cemetery."

"I'll be there."

"I know you don't have to go this far for us, Dr. Mitchel, but I appreciate it."

"I cared about your daughter very much and I would never not go, Diana. I'll see you tomorrow."

"So, the funeral is tomorrow?" I nod, tossing my phone back onto the table and falling against the couch heavily. "Who else died?"

"Her husband." Her eyes widen. "He was cheating on her and living with another woman. Their home blew up the other night with him in it, but they're still investigating."

"Fuck. That poor woman."

"She'll be better off without him. The fact he wasn't by his dying daughter's side on her birthday makes it seem like karma finally had enough of his bullshit." I have no issue being the sword karma refuses to wield against pieces of shit like him. He's not the first, and I doubt he'll be the last to fall by my hands.

"Do you still want me to go with you?"

"I won't ask that of you."

"You don't have to." She drapes herself over me again, wrapping her arms around my body, but struggling to shove them under my back. She lets out a cute sigh when she finally pins her hands under me, officially locking herself against me. "We should get up."

"Mmm, just a little longer. I'm not done recharging yet."

"Recharging?" She nuzzles her face into my neck, dragging her nose up the length of my throat on a deep inhale. "What are you doing?" I laugh.

"You smell good," she murmurs, pressing her lips against my jaw. "I want to smell like you."

Damn it, that's adorable. I love it when she wears my shit, too. I always thought it was just because she found my clothes comfortable, but maybe there's a deeper meaning to it. Is that why girls tend to steal our shit? To smell like us?

"What do I smell like to you?" I couldn't possibly smell good at the moment. Not with the fact I didn't get to shower last night and I sweat half the moisture out of my body because of the stupid nightmare that plagued me again.

"Like sandalwood and pine and vanilla and something else. Maybe musk or leather? Whatever it is, I love it. It makes me happy and your smell calms me."

I can't deny the fact I feel the same way about her, but it's not just her smell. It's her. Her just being here and willingly holding me, calms me. I definitely needed it after last night. It was one of the worst ones yet—I know it in my gut—but as I try to remember the details about it, the fractured images liquify and slip through my mental fingers. I know Avery was there, but I don't know any of the details, just this weird sense of loss and foreboding.

"Do you want to talk?" She asks, her voice timid now.

"About what exactly?"

"Who's Avery?" My hold on her tightens and panic sets in. Did I talk in my sleep? Fuck. What else did I say? "You didn't look right, Reese, and you choked out that name. Is it another patient of yours? You said your own name right after, and your eyes didn't look right."

"Were they grey?"

"What? No. They were black. At least they *looked* black. It was pretty dark and I had just woken up, but something didn't feel right."

I shouldn't feel relief in hearing that, but if my eyes weren't the colour of his, then maybe what I experienced wasn't him. I have no idea why I would call out to him though. It's not like Avery can help me with anything and he hasn't spoken to me, so what could I have possibly been experiencing in those moments? It's definitely strange that I spoke my own name as well.

"Avery is...an old acquaintance. He knows Kaine and Eden, but we haven't seen him in quite some time." The lie shouldn't come this easily. It should feel heavy in my chest and sour in my mouth, but I feel nothing but relief as I speak the words. Acquaintance is too friendly of a term. He's a reaper and a fucking hitchhiker that won't fucking leave me alone. I've done my part in whatever little plot he had planned for years, so it makes no sense why he's still clinging to me like tar on a shoe.

"So, it's a guy."

"Yeah, why?" She doesn't say anything, and then it clicks. "Ronnie," I laugh. "Trust me when I say this, there's no other girl in my life. Avery is very much male and a dick to boot. Be thankful that you don't know him." A dull throb begins to form behind my eyes and a slight ringing in my ears has me wondering if the dick heard that. Good. I hope he fucking hears me talking shit about him any way that I can. He's making my life hell right now, and if I can inconvenience him in any way, I fucking will.

"You don't talk to other girls?"

"No one of meaning. I mean, I care for Eden but that's different. Besides her, I only talk to the women at work."

"Are any of them hot?"

"Seriously?" She shrugs, nuzzling herself closer to me. "They're coworkers and nothing more. You have nothing to worry about, Ronnie. I would never be cowardly enough to cheat on you. If I have a problem within our relationship, I would at least be honest with you about it. I hope you feel the same way."

"There's no one but you."

CHAPTER TWENTY-SIX

RONNIE

He loves me. I can't believe he actually said those words to me, but the way he looked—the relief on his face—I know that he meant it. All this time he's loved me, but he's avoided saying it to me to protect me. I can't believe he thinks that he's cursed because of his mom. I can't imagine feeling that way, but knowing that now, I can't hold it against him.

I'll do whatever I can to help him and protect him, too. The first step in doing that is dealing with Dimitry and my father. I slowly pull away from him, loving the way his eyes crinkle as he stares up at me. That's the Reese I fell in love with and the one I've been missing these last few weeks. I started noticing the change in him a few months ago, but he did well to lock down whatever was going on inside his head. Now? Now, he's struggling to the point where his mental strength is waning, making it easier for that sadness to slip through his mask.

"I'm going to go grocery shopping today. Maybe we can make some pizzas for dinner. If you want to, of course."

"Yeah, we can do them on the stone in the barbecue."

"What are you up to today?"

"I have some things to take care of as well and I'm supposed to be meeting with Kaine early afternoon for a fitting."

I grin, my eyes roaming over his broad chest as he tucks his hands under his head. "Hmm, I can't wait to see you in a suit."

"Oh really?" I nod. "Do you have plans for me in the suit?"

"Well, I hear that guys tend to go for the wedding party at weddings, and I'm *really* hoping one guy in particular has eyes for the maid of honor."

"Is he good looking?"

"Very."

"Could I kick his ass?"

"I don't know, he's pretty ripped. I think you might put up a valiant effort, but you'll get hurt for sure."

"Hmm, that's unfortunate. What would this guy do to you?"

"I'd leave it up to him. Maybe he'd drag me into a corner, pin me to a wall and fuck me, or maybe he'd take me out back and tell me to run. The possibilities are endless."

His eyes light up at that and a wicked grin spreads across his face. "Veronica Halladay has a primal kink. Who knew?"

I roll my eyes at that. We may not have explored our sexual relationship to that level yet, but he knows very well that I like things some girls don't. Is it weird that I flinched internally at him calling me by my name? It could be the fact that my family has suddenly decided to take an interest in me again, threatening the life I've tried to create once I took my mother's name. I think Reese would look at me very differently if he knew the truth, and not the way he's looking at me now. Now his gaze holds kindness and affection, the love he's been trying so hard to hide burning through his amber-flecked eyes.

"I'd do anything for you," I smile.

"Hmm, we'll see. Looks like I'll have some planning to do and research."

"I'm going to take a shower and get cleaned up, if you care to join me."

He shakes his head. "You go ahead. I've got some calls to make really quick, and I'll get started on a late breakfast before you head out."

I lean down and give him a quick kiss on the lips, loving the small hum that vibrates in his throat when I do. This is what I've always wanted. I know that we're still both hiding things from each other, but the relationship feels like it's moving in the right direction now. I know that in time I'm going to have to come forward and tell him about myself and my family, but I want to cling to this reality for a little bit longer. I need to just believe that he'll take what I tell him and not run for the hills when he finds out.

Even as I walk away from him, I can feel his eyes on me, following my retreating form. My body is a bit sore from sleeping on top of him for those few precious hours, aches radiating through my back and joints, but it was worth it. It's nice to know that my company was comforting to him and that he was able to at least get a few hours of proper rest. At some point I'm going to need to talk to him about seeing someone. He needs to talk through his issues with someone, even if it's not with me.

I wonder if Kaine knows how bad it's gotten for him. I'm also curious who this Avery is and why he's haunting Reese's dreams. I grab my phone as soon as I get back into the bedroom, pulling up my chat with Eden. Gnawing on my lip, I try and come up with the best way to touch on the subject. Fuck it.

Ronnie: Hey, I have a question.

I don't think she's working right now, but I can't be sure. I didn't ask her what her schedule was going to be over the next few days, but I assume if Kaine took time off, so did Eden. I'm not expecting her to message me if she's at work, so I smile when I see that she's read the message and the typing bubble pops up.

Eden: What's up?

Ronnie: Do you know someone named Avery?

I startle when my phone starts to vibrate in my hand, Eden's name flashing across the screen. "Hello?"

"Why do you ask?" Her tone sounds clipped, almost guarded, and warning bells start sounding in my head, telling me to tread carefully.

"Reese had a nightmare last night and said his name. When I asked him about it this morning, he mentioned that he was an acquaintance of yours and Kaine's."

"You could say that. Did he say anything about seeing him recently?"

"No. He said he hasn't been around in quite a while." The sigh of relief she lets out has me questioning everything. "Should I be worried?"

"No. Avery shouldn't be coming around anytime soon. He's...overseas."

"Did he do something to Reese? He doesn't seem right, Eden, and I'm really starting to get worried about him. I'm thinking of suggesting he go see someone like a psychiatrist."

"Is he still acting strange?"

"Yeah, and he just seems really sad. I don't know what to do or how I can help him. I hate feeling like I'm not enough for him, but with this, I might not be." I make my way into the bathroom and turn on the shower to warm up. "The funeral for the little girl is tomorrow. I'm hoping that once that's over, he'll start to feel a little bit better. I know how hard it was for him to lose her. He got attached to that patient, even though I warned him it wasn't a good idea."

"He's got a very kind heart, Ronnie. There was no way you could have convinced him to pull away from that kid with everything she was going through."

"Did you hear about the mom's husband?"

"What?"

"I heard Reese talking about it on the phone. I didn't look into the details, but he said he saw the information in an article. I think it's a bit weird that he died shortly after his daughter did."

"I'm sure it's nothing. Unless he felt guilty for not being there for her and set up his own death, but who can really know for sure."

"I have to get ready to go out, but I'll send you a text later."

"Okay. I think Kaine said he wanted to go to the funeral for Reese, so I'll let him know that it's tomorrow. Can you send me the details when you have them?"

"Sure. Talk soon."

I set the phone down on the sink and strip out of the blanket, shirt, and torn pants. Fuck's sake, Reese. He seriously destroys everything, the damn neanderthal. I swear I'm never buying nice clothes again because he'll just end up destroying them. I'm learning very quickly not to have attachments to my wardrobe. I wonder if I started wearing *his* things if he would do the same thing? He wouldn't be happy ripping up his own shit, I'm sure. Scratch that, he'd probably be excited about it no matter what.

CHAPTER TWENTY-SEVEN

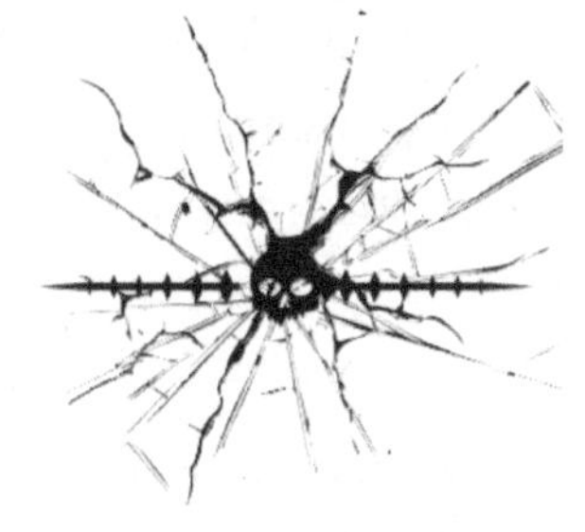

REESE

“What is it now?” Holland sighs.

I tuck the phone between my ear and my shoulder, flipping one of the pancakes before it decides to burn. “Did you get me any other information on Dimitry or Misha?”

“Is the shit I gave you not enough?”

“Not even close. It doesn’t give me any explanation as to why they’re following my fucking girlfriend, Holland.” I glance towards the hallway, straining my ears to make sure I can still hear the water running in the shower. “There has to be a reason they’re following her and you’re the only one that can get me the information I need on the fucking Bratva.”

"You could call your uncle. He's bound to have way more insight into them than I am with my research."

"I'm not calling him."

"Why not?"

"You fucking know why! I'm not going to allow myself to fall back into their shit. If I ask anything of him right now, he'll push for me owing him *another* favour. I'm so fucking done with all this nonsense it's not even funny anymore."

"If your goal was to get out from under your uncle's thumb, you wouldn't be talking to me."

"You're different."

"How am I different? I work for *him*, Reese. I'm only doing you these favours because you're still a part of this."

"Wow, okay. Here I thought we were friends, but I see how it is."

He sighs, clucking his tongue. "We *are* friends, but do you really think I would even be allowed to speak to you if you *weren't* part of the mafia? I don't exactly work as a freelance member, Reese. I'm sort of bound to your uncle, and therefore, you."

"Fine. Then do your fucking job and get me what I asked for."

I swear the fucker growls like a god damn dog, even if it sounds more like a chihuahua. "Yes, Sir," he grits out, hanging up the phone before I can tell him to do anything else.

"Asshole," I mumble, ripping the phone away from my ear and dropping it onto the counter.

"Everything okay?"

"Fuck," I gasp, spinning around to see Ronnie walking towards me, damp hair flowing down her back. She's dressed casually again today, but those damn yoga pants make her ass look so fucking good. The shirt is pretty nice, too. The way it clings to her frame and the way it stretches across her tits is perfection. "Are you a fucking ninja?"

She smiles, walking right up to me to wrap her arms around my waist. "I wasn't being *that* quiet. Were you on the phone?"

"Yeah. Just going over some shit at work since I'll be gone for a few days." I swear I was paying attention to my surroundings, so there's no way this little shit didn't purposely sneak up on me. Did she hear anything I said? I have no idea how long she'd been near me, but I tried to be as quiet as I could be, and I kept checking if she was coming out. Though, I didn't hear the shower turn off either, so maybe I'm losing my touch.

"Oh, right." She tips her head up, smiles and crinkles her nose, the motion practically begging me to kiss her. She hums happily when I press my lips to hers briefly. "Hmm, what did you make?"

"Protein pancakes with wild blueberries and white chocolate chips."

"Oh, yay!" She squeals, ripping away from me and breezing past me to check out the ones I already have plated. "Can I have these?"

"You can have as many as you want," I chuckle, smiling as she grins up at me with her plate. I cup the back of her neck and press my lips to her forehead, loving the way my body feels lighter every time I kiss her. "Go on and eat."

She breaks into a fit of giggles when I smack her ass as she walks by, and the joy in that sound fills me with so much happiness that I start to believe that what I've done is the right thing. I watch her a little longer. Watch the smile on her face while she digs into the pile of pancakes in front of her. I love watching her in general, but moments like this make me smile. I love the little hums she lets out and the way her body sways happily with each bite of food. She's never been shy about eating and can pack it away, but she tends to lean more towards the healthier choices when she has the option. The girl loves her protein but I'm not complaining because so do I.

I don't linger as long as I want to, turning back to my own pancake and frowning when I see the burnt edges as I flip it. At least hers all turned out good. I still keep stealing glances at her over my shoulder, fighting back a laugh at the fact she's swinging her feet under the table like a little kid. She's seriously adorable. Her cheeks are stuffed full, but she pauses her chewing and slowly turns her head, eyes widening when she notices me watching her.

She quickly covers her mouth, her jaw moving quicker to try and work around the stack fighting for its life in her mouth. "What?" She says, voice muffled with food.

I smirk. "Nothing."

"Why are you watching me eat?"

"Is there something wrong with that?"

She rolls her eyes, swallowing and choking slightly. I set a glass of orange juice in front of her and move back towards the stove, swapping out the pancakes. A few moments later, she sets her plate on the counter, grips into my shoulder and props herself on her toes to plant a kiss on my cheek.

"All done? You can have more."

She shakes her head. "I'm good, but I wish you would have eaten with me."

"I'll eat with you tonight, okay?"

She pouts, flopping back down and rolling her eyes. "Fine."

She squeaks in surprise when I suddenly grab her and sit her down on the counter, sneaking in between her thighs. "You're very needy," I muse.

She slides her knees up my sides and settles her forearms on my shoulders, a sneaky little smile pulling at her lips. A full shiver rips up my spine when she slowly drags her nails into my nape, tugging at the strands.

"I can't help it. I always need you."

Fuck, this girl. Normally I don't like clingy people; ones that are constantly vying for attention or getting mad when they don't get it from you. With her? She's different. She's not doing it to be clingy or controlling; she's doing it because she cares—because she *loves* me.

"You're trying to butter me up."

My fingers dig into her hips, pinning her while I roll my hips into her. Her eyes flutter closed, and that damn plump bottom lip gets pinned between her teeth in the most sensual way. The girl is a closeted sexual deviant in a way that admittedly can trump my own desires at times. There are days where I wonder if I'll be able to keep up with her appetite.

It's almost like she's been sheltered most of her life, maybe even some daddy issues thrown in there, but the girl she's turned into is someone bursting with an internal fire that knows what she wants, even if her way of getting it isn't the most forward.

Being a shy little thing in the beginning, only to open up and become this shining human in my hold, is something I'll never get tired of. "You need to go or you're not going to get anything done today."

Slowly, she opens her eyes again, frowning up at me. "Maybe I just want a me day. Is that too much to ask?"

"It's not, but you already have plans, do you not?"

"Fine." I grunt, gripping into her harder while my body curls forward towards her. The sadistic little shit leans into me, her lips brushing against my ear while her hand palms and grips at my cock. "But you better put this to good use later." Her teeth clamp down on my earlobe, nibbling the skin before she sucks it into her mouth. "Got it?" She whispers, darting her tongue out and sending a shudder through my body.

"Keep this up and I'll fuck you through a wall," I grit out.

"Don't threaten me with a good time," she giggles, finally releasing me and pulling back to look at me. I can barely keep myself composed at this rate, my body heating with each passing second while my cock throbs from the assault she just inflicted on the poor thing. She pats my hip. "Come on. Let me out of your cage." I blink, slowly backing away for her to hop back down to the floor with a smile on her face, like she didn't just manhandle my poor dick. "Your pancakes are burning."

I almost give myself whiplash when I turn my head, rushing over to the sorry state of my breakfast. "Fuck." Grabbing the pan, I quickly turn on the exhaust fan and take the blackened patty over to the trash, dumping the pathetic blob into the bag. "You should definitely go before I have nothing left to cook."

She smacks my ass hard enough to jolt me forward where I almost take out the trash can in front of me. Jesus, she has an arm on her. I can literally feel the stinging imprint of her hand on my ass cheek. I turn slowly, eyebrow lifting threateningly. She yelps, eyes widening before she takes off running towards the door.

"Be safe!" I call out, laughing at her antics. Days like this are what I look forward to. The simple things we do and experience, all while being happy within our own lives. I want more days like this—endless days where I don't need to worry about anything because I have someone in my life that cares about me. I'll fight to keep these moments, even if it takes every last shred of my soul to get it.

CHAPTER TWENTY-EIGHT

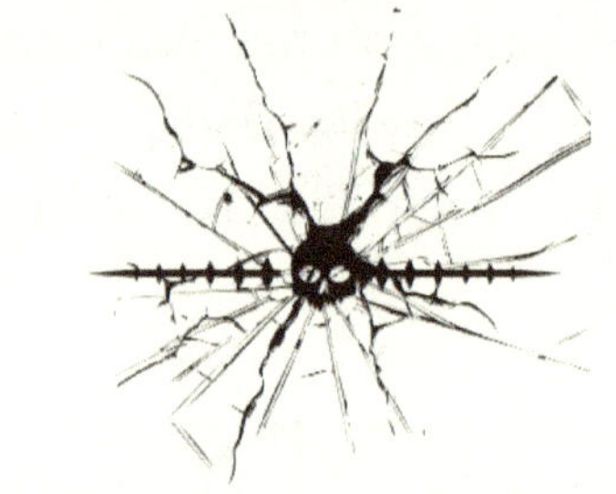

RONNIE

I see him the moment I step out of the apartment complex, his SUV parked in the same spot it was yesterday. I glare at him as I walk towards my car, expecting him to get out of the car, but he doesn't. I pull out of my space onto the road, and sure enough, Dimitry pulls out as well, following me from a distance. Rolling my eyes, I grab my phone, tapping the contact I've been wanting to avoid.

"Milaya," he says calmly.

"What are you doing?"

"Whatever could you mean?"

He's such an asshole. I can hear in his tone that he knows *exactly* what I mean, but he's being a dick about it with his false pretenses. "Why do you have Dimitry following me, papa."

"Is it so wrong of me to have someone keep an eye on my favourite daughter?"

I snort at the lie. "We both know I'm not your favourite. Try again."

"You are, even if you don't believe it. You are my youngest and you've done well for yourself. I'm proud of you and just want to make sure that you're safe."

"Why now? You're ruining everything by having Dimitry following me because it's drawing attention to me. Do you not understand?"

"Why should it matter? Are you trying to hide who you are? Are you...*lying* to someone about what you are, milaya?"

I grit my teeth in irritation, eyes glancing at the rearview mirror when I make the next turn and watching as Dimitry does the same. "You need to leave me alone."

"Why is that?" He muses, the sound of creaking leather letting me know he's in his study. The room always gave me a sense of foreboding, never comfort, even though the room was decorated in a way that exudes warmth and comfort. I hated being there because I knew what that room was for—his unsavory business.

"I'm not a part of your world anymore, papa. I haven't been for a long time, and I thought you would respect my decision."

"It's bad enough your sister has betrayed me with her endeavors, but I expected you to know better. Why do you think I trained you the way I did? I gave you everything, Veronica, and yet you turn your back on me."

"I don't want your empire. Tessa is the oldest, it should go to her. If you don't want to give it to her, give it to one of your power-hungry lackeys. Leave me the fuck alone or so help me—"

"Do not threaten me," he snarls, all fake niceness gone. "I've given you enough space and time in the hopes you would see reason, but you're leaving me with very little choice, milaya."

Well, that's not ominous at all. He has nothing to hold over me because I haven't *given* him anything. This is the reason I cut him out of my life and the reason I've avoided him for so long. Seriously, I made the biggest mistake of my life in my moment of weakness when I went to him just a few nights ago.

"I have a promising career and a life now, papa. Please don't ruin this for me."

"As I've told you before, you have a purpose within this household, and you are expected to fulfill it. I'll be contacting your sister as well, so she knows her place."

"Tessa won't do it," I whisper. I know my sister and she'll refuse him, fight him tooth and nail, even if it kills her.

"If you wish for me not to go after her, then you best do as I ask."

I love my sister, but she's fully capable of taking care of herself. I love her, but I won't sacrifice my own happiness to protect her; not when she left me to the wolves to battle my own war against him.

"Call off your hound."

"Will you do as I ask?"

"No."

"Then I refuse."

He hangs up before I can argue further, leaving me staring at the road in front of me while anger and frustration burn inside my body. I need to find a way to get him off my back before he finds out too much and ruins the life I'm trying to create. I wouldn't be able to live with myself if something happened to Reese because of this, but how am I supposed to protect him from a threat like my father. Dimitry has already tried to kill Kaine for fuck's sake. Whether that was on purpose or only because he was in the way, I'm not sure.

I pull into the parking lot of one of my favourite bookstores, grumbling as I get out of the car because there's Dimitry, parking just a few spots away from me. The fucker has the audacity to get out this time and actually follow me into the store. This fucker is going to end up getting me in trouble because this is one of my happy places and he's ruining it by being here.

Aisle after aisle he follows me, feigning nonchalance as he checks out the books on the shelves with a petty smile on his face. I've just about had enough at this point, no longer enjoying myself or the small pile of books I've collected. I dart around one of the stacks, setting my books down on the shelf while I wait.

He rounds the corner and grunts, eyes wide in surprise when I pin him to the shelf, pulling his gun out of his holster before he can react. Slowly he raises his hands, his mouth kicking up in a smirk.

"Easy there, Zara."

"Fuck off."

"I'm only doing my job."

"And what is that exactly? You're pissing me off with the way you're slinking around like a stalker."

"Are you not happy to see me? It's been quite a while since we've been this close to each other, but it's not something that I'll soon forget."

His smile widens when I shift my arm up his throat, pressing into it hard enough his breath wheezes on the next inhale. "Stay the fuck away from me."

"Would you prefer I follow your lover," he chokes out, eyes wild with savage determination. "I'm sure your father would have no issues with me removing him from your life," he laughs. "He's a distraction to our Zara."

"I am not your princess," I snarl, pressing the gun into his side, aimed up towards his heart. "I have no issues shooting you right here."

"Such a savage little thing, aren't you? Your father trained you well."

"Better than you are apparently." He winces, letting out a harsh breath when I shove the metal further into his ribs. "Back the fuck off before I kill you." I shove off of him, keeping the gun trained on him while he rubs at his throat. There once was a time I liked him; a boy that was in my life since I was young, being brought into the bratva at a young age himself. He's maybe three years older than me with eyes as pale blue as glass and dark hair that hangs in soft waves over the shorn sides of his scalp. He's breathtakingly beautiful, but undeniably deadly.

"Such a ruthless girl," he chuckles. "Bold, too, what with holding that gun in such an open space. You know they have cameras in here, don't you?" My hand wavers, my eyes shifting up to the corner, giving him time to rush me. His hand closes around mine, his other one going to my throat and squeezing just enough to threaten. "You've gotten sloppy, Zara," he whispers, his breath tickling my ear. "You've lost all sense of reason and are reacting with emotion. That should have been beaten out of you long ago."

The feel of his hand on me burns my skin and thickens the air around me. "Emotions aren't a weakness, Dimitry."

"They are when they've put you in situations such as this one. Your father would scold you for your actions. A husband would beat you into submission."

"Then it's a good thing you aren't my husband." He wheezes, breath exploding out of him before he crumples to the ground in a heap, the gun pointed at his head once more, but I make sure to shift my body, so my back is to the camera. "Touch me like that again and I'll be sure my father cuts off your hands while I castrate you." Spittle bubbles at the corners of his mouth as he laughs, gripping his crotch in clear agony.

"Is everything okay over there?"

I quickly tuck the gun into my purse, turning to see one of the workers staring wide-eyed at me and Dimitry on the floor. "Everything is fine."

"Do I need to call the police?"

I grab my books off the shelf, stepping over Dimitry as I make my way over to her. "I can handle my ex just fine. There's no reason to get the cops involved."

Her eyebrows shoot up in surprise and she leans around me, a smirk tugging at her lips as she takes in the still incapacitated Dimitry at the other end of the aisle. "He looks uncomfortable."

"Good." I brush my hair behind my ear and give her my warmest smile. "I'd like to buy these, please."

CHAPTER TWENTY-NINE

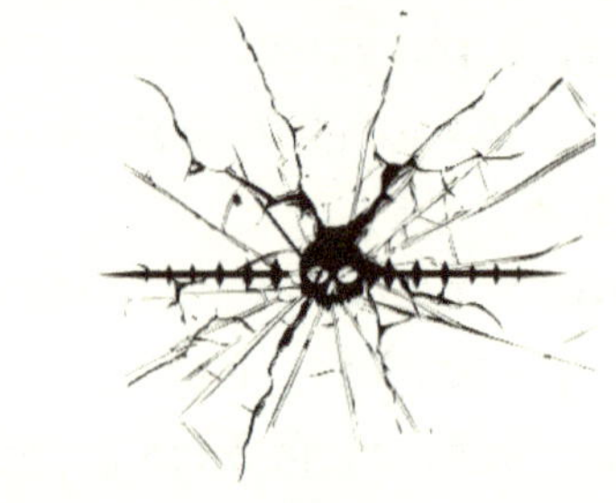

REESE

"What time do you want to meet up for the funeral tomorrow?"

The last thing I want to be talking about right now is that, but I can't exactly avoid it. I've tried on multiple occasions and in different ways to convince Kaine to just *not* go, but he's so fucking stubborn and persistent.

"I'm planning to go to the ceremony and the funeral."

"That's not what I asked."

"You're not going to the church, Kaine."

"Why not? Is there something wrong with me going to the church?"

"Aren't you scared you'll burst into flames?"

A long pause follows my comment, pulling a grin to my lips. A huff and random swearing from the other end has me laughing. "Wow, you're a dick. I'm not *tainted*."

"Really?"

"Not enough for God to smite me. He hasn't done it yet, and if anything, I've been blessed. They should worship *me* when I walk in there. Their very own real-life messiah. At least I've come back more than once. Jesus needs to bump those numbers up if he wants to keep his fan base because they're weak as fuck with the single resurrection."

"Your ego continues to astound me." I flop back on the couch, staring at the ceiling where the lights from the candles I lit just a short while ago flicker across the surface. I can feel myself getting lost in their chaotic flashes and swirls, a sense of calm washing over me.

"One of these days you'll be praying to me, just you wait."

"If you want to see me on my knees, all you have to do is ask."

He sputters on the other end, and I can imagine his face turning beet red while his mouth opens and closes like a dying fish. He's so easy to rile up, especially when it comes to sexual advances. I would never go there with Kaine, mainly because I know he doesn't swing that way. Me? I wouldn't turn my nose at it if the opportunity was there. I'm not gay exactly, but I do find certain members of the same sex attractive. Kaine might lose his shit if he realized I'm bi, but I've never made any actual moves on him that would warrant him questioning my sexual orientation. He's fun to fuck with though.

He laughs, the sound radiating through me and lightening my mood further. "You wouldn't even know what to do with my big dick swinging in front of you."

"Hmm, you underestimate my many talents. I'm sure I could make you whimper and scream."

"Fuck, dude," he snorts.

"Too much?"

"Nah, I know you're just fucking around," he cackles, going silent when I don't laugh along with him. "Right? You're just fucking with me, right? Please tell me you don't actually want my dick. I mean, it's cool if you do, but I rather not have my dick sucked by a guy. You're not like, in love with me, are you?"

His rambling is adorable, but I put the poor guy out of his misery before I actually make him uncomfortable. "I'm just fucking with you. You have nothing to worry about, and your dick is safe with me. I'm sure you get plenty of action from Eden, so you don't need some guy sucking you off just to see how it feels. Though, there's nothing wrong with being curious, Kaine, I won't hold that against you."

"Moving on," he huffs, but I can hear how flustered he is in his voice. "What time am I meeting you?"

"If you want to meet me here, be here by ten."

"Sounds good." There's shuffling on the other end and then a distinct click, like he's closing a door. "How are things with Ronnie?"

"Fine. I think we've finally worked things out."

"Good. That's good, man. Listen..." He sighs loudly. "What's going on with Avery?"

I frown at that. "What?"

"Ronnie talked to Eden earlier and she was asking who Avery was. Obviously, Eden lied to her, but that's not the point. Is there something going on?"

God damn it, Ronnie. Why the fuck did she have to go and open her mouth, and about that of all things. I was planning to avoid talking to Kaine about the reaper for as long as possible—forever if I could help it. I wanted to figure this out on my own and not have to drag Kaine or Eden back into that mess. They've been given the greenlight to live their lives without interference from the reapers, but for some reason *I'm* the one being haunted by them now. It doesn't feel like they're after me; more like I've been given special glasses that allow me to see into their world. I have a feeling that the ability to do so isn't intentional though.

"I don't want you freaking out because I don't know what it means, Kaine."

"Just tell me. I'm your best friend, Reese. You don't need to hide shit from me."

I tell him everything, right from the beginning. I tell him about the blackout moments I had as a kid, the times I wrote off as drunken stupors when I was a teen, remembering what actually happened with his professor and Avery. All those moments that had been locked away behind a dark wall, suddenly coming into the light. Every single memory made me feel as though I was losing another piece of myself, the taint of Avery's manipulation like a venomous viper sinking its teeth into me over and over again until it felt like there was nothing left of me.

Finally, I tell him about the nightmares, or at least, what I can remember about them. The small fragments that have come in on broken waves that make me feel as though I've been a part of him for a lot longer and that he's been trying to communicate with me in a fucked-up way. I tell him about the mirror and how I swear I saw someone else staring back at me from the glass, even after I obliterated it into pieces.

The shadows in the hospital and the way one of them took form, slowly drawing in Julia's soul, proving that I was useless in saving her. Of course, I am. How can a mortal being stand a chance against something supernatural that is capable of defying all the rules placed upon us. How could I possibly stop something that could tear me apart from the inside, out, without hesitation?

By the time I finish telling him everything, I'm out of breath, my body feeling both lightened and burdened. Lightened because I've finally been able to talk about it, but burdened because I just dragged Kaine back into the pit of fire. I don't want him to get involved because this is clearly something I have to deal with on my own, but I know him. I know how his mind works and the way his loyalty pushes everything else to the back of his mind.

"What can I do to help you?"

The question plows into me like a wrecking ball. This is what I was afraid of, and the hatred I have for myself for dragging him into it begins to crush me. "Nothing. Avery used *me* not you, Kaine. He has a link to me still, and I need to figure out what he wants and a way to sever this connection. I don't know why this is happening or why I'm remembering things he very obviously tried to hide from me, but I think the only way to deal with this is to face it head on and try and talk to him."

"That seems like a dangerous plan though. What if the connection you have isn't on purpose? If you're able to see into their veil, wouldn't that put a target on your back? You're not a reaper, Reese. You shouldn't be able to see them or interact with them."

"I don't know. I know nothing about any of this, but how am I supposed to figure it out if I don't ask? It's driving me insane, Kaine. It's literally destroying me and threatening to ruin my life. The way I've been acting with Ronnie has a lot to do with this because if he's coming after me, I don't want her getting caught up in it. She's innocent and doesn't know anything about the supernatural world."

"You shouldn't know about it either and I can't apologize enough, man. I'm sorry I dragged you into all of this when I told you the truth about me and Eden."

"It's not on you. It wouldn't have mattered if you had told me or not since Avery already had his claws in me from when I was a kid. One way or another, I would have found out. I was in this world anyways; I just didn't know it."

"Whatever it takes to help you figure this out and get you through it, I'm here. I know you. I know you want to keep me at arm's length when it comes to this, but you can trust me, Reese."

"I know I can," I say quietly. If there's anyone in this world that I can trust without question, it's Kaine. He's the brother I needed in my life, and I don't want to lose him. My eyes drift to the door when I hear keys jingling in the hallway and I quickly sit up. "Ronnie is home. I need to go, so I'll talk to you later."

"Okay. Try not to stress over this until we figure it out." I end the call, wishing it were that simple. I don't only have Avery to deal with, and the constant flood of stress and events is really starting to wear me out.

"Hey!" Ronnie says happily when she sees me. I quickly get up and move towards her, taking the pile of bags from one of her hands. "Thanks. I think I went a little overboard with the shopping, but I figured it's better to stock up now instead of having to make multiple trips." She sets one of the bags down on the coffee table and I follow her into the kitchen with everything else. I had hoped Holland would have gotten back to me already with any new information on the Petrov family, but so far, I've been met with radio silence.

"How was it?"

"Fine. I went to the bookstore and picked up some new stuff. I found a few books I want to give Eden to read, too."

"Did you notice anyone following you today?"

I watch her like a hawk, trying to notice any hesitation in her words or movements, but she just continues to go about her actions, pulling item after item out of the bag.

"Nope. It seemed pretty quiet."

She's lying. I don't know how I know, I just do. It's like a burning sensation in my chest, clawing its way up my throat. I'm going to have to check the CCTV feed later when she's gone to bed or something to be sure, but it still doesn't explain *why* she could be lying to me right now. If she's worried about how I'll react, she should know better. She should realize I'm concerned for her and lying to me is just going to upset me further. I can't help worrying about her, especially when some psycho mob goon is stalking her ass.

She smiles when she finishes setting out everything to make the pizzas, a soft smile tugging on her lips. "Can you get the stone out while I go put away my purse and put on some pajamas?"

"Sure."

My eyes follow her the entire time until she disappears through the door. It's interesting to see how much I notice about the way she acts, like my internal alarm is sending off warning bells, forcing my natural instincts into overdrive. I don't think I need to be worried about her in the sense she's a harm to me. She's done nothing for me to think that way and there's no way a girl like that has any ill intentions towards me. She wouldn't be pushing so hard for my affection or getting as upset as she does when I shut her out if that were the case. She has nothing to gain from earning my love, unless her goal is to break my heart in the end.

At this point, that *would* happen. The thought of her leaving me after everything causes a wave of nausea to rip through me, forcing bile to rise up my throat. I swallow around it, pushing down the acidic taste while I try to shake those fucking thoughts from my head. There's no way this is all a game to her. It can't be. She's not someone that would pretend or fake her emotions for the sake of destroying someone else mentally. I've broken her spirit as well, pushed her to the brink and watched her tumble over the edge while I scrambled to catch her while she fell. She plummeted because of me, but I won't allow myself to be the reason she ends up truly broken.

Little by little she's destroying my defense to the point I may never be able to completely keep her curious and caring nature at bay. I risk a peek into her book bag, smirking at the load of books she ended up buying. It's one of her guilty pleasures and it's something I'll never fault her for. She loves her books, falling into a hilarious relationship with Eden when it comes to them. Both Kaine and I have fallen victim to one too many of their tangents during their personal two-person book club, but they're both adorable and entertaining to watch. They laugh and squeal and cry over these fictional characters like they're being personally traumatized by them.

I can't keep the smile off my face as I move away from her treasure and into the kitchen, doing as she asked and grabbing the pizza stone we bought a few months ago. This thing is amazing and we've tried to make it a small tradition of ours, creating our own pizzas from scratch and cooking together. The girl *can* cook. Not well, but she puts in a valiant effort and is willing to learn, which of course I have no issues in teaching her. The lessons end up being pretty fun, even if the food doesn't always turn out completely edible.

I'm halfway done prepping some of the vegetables by the time she re-emerges from the bedroom, hair tossed up into a messy bun and a sheer white tank top covering her frame. My eyes widen on the expanse of leg visible under her tiny booty shorts, the creamy flesh a delicious meal of its own, waiting to be tasted.

"What?" She asks, moving in beside me to take up cutting some of the green peppers.

"What are you wearing?"

She tries and fails to hide her smirk, ducking her head down and away from me. "Pajamas."

"You've been wearing pants for the last few weeks."

She glances down at herself before shifting her gaze up to me through her lashes. "Is there something wrong with the shorts?"

"You're trying to distract me."

"With shorts?" She snorts. "How is that a distraction? Plus, why would I want to distract you? I need you to pull the weight when it comes to making these pizzas. You know I suck at making the dough."

She can't be this oblivious. Does she honestly not have a clue what she's doing to me being dressed like that? She's not even wearing a bra, and the tank top is definitely see-through because I can see her tits. Not just her nipples or the areola around them, but the actual tone of her breasts through the material of the shirt. This dinner is going to be torture when all I want to do is tear that flimsy scrap of cloth from her body and bury my face in the swell of her breasts, nipping and sucking at the plump, succulent tissue until she's moaning my name and—

"Reese?"

"Huh?" I jerk my attention back to her face, not realizing my eyes have been staring aimlessly at those gorgeous breasts of hers for who knows how long.

She laughs, smacking me on the chest playfully. "Jesus, I'll throw on a sweater."

"No!" I say quickly, hating how desperate I sound. "You're fine. I'm sorry, I was just sort of lost in thought. What did you say?"

"I asked if you wanted me to start searing the steaks. Unless you don't want steak on your pizza and something else instead."

"You can start."

She smiles, grabs the package with the steaks in them, and gets to work prepping them over at the other counter. I shift my pants as subtly as I can, cringing at the way the material is scraping against my hardening cock. I chirp her for being a sexual being, but I'm no better. It's like my body has fallen back into my teenage years, hopped up on the virility that came with it. It's pathetic, but I'm not complaining when I have to keep up with a girl like Ronnie.

When I think I've composed myself enough, I grab everything I need to make a sauce, carrying it all over to the stove to get to work. I can feel her gaze shifting to me each time I add something new and slowly stir the contents as it simmers. I risk my own glances her way, making sure she's not overcooking the meat like she tends to do. If we plan to use it on pizza, it needs to be cooked even less so it has time to finish cooking in the heat of the barbeque without turning into leather.

When she flips the steaks for the seventh time, I sigh, noticing her body stiffen. "I'm doing it wrong, aren't I?" She asks, shoulders slumping in defeat.

"You're fine. You're just working the meat a little bit too much. You won't get a proper sear if you keep doing that and you'll end up overcooking it."

"Sorry," she murmurs, stepping back when I move towards her.

"Don't be sorry. It takes time to learn things like that, okay?" She nods but still looks dejected, making me feel bad for even saying anything. I know in the end she'll appreciate it because she doesn't like her steak overcooked, but it's the fact she's done it wrong that will bother her. I grip her wrist and pull her towards me, hugging her against my side. "You're doing great, baby," I murmur against her hair, pressing my lips against her gently.

"I keep messing it up. I know you've shown me over and over again, so I think I'm just not cut out for cooking."

"You made really good penne last week though."

"Pasta is easy," she sniffles.

"So is this once you get the hang of it. Please don't be upset. Do you want to take care of the sauce? You just need to keep stirring it every few minutes until it thickens up a bit more."

"Okay." She wraps her arms around me, burying her face in my side and inhaling deeply. She's too cute, but it does upset me when she lets something so small get to her. She's done nothing wrong and it's not her fault she wasn't taught how to do these things when she was younger. Her mother must not have been great at it herself or felt like Ronnie was too you to teach before she passed away.

My own mother made sure I knew as much as I could from a young age, teaching me everything she could while she had the chance so that she could prepare me for the world and life ahead of me. I'm grateful for those moments and she turned me into the person I am today. Because of her, I care about the people closest to me and have a nagging need to take care of them any way that I can. Because of her, my heart is open enough to feel emotions, those same emotions my father claimed were a weakness.

I still remember moments from my childhood when I would cry over something upsetting, like the loss of my cat, and he would turn around and beat me until I stopped crying. Something that's nearly impossible for a child trying to shy away from pain. Every lash of his belt had new tears brimming my lashes and more sobs ripping up my throat, turning the punishment into a vicious cycle. I have plenty of scars, mostly from him, and none of which I can be proud of. Those scars are memories burned right into my flesh, whether at the hands of someone who was supposed to love me, or at the hands of those I was meant to kill and tried to fight back.

Each piece of broken flesh is a reminder of what I went through, who I was, and who I never want to be again. They're a part of me now, permanent ghosts that will forever haunt me no matter how much I may want to forget or try to run away from them. Ronnie has pointed some of them out, but hasn't pushed for the reason behind them, and I won't divulge that information to her—not yet anyways.

Never fucking willingly. The story behind them all is too dark and way too fucked up for someone like her. She would be horrified to know what I've done, the amount of blood that's on my hands. Sometimes, when I close my eyes, all I can see is red and all I can hear is the screams and pleas, begging me to spare them. Those screams mix in with my own, my useless cries for my father to spare me from the pain as well.

It made me wonder if he actually hated me. There were days that I believed it. Days where I wondered if I would finally be put out of my misery and he would end my miserable life. My only light in those moments was the glimmer of hope my mother gave me, her quiet promises that she would make it better and that she would get me out of that hell.

I hate that she still seems upset as she slowly stirs the sauce, small sniffles slipping through the silence between us. This isn't what I expected of this night. I wanted her to have fun because she seemed so excited at the prospect of making pizzas, but yet, I went ahead and ruined it for her.

I pull the meat off the pan and set it on a cutting board before moving past her, leaving her to deal with the sauce however she sees fit. I get to work on the dough, wanting to make sure it's perfect for her. Kneading it is sort of cathartic, each press of the pliable material easing some of the tension in my muscles. I cut the large clump into smaller, workable pieces, rolling it out until it somewhat resembles a circle.

I smile when I grab some of the cheese, placing it around the edges before slowly rolling the dough over it to make a thicker crust edge. The hair on the back of my neck rises and I glance over to see Ronnie standing there, watching me, her eyes on my hands as they carefully tuck the cheese in.

"What are you doing?"

"I thought you might like a cheese stuffed crust."

She looks up at me then, eyes bowing slightly in what emotion, I'm not sure. That gets cleared up pretty quickly when her bottom jaw begins to tremble. She blinks rapidly, trying her best to shut down those emotions, and turns back to the stove to continue her repetitive stirring. I don't understand why she would be upset about this.

"Do you...not *want* cheese in the crust? I'm sorry, I should have asked before I did it."

She shakes her head but refuses to look over, shoulders still and back straight. "It's—it's great, Reese."

"Have I upset you?" She shakes her head again. "You seem upset." Still no reaction. "Hey." Moving towards her, I grip her arm, trying to turn her back towards me. Her body turns, but she keeps her gaze fixed on my chest. My fingers slide under her chin, slowly tipping her head up to look at me. "You're crying."

"I'm fine."

I frown, moving my thumb across her cheek to wipe away the stray tears. Some of the flour from my hand gets on her face, coating her skin in a light dusting. "Shit," I murmur, wiping a bit harder, but I only end up making it worse. "Fuck, I got flour on you." She laughs through a hiccup and wipes her own face, which shifts into a smile. "There you are."

The way she looks up at me, her cheeks cupped in my palms as her eyes glisten with emotion, has my heart thumping louder in my chest. She's so beautiful and perfect in every way that matters. "Why are you so sweet?" She whispers.

I frown, leaning closer to her. "What have I done now?"

"The cheese."

I laugh. I can't help it, and she rolls her eyes in frustration. "So, you weren't upset about the cheese, but happy? You're so weird."

"I am not," she pouts.

I kiss those lips, humming against them when she darts her tongue out to lick mine. "You're *my* weirdo." I press her cheeks together, snorting at the disgruntled look on her face when her lips pucker out like a fish. "So cute." I kiss them again before backing away from her so I can finish prepping our dinner. "I'm going to turn on the barbecue. Keep an eye on that sauce." She stiffens, eyes darting to the bubbling pot, which she clearly forgot she was supposed to be taking care of.

The night is settling into a cooler one tonight, the darkness creeping in quicker as the year moves on. It didn't make sense to me why Kaine and Eden wanted a fall wedding, but with Eden not being a fan of heat, Kaine wasn't going to fight her on the date. If it were up to him, he would have married her the day after he proposed, but she squashed that idea pretty quickly. I can't blame the girl. She wants to make it special, a day she'll never forget, surrounded by her friends and people she loves.

My mouth pulls into a grin as I picture Ronnie doing the same thing, planning all the details for our future. It's something I want desperately, and I hope that eventually, that could happen for us as well. Not now, but I hold onto that image as something to look forward to.

I light the barbecue quickly, kicking myself for not grabbing a sweater before I came out here as the biting wind cuts through my bare arms.

"Reese."

I turn quickly at the sound of my name, not being spoken by Ronnie, but familiar all the same.

"Reese."

It comes from behind me again, pushing my body to turn once more, only to be met by nothing. It hits me then. The voice…is in my head.

"Leave me alone," I grit out, body coiling with the urge to punch something.

"Reese."

I spin again to shadows in front of me, wavering and darkening. My body moves on its own, launching at it with my fist raised, ready to destroy it in my anger. Nothing. There's nothing there but open air, the railing catching on my hips, but my momentum pushes me forward, over it. The ground comes up quickly, wind whipping past me as I descend the three-stories towards the bushes below.

"Reese!"

CHAPTER THIRTY

RONNIE

The sickening thud of his body hitting the ground below echoes all around me. What happened? What the fuck just happened? “Reese!” I scream, hoping beyond hope that he’s okay. The distance from our apartment is still pretty high up, and depending on how he fell, he could very well—

No, I can’t think like that. I spin around and bolt through the apartment, grabbing my keys and a sweater before launching through the door. “Come on!” I scream, pounding the elevator button over and over, begging it to come to our floor faster. Please be okay. Oh god, please let him be okay.

The second the elevator opens, I’m punching the button again, kicking myself that I didn’t grab my phone on the way out.

Fuck, I need to call an ambulance. Fucking hell. In my rush I wasn't thinking straight, my only thoughts on Reese and whether that fall just killed him. I just happened to look over through the doors when I thought I heard him speaking, and the next second, he was throwing his fist through empty air. What could have possibly happened for him to be acting that way?

I sprint out of the elevator into the lobby, where I come to a screeching halt. There's no way. Even if the fall didn't kill him, he shouldn't be walking around the way he is. He should have broken something at least, had some cuts and scrapes on his bare skin, but all I see is dirt and disheveled hair and clothes that are torn with remnants of blood caking him...but no visible wounds.

"Reese?" He glances up at the sound of my voice, face drawn and eyes half hooded. In this light they almost seem as black as they did last night, but he blinks quickly, opening his eyes further when he focuses on me. "Are—are you okay?"

He lifts his hands up to his face, jerky movements that clearly show the panic that's flooding him. He's shaking; full body tremors that are threatening the stability of his legs. I go to him, quickly ducking under his arm to let him lean into me for support.

"We should go to the hospital." I try to turn us back around towards the door, but he finds new strength, planting himself and jerking my body to a halt. "Reese?"

"I'm fine."

"You just fell off the balcony! There's blood on you, Reese. You are *not* fine."

He tries to pull away from me, stumbling a few steps before his body slams into the wall. "I'm not going to the hospital. I—I need to call Kaine."

What the actual fuck. Why would he need to call Kaine? He needs to see a doctor to at least make sure he doesn't have internal bleeding or anything broken that he doesn't feel at the moment because his body is hopped up on adrenaline.

"Kaine can't help you right now, Reese. You need a doctor." I mean, Kaine is a doctor and so am I, but still. A hospital would at least have the tools necessary to help him if he has internal bleeding.

He shakes his head, clambering along the wall towards the elevator. He's so fucking stubborn, but I can't exactly drag his ass out to my car to drive him there myself and I didn't grab my stupid phone. I have no choice but to follow him, trying once again to get under his arm. I half expect him to push away from me again, but he sighs and lets me take some of his weight when he realizes I'm not trying to steer him back towards the door.

He lets out a shuddering breath, leaning against the railing in the elevator while I press the button to our floor. Once it's moving, I turn around and get a better look at him. He looks awful and shaken up, body still shaking in a way that's concerning. I can see how much he wants to just let his body slide down to the floor to collapse into a heap, but he's doing well to fight that desire.

My mouth opens to ask him what happened, quickly snapping shut when I think better of it. He doesn't need me to pry into that right now, so I just shift myself closer to him and slide my hand down his arm to grip into his hand. His fingers slowly squeeze around mine, a gentle reassurance that he's here mentally. By the time the elevator opens, he looks about ready to pass out, eyes closing and body swaying with every step we take towards our home.

I barely get him to the couch before he collapses forward, face groaning into the cushions. I'll have to deal with him in a minute because there's still the pot bubbling over on the stove and the barbecue is still running. We'll have to save the pizza for a different night, or I'll have to take over making it completely if he even feels up to eating once I check him over.

Once I finish covering everything up, I run to the bedroom and grab the medical kit from the bathroom, coming back out to Reese still face planted on the couch. I touch his back gently. He flinches, his muscles jerking against the contact. His chest is heaving more rapidly with each passing second, causing panic to grip at my chest. I need to move him. I need him to sit up so I can get his shirt off. I have to get a full look at him to make sure he's not visibly injured underneath his clothes.

"Reese, can you sit up for me?"

"Maybe," he says through a shuddering breath. He braces against the couch, arms shaking as he pushes himself up slightly. He almost collapses back down, but I get my arm under him in time to help him the rest of the way. At least I got him sitting up, but he looks horrible, head tipped back against the edge of the couch, his mouth parting on each breath.

There's no point in trying to get him to lift his arms up, his body clearly weakened with the effort of even coming up here after falling off a god damn balcony. I grab the scissors from the kit, carefully cutting the cloth away from his body.

"Looks like...you're...tearing...my clothes...now," he pants.

I can't help smiling at the stupid joke, shaking my head at the ridiculousness of it. My eyes widen when I pull the shirt away, revealing the expanse of his chest, clear of any injury. I frown, running my fingers over a strange webbing along both sides of his ribcage. The pattern shifts down one of his arms as well, the black ink looking like a smokey tattoo. Is his skin necrotic? It doesn't feel damaged, and necrosis shouldn't set in that quickly. I can't figure out how this would have gotten on him either though, and he definitely didn't get a tattoo since I last saw him naked just this morning.

"I need to take off your pants."

"Getting me...naked?"

"Will you stop?" I snort. "This is serious, Reese. I need to make sure you're clean."

"I'm...filthy."

"Fucking hell," I grumble, hooking my fingers into the waistband of his pants and tugging. "A little help?" At least he lifts his hips for me. He's naked. The bastard isn't wearing any underwear so now I get to be distracted by his perfect dick settled between his thighs while I try to make sure the rest of him is okay.

More of that webbing spreads down one of his legs right down to his foot, where it wraps around the entire thing in intricate designs. His other leg seems clear, and other than the dirt caked to some areas of his skin, he physically looks fine.

"What is this?" I ask, touching the marks again.

His eyes open slowly and he carefully lifts his head enough to see what I'm pointing at. His eyes widen and his chest moves quickly again. "Kaine. I need...to talk...to Kaine."

"Fine." I don't know why he's so desperate to talk to him, but if this is what he needs, I can at least do that for him. I grab my phone, since I have no idea where his is, and quickly punch out the call. "Kaine."

"Ronnie...what's up?"

"Reese...um, Reese needs to talk to you."

"Why are you calling me and not him?"

"Something happened and I don't know what's going on but he keeps saying he needs to talk to you."

"What do you mean? What happened?"

"He sort of...fell off the balcony."

Silence ticks on for a few heartbeats, making me wonder if the connection dropped. "Where are you?"

"At home."

"Why didn't you call an ambulance? Is he okay?"

"He didn't want one!" I snap. "He seems fine, but he's got these weird marks all over his body that weren't there before."

"Marks?"

"Yeah, black webbing. It sort of looks like smoke on his skin."

"I'll be there in ten minutes."

He ends the call before I can say anything else or ask him what the fuck is going on. If Kaine is coming here, he must be worried about him. Do I need to be more concerned? I shake my head, setting my phone down on the coffee table before kneeling down in front of him. "Kaine is on his way. Let me at least get your pants back up so Kaine doesn't have to see your big dick."

He laughs, the sound pained as his head falls back onto the couch. He struggles to lift his hips up for me, but I finally manage to get his sweats over them so he's no longer naked. He starts to shiver, jaw tensing hard enough his teeth squeak together. I quickly grab the blanket off the back of the couch, tucking it in around him. He doesn't open his eyes, keeping them firmly screwed shut while I fuss over him. I take the moment of distraction and run into the kitchen, grabbing a bowl to fill with warm water and a couple of dish cloths from the drawer. I don't want to leave him for too long, especially when he looks so uncomfortable.

"I'm going to try and clean you up a bit. You've got a bunch of dirt on you and you're in no condition to be moving or I would drag your ass to the bath." He winces when I pull the blanket down, letting it pool at his waist while I sneak in between his thighs. His skin prickles with goosebumps the moment the wet cloth touches him and his eyes sneak open a fraction to look down at me.

"Thank you," he whispers.

Those two words are like a sword through my heart. They sound almost surprised but broken as well. He should know by now that I would do anything for him. I've seen him broken already on multiple occasions and I've been there for him through it all. The worst so far has been finding him in the shower, curled up like a child waiting to be beaten into submission. Seeing him like that shattered me, but seeing him like this, is almost just as bad. Now he's been physically hurt.

There's no way he's just okay after a fall like that, but he walked back into our building like he just had a heavy romp through the woods where he stumbled and got caught up on some branches. None of this makes sense. By all sense of reason, he shouldn't be here. That height didn't guarantee his death, but the possibility was too high to be leaning in favour of survival.

I try to be as gentle as possible with each pass of the cloth, taking away more and more bits of dirt and mud. His eyes flutter closed and his breathing finally evens out just as a knock comes from the door. Before I even have the chance to get up from the floor, Kaine just strolls inside, Eden on his heel.

He pauses, his eyes shifting from Reese to me settled between his legs. My hand placement isn't helping the situation any, and he's clearly thinking the same thing when his eyebrows shoot up in surprise.

"I should have waited until you answered the door," he murmurs, tipping his head up to stare at the ceiling. Eden smacks him on the back of the head, walking past him towards us.

"How's he doing?" She asks, frowning as she leans in closer to him.

"I can hear you," Reese mumbles, sneaking one eye open. "You didn't have to tag along."

Her face softens for a second before her eyes settle on the marks on his body. "Reese," she whispers.

"I know. Can you take Ronnie into the bedroom so Kaine and I can talk in private?"

"What? No! Anything you have to say, you should be able to say in front of me!"

He sighs and carefully lifts himself to sit a bit straighter, wincing at the movement. He fixes his eyes on me, filled with sadness and desperation. "Please, Ronnie. I promise to explain things to you, but not right now. I'm still trying to figure all this shit out myself?"

"What is there to figure out? You fell off a three-story balcony and walked away unscathed, Reese. If it has anything to do with that, I think I should fucking know about it."

"Ronnie, I think you need to listen to him. Please, just trust him," Eden says, placing her hand on my shoulder and giving it a gentle squeeze.

Is she in on this, too? Does *she* know what's going on with *my* boyfriend while I'm being left in the dark? It isn't fair. I shouldn't be angry about their relationship because it came before me and it's to be expected, but this still fucking hurts. I hate that he feels like he can't be honest with me, and now he's just proving that in front of his *real* friends.

"Maybe it's better if I just go," I mumble.

Reese grips my arm when I lift to my feet, stopping me from pulling away. "I love you," he says quietly. "Trust me when I say this, Ronnie. I'm trying to protect you because I love you. Please don't leave."

He's fucking cheating. How am I supposed to stay hardened when he throws that out, in front of *them* no less. He didn't even hesitate to say the words, letting them fall from his lips like it's the most natural thing to do. Kaine gasps, choking on his own air behind me while Eden stares at us with wide eyes. The fact they're surprised by his sudden change in tactics doesn't go unnoticed, and it sort of makes me feel a little smug. Clearly, he didn't tell either of them that he's finally opened himself up to me and admitted that he loves me.

I turn to face him, taking in how exhausted he looks from everything that happened. His eyes close when I brush my fingers through his hair and lean down towards him. Slowly they open, staring right at me in a way that makes my heart beat a little faster. I press my lips to his, letting myself linger a little longer than is probably appropriate in the current company.

"Call out if you need anything," I whisper against his mouth before pulling back. He swallows thickly and nods his head, watching me as I pick up the bowl and dirty towels up from the floor. "I got you some new books," I say to Eden, nodding my head at the bag on the coffee table. "Why don't you grab the bag, and we'll go to the bedroom."

She can't hide the excitement on her face as she gawks at the bag, grabbing it without hesitation and practically skipping down the hall. I follow shortly after, noticing that neither Reese nor Kaine say a word while I'm still in view. I have a strange sinking feeling growing heavy in the pit of my stomach about all of this, but he's right, I need to trust him. If I can't trust him, who *can* I trust?

CHAPTER THIRTY-ONE

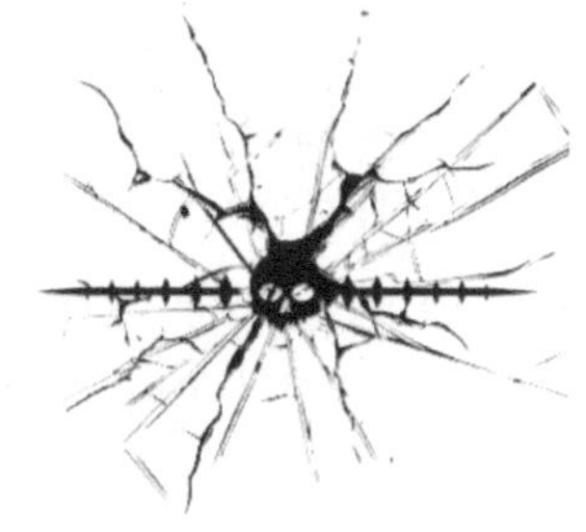

REESE

"Are you okay?" Kaine asks the moment we hear the door to the bedroom click shut. He settles down across from me, sitting on the coffee table with his elbows braced on his thighs and his hands clasped between them.

"Define okay."

"Are you hurt? Do you need to go to the hospital?" I shake my head, still trying to figure out *how* I'm okay after that. "What the fuck happened, Reese?"

"I—I fell."

"You fell? How the fuck do you just fall off your balcony like that?"

It's difficult to swallow around the dryness building in my throat, each breath and word feeling like knives scraping and clawing at me. "Can you get me something to drink?" I rasp out. Kaine frowns but does as I ask, lurching to his feet to fetch me something. I'm thankful for it. It gives me a little time to compose myself and get my thoughts in order. I'm still trying to figure out what the fuck happened myself, but there's one thing for certain. "Thanks," I whisper, taking the bottle of Gatorade from him and chugging half of it back. The cool liquid burns down my esophagus but soothes some of the deep itching that I was feeling there. One pain for another, but at least this one allows me to talk a bit easier.

"Alright, spill it."

"I heard him, Kaine. Not in a dream this time, but actually here. He's in my fucking head. He's in my *fucking* head. I'm—I'm not crazy." My voice wavers because I'm starting to doubt those words. Maybe I *am* going crazy.

"I'm not saying you are, Reese."

"I feel like I am. I feel like I'm losing my fucking mind, Kaine." My next inhale rattles my chest, everything I've been trying to hold in bubbling up to the surface. "I don't know what to do."

"I believe you." He nods his head towards my chest, to the strange marks marring my skin. He rolls up the sleeve on his shirt, exposing the mark on his own arm. "He healed you."

"Healed me?"

He nods. "Is it just the ones on your chest and arm?" I shake my head. "Show me." When I hesitate, he quirks a brow. "What?"

"It's my leg."

"Okay, and?"

"I'm not wearing underwear, dude."

He presses his lips together, but a snort still slips through. "You scared of me seeing your dick? It wouldn't be the first time, man."

I roll my eyes at that. It's not the fact he's seen my dick. "I can't exactly get up right now. My body feels really weak and Ronnie had to pull my pants down herself to check me over. If you want to see the one on my leg, you're going to have to get close to me."

"So, I need to strip you down?" I nod, fighting back a smile when his eyes widen. "Oh, um..."

"Don't strain yourself," I laugh, regretting it instantly when sharp pain rips through my chest. "It shouldn't be important."

"It could be. The one on my arm acts weird once in a while, so if you're covered in this shit, it could be a lot worse for you."

"Weird how?"

He shrugs, pushing himself up to his feet to stand in front of me. "Achy, itchy, sore. I don't know if it's random or if something causes it. I would think there's a link of some kind because when I feel it in mine, Eden feels it in hers."

My mouth pops open in surprise when he drops to his knees and settles his hands on my thighs. I swallow hard, shifting a little, but trying to hold myself back from showing him that I'm actually a bit uncomfortable. It doesn't help me any when the fucker glances up at me through his lashes, a smirk tugging at his lips.

"Never thought I would be the one to kneel in front of you," he laughs, gripping into the waistband of my sweats. "Can you lift your hips for me?" I brace my hands on the couch and lift myself up a bit, hating the way my arms shake under my weight. "Why are you half-hard."

Heat spreads up my neck and into my cheeks at the comment. Of *course* he's staring right at it. "Ronnie was where you are just moments ago, why else do you think?"

He shakes his head, laughing quietly as he pulls them down the rest of the way, exposing the thin veins of black wrapping around my left leg right down to my toes. "Damn. I think you shattered this when you fell because this is a lot. Assuming you broke some ribs on both sides and broke your distal humerus and proximal radius. It doesn't look like any of your carpals got the hit though so that's good."

"How is any of this good?"

"A doctor needs full function of their hands to do their job correctly."

"I have full function of everything because the fucker healed me. I wouldn't even be in that situation if he would just leave me the fuck alone."

"Hmm, yeah. You definitely have full function of the most important parts."

Once again, he's staring at my dick, which isn't going down in the slightest. If anything, it's standing more at attention now than it was before Kaine pulled down my pants. I slam my eyes shut when his fingers trail across the blackened skin more gently than I ever thought possible for someone like him.

"What the fuck are you doing?" Both our heads whip in the direction of the hallway, where Eden is standing with wide eyes and an open mouth. She glances back at the bedroom door before quickly shifting towards us, stopping abruptly when she notices the state of undress I'm in. "Oh my god," she whisper-yells, spinning around quickly and covering her eyes.

"It's not what it looks like," I say, panicked at the whole experience.

"Did you just see his dick?" Kaine asks.

Fuck. It's not anyone's fault but Kaine's. He's the one that insisted on looking at my leg. He's the one that decided to drop to his fucking knees to pull down my pants for me. *He's* the one that put us in this situation, and he can't blame poor Eden for thinking the worst.

I mean, it's not the *worst* thing that she could have walked in on, but I at least have some self-control, which is more than I can say for my now fully hard dick.

"You mean the dick *you're* staring at?" She snaps back. "What the *fuck* are you doing down there?"

"Why are you out here? You're supposed to keep Ronnie busy."

"She was thirsty and I insisted on grabbing her drinks so she wouldn't be tempted to come out here. Fuck, I wish I hadn't either. God damn it, Kaine."

"It's not what it looks like," I say again with a little less enthusiasm.

"Really? Because it looks like my fiancé was about to suck your dick, Reese."

"Okay, fair enough. He's not, though. He's just checking my leg out and I can't exactly function well enough to pull down my own pants at the moment."

She turns around at that, quickly diverting her eyes up to the ceiling. "You undressed him? What the fuck are you thinking, and why did you have to pull down his underwear?"

"He wasn't wearing any," Kaine sighs, settling back onto his heels. My eyes drift from her to him and then his hands, which are still awkwardly caressing my fucking thighs.

"You should probably get up," I murmur.

"Hmm, yeah. Probably a good idea." He grips my pants and starts pulling them back up my legs while I lift myself up enough for him to pull them up all the way. Fucking dick. The stupid thing just won't go down and now he's struggling to cover it. I flinch when I grab a hold of it, my ass hitting the cushion at the same time I shove it down. Kaine loses his balance from me shifting my weight, toppling on top of me and nailing me in the groin.

"Fuck," I wheeze. He scrambles to get off me, palming my already beaten dick as he leverages himself up.

"Are you decent?" Eden asks.

"Beaten, but yes," I cough, flopping down on my side and curling into myself to relieve some of the pain. "Damn it, Kaine."

"Sorry, man. I didn't mean to sack you like that."

"What's up with his leg?"

"Eden?" Ronnie calls out, the sound of the door opening like a warning bell going off.

"Coming!" She darts into the kitchen, ripping the fridge open to rummage through it, grabbing a couple of diet sodas before raiding the snack cupboard while she's at it. "You better fucking tell me later," she hisses, jogging down the hall and back into the bedroom.

"That was awkward," Kaine laughs, patting my ass before flopping down in the armchair next to the couch.

"I expected you to rip into me for that," I murmur, turning my head so I can see him.

"Meh, I'll take the blame for that one. I didn't expect her to come back out here like that so I can't exactly blame you for her seeing your dick."

"How mature."

"That happens when you get older."

"Can you please tell me if you know anything about what's going on?"

He flops back, spreading his legs wide and tilting his head back to stare at the ceiling. He stays quiet for a bit, his gaze pensive, like all the answers he's looking for might be hidden in the paint staring back at him.

"Haven't the foggiest. All I know is Avery must have stepped in and healed you before you could die from your injuries. He's a bit of a sadist since he could have probably stopped you from getting hurt to begin with, but who knows how much power he has without taking over completely. If he was only able to heal you, maybe he doesn't have as stable a connection as he did when he was squatting in you before. He used quite a bit of power when he helped me and Eden, and we're lucky he didn't burn through your body when that happened."

"Great. That makes me feel *so* much better."

"It should. If he didn't give a shit about what happened to you, he would have let you die."

"Not if I wasn't meant to die, Kaine."

"That's never stopped the reapers before. Look at my mom and Eden's dad. They both died outside their death dates. I think it's possible for them to do that, but it ends up fucking their plan. Like, one life for another; one death for another life. There could be people out there who were meant to die and ended up getting the lifespan of those people that died before their time. I'm sure they're not happy about any of it and are working their asses off to fix it, but in the meantime, they're doing what they can to prevent it from happening again. Avery was pretty pissed off at Luther for what he did, and he dragged his ass off to whatever pit he was talking about. I wonder if it's some kind of reaper hell or torture chamber, but I wouldn't want to be him either way."

He sits up quickly, brows furrowing together. "What? What is it?"

"I just thought of something...something that could explain Lazarus a bit better. Fuck, why didn't I think about this before. Eden and I are supposed to do a conference next week to talk about our research on the project and this might tip our theories in the right direction."

"Care to share with the class?"

He snaps out of his headspace, blinking rapidly before giving me a toothy grin. "If you want to know, you'll just have to come and listen to our lecture."

I roll my eyes. "I rather not."

"Come on. Come out and support us. Eden is nervous as shit about it and she's been pouring over the research we've been conducting since we submitted our dissertation. The article did well enough to draw the attention of some major scientists and even some parapsychologists. Of course we've pulled in a few anomalistic psychologists, too, but they're obviously trying to prove our theories wrong. It doesn't help that we've gone beyond the scientific explanations and have pushed the border into the supernatural. Science doesn't make sense in this instance, and it sucks that we can't prove it without exposing ourselves and basically sacrificing our bodies to science. I rather die than ever let Eden be taking by government whack jobs that just want to tear her apart and study her."

"Sort of a moot statement when you can't actually die."

"I would if I could for her. It doesn't matter that I can't, it's the intention behind it that should matter. I'd give up my pseudo-immortality if it meant Eden gets to live a little bit longer."

It's still a shock to me on how much Kaine has changed. He's always had obsessive tendencies, a side-effect of his ADHD and whatever fucked up shit is going on his head because of his trauma but seeing him so in love with someone that he would willingly throw down his life for them is something I never actually expected.

I know he would do anything for me because we're like brothers, but does his love extend to that level when it comes to me? I know he more than likely doesn't feel that way towards his father, who he still hasn't let completely back into his life. Eden has to physically drag his ass to the house for any sort of dinner, and at Christmas he lasted a whole forty-five minutes before he came up with the lame excuse of having to come over to my house just so he could get out of there faster. Eden ripped into him for that one while I tried to stay out of it. I don't care if he uses me as an excuse, but I'm not going to defend him for his actions because I've *met* Eden. She's more vindictive that he is when she's pissed off.

"Fine, I'll go."

He gives me a smug grin and settles back into the chair, relaxing his posture once more. "What do you want to do about the whole Avery thing?"

"I have no fucking clue. I can't figure out how to get rid of him, Kaine. I thought when everything was over with you guys, he would be done with me, so I can't figure out why he's still here, unless he's still keeping an eye on you."

"He has no reason to. I doubt any other reapers would be stupid enough to go against any of his orders to not come after us, and I don't think Luther has escaped or anything. If that were the case, I think he would be more upfront about it instead of lurking inside of you the way he is."

"It would help if I could talk to him properly instead of this haunting bullshit and creepy ass whispering he's doing."

"Do a séance or some shit then."

"Dude, I'm not doing that."

"Why not? I'm sure Eden has a Ouija board lying around somewhere. She's into that shit."

"That's just asking for shit to happen."

"How could it possibly get any worse? He's already stalking you and making you fall off balconies and shit. I know how much that sucks." I frown, propping myself up a bit so I can get a better look at him. "Oh, uh...Eden made me fall off my bedroom balcony the first night I met her." He shakes his head and laughs. "It was funny as fuck in the morning. I planted myself at the dining table and pretended like nothing happened. She totally thought I died and she looked horrified, like I was a ghost back from the dead."

"Did you die?"

He shrugs. "Yeah, but that's not the point. Man, it was so easy to fuck with her. She'd lose her shit if I did anything like that now, and after what she did—what she tried to do—I wouldn't put her through that. It's not a good feeling."

I'm surprised he's bringing up Eden's failed suicide attempt. He's done well to avoid it, not wanting to trigger her in any way that might push her to do something like that again. He's been good. He's kept his temper reigned in and takes the time to think things through before he speaks or reacts. I can't imagine what he went through during all of that, and it pissed me off to no end that Eden thought it was a good idea to do that to him, knowing what happened to his mother. That was the first time I held true anger towards her and the first time I've ever seen fear in her eyes when it came to me.

It was just a glimpse of the person I was, but I was already riding the high of aggression because of Stephen, and she almost tipped the scales to a point I was worried I wouldn't come back from it. If it weren't for Kaine having a level head through it, I don't know what else I would have said or done to her. I like Eden a lot, but I would do anything for Kaine, even if that meant hurting her so she wouldn't break him further.

Kaine would most definitely try to kill me for even thinking like that, but he's been my anchor for most of my life. I wouldn't survive without him. I know he wouldn't do the same for me, not when Eden is literally his other half. A destiny written by the gods themselves.

CHAPTER THIRTY-TWO

RONNIE

It's hard to enjoy myself the way Eden is when my mind keeps drifting to Reese and what he and Kaine could possibly be talking about. Eden looked a bit shaken up when she came back with her arms loaded down with drinks and snacks, dropping everything in a heap on the bed before climbing into it with me. I let her pick a movie to put on, more so she wouldn't feel as though she was being forced into awkward conversation.

That's what this is. Awkward. I know she's hiding things from me, just like Reese and apparently Kaine, and she obviously knows that I know, but she's doing well to avoid the subject, busying herself with a mindless movie instead of talking to me.

I sigh, shoving a handful of chips into my mouth and trying my best to pay attention to what's happening on the screen, but I'm already lost. I have no idea what's happening or what movie this is, but she seems happy enough with her eyes wide and mouth slightly parted before slowly sliding a chip into her mouth.

"Seriously?" I finally say.

She doesn't seem surprised by my sudden outburst, slowly putting down her bag of chips and letting out her own sigh. "I'm sorry," she murmurs, like *that's* enough of an answer. It doesn't give me shit, but it sure as fuck pisses me off more.

"Am I not good enough to be privy to whatever little secret this is? I'm worried about him, Eden, and I have a right to know what's going on with him."

"This isn't something that I can just talk about freely. All I can tell you is that something happened last year that's taking a toll on him. He just needs people to be understanding and support him while he tries to figure this out."

"Why would he need to call Kaine? He wanted him instead of going to the hospital after he fell from the fucking balcony, Eden. He could have died—he *should* have died. I thought I lost him, but I think I've been slowly losing him in a different way."

"You're not losing him. I don't know what else to say or do for you to understand how much he cares about you. He said he loved you, which after everything you said happened, I didn't think he would break down as quickly."

"I just want the truth."

"It's not my truth to share, Ronnie. If I knew one of your secrets and Reese asked me about it, how would you feel if I just told him everything?"

She's got a point there. Eden doesn't know anything outside the mask I've put on and the life I'm living being a bit of a lie. If she knew, would she leave me, too? I never really had friends growing up, everyone too scared to come near me because of who my father was. Word got around quickly on the origins of Veronica Petrov and my father liked it that way.

It's easier to control someone when they're alone and mentally broken. My mother saw it happening little by little, but she didn't know how to get us out of that situation. She was always under the watchful eyes of my father, and she took the brunt of that attention to keep it away from me and Theresa.

Tessa took on that role once our mother passed away and I hated that she did that. My father wasn't kind to her, but I was her younger sister, and she felt it was her duty to protect me, at least until she finally couldn't do it anymore and had enough. She left me. I can't blame her for that, and I give her credit for trying to get me out of that house, but she couldn't. Not without risking herself. She left me to live amongst the wolves, trapped in a den that only wanted to control me and manipulate me to do their bidding.

My father never had a son, much to his dismay, so the mantle fell to his daughters. When the eldest stepped away, shunning herself, the responsibility fell on me. He didn't want to give up his power, but he wanted to use us to gain more of it, making his name and house mean something more in this world and put fear in those around him. I don't want to be a part of it or be involved in his unsavory business, but how long can I keep running?

By now, Dimitry has gone back to him and has probably told him what I've done. I'm sure my father will still feel an inkling of pride in my actions, but he'll reprimand Dimitry for failing at the one task put on him. Good. I hope the fucker suffers and ends up beaten and bruised, something I know very well.

I flop back into the bed and stare at the ceiling, willing all the answers to just scribble across the white paint so I don't have to keep wondering what's going on. "I just want him to be okay," I whisper.

Eden flops back with me and drapes her arm across my torso, hugging me to her. "He'll be okay. Once he gets a handle on this—on his emotions—I'm sure he'll tell you everything."

I hope she's right. I hope we can *both* work past our secrets and finally be honest with each other because what kind of life can we have if it's built on deception. I'm scared to tell him who I am, but I'm more afraid of him being blindsided if Dimitry decides to try again and put Reese at risk.

He's still off their radar and I want to keep it that way. I'll tell him after the funeral. I'll give him time to grieve and then I'll sit down and tell him everything. I know he's capable of taking care of himself and protecting himself, but he's never gone up against people as deadly as them. They have no respect for human life, turning on their own when they no longer suit their needs or do what they're told to do.

A knock comes from the door and then Kaine's head peeks in, eyes finding Eden's instantly. My heart clenches in my chest at the adoration in that gaze, the unrestrained love shining in his eyes. He pushes the door further open, revealing Reese with his arm draped over his shoulder.

"He should probably take a bath to try and relax a bit more and get the dirt off himself," he says. I point towards the bathroom, quickly getting up to follow him. He's in rough shape, wincing as Kaine lowers him down onto the closed toilet lid. "Do you want me to help you?" He asks. "I know he's pretty heavy and he's not exactly helping any."

"Dick," Reese murmurs, trying and failing to lift himself back up to his feet on his own.

"Dude, just relax. Remember the last time the roles were reversed."

"Yeah, and you were a stubborn little shit that I had to manhandle to listen. At least *you* can't lift *me* up like that, so you have no leverage here."

"I'd appreciate the help." Reese turns his attention to me, glaring in a way that seems like he wants to shoot fireballs at me. "Dude, you're heavy."

"Fine," he grumbles.

I move towards the bathtub, turning the water on and tossing a bunch of Epsom salts into it before moving back to Reese. "Okay, let's get you up." Kaine helps him back to his feet to make it easier for me to slide his pants down to the floor. I bounce up, tucking myself under his other arm so we're both supporting his weight while we walk him over to the tub. I let Kaine help him into it, feeling like I'm in the way at this point, but also noticing how much care Kaine exerts while handling him. He's careful, making sure Reese is stable in the water before helping him lower himself down to settle in the tub.

"Do you want us to hang out a bit in case you need help getting him out?"

"Go home, Kaine. I can crawl out of this tub if I have to. I don't need you checking out my dick more than necessary."

Kaine laughs at that, crouching down next to him and leaning closer to whisper something I can't hear. Reese nods, dropping his eyes to the water in front of him while Kaine lifts back to his feet and ruffles his hair playfully. He stops next to me, his gaze softening as he takes in my worried expression. "He'll be okay. He just needs to sleep it off, but I checked him over and he seems fine. I'm sorry you had to go through such a scare tonight."

"Thanks for coming." I don't know what else to say. Reese wanted him here, not me, so I can't exactly tell him off for showing up here like that. I stare at Reese, no longer acknowledging Kaine, but I can feel him staring at me. He sighs, not saying anything else as he leaves the bathroom.

"Talk to you tomorrow, Ronnie!" Eden calls out.

I don't respond. I *can't* respond. I feel like my friends are only my friends because I'm with Reese. At the end of the day, they'll pick him over me at every turn, but I can't blame them. I care about them, but I know where I stand in this.

"Do you want me to get you some food or something to drink?" I ask, watching him slide further into the tub and resting his head on the edge. He turns his gaze to me, his face looking beyond tired and just over today. He's had a lot of days like this recently, ones that have drained him both physically and emotionally.

"I'm sorry I ruined our dinner."

The sadness in his voice breaks my heart. The fact he's apologizing for that after everything he just went through shows me how much he cares. He doesn't want to keep upsetting me, but he somehow keeps doing it anyways, even by accident.

"You didn't ruin anything, Reese. We can just do it another night. I'm going to go put the food away and I'll heat up some soup for you. Maybe a tea?"

He smiles at that. "That would be amazing, Ronnie."

I lean over him, pressing my lips to his forehead, the chill of his skin turning into something I don't want to get used to. He used to be so warm, like my own personal furnace, but now his body is going through something I don't understand and he's not giving me any clues to help me figure it out.

I move quickly out of the bathroom, not wanting to take longer than I need to in case he decides to be an idiot and get out of the tub by himself. I can't help the sadness that wells up in my chest when I see all the prepped toppings still spread out on the counter, a now painful reminder of what happened tonight. I don't think I'll ever think of pizza night in the same way again, and who knows if I'll end up enjoying it since it'll just remind me of seeing his body falling over the edge of that balcony.

I put some soup heating up on the stove and set the kettle up to boil, putting everything else away while I wait. I hate that this happened. I hate that shit *keeps* happening to him like a series of unfortunate events. It's like he has some weird target on his back, drawing in the weird and devastating. It's as though the world itself is trying to break him completely, throwing everything at him in an unfair test that he's struggling to complete. He may come out on the other side of these trials, but I don't know if he'll ever be the same.

Looking at him now is not like I remember. The easy smiles and joy around him seemed easy and natural. Now, it's a struggle for him to let that side of himself out and I can't blame him for it. I don't think I would be able to stay pieced together if I went through half the shit he just did. The kettle clicks, snapping me out of my thoughts and reminding me of the soup, which I somehow managed to burn. Fuck, I can't even heat up a can of soup. That should be reason enough for him to leave my ass on the curb.

I carefully carry everything to the bedroom, setting it down on the dresser before going into the bathroom to check on him. His eyes are closed, his face calm as though he's sleeping.

"Reese?" Slowly he opens his eyes, tipping his head to look at me. "Are you feeling a little better?"

"Yeah," he sighs.

"Come on. Let's get you up before you turn into a prune."

He grips the edge of the tub, lifting himself up a bit, but his arms still shake under him. I move to help him, hating how much he's struggling. "I can do it."

"Let me help you," I snap back. That shuts him up. He doesn't say anything else as I help him over the edge of the tub, pulling the plug on it to drain. He watches me as I grab a towel, putting his hand out to take it from me. I glare at him until his hand drops back down to his side, getting to work on drying him off.

"Thank you."

"Don't."

"I'm sorry."

"Stop."

"I'm sorry for everything, Ronnie. I'm sorry for pushing you away. I'm sorry for making you feel like you don't matter. I'm sorry for hiding things from you, but I'm not sorry because I care about you and I want to keep you safe for as long as possible. Most of all, I'm sorry you've had to deal with all my shit, including my depression and mental breakdowns, you don't deserve it."

I stay silent during his rant, wrapping the towel around his hips before glancing up at him. "Don't push me away, Reese. Don't cut me out when you're in pain. If you thought I was worthy of your laughter and happiness, I think I deserve to be here to help you through all the hurt and darkness, too. We're supposed to be together in everything—a team. I didn't fall in love with you to only love the light and kindness inside of you while you're fighting an internal battle in the darkest parts of yourself on your own. I love you for you. All of you."

"I don't deserve you."

"Maybe not, but if I want to be here, I think that should be my choice, too. It's one thing if you don't want me, that I can deal with in time, but if you do, don't push me away."

He looks like he's on the verge of tears, eyes glistening in the soft glow of the bathroom light. He shifts his gaze behind me, to the still broken mirror I haven't gotten around to replacing. His breath rattles out of him through pursed lips, the sadness in his eyes adding to the turmoil I'm already feeling. I hate seeing him like this. I hate seeing this side of him in this way. I appreciate him being vulnerable, but not at the expense of his mental well-being. Whatever he's going through, he's struggling, and I wish he would just let me in so I can be here for him completely.

"I don't regret loving you," he whispers. "I feel like I should. I feel like it's a selfish emotion."

"it's okay to be selfish sometimes."

"Not when it comes to you. You deserve so much more than this," he murmurs, placing his hand on his chest, right over his heart. "You deserve a heart that's whole and can love you the way you should be loved. I feel broken inside, Ronnie. Something is wrong with me, and I'm scared of dragging you down. Loving you with a fractured heart doesn't seem fair."

"I don't care if it's half, a quarter, or even just a sliver, Reese. I'll take any piece you give to me and cherish it because you're worth it. You might not see it. You might believe you're not deserving of someone caring for you the way I do, but you're wrong. You know, for being so smart, you're kind of a dumbass."

He rolls his eyes at that. "Thanks?"

"You can figure out illnesses and treatment plans with your eyes closed, but you can't see what's in front of you with your eyes wide open. It's okay to be scared. That's why you have people in your life that you can lean on and talk to."

I gnaw on my lip, trying to figure out the best way to word what I want to say without upsetting him further.

"I'm here for you, and I hope that eventually, you can trust me like you do Kaine and Eden. I know you've known them longer than me, but I'm here for you, too. I'm here for you every single day, whether you want to believe it or not. I'm the one who has been watching you breaking every day and being plagued by nightmares you can't explain every night, Reese."

"I know."

That's it. That's all I'm going to get from him. Two words that seem so simple but hold so much weight. He knows, and yet he's still hesitating to tell me anything that matters. How does he expect me to be able to help him if I don't have any idea of what's actually going on in his head. He knows. Is he saying that because he still doesn't plan to tell me anything? Can I handle another day of being left in the dark; left to wonder if when I wake up, he's no longer the Reese I fell in love with?

I have no choice but to wait it out and see what he does. I don't have the heart to leave him again, knowing that the last time nearly crushed him, pushing him to act in a way that was completely out of character. I've never known Reese to be as obsessive and possessive as he was those days I was away from him, taking on stalker tendencies that were out of the norm.

"Let's get you in bed." He nods, letting me take his hand and leaning into me as we walk out of the bathroom into the bedroom. He spots the steaming soup and tea right away, a small smile pulling at the corner of his lips. "Let me get some comfy pants for you."

"It smells amazing, Ronnie."

"Good ol' chicken noodle soup, from a can, of course."

"Still smells amazing." He settles onto the edge of the bed while I grab him some clothes, picking some of the warmest ones he owns in the hopes of heating up his chilled body. The bath barely did anything for him; his skin covered in goosebumps the second he came up out of the water.

I don't know if I'll get used to the new marks on his body, marks that I don't understand. Where did they come from? Did they have something to do with his fall? They're clearly the reason he wanted to talk to Kaine, the panic on his face when he saw them a sure sign. They suit him though. The thin strands weaving and curling across his sun-kissed skin like it belongs there. The intricate patterns twist and turn, drawing the eye along their length. I thought he would have had tattoos like Kaine, but his skin is free from any ink, outside from the marks now on him.

I settle the pants down on the bed, shifting to the heated blanket to turn it on. "Alright, let's get you up and into bed. Hopefully you sleep a bit better tonight."

He uses the bed to help himself up, still gripping my outstretched hand as I steady him. I try to move quickly, ripping the towel off of him and lowering myself down to make it easier to slip the pants over each foot. His muscles flex as my fingers graze against the skin on his thighs, shifting over his stomach once I've settled the pants over his hips. His stomach tightens, the muscles rippling on a sharp inhale when I trail my hands up to the marks along his ribs.

"They're...not very pretty," he says quietly.

I shake my head. "They look good on you. I can picture you with tattoos covering your body. Not to say I don't like your skin when it's perfectly clear, but I won't complain either way. If these are permanent, I'll love you just the same." I guide him over to his side of the bed, not expecting him to respond to my comment, and help him get settled before grabbing his food and tea.

"Did you eat?" He asks, blowing on the spoon. His eyes shutter closed, a soft hum vibrating in his throat as the warmth of the soup hits his tastebuds.

"I'm okay."

"You didn't, did you?"

"I'll grab something once you're done." He doesn't seem to like that answer, but I'm not leaving until I know he's calmed down and he's comfortable. I have plenty of time to grab something from the kitchen when I take back the dishes, and I wish he would stop worrying about me when he's the one who's going through shit.

He finishes it quickly enough. Knowing him, he was rushing it so that I would go and eat like he's insisted. A heavy warmth spreads through my body when I help him lie down and cover him up with the heated blanket. The way he smiles at me through hooded eyes is enough for me to know that I'm doing the right thing for him. I brush his hair back, running my fingers through the strands until his eyes grow heavy and his breathing steadies.

It's all I can do for him for now, and I hope that when he wakes in the morning, the pain and discomfort will be gone. He's got enough to deal with tomorrow with the funeral he insists on going to, and I plan to accompany him and support him through that hard time, too. At least he won't be alone. Eden said that her and Kaine would be meeting us here in the morning with the intention of going to both the funeral and then the cemetery. As much as that might hurt Reese, I'm sure he's grateful for the support.

I don't want him getting attached to patients, this one being one of the more difficult ones. It makes me wonder if the relationship the girl had with her mother and father brought back memories for himself. With his dad being absent and his mother getting sick, the situation must have hit him a little close to home.

CHAPTER THIRTY-THREE

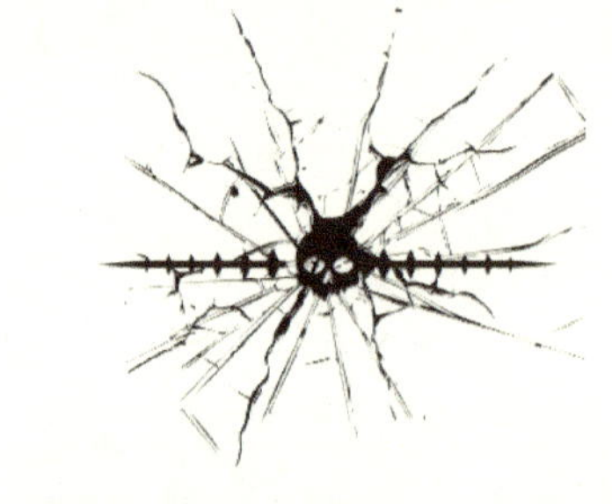

REESE

Darkness. There is nothing but darkness all around me. A stifling pressure as the blackness presses into my body and soul. There are no shadows or flickers of light, just a well of absolute nothingness. It feels like a void, all absence of joy and happiness being drained away until there's nothing but fractured thoughts and misery.

I hear him then. Through the expanse of black, his voice echoes around me. "Reese."

"Fuck you!" I spit out, my own voice barely carrying through the thickness around me. It's like the air itself is heavy, pressing into me until I feel as though my lungs will burst with the strain of breathing in.

"You shouldn't be here."

"No kidding. If you would just get the fuck out of me, I would gladly leave this hell hole."

He sighs at that, a shimmer of glittering black, somehow darker than the air around it, flickers into existence. "This is your own creation. My own world looks nothing like this, kid."

"Why are you doing this?"

"What exactly?"

The air continues to shift until a figure appears in front of me. I know it's him. I know it's the face I saw staring back at me in the mirror. He's not much taller than me, but his presence alone makes him feel huge and overwhelming. Every instinct in my body is telling me to back away, to look anywhere but at him, to fucking bow my head and submit to the ancient creature before me.

"I almost died because of you."

His face glows with an internal light, enough for me to see his pierced brow go up in question. "I'm pretty sure I saved your life."

"I wouldn't have been in that situation if it weren't for you. Why are you still haunting me?"

He tucks his hands behind his back, moving towards me with preternatural grace. A shiver rakes up my spine, goosebumps erupting along my skin as he slowly walks around me, taking me in at a distance. "I'm not haunting you. For some reason you've tapped into my soul signature, so the question is, why?"

"How the fuck should I know? I haven't done anything. I thought I would have been rid of you after you rode me like a fucking horse to punish your reaper and help Kaine and Eden. You're a liar, Avery."

I gasp at the suddenness of his hand clamped around my jaw, gripping tight enough that I think he'll shatter the bone. "I am not a liar. I've never lied to you and I never will. You're not supposed to have a tie to my realm, so please tell me how it's possible."

"I don't know," I grit out, trying to pry my face from his hand but my body won't move. It's glued to the spot, frozen in place because of him. "I have no idea why any of this is happening."

"I am not tying myself to you. You're then one hooking your human claws into my essence. Is there something you want? Greed can be a very dangerous thing, child. You need to tread carefully and explain yourself."

I have no idea what he's talking about. I haven't done anything but be myself and try to figure out all the fucked-up shit in this world. I've been trying to wrap my head around the fact that supernatural beings exist, living among us, and spying on what we do every day like it's a show they're watching on repeat.

"I don't want anything from you. All I want is to be rid of you and understand what you've done to me."

Slowly he releases my face, giving my cheek a few light taps as a small smile tugs at his lips. "I was sure I cut my ties to you after that day. It was what I promised I would do after all, but for some reason a part of me has stuck with you. The only explanation is that you're the one holding onto it. You won't let it go. Maybe, in your quest to understand, you've inadvertently siphoned a piece of me into yourself, housing me within your own soul. Again, I say, greed. Greed of the unknown. Greed for power. Greed to be more than you ever were before."

"No."

"No?" He laughs. "The proof is in the fact we keep meeting and interacting when we shouldn't. I don't have time for petty mortal ambitions. I'm trying to control an entire realm and fix the mistakes my underling has made. The chaos he's created has formed a rift in my realm, bridging portals that should not exist. He took lives that were meant to exist far longer than what he deemed fit, and because of that, the balance of souls has created a..." He licks his lips, mulling over his words in a way that makes me wonder if he should be telling me any of this, but he sighs and continues his rant. "The balance has shifted." He frowns. "Maybe you're feeling the effects of that shift."

"I told you, I'm not doing anything. All I want is to protect my friends."

He shoves his hands into the pockets of his trousers, giving me a wry grin. "How are your friends? Eden and Kaine, are they still living their lives as they should?"

"Don't you know? I thought you could spy on them through me."

"I never spied, merely observed, and I haven't checked in on them since the incident with Luthor. I don't want to possess a human body. It's not comfortable and I quite prefer my own vessel."

"Have you been to our world in that form?" I ask, nodding to his body.

He glances down at himself. "No. It takes a lot for a reaper to shift into the human realm in a physical form that is not a meat suit we borrow."

"Wow, that's rude."

"It's what you are," he laughs. "It might not be a term you like but it's what you are to us. For me to pull myself into your world I would have to exert a lot of power. To hold it for long periods of time it would take even more. I have no reason to come over there."

"Why did you save me?"

"It wasn't your time. I didn't expect you to react the way you did, but I only came to you because you pulled on me."

I frown at that. I know I wasn't subconsciously pulling on him; I've never had a reason to. I wasn't even thinking about him or anything to do with him. I was thinking about my future and how I want what Kaine and Eden have. Is that it? Is me thinking about Kaine and Eden the reason Avery is still here? Is his tie to them somehow locking him within my own body, a tie he claims to be hovering within my subconscious? I can't exactly stop thinking about them or talking to them, they're a part of my life and they're people I refuse to give up without a fight.

"Thank you."

He waves me off, tipping his head back to stare into the abyss all around us. "Your headspace sort of sucks. I didn't expect it to be quite so...desolate. I don't know anything about you or what you've been through, but seeing this makes me believe you have some heavy burdens you're trying to hide from the outside world. Does your girlfriend know about this?"

"No, and I rather she not know."

"The darkness would ease if you allowed yourself to see the light. You may not want to believe this, Reese, but it's okay to rely on others once in a while. Some burdens are too hard to bear on your own, and if you have people in your life that are capable and

willing to shoulder some of it with you, it would make it easier for you to deal with them at your own pace. If you continue to keep everything bottled up, eventually, it will overflow and cause catastrophic damage to you and everyone around you. This darkness would be better being dealt with at a trickle instead of allowing it to build and build to the point where it explodes out of you, taking down yourself and everyone around you, including the ones you love."

"So philosophical."

He smiles at that, tipping his head towards me. "I'm old, kid. If I didn't have some words of wisdom to give to you, I would be a pretty shitty being."

My emotions are at war with themselves. I hate him—I should *hate him—but for some reason, talking to him feels so easy. My heart thrums in his presence, beating in a way that makes me feel as though it's trying to match his own heartbeat. It shouldn't be this easy or comforting to be around him, but looking past my anger and frustration, I feel a kinship with him in some way. He knows more about the inky black darkness within me than my own best friend. He might have a better understanding of it than I do myself.*

"I'm sorry if I've overstepped," I murmur.

"It's fine, just tread carefully. I don't want you getting in over your head, but I promise you, whatever you're going through is not due to me interfering. I've only stepped in once now, and that was to make sure you lived to see tomorrow."

"Do you know why I'm able to see the reapers now?"

"What?"

"At the hospital. I saw a reaper a few times, and I saw the one that took my patient's soul. I've never seen them before and I've...I'm no stranger to death."

"You shouldn't be able to see them." His eyes narrow and he moves closer to me, planting himself less than a foot in front of me. "If it had to do with my presence in the past, Eden and Kaine should be witness to them as well. Have they seen any?" I shake my head. "Hmm. You're an anomaly, Reese. I'll pull my resources and see if I can find any information as to what is going on with you. In the meantime, try not to die."

CHAPTER THIRTY-FOUR

REESE

The sound of a blender running pulls me from the darkness of sleep. I feel lighter; a bit more clearheaded than I did the last few nights being tormented by nightmares that I now think were of my own creation.

Pieces of my conversation with Avery still float around in my mind, something I didn't think I would be able to hold onto. It's always difficult for me to remember the details of dreams, the details slipping through my fingers like grains of sand, but this wasn't really a dream, was it? No. It didn't feel like a dream or a nightmare, but more like a meeting of two souls with the same path and intention.

He could have let me continue to wonder, tormenting me with the constant nagging of what's going on with me, but he didn't. He reached out and spoke to me, even if I still don't fully have the answers. He was confused by what's going on as well, and I don't know if I should take comfort in that or worry more since if a reaper doesn't know why the fuck I'm tapping into reaper wave, how am I—a lowly human—supposed to know?

I curl onto my side, loving the warmth of the heated blanket that Ronnie obviously turned back on this morning. The heat of it pulls at my senses, lulling me into a haze of bliss. I wish I could just stay curled up here for a few days and let my body recalibrate. I don't want to deal with today, knowing what is coming in a few hours. I need to steel myself and keep my emotions in check so I can be there for Diana in her time of grief. I'm grieving, too, but I got my vengeance, even if it was short-lived. I shouldn't feel as much joy or pleasure in taking someone else's life, watching the light leave their eyes, but with people like Jeremy, it was euphoric. Karmic justice brought on by someone who has no issues or hesitation in doing what fate won't.

Avery didn't say anything about me taking a life before its time so it must have already been written in the stars. He must know what I've done, all the lives I've snuffed out over the years. Either that, or he agrees with my actions, not caring about the measly lives of people who don't deserve to be in this world.

The door creaks open, pulling me from my slowly spirally, depressive state. Ronnie comes bustling into the room with a tray, loaded down with food and my morning shake.

"Hey! How'd you sleep?"

"I think I slept okay," I say, rolling over onto my back and propping myself up against the headboard.

She sets the tray down in front of me, snagging a mug of tea and a breakfast wrap for herself before going over to her side and climbing back into bed. She sets the mug down to pull the covers over herself, humming cutely when the warmth of it settles into her body.

"You were pretty quiet through the night. No thrashing or talking, so I hope you get some actual rest."

"I feel better than I did last night. Thanks again for taking care of me."

She leans towards me, planting a kiss on my cheek. She cups my jaw, rubbing her fingers along the stubble starting to grow in. "You've taken care of me plenty. It's my turn to take care of you."

"I should shave today," I murmur when she keeps running her fingers over the hair.

She shakes her head and grins. "I kind of like it. You look hot and sort of like a badass," she snorts.

Settling my hand on the back of her head, I pull her towards me, pressing my lips against hers. I love the way she melts into the kiss, teasing her tongue against the seam of my lips until I part them for her. I could easily get lost in this—in her. Letting myself be consumed by the joy I feel in her company and the pleasure we can provide each other.

Slowly, I pull away, knowing I can't let myself fall into that or I'll end up locking us in this apartment until people worry about us. She licks her lips, her eyes flitting from my mouth to my eyes and back again.

"Eat your breakfast," she whispers, pulling a grin to my lips.

"Yes, ma'am."

Our relationship seems easier today, less strained and more open, even though we both know we're hiding something from each other. She's letting it go for now, allowing me to enjoy my morning so I'm in a better mood going into the funeral.

"What time are Kaine and Eden coming over?" She asks, clearing the tray from my lap.

"Oh, um, he said he'd be here around ten so we can all go over together."

"Okay. I'm going to put this away in the kitchen and then I'll take a shower. Not sure if you're planning to take one or not, but if you're up to it." She motions towards the bathroom with a nod of her head and slips out of the bedroom.

With a heavy breath, I carefully slip out from under the covers, shivering when my feet hit the floor. My skin feels electrified, my bones aching and creaking with every small movement. It doesn't hurt exactly, but I don't exactly feel right. I *feel* different. I feel like the fundamentals that made me who I am, have been genetically changed, and I wonder if Avery knows about that, too. Kaine has never mentioned feeling any different from what happened with the reapers, but he did mention that every time they die, something changes inside of them. Their bodies are slower to recover and revive, and Eden has said that there are moments where she feels her mind slipping and it can be a struggle to get a firm hold on the person she was before she died.

I don't want that. I don't want to experience any of that on top of everything else I've been through. My mind has slowly been breaking piece by agonizing piece for years, and the last thing I need is something else fucking with my already fucked up head.

My legs feel steadier under me than they did last night but still tremble a bit when they take on my full weight. I have no choice but to brace myself on the bed until I get full function of them. My body feels like it belongs to someone else and I'm trying to pilot it without proper instructions. Is this what Avery felt whenever he took over my body? My skin feels tight and itchy, a foreign feeling that I really don't like.

I need to get a hold of myself if I have any hope of looking and acting normal in front of a bunch of people today, and I don't want to have to rely on Ronnie or Kaine to carry my ass to something that they didn't even need to go to. They're all going because of me—to support *me*. They don't need to go that far, but I know that arguing with them isn't going to get me anywhere. All it will get me is anger and frustration from Ronnie and probably a punch to the gut from Kaine. The fucker nailed me in the balls last night while I was already weakened and in a fragile state and I swear my soul left my body for a fraction of a second when it happened.

I squint against the light flaring to life in the bathroom, cringing at the sorry state of the mirror. It's fucking useless at this point with only small fragments of the reflective glass clinging to the frame. Ronnie did well to clean up the mess, but that dark reminder of what I was going through is staring back at me now, pulling me into a trance that I'm struggling to break out of.

I blink, slamming my eyes shut and ripping my gaze away from it. My back cracks loudly when I shove my pants down my legs, smaller pops resonating through my system as I make my way over to the shower and turn it on.

The second I step under the flaming stream, a sigh escapes my lips and my shoulders slump in relief. The aches slowly melt away, my eyes closing as I lean my head on the cool tile of the shower wall.

The light padding of feet pulls me slightly out of my haze, but I don't bother to look over, knowing Ronnie has come back. Will she get in with me, or will she give me time to myself? I rather not be alone, giving time to my constant wheel of thoughts rolling around in my head.

My muscles relax further when I hear the shower door slide open, then closed, followed by the gentle touch of her fingers down my spine. Even with the heat of the water pelting into me and fogging up the air around us in thick plumes, her touch sends a shiver through me and goosebumps rising along my skin. I've always reacted to her touch. Whether gentle or aggressive, my body vibrates like the hum from a tuning fork being struck.

My entire body shudders at the feel of her pressing a washcloth against my back, gently scrubbing it into my shoulder blades, along my spine, and across my hips. I smirk when she shifts a bit lower and rubs it across my ass cheeks, lingering longer than she should, but I'm not complaining.

"All clean," she whispers, pressing her lips to my back and wrapping her arms around me. The cloth is still gripped in her hands, now moving slowly up and down my stomach. "Want me to do the front?"

I push away from the wall, gently gripping her wrist as I turn to face her. Her damp hair clings to her cheeks, urging me to tuck the strands back, exposing her beautiful face to me. She's breathtaking. No matter how many times I look at her and drink her in, it's like I see something new and fresh within her that makes me fall harder.

She's everything anyone could ever want and more, wrapped up in a perfect package of soft, creamy skin, cradled around tight muscle. The girl is fit and stronger than she looks, sporting her own little six-pack and biceps that would make weaker men weep. Her thighs are thick and toned, lines of muscle definition peeking through with every subtle movement. She could be a deadly little thing if she set her mind to it. A femme fatale that could easily render her enemies weak in the knees and headless.

She gently tugs her hand from my grip, peeking up at me through sodden lashes as she shifts the cloth back up my stomach and across my chest. I can't stop my heart from beating harder and faster with each passing second, heat spreading through my body with each swipe. Suds form against my skin, washing away all the darkness of my soul clinging to the surface. Each swipe eases my worry and gives me a little glimpse of what could be.

"Can I wash your hair?" Her hand pauses and she tips her head up to look at me fully. "If you don't want me to..."

She shakes her head, dropping the washcloth to the ground and turning her back to me. I'll admit, I've never actually done this for her. She has her routine, something I've watched countless times and enjoyed every second of it. I've wanted to do it; wanted to scrape at her scalp and lather her locks, tugging the strands gently through my fingers. Why haven't I asked her before? She didn't even hesitate to say yes, making me wonder if this was something she wanted as well.

I grab her shampoo, smiling when the scent of it wafts into my nostrils. I love the subtle scent of lavender and vanilla, a smell that clings to her and drifts in every movement. I love the smell of it, but I love it more when my own scent mingles with hers. A combination of softness and light merging with the musk and darkness of my own notes.

She hums out a breath, letting her chin drop to her chest as my fingers work through her locks until they lather. "That feels so good," she whispers, shakily bracing her hands on the opposite wall. I grip her hips and shift a bit, settling her under the stream of water to wash out the suds before grabbing the conditioner. I work it onto her ends, gently massaging the strands and letting them settle along her back to soak in a bit. I take the time given to me and move my hands to her shoulders, squeezing the muscles and massaging into them. Her skin pebbles and her legs wobble under her, forcing her to shift her grip on the wall to something more stable.

The girl actually spreads her legs farther apart, leaning into my touch and shifting her hips enough that her pert ass grazes against my cock. Fuck. When did it get hard? I was too distracted with my task that I didn't even notice the little fucker went off on its own. Clearly, I'm not the one controlling it, not when its master is standing naked in front of it. What I wouldn't give to bury myself inside her heat, feeling her tight walls clamping around me while I rut into her. She wants it. I know she does in the way she rocks back into me and lets out a soft whimper.

"Don't tease me," I breathe, stepping into her. I grip her throat, pulling her up and back against my chest. "If you keep wiggling that ass of yours, all I'm going to want to do is fuck you."

"You say that like it's a bad thing," she pants, reaching one of her hands up to cup the back of my head and bring me down closer to her neck. She leans to the side, giving into the pressure I put on her jaw and exposing the delicate flesh to my heated mouth. "Reese," she whispers, reaching back her other hand to grip into my thigh.

I nip and suck my way up the creamy expanse, biting into her jaw playfully while my fingers press into the side of her neck. She moans. The little deviant moans at the restriction around her throat and the subtle stemming of her blood flow. "What will the little rabbit do now that I have her caught in my trap? Do you want to run?" A subtle shake of her head. "Do you want to cry?" Another shake. I bite down on her earlobe, loving the way her legs buckle, forcing her to lean further into me for balance. "Do you want to whimper and moan?"

"Yes," she says quickly.

I grind against her ass, gripping my other hand on her hip harshly and pinning her to me. My cock throbs against the feel of her and the need to be inside of her. "What do you want, little rabbit?"

"I want you. I want you to fuck me."

"You always want me to fuck you," I muse, shifting my hand around to cup her pussy. She gasps when I strum my fingers lightly against her clit, tipping her head back against my shoulder. "What do you want?"

"Please, fuck me."

Smack.

She jolts at the sudden slap to her pussy, her legs almost giving out under her. She always wants to fuck, but there's one thing I know she wants more. Something she's been aching for since the moment she spoke those three little words to me. "What. Do. You. *Want*?"

"Ma—make love to me," she whispers. She says it cautiously, as though I'm setting her up to fail and she's worried that it's the wrong answer. It's not, and the little rabbit deserves to be rewarded for being so good. "Oh, god," she whimpers sinking into my touch when I curl my fingers into her and strum her clit with my thumb.

"Don't call out another man's name when I'm the one about to make you come."

"Reese," she says breathlessly.

"Again."

"Reese!" She cries out, curling her fingers around my wrist, pulling my grip tighter around her throat. She's slick between her thighs, warm and wet and sucking my fingers in so greedily. Every thrust into her has her hips bucking into me and bumping against my cock. She grinds her ass against it, teasing my member until it's hard as steel and ready to plunge into her. "Fuck!"

"That's it. That's a good girl. Come for me, baby." She collapses against me, the only thing holding her up is my grip on her throat and the fingers still curled into her cunt. Slowly, I slide them out of her and walk her closer to the wall, turning her around to face me.

"What are you—"

"I want to see your face while I fuck you. I want to see your lips part, your eyes glaze over, and the ecstasy spreading across your face while you come with my cock buried so far inside of you, you'll think you've been impaled. I'm going to make love to you, but I'm going to make you scream for me, Ronnie. I'm going to make you cry out so loud that even the dead will hear you."

Gripping her hips, I lift her up the wall and slowly lower her onto my cock, groaning against her mouth. I'll never get tired of this. Not the feel of her around me or how she clings to me desperately, begging me with her body to get closer to her. This is as close as someone can get to another person without ripping off their skin and wearing it like a suit, but that's gross as fuck and not remotely sexy or appealing. Pretty fucked up of me to think of something like that while I'm buried inside my girlfriend, but I've never pretended to have a normal brain.

If anything, my thoughts are usually skewed more to the weird and deranged, even if I don't show any outward signs of how mentally fucked I really am. Intrusive thoughts; some that would surely get me committed if they ever saw the light of day, but that's why I keep the inside thoughts *inside*.

She curls her legs around me, drawing me into her until I'm completed seated inside her. Fuck, she feels amazing, her chest heaving against mine, every panting breath a ghostly touch against my lips. Her eyes are locked on mine, her hand digging through my hair, scraping and clawing at my scalp as I slowly draw my cock out and slam back into her.

Her head thunks against the wall, mouth parting on a deep moan as I do it again and again until our bodies thrum together in a chaotic rhythm. We're both clawing and gripping each other, my mouth moving up her neck while my own hand buries into her hair, pulling her head towards me so I can claim her mouth with mine.

The kiss is electric and all consuming. A clash of tongues and teeth, nipping and sucking and devouring. She tastes like sweet heaven on my tongue, an aphrodisiac I'll never get enough of. She tastes like life itself, an elixir that should be so far out of reach that only the gods should be blessed to taste her, but she's mine. *Mine.* All fucking mine, and I'll kill anyone who dares to try and take her from me. She's an addiction I'll never break; one I'd never want to be rid of because the ecstasy I feel when I'm with her is terrifyingly euphoric.

It's like I can't get close enough to her. I can feel her body heat burning into me, bypassing the steam and warmth of the water still cascading around us. It pelts against my back, tingling against my skin and merging with the already building vibration along my spine. The heat pools down in my lower back, my cock throbbing and balls tightening with the need to spill into her.

"Reese!" She screams, biting at my lip hard enough that I taste iron blooming on my tongue. "Fuck!"

"Rabbit has teeth," I pant, slamming into her again, diving my tongue into her mouth so she can taste the blood she's drawn from me. She hums into my mouth, sucking on my tongue greedily and lapping at the lip she's spilt open. Such a little sadist, the perfect match to my psycho ass and she doesn't even realize it. "Fuck," I growl, wrapping my arms around her as my cock spurts and fills her with my cum. My entire body coils, muscles tightening around her while she claws at my scalp and back, her nails scraping against my skin and leaving hot trails in their wake.

We stay wrapped around each other for a few precious moments, our hearts pounding viciously against our chests. I don't want to let her go. I want to hold her for as long as possible and pretend that everything is okay when I know it isn't. I want to stay locked in our home and not worry about what's going on in the world around us, focusing on the here and now and making our relationship better.

"Reese," she wheezes, lightly trailing her fingers up the back of my neck into my hair. Fuck, I'm squeezing the shit out of her. I didn't realize that my grip on her tightened as much as it did while my thoughts went from peaceful to chaotic in my desperate attempt to hang onto her any way I can.

"Sorry." Slowly lowering her back down to the ground, I keep my hold on her, watching her legs buckle under her a bit as she tries to regain her footing.

She settles her forearms on my shoulders, frowning up at me. "I'm not going anywhere," she says quietly. "Why does it feel like you're worried that I'll disappear on you?"

Because you will. They always do.

I shrug. I can't voice what my mind is screaming at me to tell her, but it's the truth. It's a fear that will never go away, no matter how much time passes. It's not even a conditioning, more like an expectation at this point.

"I promise, Reese. I promise you, I won't leave you again."

CHAPTER THIRTY-FIVE

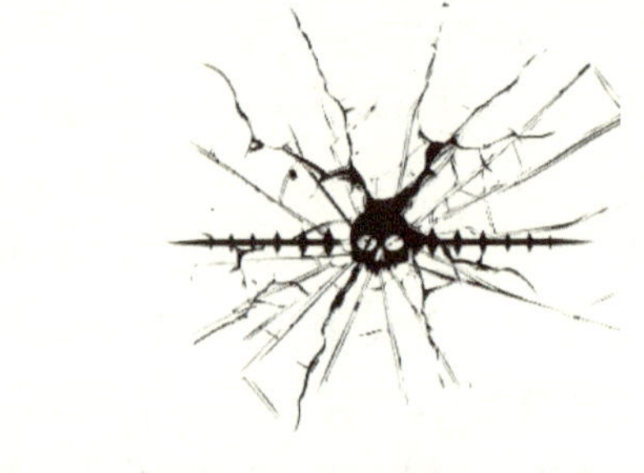

RONNIE

"You look flustered."

My eyes snap up in the mirror, meeting Eden's as she sits on the bed and watches me finishing up getting ready. Of course they ended up showing up early, and I'm pretty sure Kaine and Reese are already drinking in the other room. Kaine's reasoning, *'it's five o'clock somewhere'*.

"I'm fine, just trying to keep myself in a good headspace for Reese's sake."

"Really? It looks like you're freshly fucked."

Heat crawls up my neck and into my cheeks. I can see it in the mirror, pushing through the light makeup I've put on. Is she a fucking truffle pig for sexual encounters? I don't think I've done anything to make her believe that's what happened, even if it is. Fuck, that was some good sex. Feral Reese is a whole other beast, and I'll admit, I want more of it. I thought I took it too far when I made him bleed but his actions surprised me and turned me on more than I thought possible. Why was it so hot? I want to do it again. I want to see how far I can push him before his limit is actually hit, if he even *has* a limit.

"Pretty sure my sex life isn't any of your business." I cringe at the fact that I took the defensive route. Like *why*? Why would I do that? Eden has talked about her own sex life plenty of times and I've divulged a bit of my own as well. It's nothing new, so why would I think saying that now is appropriate?

"Are you good?"

"Sorry," I sigh. "I'm just a bit on edge still with everything. Reese and I are fine, and he was feeling better this morning so we...we ended up fucking in the shower."

Her eyes widen and she squeals, jumping off the bed to come over and stand next to me. "Oh my god, how was it?"

My eyes close at the memory, the phantom feeling of him railing me and clinging to me like a lifeline burned into my body. "So fucking good."

"He seems like the type that would be good in bed. He's way too strait-laced in the streets to not be a freak in the sheets. He's got a bit of a temper, too, so I would just assume he's got a bit more of a dominating personality."

"He's definitely not holding back in the bedroom."

I smile, shaking my head at her ridiculous exuberance. She's actually bouncing on her feet like I just told her the most amazing secret. I know for a fact that Kaine is pretty fucked up and adventurous in the bedroom thanks to the fact that Eden is pretty open about it. I can't blame her. She's had no real friends since she moved here—none in Chicago either from what she told me—the only person she really had to talk to was Reese.

The poor girl is desperate for any attention she can get, pushing through her social awkwardness to allow people into her life after suffering from trust issues. Her mom is a real piece of work, too. Kaine's not a fan of her at all, arguing with her on multiple occasions when she still tries to explain her actions. She's never truly defended her, but she still comes up with reasons behind all her harsh actions and words in the past. I'm with Kaine on that one though. She would be better off cutting her out of her life until she learns to be a better person, one that's more understanding and less judgmental.

"I'm glad you two are doing better, and hopefully after today, things will continue moving in the right direction."

"That's what I'm hoping for."

"I can see you two being together for a long time, Ronnie. You two are so good together, and even though you two have been having some rough moments, you balance each other out. I can see you two getting married and all of us being friends through it all."

She has a vision for a brighter future than I do. Those are my hopes and dreams, but they seem so far out of reach to ever become a reality. It took me fighting with Reese to finally get him to admit how he felt about me—to tell me he loves me. I don't want to be fighting every aspect of our relationship with him and practically begging him to feel the same things I do and want the same things I do. If I want to be with him, I need to be happy with what I have now and enjoy everything he decides to give me. If this is the extent of it, then so be it.

"We'll be friends for as long as you want to be, Eden." I can't tell her I hope for all those things as well. It's better to hope for less and not expect more, that way when the possibility of more is there, I can feel the happiness of him evolving past the shutdown person he's pretending not to be. They don't see it. They don't know what's going on inside his head. I don't either, but I feel like I have a better grasp and understanding of it than they do because I'm with him every day.

She gives me a sad smile, like she knows where my mind just went, but I'm thankful she doesn't push it. "You look really pretty," she says quietly, tucking a stray strand of hair that slipped from my braid back behind my ear. "You've always been really pretty, Ronnie."

"You're really pretty, too, Eden, don't ever think you're not."

She shakes her head. "I feel like you underestimate yourself a lot of the times, you're like me in that way, but you have more power than you realize, Ronnie. Reese wouldn't have given you a second glance if he didn't believe you were different from everyone else who tried to throw themselves at him. He sees the good in you. He sees through the outside, tears through the mask you might put on for everyone else and sees the real you. That person, the one in your heart, is a good person and really pretty, inside and out."

I blink rapidly at her words, trying to stem the buildup of tears burning at the back of my throat and rimming my lashes. Her words were so simple, but they feel heavy in my chest, like a weight pressing into me, forcing me to acknowledge them as the truth.

"Shit. I'm sorry, Ronnie. Please, don't cry. I didn't say that to make you cry."

"You're too good of a person, Eden," I sniffle, quickly grabbing a tissue to blot at my eyes before I ruin the makeup I meticulously put on.

"I'm just me. I would rather tell you what I think about you instead of not saying it and letting you feel as though you don't mean as much as you do to me. I know you're questioning my friendship because I'm keeping things from you for Reese, but it's for a good reason. I never want you to feel like you're not a part of our group."

"I get it. I do. It just sucks knowing there's something going on and being on the outside of it."

"I'll talk to Reese. I'll try and get him to find a way to talk to you about everything that's going on with him, but you have to promise to keep an open mind and not run away when he tells you. He won't be able to handle it if he ends up scaring you away, Ronnie."

"Is it bad? Did he *do* something bad?"

She shakes her head. "He's done nothing wrong; he's just stumbled into something without realizing it and he's trying to work through everything as best he can."

"I promise I'll listen to whatever he tells me without judging him." I'm *in* no position to judge him. I'm not innocent either, doing plenty of things that would make any sane person turn tail and run. I doubt Reese could possibly have a worse background than my own, what with me being a runaway mafia princess that would rather kill her own father than go back to that life.

CHAPTER THIRTY-SIX

REESE

The drive over to the church is quiet. Kaine and Eden are whispering in the back seat, trying their best to keep their conversation to themselves. Ronnie is next to me in the front; her hand gently gripped in mine on her thigh. She looks beautiful in her tasteful black dress, hair swept back in a gorgeous braid, and the subtle makeup rimming her eyes. Those eyes seemed sad and slightly distant when she came out of the bedroom, a soft smile on her face, a clear sign she was faking the emotion she was displaying.

I don't know what happened between her and Eden in that amount of time, but something *did* happen. I hate the feeling of being angry at Eden for upsetting her, especially since I don't know the reason for it. Ronnie showed no outward signs that it had anything to do with me, coming over to me right away and wrapping her arms around me, the way she normally does.

Now, she sits in her seat, quiet as a mouse, staring off into the city as it sweeps by. I brush my thumb against the back of her hand, trying to show her reassurance and appreciation at the fact she's here with me right now. I catch the slight tip of her head towards me out of the corner of my eye and risk a glance her way. Those eyes seem so empty and lost, that weak smile painting her lips again. My heart tightens in my chest at that. I don't like it. I don't like the lack of warmth in her smile or the lack of life in her hazel eyes as they stare at me. She shouldn't look at me like that. Not in a way that mimics or proves I'm losing her again.

"Are you okay?" I finally ask.

That forced smile stretches further, not reaching her eyes. "I'm fine."

I squeeze her hand tighter, trying to encourage her to open up to me. It doesn't work. She turns her head away from me to stare out the side window again. We spend the rest of the ride like this, so close to each other but a chasm of distance between us.

I frown when we pull up to the church, easily finding a parking spot near the entrance. I expected more people to be here, the spots full and people streaming in to celebrate a child's life and to mourn the loss of it.

"Did you get the right time?" Kaine asks from the back, leaning through the gap in the seats with his hand resting on the center console.

"I got the time straight from Diana. This doesn't make any sense."

We get out of the truck, and I move quickly around the front to help Ronnie out, taking her hand in mine and closing the door once she's clear of it. We all walk up to the church together, but my unease grows the closer we get to the doors.

Soft music echoes around us once we get inside, and I see Diana right away, stationed near the entrance with who I assume are her parents. She gives me a warm smile once she sees me and I quickly make my way over to her, dropping Ronnie's hand to pull the woman into a tight embrace.

"Thank you for coming," she sniffles into my chest, pulling back and wiping at her eyes.

"Where is everyone?" My eyes drift into the church, only seeing maybe twenty people in there, some children with their parents sitting next to them. The small casket in front of the dais is covered in white roses and a soft purple tapestry. There's a child up front with her parents, standing next to it, and their soft sobs filter through and mingle with the music to create a somber setting.

"Jeremy's mistress decided to hold his funeral today as well. His parents are there...same with a lot of our friends."

"Some friends," I murmur. "They rather attend the funeral of an adulterer than that of an innocent child." Looks like my list of victims is growing by the second. How dare those fuckers leave this poor woman to grieve on her own. The ones here must be kids from her school; her friends and their parents who wanted to show their support. She was cared for and loved, but this is not enough.

"I'm sorry for your loss," Kaine says, bowing his head to Diana and taking Eden's hand to lead her into the church.

Ronnie stays by my side, her body pressed against me with her arms curled around my arm. Diana's attention gets pulled to her and her expression softens. "Is this your better half?"

I smile at that. "Yes. This is Veronica Halladay, my girlfriend."

"Ronnie," she says, holding out one of her hands to Diana. "It's nice to meet you, but I do wish it were under better circumstances."

"I wish that were the case as well. Hang onto this one," she says, nodding towards me. "He's an amazing man with a kind heart."

"He is," she says, leaning her cheek against my arm. "He's one of a kind."

She's acting like everything is okay, so maybe I'm reading too much into her behaviour from before. She could have just been feeling the weight of today and the somberness of the funeral. That has to be it. She wouldn't be clinging to me in this way if she were upset with me or with something I've said or done.

We leave Diana to greet the next couple that come through the door and make our way to the pew Kaine and Eden have claimed. I slide in next to him, feeling the weight of his stare as I take my seat. He doesn't *stop* staring. Finally giving into the heavy observation, I look over to him, and I'm met with furrowed brows and lips pressed into a hard line.

"What?" I murmur, settling back into the seat.

"Are you okay?"

"I'm fine."

"Really? You seemed pretty upset when she said the rest of family was off at the other funeral."

"Because it's upsetting. What did you want me to do? Did you want me to feel sorry for the stupid fuck? He wasn't a good person, Kaine, and clearly his friends and family are no better."

"You're letting it get too personal, man. I can see it on your face. You're not—" He sighs, leaning closer to me and lowering his voice further. "You're not thinking straight and I have a bad feeling that you're up to something in that head of yours."

If he only knew the things that were currently being planned in my head. Kaine only knows what I've allowed him to see of myself. He has no idea how dark and deranged I can be, or the murderous plans I'm concocting in my mind. Murdering a large group of people at the same time is rarely easy and never smart, but I want justice. I don't *want* to drag it on over months until they're all wiped from the face of this earth to join the bastard I've already killed. I want them all to burn in the funeral pyre of their own making. I want them to suffer and scream and try to repent for their actions and bad decisions. Could they be good people? Possibly. Do I care? At the moment, in my current state, absolutely not.

"I'm not up to anything. I just think it's bullshit that they can't find the common decency to come to a child's funeral. She's a fucking kid, Kaine. She was sick and feared being alone and looking at what that got her. Her own family can't even be here. No wonder Jermey was such a piece of shit, he learned it from his parents."

"It's not your place to judge the actions of others. You don't know what they're feeling. They lost a child, too, Reese."

My teeth grit together painfully, making my jaw pop with irritation. He's right, they *did* lose a child of their own, but it's not the same. He's had years to grow and become a better person. He's lived a life already and had the audacity to want more and create a second life hidden away from those he claimed to love. He's had *years* to do the right thing, but he's made mistake after mistake, never once feeling regret or remorse in his actions. Julia had none of that. She didn't get to live even a single life. She never even got to make mistakes to have the opportunity to make things right. She was taken from this world too soon and deserves to have people around her.

I don't say anything else to him, there's no point. Kaine has a vengeful side, but nothing compared to mine. He doesn't understand or see the misguided actions of these people who claim to be friends and family. I'm glad I came and showed Diana that sometimes the ones who have been in your life for a brief moment can be the ones that will mean more to you in the end. I haven't known her or Julia for long, but it was long enough for them to impact my life.

The funeral is difficult once it gets started. Broken sobs and cries of anguish echo around the vast, high-ceiling church. Ronnie cries quietly next to me, pushing my own tears to brim my lashes. I thought I was ready for this. I'm not. I can't take my eyes off the small casket at the front, hating the fact I couldn't do anything to save her.

Once it's finished, we follow the line of procession out, Julia's casket being carried by her grandfather and a few other men that I don't know. It's beyond depressing, but once she's settled into the back of the hearse, we all pile into our vehicles and follow it to the cemetery. The drive is silent once again, aside from the quiet crying still coming from Ronnie and Eden. Neither of them knew her, but they still felt the loss of such an innocent soul.

The day shouldn't be as bright and cheerful as it is. In movies, they make funeral scenes gloomy and cold, with rain cascading down from the sky. Today the sun is shining brightly in the sky, a beacon of light and hope, and the complete opposite of what everyone is feeling.

We exit the truck once we're there, Ronnie quickly moving to my side and gripping my hand in hers tightly. The already fallen leaves crunch beneath our feet as we follow everyone to the plot chosen for Julia. My heart breaks for Diana as they slowly lower the casket down into the ground, each person around taking a handful of dirt and sprinkling it over the mahogany wood below.

My body feels stiff when I move forward myself, following Ronnie. I bend down, grabbing a large handful before bringing it to my lips. "May you find peace and joy in your next life, Julia," I whisper, opening my hand and watching the dark soil drop from my fingers to clunk softly against the wood.

I freeze to the spot when I lift my head, a wave of cold settling into my bones. "Reese?" Ronnie settles her hand on my shoulder, squeezing gently. "Come on."

I want to move—I *need* to—but I can't, my eyes locked on the line of flickering shadowy forms in the distance. None of them come into full focus, but I don't need them to. I know what they are, but I don't know why they would be here. There are no souls here for them to collect, unless there's going to be a mass murder I'm about to be witness to.

I can *feel* them. I don't know how to explain it, but it's not just being able to see them, but feeling their presence here. If I were to close my eyes, I know they would be there. It's like a subtle hum in my chest, a flicker of electricity sparking through my nerves. I swear, even in their shadowy forms, their eyes are all locked on me. I don't feel Avery in their crowd, whether that's a good thing or a bad thing, I'm not sure.

"Reese," Ronnie whispers a little louder. "We need to move." She ducks down and helps me to my feet, and that's when I notice everyone staring at me. Eyes widen and some hands go to their mouths, forcing me to duck my head in embarrassment. Ronnie pulls me along behind her until we're standing with Kaine and Eden again, both of which frown as well. "Oh my god," Ronnie gasps when she turns to face me. She reaches up and swipes her thumbs under my eyes, wiping away the tears that broke through. "Are you okay?"

"I'm fine," I mumble, shifting my face away when she just won't fucking stop. That's when I notice it, the red stains on her thumbs. I quickly reach up to my own face, wiping at my eyes and feeling bile rising in my throat when my palms come away red. "What—"

"Dude, maybe you should go to the hospital. You shouldn't be crying blood."

"No shit," I snap back, quickly turning to look over my shoulder, to where the reapers stood moments ago. They're gone. Not a single trace of their presence left behind. Is this because of them? Anxiety gnaws at my insides and my body sways as true panic sets in.

What the fuck is happening to me?

CHAPTER THIRTY-SEVEN

REESE

I flinch at the blinding light flickering across my retinas, glaring at the doctor when he pulls it away. "Have you been experiencing any headaches, nausea, vomiting, sharp pains in the eyes, temporary loss of vision, taste, or smell?"

"No."

"Have you had this happen before?"

"No."

"Are you—"

"I'm fucking fine!" I snarl. "I feel fine and there's nothing wrong with me, so I don't know why my eyes randomly decided to bleed." I didn't even want to fucking come here, but when you have three people arguing with you, you tend to give in just to shut them up.

"Fine," he huffs. "I think we should still run some labs to make sure there isn't something we've missed. I'd suggest an MRI or at the very least a CT scan of your head to rule out any tumors or cerebral bleeds."

"I rather not."

"Mr. Mitchel, this is serious. You're a doctor yourself so you should understand the gravity of this situation. If you were your own patient, would you allow yourself to just leave this hospital without at least running some tests?"

He's got me there. I would definitely be running every test possible until I found the reason behind the symptoms. This is why I'm a doctor and not a patient. I'd make a terrible patient because I don't fucking listen to what's good for me.

"Fine. Run the tests."

"I'll pull the bloodwork now and then you can go wait with your friends while we open up one of the scanners for you."

I roll up my sleeve and give him my arm, half expecting the blood he draws out of me to come out like black ink instead of the deep red that settles into the tubes. He tapes off the puncture once he's gotten what he needs, staring at me when I don't move.

"I want a lollipop." His lip twitches with the threat of a smile, but he gives in to my pathetic demand, holding out the container for me to pick one. I pop it in my mouth, smirking as I walk past him.

Ronnie jumps to her feet and rushes me the second she sees me heading into the waiting room. "Are you okay? What did the doctor say?"

I pop the sucker out of my mouth and hold it out to her. She stares at it for a second, quirking a brow. Her eyes widen in surprise when I press it against her lips, waiting for her to open her mouth for me. She does because she's a good girl, and smiles around the lollipop.

"They're running some blood work, but I need to wait around a bit since they want to run some tests and do some scans on my head."

"You're going to end up breaking the machine," Kaine snorts.

"I'm not *that* big."

"I meant because your head is fucked up, but that, too," he laughs.

Ronnie doesn't seem impressed by our banter, the earlier smile fading, replaced by worry creasing her brow. I sigh, cupping her cheek. "It'll be fine. He couldn't find anything wrong with me so he's just being overcautious with the tests. Why don't you go grab yourself some tea from the cafeteria?"

"What if you get called in while I'm gone?"

"It's still going to take them a bit, and I promise I won't go in until you're back, okay?" She nods. I lean down, pressing my lips to her forehead. "I love you," I whisper. Colour paints her cheeks and she ducks her head the second I pull my hand away from her, scurrying off down the hall. I watch her retreating form until she turns the next corner and then turn my attention back to Kaine and Eden. "Did you notice anything weird at the cemetery?"

Kaine lifts to his feet, shoving his hands in his pockets as he walks towards me. Eden's eyes drift from me to him, confusion written all over her face. "What do you mean?"

"There were reapers there. They weren't in full form, but there were at least ten of them standing by one of the trees, watching us." I keep my voice low so the other people in the waiting room don't think I'm insane, even though I feel like I am. Leaving out the fact that the reapers seemed to be watching *me* might be a dumb move on my part, but I think I've freaked out Kaine enough to last a little while.

He shakes his head. "I didn't see anything. Was that before or after you started bleeding out?"

"Just before. It felt like my body was frozen when I saw them. I wanted to move but I just...couldn't."

"Well, hopefully you come back with a clean bill of health. I know today has been rough for you as it is, Reese, you don't need more shit thrown on top of it all."

He doesn't even know the half of it. My life lately seems to be a chaotic stream of unfortunate events that keep piling on top of me, like the universe itself is trying to crush me under its metaphysical thumb. I know I need to keep pushing through and fight it, but it's so fucking hard when the stress of it all is stifling. Kaine nods behind me and I turn at the motion. Ronnie is on her way back with a tray full of drinks and a bag with what I can only assume is some type of treat on top of everything. The conversation is officially over, or so I think.

"Reese, can I talk to you for a second?"

Ronnie pauses next to me at Eden's question, and even Kaine looks confused. "Uh, sure." I follow her a few feet away, a distance she seems satisfied of from the others. "What's up?"

"You need to tell Ronnie what's going on with you."

"Excuse me?"

She rolls her eyes, crossing her arms across her chest. "She feels like none of us trust her because we're all sharing this secret and keeping her out of it. We can't keep doing this to her, Reese. She deserves to know."

"This isn't exactly something I can bring up in casual conversation, Eden."

"You handled it fine."

"Did I?" Her eyes widen at the sudden rise in my voice, and I quickly step towards her, leaning closer to her ear. "Finding out about you and Kaine and all this shit going on wasn't something I just *handled*. I had no choice but to listen because Kaine was frantic when you fucking died, Eden. What was I supposed to do? Did you want me to call him crazy and leave his ass to deal with it all on his own?"

"That would have been the normal reaction, yes, but he meant something to you, so you listened. Ronnie will be the same. She loves you, Reese, and if you love her back, you need to start trusting her a bit more. She can't be there for you if she doesn't know what's going on."

"Maybe I don't need her to be there for me. Did you ever think of that? Maybe it's better for her to stay out of this shit so she stays safe."

"It should be her decision. I know you. I know you're scared to lose her, but she's not like that. Keeping her at arm's length is breaking her, not helping her."

"Fine, I'll tell her." I think it's a stupid idea. I think Ronnie will fucking run when she finds out what's haunting me, and it's just one more thing to add to the list of reasons she shouldn't be with me. It's bad enough she's in love with someone that's secretly part of the mob, something she would *also* run away from.

Kaine and Eden leave after that, but only once I promise to call them once I get my results, so they know for sure that I'm okay. I know they're not going to find anything on the scans. Whatever is going on with me has to be a side effect of the hitchhiker still attached to me. Not only do I have to deal with Avery at every turn, now I have his stupid reaper legion following me, too.

Ronnie stays with me the entire time, looking more and more exhausted as the time passes. "Why don't you go home and get some rest. You've barely eaten anything and you can't survive on some tea and a muffin."

"You haven't eaten yet either."

"I *have* to be here. You don't. Please, just go home."

"I don't want to leave you," she whispers. Curling against my side and resting her cheek on my arm. The chairs in the waiting room are uncomfortable as shit, and I rather sit on the floor at this point instead of having my back and ass suffer against the restrictive plastic encasing me.

"I know, baby, but you look really tired and I don't want you feeling like shit because you're stuck in this hospital with me."

"Reese Mitchel!"

A nurse calls out my name and Ronnie squeezes my hand. "We're going home soon. I'll be here once you get out."

I grip the back of her neck, holding her while I press my lips against hers. The kiss is a silent plea, a prayer that everything will be alright. "I'll see you soon."

As much as I wish she would just leave me here, I'm thankful she's staying. I know how much she cares and how much she wants to be here for me, every action from her a desperate attempt at getting me to open up to her. I have no choice but to do as Eden suggested and tell her about Avery and the reapers. I didn't confirm what I would be allowed to tell her, and now I'm kicking myself for not asking Eden if it was okay to tell Ronnie about them, too. Better to ask for forgiveness than permission. She wants it done, so it will be done.

"You can change into one of the gowns in here and then we'll take you over to the MRI lab." The nurse points to a small room down one of the back hallways and I quickly slip inside, undressing and slipping on the pathetic gown over my frame. No way in hell was I taking off my underwear when the damn thing isn't big enough to cover my back. They really need to invest in a better distributor for this shit.

The nurse's eyes widen when I pop out of the room, awkwardly adjusting the garment around me while she leads me to the next room. I catch sight of the doctor through the glass barrier while the nurse gets me settled on the slab. The table is cold enough I feel the chill of it seeping through every muscle right down to the marrow of my bones.

"Make sure you don't move during the procedure so that we can get as clear of an image as possible of your brain."

"I know," I mumble, not appreciating the fact she's talking to me like I'm *not* a doctor myself.

The table shifts, sliding me into the machine. I stare up at the entrance, getting lost in the lights before the machine starts ticking its monotonous drone. I frown when the lights begin to flicker, the *wump wump wump wump* drumming into my brain louder and louder until I can't take it anymore. My eyes slam shut, teeth gritting together as sharp pain lances through my skull.

I want to scream. I want to lash out and tear this infernal machine apart piece by piece until it stops. Something isn't right. Something isn't—

"Oh my god!"

A high-pitched screeching scrapes at my eardrums, digging right into my skull to the point it feels like it'll tear it open like a fucking watermelon. Even through my closed lids I can see the lights continue to flicker, strobing faster, brighter and darker, until there's nothing but blackness behind my lids. Metal groans and screams erupt and then I'm falling. The table beneath me pitches, lurching from side to side, forcing me to open my eyes.

I stare in horror. Not only because I can see clearly through the pitch-black blanketing the room, but because the machine around me ripples and jerks, caving in and ripping away until my body is free of its confines. The table I'm on slams onto the floor, the metal around me dropping in a cacophony of metal and plastic on cold broken tiles.

The emergency lights flare to life in the corners, bathing the horrific scene in a muted red glow. "Mr. Mitchel, are you alright?" The doctor and nurses come rushing into the room, their shadows lengthening along the floor and up the walls as they get closer to me. Those shadows almost seem alive, ready and waiting to wrap around the bodies they're tethered to with just a single thought. "Here, let's get you up. Be careful now."

"What the fuck happened?" I grumble, taking his hand and letting him pull me up to my feet, being careful not to step on any of the debris littered around me.

"I'm not sure. We got a couple of scans done before the images lit up like a Christmas tree. It was chaos after that, so we'll have to pull the camera footage to get a better idea of what happened."

I don't know how I know, but the camera feed will come up empty. I did this. I don't know how or why it happened, but I'm the reason this lab is destroyed. "Can I see the scans you got?"

"Well, technically I shouldn't."

"Please."

"Very well. I don't think the scans are accurate. There seemed to be too much neuro-firing for it to be conclusive."

I'm sure they're completely accurate for me, just not for a normal human. Whatever is going on with me, it's physically changing my system. It's as though this shadow inside of me, whether it's Avery's doing or not, is trying to protect me from outside interference. Whatever it is, it doesn't want me to know any of the inner workings of this supernatural blueprint etched into my soul.

"I need to check you over and make sure you're not injured."

"I'm not."

"That's not possible. The machine practically imploded around you and with all that scattered steel and—"

"I'm fine," I grit out. I know I'm unharmed. I would feel it if I were hurt in any way, but if anything, I feel better than I did before going into the stupid thing. He doesn't argue with me any further, leading me to the room behind the glass, which is spider cracked so badly I have no idea how it's still within its frame. It's the only thing that protected the people in the observation room from the blast of energy that careened through me.

The doctor doesn't even bother stepping in to help me once I'm in front of the monitors, quickly bringing up the feed and the scans. Fucking hell, he's right. My entire brain is lit up, flickers of electricity snapping around the frontal lobe and parietal. The next image shows more activity in the frontal as well at the premotor cortex, as though preparing for whatever intention my subconscious was trying to bring to fruition. The last image before everything is just an explosion of light on the screen, showing my limbic system lighting up, those flickers of electricity focusing in on the hypothalamus. The fact that my parahippocampal gyrus is lit up as well makes sense, the area being one for memory processing and emotional processing, which I've been getting heavy doses of over the last week.

"The scans are garbage," I murmur, trying to hide the tremors running through my body. "From what I can tell there's no bleed at least, so it's good enough for me."

"If they're garbage then we need to do another scan."

"No. We're done here."

"Mr. Mitchel—"

"It's *Doctor* Mitchel, and if I say we're done here, we're fucking done. Do you understand me?" Heat builds in my chest, burning through every rational thought trying to stay glued to the front of my mind. I know I'm being ridiculous, but I'm not putting myself through that again and I'm not risking *that* happening again. This was a mistake, one that almost cost them their lives.

"Reese—"

"We are *done*!" The emergency lights flicker with my increased anger, threatening to go out as well. The computers aren't so lucky, not with being as close to me as they are. The monitors flare with light before going out, plunging the room into an even deeper darkness. "I'm going home."

CHAPTER THIRTY-EIGHT

RONNIE

The lights in the hospital dim and flare, spiking my anxiety. What the fuck is happening? Reese has been gone for about twenty minutes now and should be out soon, but a strange feeling of dread settles into the pit of my stomach. I feel like something is wrong, and when the lights start going out one by one, plunging the hospital into darkness, I know I'm right.

People gasp and scream all around me, the emergency lights coming to life in the corners of every room and hallway. The nurses are frantically telling people to calm down and making calls to the emergency wards to make sure the generators are kicking on for the patients in intensive care.

I'm on my feet now, pacing the waiting room while my eyes stay fixed on the hallway Reese went down. He needs to be okay. Any minute now he'll come through that door, clear to go home, and that's what we'll do. We'll go home and forget about this day because he's okay...he has to be.

Seconds tick by, then minutes, on and on and still no sign of him. I start moving down the hallway, resolving myself to just go in there and find him myself, but I'm jerked back by the arm. "You can't go down there," one of the nurses says, trying to pull me back towards the waiting room.

"Take your hand off of me right now before I break every single bone in it."

Her eyes widen at the cool, deadly tone of my voice, and I can see her fighting with herself. The need to complete her duty and not let me go and the fear of not letting me go and suffering the consequences. I've left no room for doubt in my words, and if she doesn't fucking take her hand off of me right now, I *will* crush every single one of those bones until they're irreparable.

"Ronnie?" The nurse's eyes snap up behind me, her face pale already, but the way it becomes more ashen as her eyes widen, has me spinning around and ripping out of her grip. "What's going on?" Reese asks, grunting when I launch myself at him, wrapping my arms around his back.

"You're okay," I murmur against his chest, breathing in the smell of him clinging to his clothes.

Slowly, he lifts his arms and curls them around me, hugging me to him tightly. "I'm fine. Everything is good so we can go home. Why are the lights off up here?"

I pull back enough to look up at him, his brows dipped in confusion, but his eyes gleam in the dim light, reflecting like a predator. Seeing that has me swallowing thickly, a nervous tremor radiating through my body. "I—I don't know," I stutter, trying to compose myself so I don't show the slight fear I'm getting from looking at him. "They just went out all of a sudden."

He kisses my forehead and steps back, taking my hand in his. "Let's go home."

I don't respond, following him aimlessly and watching the way his muscles bunch through his dress shirt as he leads me out of the hospital. It's late afternoon now, most of our day spent here while they ran tests on him. Eden checked in about ten minutes ago, wanting to know if I had heard anything yet, but I had nothing to tell her at that point.

Reese is quiet as he leads us to the truck, opening the door for me to hop in. I fumble with the seatbelt, going deathly still when he leans in and buckles me in. The moment the door closes, my eyes are on him, following every movement as he walks to the driver's side in front of the truck.

He seems better, surer in his steps and not as curled in on himself, but his expression tells me something is still off with him. He doesn't seem sad or upset, more so angry. I hope he's not mad at me. I haven't done anything to warrant that type of emotion—at least I don't *think* I have.

I stare straight ahead when he gets in the truck, flinching at the sound of the door closing. Fuck, I'm so on edge right now and I can't figure out why. He hasn't said or done anything to make me feel this way, but I suddenly feel like I'm in a tight space with a fucking jaguar.

I practically jump out of my skin when his hand settles on my thigh, my head snapping in his direction. His brows knit together, his hand slowly pulling away from me. I quickly grab it, settling it back down. "Are you okay? You're weirdly jumpy."

"I—I'm just a bit shaken up from the power going out like that. Everyone started freaking out and screaming and it just amped up my nerves." Not a total lie and hopefully one that's believable.

"I'm sorry you had to experience that. Why don't we grab some take out and eat it at home. I could use a beer."

I plaster my best smile and nod my head. "Sounds good."

CHAPTER THIRTY-NINE

RONNIE

The heat from the takeout container seeps into my legs, hiding the fact I'm still shaking as we pull up to our apartment. Reese quickly grabs it from me, hopping out of the truck and waiting for me to get out as well. I can't get over the silence that keeps stretching on between us, the small talk we had doing nothing to ease my anxiety.

The moment the elevator door closes he lets out a sigh. "Listen, I want to talk to you about something over dinner, if that's okay with you?"

"Sure. Do I need to be worried about this conversation?"

"It...doesn't have anything to do with you, it has to do with me. I have some things to explain to you, and I hope you take what I give you with an open mind."

"Oh, okay." I feel a bit nervous about what he could possibly want to tell me now. I wonder if Eden ended up talking to him and finally convinced him to tell me what's been going on with him and the reason he has those strange marks on him now.

The elevator pings, the door opening to our floor. Reese reaches for me, waiting for me to take his hand. I don't hesitate this time or flinch away, the excitement that he's finally going to tell me something about himself that he's been trying to keep guarded from me for who knows how long, fluttering through me. He makes me giggle when he tries to pull out his keys without letting go of my hand, juggling the food awkwardly.

"Let me get it," I snort, digging my free hand into his pocket to pull them out. He quirks a brow, a smile tugging the corner of his lip. "Don't start," I huff, opening the door for him.

"I didn't say anything."

"You didn't have to. I know that look."

He practically drags me over towards the table, only letting go of my hand once I sit myself into one of the chairs. He sets down the containers and jogs into the kitchen to grab some napkins and ketchup for the fries we got with our burgers.

He sits down in the chair next to me, smiling as he pulls all the food from the bag and pushes my container towards me. "I hope you're hungry."

"Starving." He's being really nice and caring, which is sort of throwing me off a bit because I wonder if he's acting this way to lessen the blow of whatever he's planning to tell me. I wish he would just say it already, get it over with, but he bites into his own burger, letting out a soft moan.

His phone vibrates on the table, and he gives it a quick glance before flipping it over, so the screen is down. “So…”

“So.”

“Do you believe in the supernatural?”

My fry freezes halfway to my mouth, my eyes drifting to him slowly. “Um, like vampires and shit?”

“In general. Is there anything you believe in?”

“I mean, I believe in ghosts and aliens. I don’t think we’re the only things out there.”

“Do you believe in reapers?”

“Like the grim reaper?” He nods. “I don’t see why not.” I shrug, not really understanding why he’s talking about this. I thought he had something important to tell me, but he’s talking about weird shit.

“You know about Kaine and Eden’s dissertation, right?” I frown, nodding my head slowly. “Did you actually read it?”

“I skimmed it.”

“Did you ever wonder *why* they both picked that as their topic?”

“Reese, what is this about? Just get to the point.”

“Lazarus is a phenomenon where the body self-resuscitate once outside intervention ceases. Eden and Kaine took their research further, covering supernatural elements as well and not just science-based findings. The reason they went that route is because they’re both Lazarus.”

That gets my attention. “Wait, they’ve died?”

He nods. "The thing is, Lazarus syndrome is a one-time thing, and the findings have shown that the people who have come back have died officially shortly after. Whether that's days or months later, they never live a full life."

"Okay? I still don't understand what this has to do with you. I thought you were going to tell me about what's been going on with you and some sort of explanation for those marks on you."

"I'm getting to that, I promise." I settle back into my seat and let him continue. He almost seems nervous, his hands fidgeting with his napkin more and more the longer he sits there until he starts tearing small pieces off of it to scatter across the table. "Eden and Kaine can't die. I mean, they do, but they *keep* coming back. Their Lazarus doesn't have a limit to it."

"Wait, are you trying to tell me they're immortal?" I snort.

"Not exactly. They're what's considered split souls. Now that they're together, their Lazarus is weaker but still functioning. Over time they'll die, but they're also more vulnerable at a specific time of the year."

"How do you know all of this?"

"They almost died for real last year. There was a rogue reaper that went after them and tried to claim their souls. Another reaper showed up and banished him, saving both of them in the process and explaining to them what they are."

"You were there for all of this?" I'm still having a hard time believing everything he's saying, but his face is so serious and the way his hands tremble as he continues to rip and tear at the napkin is telling me he believes every word out of his mouth.

"I was technically involved. The reaper..." He pulls in a shuddering breath, dropping the shredded napkin to the table.

"Avery. Avery took over my body. He's done it at least twice that I'm now aware of but he's—he's still here." He taps his trembling fingers to his temple. "Right here."

"The other night, when you said his name—"

"He was in my head, Ronnie. I can't get rid of him, and I don't know what he wants. I've talked to him, but he's given me no answers."

"Is he the one that gave you those marks?" I can't believe I'm buying into what he's saying, but I feel it in my heart, he's telling me the truth. At least the truth he believes in.

"Yes. They're healing marks. Kaine and Eden have them as well from the incident last fall. I would have died yesterday if Avery hadn't taken over."

Knowing that sends my heartrate skyrocketing. I could have lost him yesterday if it weren't for the fact that he's being haunted by this...reaper. A fucking *reaper*. How is this real life? He's blowing everything I've ever known out of the water, shattering everything I've ever thought I knew.

"Is this all that you've been keeping from me?"

"The most relevant thing, yes."

"Okay."

He quirks a brow at that. "You believe me?"

"Do I have a choice? It seems pretty extreme, but it wouldn't make sense for you to be making up such an extravagant story just to be lying to me anyways."

His shoulders sag in relief and he lets out a long, shaky breath. "I thought you would freak out more than this. I didn't exactly take the news well myself when Kaine first told me what was going on."

"I believe you."

His phone vibrates on the table again, pulling his attention back to it. My own goes off as well, eyes narrowing at the '*unknown number*' flashing across the screen. I watch as he flips his over to check the screen again while my own continues to buzz.

"I should get this."

"Okay." He takes the opportunity to answer his own phone this time while I step away to answer mine.

"Hello?"

"Don't react." My body stiffens at the sound of Dimitry's voice on the other end. "If you try to say or do anything, I'll kill your boyfriend." I turn slowly to look at Reese, wondering how the fuck Dimitry found out about him. My heart jolts up into my throat when I see a small green dot glowing against Reese's temple. "You're going to do exactly what I say, or you won't even get the chance to say goodbye to him."

"What do you want?" I whisper, trying to put myself into the line of fire.

"Stop fucking moving, Zara." I freeze. "Get out of the way." I don't want to, but I do as he says, exposing Reese to the laser once more.

"Please, don't."

"Hmm, I do like it when you beg," he chuckles. "If you do what I say, I'll let your little fuck toy live to see another day. If you *continue* to do as I say, he might get to see next week."

"Fine."

"You're going to tell him you need to leave and you're never going to come back. You're going to break his little heart if you want to save him. Your father wasn't too happy to find out you've been living with a male that isn't of his choosing, little Zara."

"I—I can't do that."

"Can't? Oh, you can and you will." I hear the distinct click of the safety sliding out of place.

"Okay. Please, don't hurt him." I try to pull the phone away from my ear, but I hear him screaming at me to stop.

"Don't hang up. You're going to do this while I'm on the line with you. You're not going to take anything with you and you're going to walk out that door and meet me downstairs so I can take you to your father."

Reese glances at me, his brows furrowing as he stares at me. "Reese."

"Let me call you back," he murmurs into the phone before ending the call and settling the phone back down on the table. The light from the rifle disappears from view, but I know Dimitry is still locked in and ready to fire if I fuck this up.

"Reese, I'm sorry but I need to leave."

"Oh. Do you want me to come with you?"

"You better fucking sell this, Zara," Dimitry hisses.

"No, Reese. I—I can't do this. I thought I could, but I just—I can't be here anymore."

His face pales and his jaw goes slack. "What—what are you trying to say?"

"We're over. I can't be with you. This is just too much, and I can't wrap my head around any of this. I can't be with someone that speaks nonsense and hides things from me."

He lurches to his feet and stumbles towards me, stopping dead when I step back. He sways and drops to his knees, arms falling limply at his sides. "I thought...you understood. I thought you were going to...stay—stay with me."

My heart shatters at hearing his voice break, at the look of absolute defeat and misery spreading across his face. I never wanted this. I want to stay. I want to fucking *stay* with him and be here for him and help him through whatever misery he's feeling. He's called me his light in the darkness, and here I am snuffing out the only beacon that's held him up.

"I can't. I can't do this."

"Good girl. I think he might actually cry. You're a little savage, just like you were raised to be. Now, get out of there." I'm going to fucking *murder* Dimitry the moment I get the chance.

"Goodbye, Reese," I whisper, fighting back the rise of bile in my throat and the burn of tears behind my eyes.

"Please, don't go," he whimpers when I walk past him. I want to stop and throw myself down on my knees beside him, pulling him into my arms and apologize over and over again until he can forgive me for this. I don't. I *can't*. I won't be the reason he gets killed, not here, not right now. I keep going, not letting my steps hesitate or stop until I'm through the door.

"See you in a few," Dimitry says happily, ending the call.

Hopefully he leaves Reese alone and is satisfied with me doing as he said. I can't hold myself up any longer, crumpling to the ground the second the elevator door closes. The sound of the metal is so loud in my ears, cutting me off from the man I love and always will. I hope he at least calls Kaine so he can talk through this and not be alone. He's going to break—No. He's already broken. I fucking broke him beyond repair. He opened himself up to me and told me something that was tearing him up inside. He was vulnerable, and because of Dimitry, I took that vulnerability and beat him with it until there was nothing left of him except a shell.

I stagger to my feet, stumbling through the lobby until I'm outside the building, glancing around for the prick that just ruined my life. "Dimitry!" I scream. "Show your fucking face, you coward!"

I gasp, clawing at the gloved hand clamped over my mouth, realizing too late that there's a cloth in his hand. The sweet smell hits my senses instantly, my body going numb, mind going dizzy, and my eyes growing heavy. "Night, night, Zara."

CHAPTER FORTY

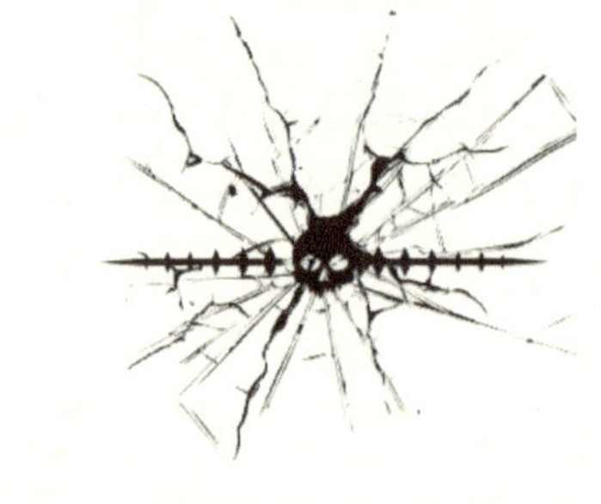

REESE

I can't breathe.

I can't breathe.

I can't *fucking* breathe.

She left me.

She fucking left me after she made me believe that she would be here for me. I told her everything, and she seemed to have believed me, but I don't even know if it was all a lie. What happened in those few minutes to make her change her mind? Who was on the phone? Did they have something to do with it?

Get up. Get up. Get the fuck up.

I need to go after her. I need to make her see that this is real. I need her to be here; I can't fucking lose her. Fuck, I can't think straight. My head is spinning and I can't feel my body. My knees ache and my fingers are numb, my entire body swaying with the weight of being rejected by the one person that I've allowed completely into my life.

Vibration draws me from my mental breakdown. My phone. Fuck. I was on the phone with Holland before all of that went down. He was about to tell me something, but I cut him off. I can't deal with him right now, but he keeps calling, over and over again. I barely get myself to my feet, stumbling towards the table and almost taking the whole thing out when I fall into it. I slam my hand over my phone, dragging it towards me and answering the stupid thing.

I still can't breathe, my chest tightening so viciously that it feels like I'm going to pass out. "I can't talk right now, Holland," I wheeze, clawing at my chest in a desperate attempt to draw in a proper breath.

"Are you okay? You don't sound right."

"I—I can't breathe. Just leave me alone."

"I can't. The information I was able to get is really important, especially since there's word out on the street that the bratva has a hit out on you under certain circumstances."

"What?"

"They haven't figured out who you are exactly, but I found your name on the dark web with a hit out. Reese Mitchel, 4357 Legacy Drive, Apartment 302."

Fucking hell, the Russian mafia knows where I live. This has to be because of Ronnie, but it still doesn't make any sense why they would be after her. "I don't care about me, tell me why they're after Ronnie."

"So, you're not going to like this. Your girlfriend has been lying to you the same way you've been lying to her."

"Excuse me?"

"Veronica Halladay is actually Veronica Petrov, youngest daughter of Misha Petrov, princess to the Russian mafia. Her father has been trying to marry her off to a mafia prince from a different city, Mikail Ivanov. Dimitry used to be her bodyguard, and word on the street is he got a bit handsy with the girl in her early teen years."

This is the last thing I expected him to tell me. What are the chances that I get involved with someone hiding from a rival mafia? Why was she hiding? Is she like me? Is she trying to escape the chains of the mafia, trying to start a new life outside the confines of the path they've tried to set for us? She goes by a different last name, just like me.

"Send me all the information you got and send the feed from the CCTV system to my phone with Dimitry's vehicle plugged into the database."

"What's going on?"

"I think he took her. She...left me tonight, but the way she left didn't seem right. She was cruel and seemed to be fighting the words she was saying to me. I think something is wrong, Holland."

"Well, this hit that they put out on you has stipulations. Oh, wait. The hit's been removed. That's so fucking weird."

"Fuck." I grab my keys and head for the door, wishing I would have been strong enough in the head to see through the fucking lies she was spewing. She didn't leave me; she was being threatened. "I need to go."

"Alright, I'll keep you posted if anything else comes in. If you get in too deep, you might need to consider contacting your uncle."

"That will never happen."

"Never say never. If it's your girl on the line, would you seriously turn your nose up at that kind of help?"

"I can deal with this on my own, Holland, as long as you continue to do your job and help me out."

"Fine, but I think you'll end up reconsidering."

I hang up on him and get on the elevator, trying Ronnie's phone. It's off, going straight to voicemail. "Fuck's sake, Ronnie." I swear to god if something happened to her, I'm going to fucking kill them all. I don't give a fuck who they are or how many people they have under their thumb, I'm going to wipe them from the face of this earth. The lights in the elevator flicker, reacting to my anger.

"Not now," I grit out.

The last thing I need is the power going out and my ass getting stuck on this elevator when I'm desperately trying to get to Ronnie before it's too late. Thankfully, I make it to the lobby, rushing through the entrance and bursting out into the street. I stop short when I see Ronnie's car still parked in her spot next to my truck. I step towards it, stopping at the crunch of metal under my foot.

"No." Slowly, I bend down, picking up her keys. She's been taken. Whatever happened upstairs led to this moment, and now I've lost her. "Fuck."

CHAPTER FORTY-ONE

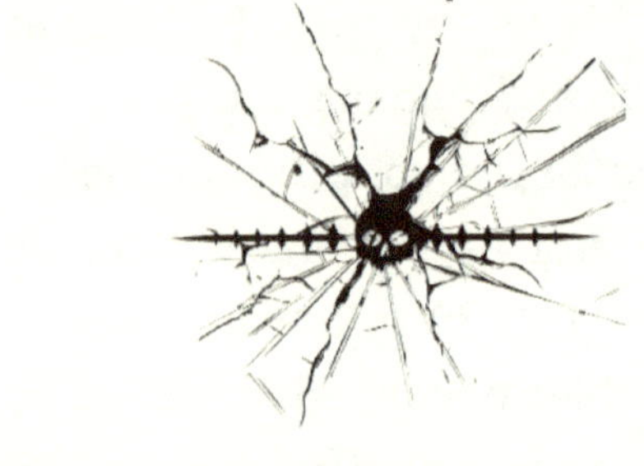

RONNIE

My head throbs and my eyelids feel like lead as I struggle to open my eyes. It's like shards of glass cutting into me with every heavy blink. Fucking Dimitry. The stupid bastard drugged me, and I highly doubt my dad would approve of such things.

I'm in a dark room, but it's familiar, a sense of panic settling into me. I jolt up in bed, regretting it instantly when my head spins and nausea burns in my throat. My feet settle onto the cold, warn wooden floor, my steps sluggish. I brace against the wall until I reach the door. Locked. I jerk on the handle, the rattling metal groaning in protest as I try to rip the stupid thing open.

"No," I whimper, letting my forehead smack against the wood.

I'm fucking trapped in my own home; a house I should have never come back to when I was at a low point in my life. That decision has created a horrible snowball effect, pulling me back into the lies and deception of the Russian mafia. I thought I could run away from my past and my father, but I've been dragged back and have put Reese at risk because of my actions.

Reese called it right, I'm a brat, and because of that, I've fucked up our lives. I bang on the door, jerking the doorknob over and over. "Let me out!" I scream. "Let me the fuck out of here!" I pound on the door until my knuckles bruise and turn bloody, tears streaming down my cheeks in hot waves. I slam into it, my shoulder screaming from the blow, but the stupid thing just won't give way. I can't breathe, panic clawing at my insides and tightening my chest so hard that it feels like my ribcage is shrinking and crushing my lungs.

My body sways, dropping to the ground where my knees slam against the unforgiving wood beneath me. I'm fucking trapped here with no way out, not until my father decides to grant me leniency and wishes to speak to me. I can only imagine what he wants from me. What could possibly make him go this far?

I curl onto my side on the floor, my back pressed up against the door while my mind flashes images of Reese behind my closed lids. All the good memories I have of him are overwritten by the last moments I saw him. The pain on his face, the heartbreak written all over his defeated body, what *I* did to him. I hurt him far worse than I ever thought possible, speaking harsh words to him and gutting every ounce of love he's held for me right out of his chest.

I should have stayed away from him. I should have gone about my life and kept to myself, but my selfishness and need to have something to call my own pushed me towards him. Because of me, he's hurting. Because of me, he almost died today. I did what I had to, breaking his heart so that I could save his life. I couldn't bear to watch him being shot, disposed of like countless others before him just for being with me. My existence is a fucking tragedy, a life of hidden shackles and chains.

CHAPTER FORTY-TWO

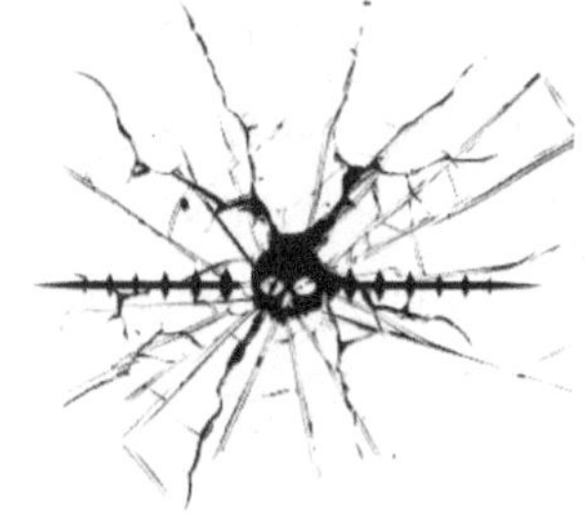

REESE

Dimitry's vehicle got flagged on the feed after being missing for what felt like hours. Now, I'm sitting outside the warehouse from before, in the middle of the night, wanting nothing more than to go in there and bash his head in. I'm thankful I've calmed down enough to think rationally, knowing the best course of action is to sit and wait. They won't hurt her. They have no *reason* to hurt her because she's one of them.

I pull up all the information Holland sent to my email, kicking myself for not having grabbed my laptop in my rush to get out of the apartment. I'll have to go over everything in better detail, but for now, I skim through all the files, pulling up the one on Ronnie. She looks different in the photo; younger and more innocent than the girl she is today. The fact he doesn't have any recent photos tells me she's been out of that life for a while. She's probably kept under the radar for the last few years at least, but she broke down and went to her father just a few days ago.

This feels like my fault. She wouldn't have resorted to doing something so stupid if I had just told her I loved her that night and prevented all this shit from happening. Because of me, she was taken. The fact they had a hit out on me—although temporary—just goes to show they've been watching her for a little while. They would have had to see us together at some point, maybe even seeing us coming into the apartment together.

The fact I didn't fucking know we were being followed sort of pisses me off. I clocked that shit when it was Ronnie, but when it came to me, I figured she was safe with me. Did she allow them to bring her in because of me? She's such an idiot for doing something so reckless. I'm perfectly capable of taking care of myself, and if I go off what Avery has told me, I'm pretty sure my time isn't coming up anytime soon.

I startle when my phone vibrates in my hand. "What?" I mutter.

"My sources tell me that Mikail is on his way into the city. This is serious, Reese. You need to talk to your uncle."

"I can handle it."

"He needs to know. Not even because this involves your girlfriend, but if there's an alliance like this forming, it could mean trouble for our organization. If you won't tell him, I have no choice but to do it myself. I'm only telling you this, so you make the right decision because I respect you."

Mother fucker. Of *course,* this all comes down to power. The fact Misha is using his own daughter to accomplish that isn't that surprising, but I thought for sure he would use his eldest, Tessa. How the fuck is she getting away with being with someone else that doesn't get them any form of territorial gain? Unless he doesn't know. Theresa could be doing a better job than Ronnie at staying off his radar, not being stupid enough to run back to daddy when things get a little tough.

No, I can't think like that. She had nowhere else to go, and once she realized her mistake, she reached out to Eden. It was too late at that point, but she tried her best to fix it. Now, it's my turn to fix everything else. I'll get her back, one way or another.

"You can tell him whatever the fuck you want, but you're not to tell him that Ronnie Petrov is Ronnie Halladay. I don't want him interfering in this and I'll handle it on my own. If I see any of my uncle's men anywhere near this, I'll fucking murder all of them and send him all their heads in cardboard boxes."

Holland sighs. "Reese, you can't handle this by yourself. Taking on an entire mob is fucking suicide."

"You don't know what I'm capable."

"I do and I know that you're way out of your league, kid."

"Do as I say, Holland."

"As you wish."

He ends the call, leaving me with my thoughts once more. I see no reason for them to be holding Ronnie here, but that won't matter. I'm planning to create a lot of noise for these fuckers, I just need to be patient and plan this out properly, so I don't get myself killed. My phone vibrates again, this time, it's Kaine.

"Why are you calling me so late?"

"It's like, ten."

"What do you need, Kaine?"

"Why do you assume I need anything?"

"You wouldn't be calling me right now if you didn't."

"Maybe I'm just calling to check in on you. Today was a rough day and we didn't hear back from Ronnie after you left the hospital."

Fuck. Was she supposed to check in with them? "I'm fine. There was a small incident at the hospital, but no one was hurt."

"What happened?"

"I blew up the MRI machine, and the few scans they were able to grab showed a shit ton of activity leading up to the incident."

"What the fuck, Reese."

"Good news is I feel better than I did before. Whatever is going on with me is doing something to my body."

A car horn blares a few blocks over and I duck down further in my truck in case anyone comes out of the warehouse to check on it. "Where are you?"

"Uh—"

"Where the fuck are you, Reese."

"There's some shit I need to tell you but now isn't a good time."

"We can talk tomorrow then. The conference has been moved up, so now it's tomorrow morning. Eden and I would really appreciate it if you and Ronnie came."

I swallow around the lump forming in my throat. I know I need to tell him, but now isn't the best time. I don't need him or Eden worrying about any of this when they have something so important coming up. "Ronnie won't be able to make it tomorrow. She has...some prior engagements, but I'll definitely be there."

"Alright. It's at nine tomorrow at the Pollack Plaza, third floor, in the Lexington conference room."

"Sounds good."

"Are you going to tell me where you are?"

"Goodbye, Kaine."

I hang up before he can pester me any further, not that it stops him from sending me rapid fire text messages telling me off for hanging up on him and still asking me over and over where I am. I love the guy, but he infuriates me sometimes. I can't exactly fault him for acting this way, his concern blatantly obvious with his words and actions.

We're two sides to the same coin, and even though Kaine thinks he's the fucked up one, he's wrong. He has more trauma association because of what he's been through in his life, but his soul is good and pure. Me? I've had my fair share of trauma as well, but my traumas have tainted me. Where he does bad things because he has to or has been pushed into a corner where he's left with no other choice, I have no qualms in doing bad things just for the fun of it, too. For myself, for Ronnie, for Eden, and especially for him.

I should get home and get a plan put together so I'm not going into this blindly on just instinct. I need to be smart about my actions because if I fuck this up in any way, it could end up getting Ronnie hurt, or worse, killed.

CHAPTER FORTY-THREE

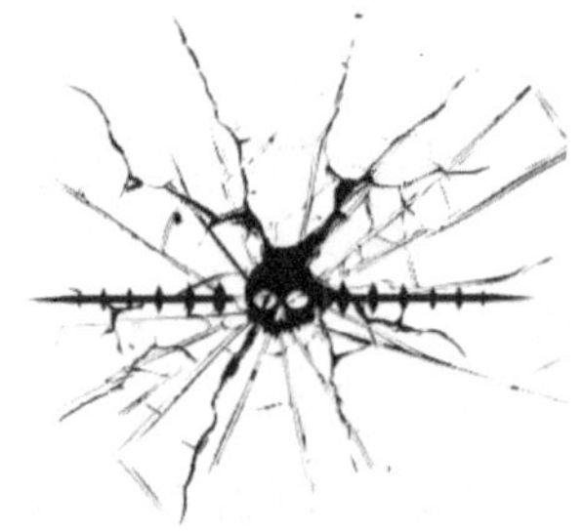

RONNIE

"You look pathetic." I'm still on the floor, but I glance over my shoulder and see Dimitry looming over me, a smirk tugging at his lips. "Did you sleep there all night?" I turn away from him, curling into myself and ignoring him. A small cry slips from my lips when he grips into my hair, tugging my head back up. "Look at me when I'm talking to you and answer the fucking question."

"My father is going to kill you," I snarl, spitting in his face.

A wicked grin turns his features deranged, and the sick bastard actually wipes the spit from his face and licks it off his finger. "Careful, Zara, I'm big on the foreplay, but if you keep this up, I'll fuck your ass until you bleed."

"My father—"

"Doesn't give a fuck about you. You're here for one reason and one reason only, to sell that pretty body of yours and get himself a bit more territory. You're a bargaining chip, but there's nothing in the contract that states you have to be pure, and we both know you're not anyways. Such a little whore, galivanting with the common folk. You have no problems spreading your legs for someone like your precious Reese, but yet you denied me at every turn."

"Because you're a crazy fuck with a psychotic obsession. You don't give a fuck about me. All I am to you is some conquest, a notch on your bedpost. I want nothing to do with you, and my father should have fired your ass years ago."

"Your father would never get rid of me because my daddy and your daddy are best friends. That gives me a free pass to do whatever I want with you until you're sold." He tugs on my hair, forcing me to grip into his wrist to ease some of the ache, my body following the pull until I'm up on my feet. "In the meantime, you're going to be a good little girl and do as your told. Your father wants to see you in his office."

He shoves me so hard that I stumble and slam into the doorframe, barely catching myself before my face cracks off the wood frame. I'm going to murder this fucker in his sleep. No, not in his sleep. I want him to watch me fucking gut him and cut off his dick before I shove it down his throat. I want to see him choke on the tiny pecker with wide eyes, and then I'm going to scoop them out with a fucking spoon.

Ugh, I hate him so much. I hate the fact he's still allowed to be here and is still breathing after everything I told my father about him. He tried to rape me when I was sixteen and then I still had to be in the same room as him for another year before I finally left.

My skin crawls knowing he's at my back, his footfalls heavy and echoing in the hallway as I head to my father's office. He reaches past me and knocks on the door, my heartrate skyrocketing at the sound of my father's voice. "Come in." He opens the door for me, gripping my elbow harshly and pushing me inside. "You can go, Dimitry."

I yank my arm away from him, shooting him a death glare. It doesn't faze him; it only pushes him to plaster an evil grin on his face before closing the door between us. "Why him?" I mutter, turning back to face my father.

"Have a seat, milaya." He motions to the chair across from him. I don't move, keeping myself rooted at the entrance and crossing my arms across my chest. If he wants me to sit, he'll have to *make* me sit. He sighs, his chair creaking as he settles back into it. His fingers tap on the dark mahogany desk; aged and worn from all the years he's owned it. "Sit," he snaps.

"I rather stand."

"Why must you make this difficult?"

"Why must you kidnap me? I don't want to be here, and I don't have any reason to be." I storm towards him, stopping in front of his desk and swiping my arm across it, scattering all the neatly piled papers there onto the floor.

"I'm calling you to do your duty."

"My duty? I scoff. "I'm not some broodmare you can sell at your leisure. If you try to pawn me off on some random man, you won't be getting territory, you'll have a war on your doorstep."

He quirks a brow at that. “I’ll kill him. If he comes anywhere near me, I’ll kill him, papa. You can’t force me to do this.”

He rises from his chair and bends down to the mess scattered across the floor, digging through everything until he finds a file he’s looking for. He slides it across the table, tapping it with his finger. “I think I can force you to do whatever I wish.” He sits back in his seat, nodding towards the folder. “Open it.”

Hesitantly, I flip the cover open, my knees buckling under me and forcing me into the chair I originally refused. My fingers tremble as they graze the photos clipped to the file and page upon page of information on Reese.

“I was curious. I wanted to know who was able to woo my daughter and capture her undivided attention. What kind of man could this Reese Mitchel be if my own daughter—ruthless and merciless—was willing to step in front of a bullet for him. Imagine my surprise when I dug a little deeper. Tell me, milaya. Did you know who he was when you got into bed with him, or were you kept in the dark?”

Reese Mitchel. Doctor specializing in pediatrics, 6’2, 230lbs, dark brown hair, hazel eyes. Date of birth: December 13th. Mother: Rory Mitchel. Deceased. I flip to the next page and my heart drops into my stomach. Reese Brennan, son of Kiernan Brennan(deceased) and Rory Brennan (deceased), maiden name, Mitchel. 6’2, dark brown hair, hazel eyes. Date of birth: December 13th. Nephew to Declan Brennan, current leader of the Irish mafia in Cameron.

No. This can’t be true. If it is, Reese has been hiding his identity this whole time...just like me. How did this happen? How did my father find all this information in such a short amount of time?

"Normally, I would be impressed with you and bless such a union, but the *Irish* mafia, milaya?" He scoffs. "You should be ashamed of yourself for associating with heathens like them.

"Heathens. You're no better, Papa. You've murdered plenty, including innocent people just for your power and financial gain."

"If I were a heathen, I would have had Dimitry kill him in the apartment and then had you dragged out of there after you watched the light leave his eyes. As you can see, I'm not cruel. You're my daughter—my milaya—my precious darling. I do not wish to bring you unjustified sadness."

"Then let me go. Keeping me here is doing just that, Papa. I don't want to be here, and I don't want to marry some random man just for power. I love Reese and I want to be with him."

"Mikail is not some random man; he's set to inherit the Chicago branch once his father steps down. We need powerful allies, Veronica." I swallow, hating it when he calls me by my name. He only does that when he cuts off emotion in his words, making the conversation impersonal. "You *will* marry, Mikail. He'll be here tomorrow and you will meet him and speak to him in a civilized tone."

"And what if I refuse?"

"Then I hand you off to Dimitry until you change your mind. It's your choice."

My blood freezes in my veins at the threat. My own father is willing to pawn me off on a psychopath that is supposed to be protecting me, just so that I can be broken and more compliant.

That's what he'll do, he'll fucking break me until I don't even know who I am anymore.

I don't want to do this, but I won't become Dimitry's plaything in the meantime. I need to pick my battles and make a plan to get myself out of this situation. I wish I had told Reese who I am, maybe then he would have been open with me about his own past and I would have had a better chance of escaping this mess. If we would have been honest with each other right from the beginning, I would have never left him and I would have never ended up running home with a broken heart.

"Fine. I'll meet with Mikail."

He smiles, lifting to his feet and moving towards the side table where he keeps his decanter filled with the finest whisky. "Let's have a drink to celebrate the prodigal daughter returning to the fold."

"Make it a double."

He grins, pouring out two glasses and handing one to me. He clinks his glass against mine, smirking as he takes a sip of his liquor. I chug mine back, going through ideas in my head while I keep eye contact with him the entire time. I need to talk to Tessa and tell her to stay away from here. If father finds out she's coming back into the city, he might go after her as well. I think the only way out of this is to kill him—I need to kill my father and anyone who poses a threat to me and the one I love.

CHAPTER FORTY-FOUR

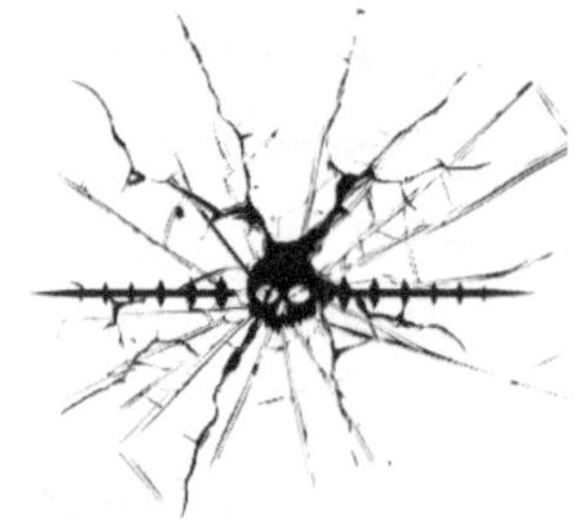

REESE

I look like absolute ass. Once again, I slept like shit, tossing and turning because of the nightmares plaguing me. This time, I remember them clearly and none of them were of Avery or the reapers haunting me, but of Ronnie. Scenes of her being ripped away from me, caught in the crossfire of the war I'm about to create and dying in my arms. That's one image I can't get out of my head.

It's like it's permanently burned into my retinas, so every time I blink or close my eyes, all I see is her. Her pale and bloodied face, her wide eyes briming with tears, but vacant and void of light or life. The silence of her still heart resonates in my mind, the only sound echoing in my psyche is my own screams and cries of anguish. Fuck, I need to get a hold of myself. Ronnie isn't dead and she's not going to be. Not for a very long time. I have plans for her—a future I now want, no matter the cost.

I want to grow old with her. I want to move out of this apartment and get ourselves a home where we can sit on the porch and watch the storms rolling in on the horizon while we snuggle up together on a porch swing sipping on her favourite tea. I want a huge yard so our dogs can run and play with our children, their barks and laughter the only thing drowning out the screams in my nightmare.

I want to see her smile and laugh and grow old with me; watching her beautiful face age and change and continue to be the most beautiful thing I'll see every single day. I want to love her with all my heart and never keep secrets from her again. I want to be able to tell her everything. All my truths and traumas and the darkness that clings to me like a symbiotic veil, morphing and changing with every action I take and every stupid decision I make.

I'll take it all on. I'll welcome the darkness and become the monster both my father and uncle hoped I would become if it means saving her from whatever torturous future her father has planned for her. I'll kill Dimitry without hesitation for taking her, for stalking her, for *hurting* her. I know he has. I know it in my gut and from the small bits of information Holland was able to gather. The mother fucker touched my girl, and I plan to rip off every fingernail, cut off every digit, and sever each hand before I'm even close to being satisfied.

Working for the mafia, he has no issues inflicting pain and inciting fear into those around them. It's time he gets a taste of his own medicine from someone far more deranged and diabolical than he's ever met before. He may think I'm weak, he may already know who I really am, but they'll know I've excommunicated myself. I'll come back for this—one final battle to end all battles. After this, even my uncle will fear me, and if he doesn't back the fuck off, I'll kill *him*, too. No one else matters but her. He's not my family and he never was. I've *chosen* my family now, a select few that I'd trust with my life.

No one fucks with what is mine, and if it means becoming my own version of a reaper, I'll gladly grip that scythe and let it careen down on my enemies without hesitation. For once, I welcome Avery's mindset and power, I'll embrace it if it means doing what I need to do without anything happening to Ronnie or anyone else. For all I know, they know about Kaine and Eden, association creating a target on their backs if they're hoping to get to me and use them as leverage against me. Sucks for them that the two are basically immortal, and they have almost two months before they're in their weakened and most vulnerable state.

I grab a breakfast bar and head out the door, not wanting to be late to Kaine and Eden's presentation. I instinctively look around, trying to spot Dimitry's vehicle in case he's still watching me, but he got what he wanted.

The drive over takes longer than I anticipated, the morning traffic moving at a fucking snail's pace. I could walk faster than the speed I'm going, but at least it gives me time to think—to plan. I need to do something *today*. With Mikail coming into the city, it doesn't leave me much time to do what I need to do in order to get Ronnie back before he whisks her away, out of my reach.

I'd still follow her. He could take her to the other side of the world, and I would still stop at nothing to get to her. My best chance of succeeding quickly is doing this while she's still within reach.

The parking structure is packed by the time I pull in, having to park on one of the upper floors and trek my way back down since the elevator is broken. A thin sheen of sweat is making my clothes cling to my skin by the time I make it into the lobby of the building, ignoring the people there asking me if I need help. I go right for the elevator, taking it up to the floor Kain told me, and finding the room easily enough from the crowd slowly piling in.

I settle myself into one of the seats closer to the front, wanting Eden and Kaine to spot me if they happen to look out into the crowd. I keep to myself, listening to the quiet murmurs and broken conversations around me.

"This should be interesting," an older man in front of me says to his colleague next to him.

"Interesting or stupid. It's one thing to research the medical aspects, but have you seen where they've taken their findings?" He shakes what looks like a pamphlet in his hand. "Hey!" He says in shock when I reach forward and pull it away from him. "What do you think you're doing?"

"Clearly you don't need it. Maybe you should keep an open mind instead of staying locked in your stagnant mentality. You might learn something today because you might not believe it, but the supernatural exists." I smirk when the lights in the auditorium flicker as though answering my call for proof on what

I claim. I lean in closer to the man, giving him my best sinister smile. "We're all doctors in some way, and the good ones aren't exactly sane."

He shies away from me, eyes widening and face going pale. Even his buddy seems like he's seen a ghost at this point, but I just lean back into my chair, exuding as much nonchalance I can muster, even though my current urges are pushing me to punch the old fuck in the face for talking shit about my friends and the hard work they put into their research. If what they claimed had no ground, they wouldn't have asked them to speak at such a gathering. Someone higher up must believe in what they've done and what they've found, and I feel a flutter of pride in my chest at calling them my friends.

The auditorium is filled to the brim, every seat taken, leaving the late few to stand against the back walls. I didn't realize how big this was going to be, and I can't help smiling when I see Eden and Kaine standing off to the side on the stage as an older man with salt and pepper hair walks towards the center. He's on the shorter side, his head barely making it over the podium. I stifle a laugh as I watch him reach up and shift the microphone down so he can actually speak into it.

He taps the stupid thing, sending a wave of squealing reverb through the entire room. "Welcome, everyone. I'm very excited to introduce you all today to Kaine Montgomery and Eden Taylor. They're known for their research on the Lazarus Syndrome and have agreed to speak today on their latest findings and theories." He turns towards them, motioning them forward.

Kaine exudes his normal cocky and confident persona, while Eden looks about ready to throw up. Her hand is gripped in his as he pulls her next to his side, the subtle tightening of his grip not going unnoticed. He does well to reassure her, her eyes drifting from the floor, up to his face. He glances down at her and gives her a small smile, guiding her up to the podium in front of her.

The poor girl looks so nervous, awkwardly setting down her notes on the stand and shuffling them around as she clears her throat. Kaine steps up and adjusts the mic to her level, leaning down into it and giving the crowd his best, shit eating grin.

"Hello, everyone. Thank you for coming. We'll be going over our original dissertation and then progressing into our latest research before opening the floor up to any questions you might have. I'd like to keep this as casual as possible but still professional, and I hope you all can keep an open mind since this goes well beyond covering just the medical aspects associated with such a rare phenomenon."

He nudges Eden, bending further down to say something into her ear. She nods her head and then stiffens, shifting back to stare at him with wide eyes. He grins when heat creeps up her cheeks and steps back from her, settling his hand on the small of her back. This shithead really knows how to rile her up. I'm sure he said something dirty to her, but at least it's shifted her attention away from nervousness. She glares at him but steps closer to the mic, clearing her throat again.

"Hello," she says in a meek voice. "I—I'm Eden Taylor."

"You got this," Kaine whispers, but the mic picks it up.

She nods again, clenching her jaw and lifting her chin with as much confidence as she can. She carefully moves the papers around and takes a deep breath. "If you're all here today, you've already read our paper on *'The cause and effect of Lazarus Syndrome'*. We've exhausted every possible medical reasoning behind the phenomenon, covering build ups of electric current that choose that moment to fire, like the final energy burst from a dying star. Those residual pulses can be known to send a last-ditch effort for survival and in cases where Lazarus has been successful, it works, but only for a short time. With that energy being used up, it makes sense that the cells can no longer regenerate that level of energy to keep the body functioning the way it's supposed to, explaining why those who have experienced Lazarus die shortly after the incident."

I'm glad she's finally feeling comfortable in speaking, falling into the natural rhythm that comes from speaking on things you're knowledgeable in. This is what she's been working towards—they both have. The audience is deathly silent as they listen to her, hanging on every word and taking notes where they find it appropriate. I'm sure some of them are taking points where they might be able to further dive into those aspects in the hopes of solving the mystery that is still so widely unknown.

"Every time we've come close to finding and speaking to someone who has experienced this phenomenon, we end up too late. We still haven't found anyone who has publicly admitted to coming back from the dead without assistance from medical intervention and has survived long enough to be questioned or studied. We've resorted to running tests on those who have experienced death before being brought back by medical means, doing brain scans and monitoring the electric pulses that run naturally through the brain. The findings will be explained in the next paper we're currently working on, which I think you'll all find quite interesting. The subjects have all had different experiences and flashes of memory from their time on the other side, but they all have one thing in common."

She takes a heavy breath, shuffling her papers together and closing the folder on them. Here we go. This is the part that they were the most concerned with talking about, and the reason so many different doctors and scientists decided to come to this conference. I don't know the full details of what they found, but I might be able to find some answers to my own questions within whatever they have to say. It would be so much easier if they were able to just talk to the reapers and get the answers straight from the source of those who control death, but they've done well to piece everything together on their own, at least, in part.

"They all experience some form of life reel and claim to be taken to a world just like ours, but...different. One patient described it as though the world around them was in reverse and everything was dark but bright at the same time. This world had something that resembled a sun, but there was no heat like you would experience from ours and that it seemed to be alive. It moved and flickered like it was its own being, something that was in a way omnipotent, following none of the usual laws we know on the mortal plane. After that, there's darkness before being thrown into a world they describe as feeling as though they were in a dream. Now, religious norms would most likely classify that as heaven; a place where they only feel happiness and peace and where their dreams become a reality. Our goal is to focus on the in-between, the world between worlds because it seems as though that landing place is the deciding factor.

"Clever girl."

I stiffen in my seat at the voice in my head, a strange pressure clawing at the wall I've attempted to put up. Of *course* he's listening in during something like this. "You're a nosy fuck, aren't you," I murmur. The men in front of me glance back, but I just glare at them.

"Call it curiosity. I wondered if the soul bound would eventually stumble upon information like this."

"Are they right?"

"They're getting close, but there are some details they won't be able to uncover. That information is only privy to those who reside in the in-between as they put it."

"What is it?"

Avery laughs, the sound making me flinch. *"Why would I tell you that? You are not one of us, but when you die, I might allow you the grace of the information because I like you."*

"Who am I going to tell? It's not like it benefits me in any way."

"No, but you would end up telling Kaine, and I don't need people digging into that world. It's not meant to be seen by mortals. It's bad enough that those who are not meant to die still happen to fall into the realm that is for souls."

"You have a city of souls. What the fuck do you do with them?"

"The divide is not just a city, but a beating heart. That's all I can tell you."

The pressure in my head recedes, telling me that Avery has decided he's done with the conversation. Stupid fuck. I hate that he can just drop in unannounced and fucking spy on me and my friends. So much for not interfering. He must be bored or something since he keeps fucking coming around and messing with me and my life.

Kaine glances my way, eyes widening and a smile spreading across his face. I smile back, giving him a small nod. He steps forward next, leaning down to the mic again, and I realize he's doing it so Eden can still speak if she needs to. "We'll open the floor up to any questions you might have now." Hands shoot up instantly and Kaine scans the room, pointing to a young woman in the from row. "Yes?"

"Some of your research has stated that those who have died shortly after their Lazarus have experienced more extreme deaths. Do you have any theories in regard to that?"

"I wouldn't say that *all* their deaths have been extreme, just ones outside of the norm. Situations where the cause of death are unlikely or a very low percentage, but yet, a Lazarus is the one to be that low percent. It could be anything from vengeful behaviour from death itself, or a right of passage for getting a second chance at life." More hands shoot up and Kaine picks another one, an older gentleman a few rows over from me. "Yes?"

"Do you have any theories as to why Lazarus occurs in the first place? If someone comes back to life without the help of outside means, what could be the supernatural reason behind that?"

"We're exploring the idea of untethered souls. A Lazarus could very well be a mistake made by death, where they aren't meant to die at that time and they're trying to correct it, putting the soul back on the path to their true death date. The thing about taking a soul that isn't meant to be reaped is that it can create a domino effect. It changes the very fabric of fate, morphing the paths of everyone around them. If someone close to you died but you find out they weren't meant to in that moment, it puts you on a new path where you might do things that weren't meant to happen, or at least, not for a while. It changes the path you were meant to be on."

I know he's speaking from experience on that one. The death of his mother put him and his father on a different path and affected me as well. I don't know if I would have become such close friends with Kaine if his mother *hadn't* died. It may have happened, but it might not have happened until we were older. Eden's path was changed as well. The death of her father forced her hand and pushed her to move here from Chicago. The trauma she went through wasn't in her original plan, but because of it, people died at her hands as well. That might have been a way to correct the error made by Luther, a sort of forced balance to make up for the fact a soul was collected outside the set death date, but it put her on a collision path to Kaine.

More and more hands go up, and more and more questions get answered. I check my watch, deciding that I've been here long enough and quietly get up, sneaking out along the side and out of the auditorium. I'll apologize to Kaine later for leaving like that, but I have more important things I need to take care of. They both did well, something I plan to tell them when I get the chance to. I'm seriously proud of both of them, accomplishing so much in such a short amount of time and gaining the respect of so many of their peers.

Me? I'm just trying to get by. I'm not a bad doctor, not even close, but I don't have the same ambitions that they do. I just want a life that I can be happy with and live fully, and that includes Ronnie. My entire future has her in it. I can't picture it any other way and I don't want to. I need to get her back. I fucking *need* to save her from whatever bullshit her father has planned for her.

My phone buzzes in my pocket the second I sit down in my truck. I frown at the display, contemplating either ignoring it or answering it and telling him off right off the get go. I sigh, answering the call and bringing it to my ear, holding back everything I want to say.

"What do you think you're doing?"

"Hello, uncle."

"Reese, tell me what the fuck you're doing. Why am I finding out from Holland that you're planning to start a war against the fucking bratva?"

"Fucking Holland. What did he tell you?"

"I hope he told me everything or we're going to have some words. Why are you using my connections for your own personal gain? You said you wanted out, yet you're still keeping one foot on my territory."

"I don't need your help. Holland is enough for what I need, uncle."

"Holland is mine. If you're using him, you're also using me, and I don't like being used without knowing about it. Why are you involved with the bratva? What could you have possibly done to piss them off to this level?"

So, Holland didn't tell him about Ronnie. I half expected him to do it anyways, but maybe my threat was enough for him to think better of it. In the end, it doesn't even matter because this could still come back on him, and uncle Declan could very well punish him for not only helping me but also keeping things from him.

"Leave Holland out of this."

"Then tell me the truth."

"Mikail Ivanov is on his way to the city. He's apparently set to marry Veronica Petrov, Misha's youngest daughter. The thing is...Veronica...is my girlfriend."

"Excuse me?"

"They took her from me. They used me to threaten her and fucking kidnapped her, Declan. I can't let them take her. She's—she's everything I have. She's all I have left that I care about."

"You're in love with the girl? If she's set to marry Mikail, that will shift power in their favour. That's a problem for us, Reese."

"I know. Please, don't interfere. I can handle this on my own without risking her safety."

"How do you plan to accomplish that without any casualties?"

"Who said anything about not having casualties? I'm planning to wipe them all from the face of this earth. I plan to make everyone who has hurt her suffer unimaginably. This isn't something I would want anyone to be involved in because I want the satisfaction of taking every single one of their lives with my own hands."

"And what happens when you end up getting killed? What then? You will have lost your life, and your girlfriend will still be captured within that world. There's nothing wrong with accepting help, Reese, especially when it's being freely given."

"Freely given?" I snort. "Nothing with you is free. If I were to accept your help, it would mean being locked down in your organization. I will get this done my own way without your help, and you can just sit back and reap the rewards being granted to you. With the bratva out of the way, you'll be able to gain more power for yourself and take over the territories that they'll lose before anyone else can come in and claim them."

"What do you want me to do, Reese?" He sighs.

"Nothing. Stay out of my way or you'll end up collateral damage. Anyone who comes near me when I'm trying to do this will end up in a shallow grave, and it doesn't matter what side they're coming from."

I hang up on him before he can say anything else. I don't *need* to hear anything else from him, and if he still doesn't listen and tries to send in a team to either help me or overrule what I'm trying to accomplish, they'll all end up dead as well.

CHAPTER FORTY-FIVE

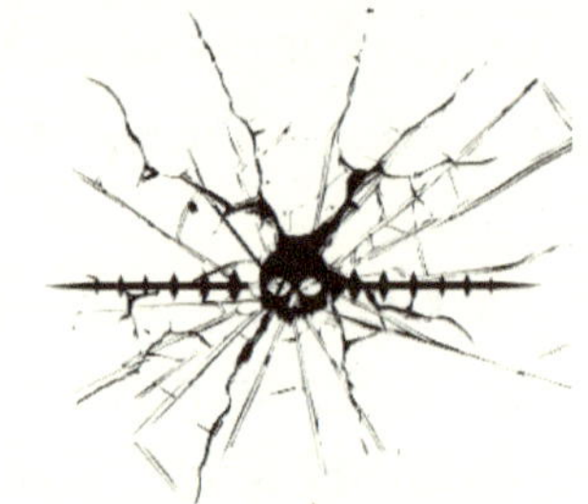

REESE

My mind is slotting away everything I need to do and everything I need to accomplish the task set before me. I watch the elevator ticking up to my apartment floor, using the monotonous droning of metal clinking on metal to try and ease my anxiety. A heavy breath escapes me when it finally opens, and my determination pushes me towards my door.

"For fuck's sake," I snarl when my phone vibrates in my pocket the second I'm in front of the door. "What?"

"Are you good? Why the fuck are you snapping at me?"

"Kaine." I drag my hand down my face and push into my apartment, heading for the hidden safe under my speaker system. "I can't really talk right now."

"You left before we could talk to you. I thought you were going to stay for the whole thing."

"I'm sorry. I have some stuff I need to do today that's really important and I needed to get out of there."

"Is everything okay?" He says quietly. "You sound off. Is there something going on?"

I don't actually see the harm in telling him since it's not like he can do anything about it or do or say anything to stop me.

"I'm about to start a war against the Russian mafia."

A long pause stretches between us, and I pull the phone away from my ear to see if the call got dropped. The time is still ticking by, showing me that he's still on the line, but he's weirdly quiet with no sound or breath from the other end.

"Why?" He says carefully.

"They took Ronnie."

"That dude that was following her..."

"So, here's the thing. I found out that Ronnie is actually a Russian mafia princess and that dude that was following her used to be her bodyguard. He kidnapped her last night and now I need to go and get her back. I'm only telling you this in case something happens to me along the way and I don't want you to think I'm ghosting you or something." I hear metal clinking on the other end of the line and frown. "What are you doing right now?"

"Nothing," he says quickly. "So, you're going after an entire mafia. Is your uncle helping you with this? Is our city about to be the center of a mafia war?"

"No. I told him I didn't want him to get involved and I threatened to kill him if he tried to get in my way."

"You're going to get yourself killed."

"Not before I get her out of there." I pull out the stash of guns tucked away and all the ammo I have in stock, snagging a couple of my favourite blades as well before locking the safe again. I make my way to the bedroom, pulling out a duffel bag from the closet before moving to my drawers. "Listen, I need to go. I'll talk to you soon, Kaine."

"Reese!"

I hang up on him, my heart tightening in my chest at the panic in his voice as he called out my name like a silent plea. I quickly get changed into a pair of black tactical pants and a black long sleeve henley. I crouch down to open the lower drawer, moving the clothes out of the way to lift up the false bottom, pulling out a few of the holsters and harnesses I have hidden there.

I strap everything to my body, grab the duffel, and make my way out of the room. One by one, I strap the various blades to my body, sliding a few of the guns into the holsters. I check over my favourite ones, popping in the mag before slipping it into the holster on my thigh. Everything else goes into the bag, including a few semi-automatics and the magazines to everything I'm armed with.

I think I'm ready, at least as ready as I'll ever be. I don't think Ronnie will be at the warehouse, but it doesn't even matter, the answers I need will be there, one way or another. I check my phone one last time, pulling up the CCTV feed. I don't know how I know, but Dimitry is there. The only thing left to pack is my laptop, so that once I'm done with the warehouse, I can move onto the next location with the means to be able to surveillance it with ease.

I sling the bag over my shoulder and head for the door, giving the apartment one last look. This has been my home for the last few years, becoming even more of a home once Ronnie moved in. It's everything I could have ever wanted, and now looking at it with the thought this might be the last time I lay eyes on it, fills my chest with crushing sadness. I want to come back here, I do, but not if I'm alone. I won't come back here if I don't have Ronnie with me. I won't go anywhere without her. I either succeed in the mission, or I end up dead, but either way, I won't live without her.

CHAPTER FORTY-SIX

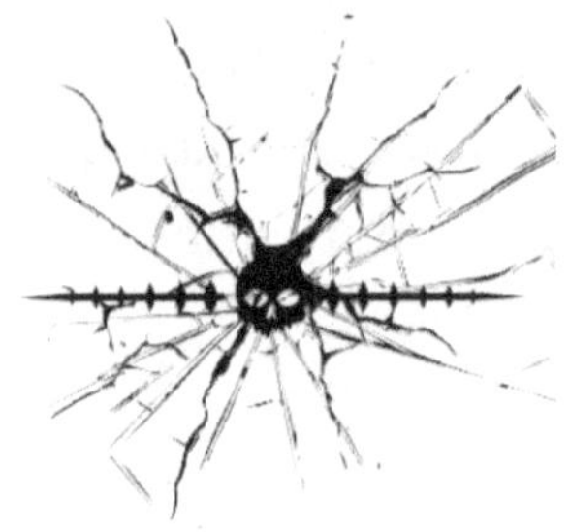

REESE

"What the fuck are you doing here?" I swear to god I'm going to punch this mother fucker. He grins at me, hiking a backpack higher on his shoulder. "What the *fuck* are you doing here, Kaine?" I can't keep the anger out of my voice, pushing past him in the lobby and out the door.

His feet slap against the ground as he jogs to catch up to me, falling into step beside me as I make my way to the truck. "I'm here to help you," he says, like it's the most obvious thing in the world. He says it like we're going on a fucking road trip instead of into a fucking war where I'm starting to doubt if I'll come out of it alive. He jerks on the passenger side door, glaring at me when it doesn’t open. “Hello?” He points to the door, pulling on the handle again.

“You’re not coming with me, Kaine. Do you have any idea how dangerous this is? This isn’t like Stephen. These are people that will fight back and are trained to kill, and they will have no hesitation in shooting you in the head. I can’t worry about them and worry about you at the same time. I need to go into this without any distractions.”

“Well, that’s fucking rude. I’m not a distraction. Plus, I can’t die, so you really don’t have to worry about me.”

“We *assume* you can’t die, Kaine. We don’t actually know when your death date is so we can’t be sure that your Lazarus won’t just stop working. How do you expect me to explain that to Eden? How do you think she’s going to take it when she finds out I let you go off to do something so stupid that you ended up getting yourself killed.”

“So, you admit that this is stupid.” That shuts me up. It *is* stupid, but it’s still my decision and my job to protect and save Ronnie. It’s not on him; never has been. “I think I should go with you, so you don’t end up getting *yourself* killed. I think you need me not just as backup, but as emotional support. Plus, someone needs to provide the epic tunes while you’re kicking ass.” He pulls out his phone, tapping the screen until music blares from the tiny speaker.

I blink. He can’t be serious. This mother fucker is actually insane. He might even be crazier than I am but in a completely different way. He has zero self-preservation and a weird attachment to me since coming here is probably one of the dumbest things he could have done. “Go home, Kaine.”

I slide into the truck, tossing my bag into the back and trying to ignore his incessant pounding on the glass. "Let me in, Reese!" Another bang. "Let me in!" I glance over, cringing when the idiot actually licks the fucking glass like a dog. "Let me in!" He says again, the words garbled because his mouth is still open on the glass, tongue half hanging out.

He starts jerking on the door handle hard enough that I think he's going to end up ripping the damn thing off. I could just drive away. I *should* just drive away. He wouldn't be able to follow me if I gunned it out of here fast enough that it wouldn't give him enough time to get to his own car and follow me. But what if he does. If he follows me, it would be far worse for him and way harder for me to protect him. I'm starting to compete with his stupidity levels because I push the unlock button, scowling at him when he hops into the truck with a happy-ass grin on his face. He's practically bouncing in his set with excitement; the backpack now nestled between his legs on the floor.

"I'm going to set some ground rules. Rule number one, whatever I say, goes. You are not to step out of line or do shit on your own. You're going to listen to what I say and you're going to fucking do it without your sassy fucking mouth getting in the way."

"What's rule number two?"

"Rule number two, you follow rule number one, or I beat you within an inch of your life."

He snaps his mouth closed, his eyes widening when he takes in my clothes and the various weapons strapped to my frame. "Are those real?"

"Why the fuck would I take fake weapons with me, Kaine?"

"Do I get a gun?"

I quirk a brow at that. "Do you know *how* to use a gun?"

He shrugs. I take the nonchalance as a no and put the truck in reverse, backing out of my spot and pulling out onto the road. I pull up the GPS on my phone, sliding it into the holder as it guides me through the city towards the warehouse.

"Where are we going?"

"To a warehouse."

"Are we almost there?"

My eye twitches. "I swear to fucking god if you start with the 'are we there yet' bullshit, I'm going to pull this truck over and throw you out of it."

"Fine," he huffs, sliding down into the seat and crossing his arms across his chest. "You're a mean dad."

"Kaine," I groan. "This isn't some fucking vacation. This is serious."

"I know it is, but I also know that when you get too far into your own head, you tend to make mistakes. You zone out and start doing things you wouldn't normally do."

"You think that joking around right now is going to help me?"

"Isn't it?" He asks, pointing to my hands. They're no longer gripping the steering wheel so tightly that my knuckles are white but loosely holding the smooth leather. "You've already calmed down in my presence. I'm your own personal brand of Valium."

I hate that he's right. Even though Kaine irritates me with his behaviour a lot of the time, he uses his fun attitude to cover up the darkness that's constantly swirling around inside of him. Another ten minutes in and his leg is bouncing erratically, his thumb in his mouth as he chews on the cuticle. I'm waiting for the inevitable 'are we there yet', but before he can say the words, I'm pulling over a few blocks away from the warehouse. I grab my laptop from the bag in the back and put in the call to Holland.

"What is it, Reese?"

"I need you to hack into the security system at the warehouse on Cassidy drive. If you need an exact location, just use my GPS to triangulate."

"You're going through with this on your own?"

"Declan doesn't have any other choice. Either he stays away or he ends up dead himself."

"Fine, I'll put the feed through to you."

It takes him a few minutes, but soon the camera footage lights up my monitor, showing me at least ten men inside and what seems like some sort of packing facility. They're either dealing in drugs or money or both, and they're definitely not expecting any company. "Thanks, Holland."

"Reese?"

"Yeah?"

"Be careful."

"Goodbye, Holland."

"Why does it sound like he's expecting you to die in there?" Kaine asks.

"Because going in there the way I am would normally get anyone else killed."

"But you're not normal, is that it?"

"Far from it." I take account of everyone in the building, clocking their locations before closing the laptop and grabbing one of the rifles from the bag.

"Do I get a gun?"

I roll my eyes and grab one of the smaller handguns, pausing when I settle back into my seat. "What the fuck is that?"

"What?"

"That," I say, pointing to the mask on his face.

"I figured we were going in disguised. You know, all incognito and shit."

"You're wearing a fucking Batman mask, Kaine. You look ridiculous."

"I'm Batman," he chirps, lowering his voice in a way that he sounds like he's choking on a frog.

"You're an idiot. Can you even see out of that thing?"

"I see...shapes."

"Fucking hell." I shove the gun towards him, watching as he struggles to tip his head down to look at it and scramble with the fucking thing in his hand. "You don't know anything about guns, do you?"

"I mean, I know a little bit."

"Video games don't count."

"Okay, I know nothing."

"Jesus, okay. The main thing is don't fucking shoot me. This right here is the safety; you need to slide this out of the way when you want to shoot someone. Make sure you're aiming and not squinting through your god damn mask. Better yet, take the stupid thing off."

"No. I like my mask."

"Fine, but I swear to god if you shoot me because you can't fucking tell who you're aiming at I'm going to murder you."

"Noted."

"Don't pull the trigger, squeeze it gently, and make sure you use both hands and don't try to be some badass shooting with one hand. You're not some gangster popping a cap in someone's ass. You have zero experience and you're going to end up smacking yourself in the head with the recoil if you do that. One hand here, the other here and lock your elbows to absorb some of the blow."

I move his hands around, curling his fingers under the butt of it to support his other hand and gently settling his finger over the trigger.

"Don't shoot unless you absolutely want to, Kaine. If you don't want to have the guilt of it eating away at you, just stay in the car."

"No, I'm doing this. You're not going in there for shits and giggles; you're going in there because of Ronnie. You didn't hesitate to help me so now it's my turn to help you."

"I don't want you doing this because you feel indebted to me in some way."

He shakes his head, lowering the gun down into his lap. "I would do anything for you, man. I don't know when you're going to realize that. Even if you hadn't helped me in the past, I would still help you right now because it's the right thing to do. I know you. I know you're doing this because you love her, and if anyone can understand what you're feeling and what you're going through, it's me."

His words settle into me heavily, words that affect me more than I care to admit. No one should care about someone who isn't their own blood to this extent. It's not naturally ingrained into us to want to sacrifice and protect another that isn't our kin, even then, some wouldn't give two shits about their blood relatives at all—me being one, other than my mother. Humans are selfish beings, driven by greed and self-preservation.

"I would do anything for you, too, Kaine. This is why I'm going to ask you again. Stay behind. Don't do this. Don't come with me."

He shakes his head, the stupid Batman mask slipping sideways and covering his eyes. I swear, that thing is going to end up getting him killed. I don't understand why he wants to wear it.

He adjusts the mask, tightening the hidden strap at the nape of his neck before locking his eyes on mine. They shine brightly through the mask, filled with determination. "We're a team. We'll always be a team, Robin."

I stare at him, deadpan. This mother fucker is trying to make *me* his sidekick? "You know Robin is the one that's always saving Batman's ass, right?"

He grins at that, nodding his head. "But they still work well together. Batman motivates Robin to be better, and Batman is the one with the cool toys." He waves his gun around, pretending to shoot at imaginary enemies.

I shake my head, turning my attention back to the warehouse. This would be easier under the cover of night, but I'm hoping for the element of surprise by doing this during the day. The sunlight doesn't stop the sudden flow of shadows undulating around the building, rising up until they form humanoid figures in the distance.

The reapers are here. I'm not sure if that's a good thing, but I'm hoping it's a sign that this is meant to happen. Hopefully none of those assholes are here for us, but for the sorry fucks that are trapped inside.

"Dude, your eyes."

"What?" I ask, pulling my gaze away from the building to look back at Kaine.

His eyes widen, his hand slowly coming up towards my face. "That's...not fucking weird at all."

I flip down the visor, popping open the mirror to stare at myself. "Fuck." I gently touch under my eyes, noticing the swirl of darkness flowing into my irises and taking over the brown hue completely, spreading until the whites of my eyes are completely gone. "I think the reapers are triggering whatever is still lying dormant inside of me."

"Reapers? What the fuck are you talking about?"

"They're here. They've sort of surrounded the building."

"You can see them?" I nod. "What do the look like?"

"The same way they looked at the cemetery. They're not in full form, more like shadow beings just standing there like fucking creepers."

"Is—is Avery here?"

"Not that I'm aware of." I don't want to tell him that Avery was listening in on Kaine and Eden's presentation. I feel like he would be pretty pissed if I brought that up, especially since he doesn't want them to know the truth about his little reaper village.

"Those guys are going to shit their pants if they see you walking in like that. You look scary as fuck, dude."

"Good. I want them to be afraid. I want them to know that I'm there to kill them and rip their heads from their bodies. Clearly, the reapers know what I'm planning and are chomping at the bit to take their pathetic souls. If they're here, this was part of their plan all along. Their deaths were written in the stars."

"I...don't feel like that's true."

"What do you mean? How else would you explain this?"

"Maybe the reapers are reacting to *you*. You're tied to Avery. He's their leader, so wouldn't that make *you* their leader now, too?"

"I don't think that's how it works, Kaine." I slip out of the truck and make my way down the street. Kaine's footsteps aren't as quiet as mine. Actually, nothing about him is quiet, the mother fucker is *humming*. I turn around suddenly, Kaine almost running right into me. "Why the fuck are you humming the song to Pink Panther right now?"

"That's the Batman song."

My eye twitches as I squint at him, trying to figure out if he's fucking with me. "No, it's not."

"Yes, it is."

I hum the Batman song for him, watching as his face slowly breaks into a smile. "You're such a good Robin, giving me a soundtrack to be a badass. I should have brought a cape."

I shove him back, making him grunt out in surprise before breaking out into quiet laughter. I shake my head and smile, hating the fact he's fucking around right now, but sort of loving it at the same time. He either doesn't understand the danger we're putting ourselves in or he really doesn't care. I feel like it's leaning more towards the latter. Kaine wouldn't care. He truly believes he won't die any time soon and would willingly take a bullet for me and suffer through another resurrection if it meant saving me or at least giving me more time.

He looks like an absolute idiot, slinking down the street dressed in all black with a cheap-ass Batman masked strapped to his face, but he's my idiot. He's holding the gun just like I showed him, keeping it down at his side and moving along with his body in a slight crouch. He's moving like he's done this before, but maybe his stupid adventures included shit like paintballing or something. I could train him up to be better at this, even if it isn't a life I want him to live, but knowing how to defend yourself is really important, especially when being thrown into random situations like this one.

CHAPTER FORTY-SEVEN

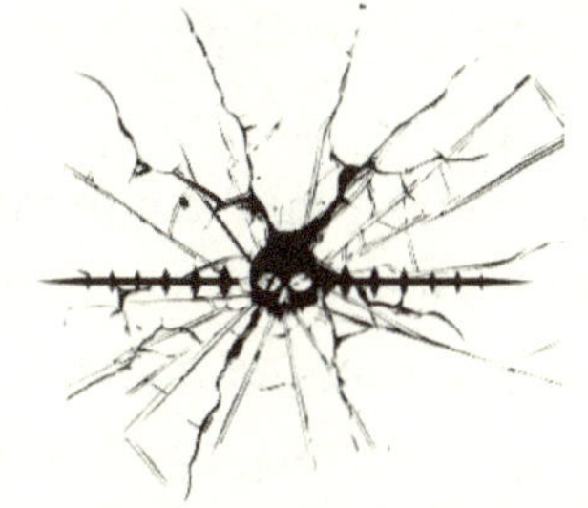

REESE

"Fucking hell. Why is it so cold all of a sudden?"

I palm his chest, pushing him back into the wall while I glance around the corner of the building. I picked my way through the reapers, some of them turning their void heads towards me as I passed, while Kaine—none the wiser—walked right through a few of them. I should have been more mindful of it, not really thinking anything about it until his teeth started chattering and his body shook with small tremors.

I turn to face him, rubbing my hands up and down his arms to bring more heat back into his body. "Sorry, man. I didn't think it would affect you that badly, but you walked through a few of the reapers on our way over here."

"Fuck," he murmurs, teeth still chattering. I wrap my arms around him, pulling him into my chest and willing my own body heat into him. After a few moments, his body relaxes against mine and he lets out a little sigh. "Thanks."

"Of course." I slowly back away from him, his eyes on the ground between us. I adjust his mask, tapping him under the chin so he'll look at me. "Last chance. If you want to back out, now is the time, Kaine."

He shakes his head, readjusting the gun in his hand. "Let's go."

I should have been honest with him. I think he's under the impression that Ronnie is in there and we're on a mission to save her. The thought that he would back out of this because of that fact has me pausing once more. "This isn't a rescue, Kaine. I know Ronnie isn't here, but at least one of the guys in there knows where she is."

"It doesn't matter. Whatever you need to do, I'll do it with you."

I cup the back of his head and press my forehead against his, pulling in a rattling breath. I really want to make it out of this, and because of the fact he's here with me, I know I *need* to make it out alive. "You're the brother I wish I had," I murmur quietly. "I want you to know how much I care about you. I fucking love you, Kaine."

"Stop talking like you're going to die."

"I'm sorry."

I pull away from him again, turning, but he stops me with his hand on my arm. "I love you, too, Reese."

My heart swells in my chest and tears burn the back of my throat. It's an emotion we've felt towards each other since we were younger, but I don't think we've actually ever spoken the words. Why is it that people always wait until dire moments to say how they truly feel about someone. We should have said it long ago. I should have made it completely clear to him that he's been my anchor since my mom died. I was there for him when he needed someone to lean on, and he was there for me at every turn as well.

As much as I want to go in there like a fucking bomb, I need to protect Kaine. This was the biggest reason I didn't want him coming with me, but his presence is making me think about my actions more. Him being here is pushing me to not be reckless.

I pull the gun from my holster, reaching into one of the pockets on my pants and screwing the silencer onto the tip. A few of the reapers phase through the wall ahead of me, three of them to be exact. Is that a sign that the guards have shifted closer to this wall? I don't question it, letting my instincts take over. "Stay behind me. There should be three guards just on the other side of this door to the left."

"You got all that from the video stream?"

"No. The reapers have gone in."

"What the fuck."

I try to be as quiet as possible as I open the door, a weird snap sounding. Did I just break the lock? I barely put any effort behind it, but the cheap steal broke away like it was made of paper. Thankfully, the noise wasn't enough to draw the guards' attention, and I sneak inside with Kaine close on my heels.

I spot them right away, the shimmer of shadows hovering behind each one and drawing my attention to them. Two more reapers phase through the wall, smoking past me further into the warehouse.

Pop.

Down goes the first one, my hand snapping out to catch him as his body gravitates to the ground, blood and brain matter oozing out of his skull. Kaine pulls in a sharp breath behind me, finally realizing what I've done. The flicker of soul catches my eye, slowly being pulled to the reaper standing guard a foot away from the body.

I move forward quietly, noticing the two standing closer together, speaking to one another. I stop and lean towards Kaine to whisper in his ear. "I need to take out both of them at once, but I don't want their bodies dropping to the ground and making noise which would possibly draw the others' attention."

"You want me to catch a dead body?"

"Aren't you batman?" His chest puffs out at that, and I fight back a smile, hoping he doesn't hesitate as I raise the gun, aiming at one, and then the other.

Pop. Pop.

Kaine and I both rush forward, his grunt of surprise making me realize too late that he ended up with the bigger of the two, and dead weight is a lot more surprising than you realize. He starts to go down with him, his back smacking against the wall while he tries to hold the big fuck up under his arms. Their souls get sucked out as well, disappearing into the shadowy forms before the reapers slip out through the wall.

I roll my eyes, setting down my own body before going back over to him and helping him place him down. "You need to start working out again. You've gotten lazy since you and Eden got together."

"I wish I could tell you to fuck off," he pants. "But I think you're right."

I tap his gut playfully. "Is that six pack turning into a keg?"

He lifts his shirt, showing me his slowly fading six pack. "I mean, it's not quite a keg yet, but making Eden eat has made me eat a lot more than I usually do. I'm not complaining, though."

I shake my head, knowing what he means by all of that. Eden still struggles with food and her eating disorder, but he's done well to break through that behemoth wall she's put around herself.

I motion for him to follow me down a small corridor, where flickers of shadow signal me towards them. Two more guards come into view, their reapers hovering behind them. This seems like such a harder task with Kaine trailing behind me. To be fair, if Kaine hadn't been here, I would have struggled with those last two. It would have been doable, but a pain in the ass.

My rage boils to the surface as my steps quicken, my hand moving quickly to switch out the gun for one of my blades instead. I need to feel something more than the quick deaths I'm handing out, and I still haven't seen Dimitry. Three down, another seven to go. Between the camera feed and the reaper count, I know that there's only ten people currently in this building. Only five have come inside so far, so the other five humans must be further inside the warehouse and not close enough for death to be imminent.

The one closest to me turns and I rush behind him, covering his mouth and jamming the blade down between his clavicle, piercing his upper lung. His body jerks then goes still and limp in my hold. Still a quick death but the ooze of blood satiates a bit of my murderous hunger.

"That was so fucking badass," Kaine whispers behind me.

I set the body down on the ground and glance up at him. The fucker is actually grinning, like what I just did wasn't the most deranged thing he's experienced recently. His head jerks up before he lifts the gun in both hands and fires. I flinch, ducking at the sudden blast of the bullet flying past me. A grunt and a thud echoes behind the shot being fired, and I turn slowly to see one of the other guards now dead behind me, a bullet hole right between his eyes. The reaper latched to him stares at Kaine, phantom head tipping in question.

Heavy footsteps sound and the other guard rounds the corner, pointing his gun at Kaine. I lurch to my feet, flipping the blade in my hand and launching it towards him. It whistles through the air, hitting its target with a bone crunching thunk. The guard stares at the blade protruding from his chest, blood oozing from the wound and from the corner of his mouth before his wide eyes look back up and lock on mine. His mouth moves, but only whispered breaths come out. He crumples to the ground the next second, unmoving.

I know I should feel some ounce of guilt in killing these men. I know nothing about them, no history into their lives and who they are as people. I don't know if they're leaving anyone behind with nothing but their memories. They could be like me, being pulled into this life without a choice, but the difference between me and them is I'm better trained.

I can't let the thought of them being innocent victims of the mafia system taint my actions. I came here with one goal, and I can't save Ronnie if I don't follow through. Letting any of them go could risk everything. They could go back to Misha and warn him of what's coming, and that would end up destroying any chance of me getting to him before he sells Ronnie off.

Five more bodies need to be taken care of, but my main goal is the last one. I know he's protected, using the lesser grunts as a barrier to anything or anyone reaching him. He's not just a bodyguard either. From the information Holland gathered, the fucker is the son of Misha's best friend and the eldest cousin to Mikail Ivanov. It's all connected. Misha has done well to weave himself into every Russian family possible and secure his place on the food chain.

I know that the sound of Kaine's gunshot will warn them that something is wrong, but I can't think about that right now. I didn't expect to be able to take them all out quietly, but I'm glad at least half of them are down.

I rush towards Kaine, taking in his frozen form. "Are you okay?" I ask, gripping into his arms and giving him a shake when he doesn't respond. "Kaine, are you okay?"

"Ye—yeah," he chokes out. "I—I shot him."

"You did. You saved me by doing that." He tips his head up to look at me, his green eyes wide behind the mask. "You did good. You shot that gun for the first time without hesitation, and you hit your mark. You should be proud of yourself."

"I shot him," he says again.

Fuck, is he going into shock? I pull the mask off his head, taking in his ashen face. Some of his hair is sticking to his forehead, damp with sweat, and his lips are parted as small puffs of breath slip through. "Focus, Kaine. You knew what would happen when you came here with me."

"I didn't think I would actually shoot anyone. I thought I would just get to see you taking everyone out."

"Kaine." He blinks, ripping his gaze away from the man he killed lying behind me and focusing in on me again. "I'm glad you're here." I brush his hair back and his eyes flutter closed on a heavy breath. "Just a few more and then we can go home, okay?"

"Okay," he whispers.

Footsteps sound in the distance, no doubt drawn to the sound of the gun going off. We don't have time to stand here, so I tuck the mask back onto his head and walk towards the dead guards, ripping my blade out from the one guy's chest. I don't need to check behind me to know that Kaine is following me, I can hear his footsteps keeping up with every one of mine.

They all come at us as once, the last four guards rushing towards us and sending our movements into chaos. Kaine shoots at one, clipping him in the shoulder this time and stalling him but not taking him down. I rush forward, grabbing my gun off my hip at the same moment I slam the blade under another one's jaw. His mouth gapes open, showing the blade running through his mouth and piercing his tongue. I use his body as a shield, shooting the one behind him. Two to the chest, one to the head. He falls and I rip the blade out, shoving that dead body into the one Kaine clipped.

Kaine's gun goes off again, hitting the next one in the kneecap of all places and forcing him to slam into the ground with a cry of pain. The one with the shoulder wound looks up at me, eyes wide in panic. "Please," he whispers. *Pop*. I have no time for begging and no time for mercy.

I step over him, hovering above the one with the leg wound. He grips at the bleeding limb, trying to scramble away from me while trying to grab the gun he dropped a few feet away. I press into his knee with my foot, his blood-curdling scream vibrating off the walls as he writhes and claws at my foot.

"Where is he?" I snarl.

"Fuck you!" I press down harder, blood spilling from the open hole. Bone snaps and he gasps, eyes wide and face turning death pale. "No! Get off!" He wails, tears springing to his eyes as blood and spittle foam at the corner of his mouth.

I press down further until I feel the bone complete crush beneath my boot. "Where. Is. He?"

"Wh—who?"

"Dimitry. Tell me where he is and I'll show you mercy."

"He's in—in the pit. In the office."

"Was that so hard?"

"No. Wait—"

His body hits the floor, eyes blank and unseeing and turning red as the blood from the bullet wound in his forehead trickles into them. "You said you would show him mercy," Kaine whispers behind me.

"I did. I gave him a quick death instead of dragging it out and torturing him further. He wouldn't have lasted long anyways. The way his femur snapped clipped his femoral artery." I point to the pool of blood around him. I noticed it right away, how the slow dribble from the gunshot wound quickly turned into a flood of red the moment I crushed his leg.

"Reese, are you okay?"

I glance at him over my shoulder, watching him as he carefully walks towards me. "Why wouldn't I be?"

"I mean...mentally."

A dark bark of a laugh bubbles up my throat as I turn away from him, tipping my head back to look up at the ceiling. I get lost in the rusted metal beams crisscrossing above me, mulling over his question. "I've never been okay, Kaine," I finally say. "You've kept me grounded all these years, but I never changed. What I am was just buried deep inside me, and now—to do what I need to—that monster needs to be let out."

He pats me on the back and grips my shoulder, drawing my attention back to him. "Just don't lose sight of the you you've become."

CHAPTER FORTY-EIGHT

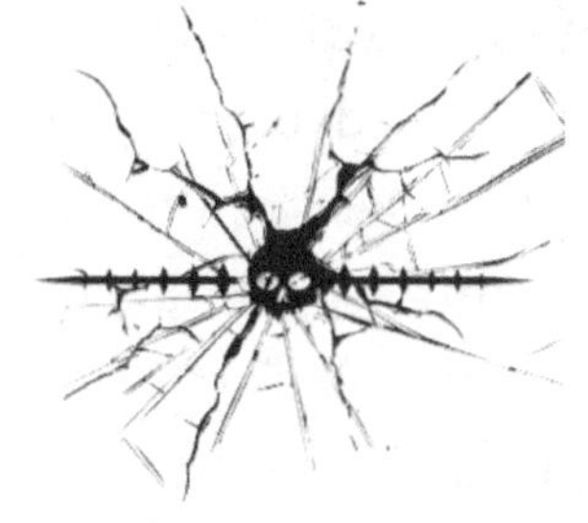

REESE

We walk out into the open and I spot the so-called pit right away. Dimitry doesn't seem bothered in the slightest, standing at the window in his office with his hands casually tucked into the pockets of his trousers and a smirk on his face. I step in front of Kaine, but he moves around me, pointing the gun towards him. I slide my knife back into my holsters and pull my second gun, gripping into it when Dimitry's smile widens.

His reaper is here, but he's hanging off to the side—hesitating. He stands watch farther away than any of the others, his shadowy gaze drifting from Kaine, up to the window. A strange hollowness settles into my chest, the feeling of doubt creeping into my senses.

Kaine fires first, bullet after bullet slamming into the glass, but barely making a mark on it. Of course, this fucker would be behind bulletproof glass. His gun clicks, signaling the empty magazine. I keep my eyes locked on Dimitry while I shift both guns into one hand and reach into one of my pockets to grab him another loaded magazine.

"I don't know what to do with that."

Fuck, I didn't think I needed to show him how to use it because I didn't actually expect him to be firing a single bullet, let alone emptying an entire magazine. I hand him my other gun instead, turning my attention back to Dimitry. He leans forward, reaching for something, and the squeal of a speaker system has me flinching.

"What do you expect to accomplish in coming here? She's not here you know."

I stand up taller, my hold on my own gun tightening further. "Who says I came here for her? I never expected to find her here, Dimitry Sokolov, but I did expect to find *you* here."

His brow lifts at that, a sinister grin spreading across his face. "And what does a nobody like you want with me?"

"You took her from me!" I roar, stepping towards the room, slightly elevated above me. "I know what you've done to that girl."

"Do you now? What is that exactly?"

Anger coils in the pit of my stomach, the words burning like bile up my throat. "You touched her. She was a child and you fucking touched her."

"Wait. What?" Kaine hisses behind me, tugging at the back of my shirt. "Reese—"

I brush him off, stepping further in front of him and blocking him from Dimitry's view. This is all about Ronnie. It's not just a rescue mission for me but revenge for her. Hearing about what he did to her and how her father didn't do a single thing about it, turned my throat into ash. I couldn't breathe. I couldn't understand how someone could just be okay with his daughter being sexually abused and assaulted. It's like he believed he had a claim to her because of who his father was to Misha, and that doesn't sit well with me. Dimitry is just a steppingstone to the bigger picture. The fact Misha still allowed him anywhere near his daughter and actually assigned him to be her bodyguard is just the poisonous icing on the cake.

"Hmm, you would have done the same thing if you were in my shoes. She was such a lovely thing—still is. Watching her bleed and cry while I made her come for the first time is a memory I won't soon forget."

All I see is red. My ears ring and vibrate with the blood pulsing through my veins. I take off towards him, firing bullet after bullet against the glass while I try to make my way towards the door. Kaine's scream sounds distant and garbled, my focus only on the piece of shit in front of me.

Out of the corner of my eye, I notice the reaper shift, not towards Dimitry, but towards Kaine. Panic hits me then, the scene in front of me coming into focus as Dimitry holds up a switch in his hand. He flicks it, red light gleaming before his thumb comes down on the button.

No.

I spin, my focus shifting to Kaine. I need to get to Kaine. Fuck, the reaper is getting closer. He should have more time. He has

Lazarus so he can't fucking die here. Blinding light flares in front of me and then I'm blown back, thrown into the wall while steal and debris rains down around me. My body feels like lead, my eyes unfocused and burning from the heat of the flames spreading around me.

"Kaine?" I croak out, trying to see through the chaos. A body. I see his body and the reaper standing right next to it. "Kaine!" I scream when I see his batman mask lying on the floor, cracked and covered in blood. This can't be happening. This can't be it for him. The reaper turns to look at me, and I swear I feel pity coming from the fucker.

A door creaks to my left, pulling my attention for a fraction of a second. Dimitry walks through it without a care in the world and completely unharmed. He looks at me with that stupid grin while I struggle to get my bearings, my arms shaking under me as I try to lift myself up. This is my fault. Kaine would never have been here if I had just put my foot down and drove away without him.

"No!" I scream, my voice hoarse and broken as Dimitry walks towards him, pulling a gun from the holster on his chest. "Not, Kaine. Please, not Kaine. It's not his time."

"It isn't for you to decide," Avery whispers in my head.

"You asshole. He has Lazarus. You told him he had time."

"I didn't tell him how much time, and your actions are shifting fate."

"He's getting married. He's—he's, my brother."

"Brother in trauma, not in blood."

"It doesn't matter!" I scream, no longer caring if I speak to him in my head or out loud. "It doesn't fucking matter." I stumble to my feet, hand slamming into the wall to balance myself. Everything hurts. Blood trickles down my face and I swear my other arm is either broken or dislocated. "You won't take him!"

Dimitry turns back to look at me, but my eyes are burning into the reaper still hovering next to Kaine. Kaine twitches and groans, the relief I feel quickly being snuffed out when Dimitry points the gun at him.

"What will you do, Reese?"

"You seem attached to the weirdo. What kind of idiot comes in here dressed like batman? Is he a fucking child? I think I should put him out of his misery," Dimitry cackles, cocking the gun.

I stumble forward, trying to reach them—to reach *him*—but my feet don't want to work. My knees slam into the ground, sharp pain shooting through my hands from landing on the debris.

"You won't take him," I grit out, body vibrating with rage.

"Reese."

"You won't fucking take him."

"What are you going to do about it?" Dimitry snorts. "You're already on your way to an early grave as well. You came in here thinking you could outsmart me, but I've been watching you. Did you really think you were the only one running surveillance? I knew you were coming the moment you left your apartment."

My eyes lock on Dimitry's and his grin fades as panic starts to take over his features. "A life for a life," I whisper, dropping the walls around my mind and allowing the darkness in. It writhes at the sudden space, now trying to flee as I reach out my mental hooks and slam into it, dragging it to the surface.

"Reese!" Avery screams, but it's too late now. He no longer has control, but honestly, I don't think he ever did. I pull and pull until I'm completely consumed by it. Lightning skitters through my veins, heating my blood so viciously that I can't help but scream out in agony.

Shadows ripple out of me, rushing across the ground in a tidal wave of black and slamming into Dimitry like a solid wall. They slither around him as he struggles to stay on his feet, weaving their way around his entire body.

The reaper's shadows shudder and he takes a step back from Kaine. "Back the fuck away," I snarl, slowly lifting myself to my feet. The pain I was feeling before burns away as everything around me shimmers and my vision takes on a hazy hue of blue and green.

"Damn it, Reese."

"Fuck off, Avery. You're no longer needed here."

I slam the wall down on his voice, snuffing out the nagging existence that has been poking and prodding at me for the last few months. This is *his* fault. If he had left me alone when I asked, I wouldn't be using him in this way. Whatever link we have to each other is now under my control, even if it's temporary. I don't care. I would love to lose all connection to him after this as long as I get my revenge and I get to save Kaine.

Dimitry struggles in the bindings as I walk towards him, mouth gaped open in horror. I spare a glance at Kaine when he coughs and lifts himself to his hands and knees. The reaper tries to surge forward towards him, but I throw my hand up, stopping it in its tracks. It claws at the invisible grip I have around it's throat, its form shifting and morphing until a young woman with dark hair and sharp features comes into focus.

"You have no power here!" She snarls.

"Don't I? Your leader is squatting inside me. I think it's time he pays rent." I squeeze my hand until she's gasping and wheezing, her electric blue eyes bulging at the pressure. "Who said you could collect him? He's Lazarus."

"I—" Her eyes dart a few inches past me, then snap back to me, her pale face turning ashen. "I didn't...know."

"You're going to take him," I say coldly, jerking my chin towards Dimitry. "When I'm done with him." I release her, watching as her knees slam into the ground, sputtering shadows scattering around her like she can't fully hold her form. I turn back towards Dimitry, feeling the shadows around him like an extension of myself. I turn my hand palm up, watching as Dimitry's body spins to face me. "Where is she?"

"Fuck you, you freak."

I close my hand slightly, watching the black tendrils tighten around him. Something snaps and he lets out a cry of pain. "Where the fuck is she?"

"You're too late," he laughs. "She's no longer yours. She was *never* yours, and I had her first," he spits out.

I'm in front of him in an instant; my hand gripped around his throat in a punishing hold. His breath wheezes out of him, eyes bulging while the shadows slither up my arm to claw at his jaw, prying his mouth open. They slide up his cheeks, digging into his eyeballs until they start to lift from the sockets.

"No! Nooo!" His screams are muffled from his mouth being pried open. He's trying his hardest to writhe and break free from the prison I've created for him. They rip out with a sicken squelch, dangling down his cheeks by the optic nerve.

"Reese?" Kaine croaks behind me. "What—what happened?"

"Stay there. Don't fucking move."

I don't need him stumbling around disoriented from a resurrection and getting himself hurt on the debris or falling into the flames that are still spreading around us. I need to finish this and get us the fuck out of here before we both end up crushed by the building coming down on us. This psychopath had the nerve to set off a bomb within the building with himself inside, not knowing the extent of the damage.

"I'll ask again. Where is she?"

He doesn't respond, too focused on the pain I've already inflicted on him. The poor bastard can't even cry, but rivulets of blood cascade down his cheeks, merging with the shadows clinging to his skin. They shudder as though excited, lapping and swirling against the red liquid.

A whimper chokes out of his throat when I tighten my hand around his neck further, the shadows responding to my growing agitation and crushing his body until I hear more snapping bones.

"Where is she."

"Ho—home." The words are gurgled, getting caught on the mix of saliva and blood pooling in his mouth as the claw-like shadows continue to pry his jaw open.

"Look at that. You finally did something good in your life."

His jaws snap, dangling from thin strands of skin and sinew, revealing every tooth and his vicious tongue that had no hesitation in spewing filth and degradation about my girl. It's not enough. I'm not satisfied enough with his death.

"S—Sir." The female's voice is quiet behind me, hesitant, if not a bit nervous.

"I said when I'm done with him." I glance back at her, pinning her with an icy glare. "Do I look like I'm done?"

"Who the fuck are you talking to?" Kaine asks, looking around in confusion. He points to himself and blinks. "Are you talking to me?"

"No. I'm talking to the reaper bitch who tried to take your fucking soul."

"I didn't know," she chokes out.

"Are you new? Looks like I need to have a little chat with Avery, so he gets a better handle on his reapers again. This is unacceptable."

"N—no! You don't need to contact him. Please don't contact him! I don't want to go to the pits!"

"You're lucky I don't try to send you there myself. Can reapers die?"

She swallows hard, dropping her eyes to the ground. "In a way, yes. We're reintroduced into the cycle of the Divide."

I stiffen, the scratching sensation at my mind letting me know that Avery is trying to push through. I don't have a lot of time, and I can't afford for him to take over my body right now in his attempt to end this girl. I know she's said too much, his anger flooding through me like a hot wave. The Divide. The world between worlds that Eden and Kaine have come so close to understanding.

"Reese? You're Reese, right?" Kaine asks quietly, taking a cautious step towards me.

"It's me," I whisper, hating the state of his body.

If he didn't have Lazarus, he would be dead right now. If I hadn't stopped that reaper from claiming him, he would no longer be here with me, and Eden would follow soon after. I don't understand it because I thought he had more time than this. There's no way this is his last life. There's blood all over his face and clothes, dirt and debris clinging to every particle of clothing.

"Just...stay there, Kaine."

I've bought him a bit more time by trading Dimitry's life for his, but I need to fix this. I would have failed in the worst way today if it weren't for the fact I'm tied to a reaper. I've never been so thankful in my life for being possessed by an otherworldly being that could kill me at a moment's notice without hesitation, but I'm sure he's regretting that fact right now.

The flow of power is addictive, where one hit of it isn't enough. I'm enamored with the way the shadows bend to my will, submitting and responding with a single thought. This power is dangerous; something someone like me shouldn't wield.

Those shadows flex and bend now, snapping every bone within his body, echoing and merging with the roaring flames around us. The heat of them doesn't even phase me, my eyes glued to the body in front of me, breaking and bending into a mutilated husk. It's still not enough. He didn't suffer enough; didn't feel enough pain, but it's too late now.

"What's your name?" I mutter, allowing the shadows to recede and drop Dimitry's body to the floor.

"Anna," she whispers. "My name is Annabeth."

"You may claim your soul as well as a warning to take back to your reaper hoard. You are never to reap Kaine, Eden, Ronnie, or myself."

"That's not possible," she says quickly.

"I decide when I'm ready to die. Not you, not fate, and not fucking Avery. You will not touch me or those I love, or I will end you where you stand. You know very well that I'm tapping into Avery's power; I know you can feel it. With knowing that, you know what I'm capable of, and as you can see, I have no issues with killing people. I'll keep your little soul reserve full, but with souls of my choosing." I turn to look at her, not even attempting to hold back the pressure of power trying to uncoil out of me. "Do you understand me?"

"I—" Her eyes dart around, wide and panicked. For having such harsh features, her personality reminds me of a doe being cornered against a cliff's edge. I sort of feel bad—just a little bit—but not enough to ease up on her.

"Do you understand me?" I snarl, letting the shadows pulse and coil around my feet.

"Yes," she says quickly. "Yes, I understand."

"Good. Now do your job and get out of here." She lurches to her feet, running past me to deal with Dimitry's tainted soul while I deal with Kaine. He doesn't look fearful exactly, but he can't quite meet my eyes, looking everywhere but at me. "Kaine?" He freezes his fidgeting and shoves his hands into his pocket, swallowing hard. "Are you okay?"

That finally gets his attention, and he slowly shifts his gaze to meet mine. It hits me then. I almost lost this. If I didn't do what I did today, I would have never seen those green eyes staring back at me ever again. I step towards him, wrapping my arms around him in a tight embrace, fighting back the tears threatening to bubble over at knowing I wouldn't have been able to hold him like this ever again.

"I thought I lost you," I murmur, my words spilling out of me without meaning to.

He grips into the back of my shirt and pulls in a rattling breath. "I'm on my last life, aren't I?"

I pull back from him, and he quickly wipes at his eyes, the gravity of today's events finally hitting him. I pick up his broken mask and press it against his chest, where he carefully takes it from me. Gripping his face in my hands, I force his eyes on me, pouring as much conviction into my words as I can. "I won't let it be. I won't let them take you from me."

He tries to shake his head, but I stop him, curling my fingers into his jaw. "I—I should have been more careful. Eden...Eden is going to hate me."

"She's not. I'm going to fix this, Kaine. You're going to get married and you're going to live a long and happy life." He flinches when sections on the ceiling come crashing down in one of the corners. His breathing is harsh and those tears keep streaming down his cheeks. All his life he's wondered if he would die and has been living recklessly because he can't. Now, it's caught up to him, and I can see the regret on his face.

"There's nothing you can do," he whispers.

"I already did. Avery won't touch you."

"You can't control a reaper, Reese."

"I might not be able to control him, but I'm able to access his power. If he wants a war, I'll give him a fucking war." Another section of ceiling falls and I pull him into me, pressing my lips to his bloodied forehead. "Let's go."

I keep him tucked against me, weaving our way through the slowly crumbling building while he stumbles along beside me, clinging to his mask. This isn't the Kaine I know. The Kaine I know is cocky and funny and filled with life. This version of him reminds me of the version I first met when his mother killed herself. This is the version he was when he was killed by her over and over, made to believe that he was a monster. I can't let him fall back into that mindset after he's worked so hard to drag himself up from the grave of his past. Eden would never forgive me if I let him fall.

This is my fault.

All of it.

Every single thing that has happened over the last week is because of me. No, not just the last week, since the beginning. All my own lies are catching up to me, including hiding the fact Avery has been haunting me. If I had been honest with Ronnie about who I am, she might have been confident enough to tell me about who she is as well. It would have been so much easier to protect ourselves if this situation had come to happen, but it might not have ever happened because if we hadn't fought, she wouldn't have felt the need to run back to her father in her moment of weakness.

Kaine is quiet as we exit the building, but he still clings to the edge of my shirt like a child. I fucking broke him. I should have pushed him harder to stay behind and gone in there alone. I never wanted this, and I don't know how to fix it—fix *him*. He doesn't argue with me or fight me as I help him into the passenger seat of the truck and buckle him in, his eyes staring off into the distance.

What could he be thinking about right now? I close the door on him, hating the way he seems almost catatonic now, clinging to that stupid mask. It's not stupid. He wanted to be a hero. He wanted to help me and help Ronnie, even if that meant shattering his own soul in the process. I fucking broke him, but I'll use the pieces of myself to mend him if that's what it takes.

CHAPTER FORTY-NINE

RONNIE

My childhood home is a prison. It's always been that way, but now it's definitely worse than before. I'm still locked in my room with meals being brought to me throughout the day. My father hasn't called for me since this morning, and thankfully, I haven't seen Dimitry either. The last thing I want is that fucker anywhere near me, and I hate that papa still trusts him after everything he's done to me.

I'm surprised the asshole didn't ask for me himself. He still has ties to the same family as Mikail, though his side of the family isn't as notorious. I hate all of them. Every single member of the bratva is a piece of shit and I hate that I was born into this family.

I miss my mom and the comfort she gave me growing up. She would have never allowed Dimitry to come near me to begin with, but she died too soon, leaving me at the hands of corruption, privilege, and heavy hands. If she were still alive now, she would castrate Dimitry and send his shriveled balls to his father just because she could. Sloane Halladay was a light in the darkness and a collar for the vicious Misha Petrov. He was calmer with her around, allowing her to have her say and giving into some of her request, mainly when it came to me.

Losing her was not only like losing a piece of myself but losing all hope for a better future. I should have stayed away. I should have kept under the radar and avoided this family for the rest of my life, but I didn't, and now I need to live with the consequences.

I wouldn't be in this situation if I never told Reese how I felt about him and then freaked out when he didn't feel the same way. This would have never happened if I had trusted Eden right from the beginning and went to her when it happened instead of running home.

Now I've lost everything; my freedom, my life...Reese. That one hurts the most. I would give everything up if it meant I could have him, but to keep him safe, I need to stay away from him and follow the path my father has set before me.

It's only been a day, but I already miss him so much. I wish I had my phone so I could at least scroll through the picture I have of him, but they won't even grant me that one small thing. Work won't even try to check in on me because I took a few days off to spend time with Reese while he grieved the loss of his patient, but it wasn't just about that. I wanted to be there for him through everything. I want to be there for him more now because of everything he told me. I can't imagine what he's feeling or what he's going through when being burdened by the haunting of a supernatural being like that.

All this time I've been friends with people that aren't fully human and I didn't know it. It makes me wonder what else is out there and if I've ever come in contact with any of them. It opens up an entirely different world, one where creatures that go bump in the night exist. Have the others met anything like that? Vampires, demons, witches, and whatever else might be real and hiding among us. Supernatural beings that could whisk us away or completely destroy us if they chose to.

I'm so fucking bored. They could have at least brought me a television or something instead of leaving me with the few measly books I collected as a kid. I get it, I haven't lived here in a long time, but the fact no one thought of providing me with a means of entertainment when they've clearly been planning my return for a little while now.

I flop back on my bed and stare at the ceiling, wondering what Reese is doing at this moment. Every time I close my eyes, all I see is his face and the way I shattered his heart. "I didn't mean it, Reese," I whisper, wishing the wind would carry my words to him. I curl onto my side, hugging one of my stuffed animals to my chest. "I didn't mean it."

The tears burning in the back of my throat break through, flowing freely down my cheeks and soaking the pillow beneath my head. I want to go home. I want to feel Reese's arms wrapped around me while he tells me it'll be okay. It's almost like I can hear him whispering the words in my ear, his warm breath caressing my skin. I close my eyes, ignoring the sound of the door opening and someone walking inside.

"Milaya." My body stiffens. "Get up and get dressed. We have guests arriving shortly for dinner and I need you presentable."

He doesn't wait around to hear any form of argument or response, he knows I won't give him one. He's trapped me—forced me to submit to his will because if I don't comply, he'll go after Reese again. He has no reason not to, in general, what with him being the nephew of a rival mafia family, but he's using his false mercy as a bargaining chip to manipulate my compliance. I have no choice but to listen to him and hope he holds his end of the deal. It's the least I can do for the man I fell in love with, and whose heart I ended up breaking.

I roll out of bed, dragging my feet towards the closet. "Of course." They had no issues providing me with some form of wardrobe, but heaven forbid I get anything to make my pitiful stay here any better. It's all about control, it always has been, and it won't ever change. I wish it were different, but that's just who my father is. He always needs to be the most powerful man in the room no matter who's in attendance, and the only way he knows how to accomplish that is by making everyone else feel small and useless.

He'll break me. It's his goal after all, a daughter that finally does what he asks without question. Tessa truly escaped, finding her own path in life and sticking to it no matter how hard things got for her. She never once felt the need or urge to reach out to the family to get her out of anything, or to try and find any form of familial comfort. I tried to call her that day, too, but she pushed the call to voicemail, only choosing to speak to me when it fits into her schedule.

I can't exactly blame her for that. Sure, we've gotten close again, both of us trying our hardest to pave our own paths because we learned the hard way that we can't trust anyone except ourselves. I thought I had grown from that mentality myself, learning to let people in and learning to trust others, but I never truly let that wall down around myself. If I had, Reese would know about me. I'll admit that I was scared—still am. Scared that he wouldn't like who I am and would turn away from me. I never gave him that chance though, and now, it's too late.

I slip on one of the plain black dresses hanging in the closet and move to my vanity to try and bring some semblance of life back into my face. My hair is messy, tangled, and dull, like my soul. A bitter laugh bubbles up my throat at that thought. The mask has fallen. All my attempts at hiding what was lurking inside of me has sprung to the surface, visible for everyone to see. There is no light, no hope, and no love in my future.

CHAPTER FIFTY

RONNIE

It's like I'm in a daze as I follow the guard that let me out of my room, my steps slow, eyes unfocused. He motions me into the dining room and I freeze.

What the fuck is she doing here?

Tessa's eyes meet mine, a forced smile pulling at her lips. "Ronnie," she says, giving me a curt nod. I recognize the man next to her because of the pictures she's sent me, but now seeing him up close, he seems a bit more familiar.

"Have a seat, milaya," papa says, motioning to the seat on his other side, between him and a man I've never met before. He turns, brown eyes so dark they seem void-like meeting my own. "This is your betrothed, Mikail Ivanov."

I swallow down the bile rising in my throat and fight the sudden chill pebbling my skin as I slowly walk towards the table. I sit stiffly in my seat, not wanting to make eye contact with any of them. Why is my sister here and why would she bring her fiancé with her? Isn't she afraid that papa will rip him away from her like he's done to me?

My back stiffens when Mikail's hand settles at the small of my back and he leans into me. "You can relax, Mushka. I don't bite."

I want to throw up; projectile vomit all over this fucker and break that hand that he's so casually put on me. I dart my eyes towards papa, noticing the smile there. I hate him. I hate him for doing this to me and trying to control my life. I swallow around the lump in my throat and turn my attention to Tessa, ignoring Mikail and his creepy advances.

"Surprised to see you here," I say, not even trying to hide the disappointment and anger in my voice.

"I'm surprised to be here." She gives me a pleading look, and that's when I know, she's not here by choice. Did papa threaten her, too? What is he using against her that would make her come here? She clears her throat, giving papa the fake smile I know so well. "Papa was very...persuasive in getting me here and insisted on meeting Cillian."

"Yes, I was very interested in meeting you, Cillian. Why don't you tell me a little bit about yourself."

Cillian seems unphased and unbothered by the building tension at the table, shifting back slightly to allow the waitstaff to set down a plate in front of him. "Thank you for having me. A little bit about myself, hmm. I'm a junior associate at Reed & Michaels Law Firm, which specializes in criminal law, and I'm hoping to move up to Senior associate within the year. My goal is to become a partner the year after that."

Papa laughs, leaning back in his chair. "You're ambitious. I like that. What kind of clientele do you take on?"

"We don't discriminate," Cillian grins. "Personally, I'll take on anything that I know I can win."

"Such confidence. I might have to put you on my team if you're as good as you claim."

Cillian looks thrilled with the idea while Tessa looks horrified. She quickly ducks her head, covering her expression from papa, but I can see the panic in her eyes. She didn't want this, and now, she's trapped but in a different way. He's playing the both of them and I'm sure he knows full well what Cillian does and is using it as leverage against her. I'm sure if she didn't come here, he would have killed him out of spite. What I want to know is how he knew she was coming back into the city to begin with, or has he been watching us this whole time? Maybe Dimitry putting himself into view was all a game, a ruse to get me to react and give them the opportunity to fight back for my insolence.

Father's attention turns back to me, his little interrogation of Cillian minimal but productive. "Why don't you speak with your future husband, milaya? I'm sure he would love to get to know you. The wedding is planned for next week, so it's best you get...acquainted."

The way he says that makes my skin crawl and anxiety spike through my chest. Mikail's hand is still on my back, rubbing slow circles in fake attention or comfort, I'm not sure which, but I don't like it.

"I don't see a point. I'm sure Mikail doesn't give a shit about what I think or what I have to say." I turn my glare to Mikail. "He just wants a wife who will sit down and shut up. Isn't that right, Mikail?"

His smile falters and his eyes shift to my father before clearing his throat. "I *would* like to get to know you, actually. Maybe don't judge someone based on their familial ties and upbringing."

"I'm sure my judgment of you is sound. You're Dimitry's cousin after all."

"Veronica." I flinch at papa's angry tone, the ingrained fear tightening my throat and preventing me from snapping back like I want to.

"Where *is* my cousin?" Mikail asks.

"I'm not sure. He went to one of our warehouses to deal with some business, but he hasn't returned yet. I'm sure he'll be back shortly and then you both can catch up."

Having both of them here at the same time is the last thing I want right now. While one has no issues projecting his hatred for me but unwanted obsession, the other is trying to butter me up with kindness and false niceties. I want Reese. I want to be with *him*. I want to see him, smell him, *feel* him. I want to escape this fucking house and never come back, but I can't, especially now. Tessa being here makes things more difficult, turning a nearly impossible situation into one that has absolutely no escape. With her here, we'll be used against each other, threatened and broken until there's nothing left of us.

We're fucked.

I poke around my food, barely listening to the monotonous conversation between my father, Mikail, and Cillian. I keep stealing glances at Tessa, but she hasn't looked up from her still full plate even once. She's probably thinking the same thing as I am or trying to come up with solutions and finding none that would get us all out of here unscathed.

A knock from the entryway makes my father cluck his tongue, interrupting his conversation with Cillian. "What is it?"

The guard from my room—I think his name was Ivan, but I can't be sure—walks into the room, bowing his head to my father. "We have a situation," he says quietly.

"What is it?"

I peek up at him when he doesn't respond, noticing the way his eyes drift around the table to the mixed company. "I'm not sure if I should speak about it freely. It's about the warehouse." My father motions him closer and he bends down to whisper in his ear. I catch bits and pieces of it, voice too hushed to get the full story, but it sounds like he just said Dimitry is dead. If only I could be so lucky.

Papa clears his throat, sets his napkin down on his plate, and pushes his chair back from the table. "I have some pressing matters to attend to. Ivan, can you please show Mikail to his room and escort Veronica back to hers for the night. Theresa, I expect you to be back here tomorrow evening once you've finished with whatever it is you're doing tomorrow."

"We're finalizing the venue details tomorrow for our wedding," she says harshly.

"As I said, whatever it is you're doing." He does up the button on his suit jacket, composing himself, even though I can tell whatever Ivan told him is bothering him.

"Let's go," Ivan says, lightly gripping my arm.

"I'd like a word with my sister."

"Your father said—"

"She is my sister and I have a right to speak to her," I snap, ripping my arm away from him. My sudden movement has me pushing into Mikail and moving away from him just as quickly when he tries to steady me. "Don't touch me," I snarl.

"Mushka—"

"Don't call me that. I am *not* your sweetheart." I shove the chair back hard enough that it topples over, the wood backing smacking off the tile floor and echoing around the room. "Tessa."

She blinks at me, mouth popped open in surprise. She glances around like she doesn't know what to do with herself but slowly gets to her feet. I motion toward the door, glaring at Ivan when he tries to follow. She steps out into the hallway first, and the second I join her, she wraps her arms around me in a death grip.

"Ronnie," she sobs. "I'm so sorry."

I hug her back. "What happened?"

"I don't know. I have no idea how dad found out I was coming back into the city, but he had people waiting outside our hotel. I'm glad they don't know what house we just bought because that would have been horrible for the people in that community."

"He must have been keeping an eye on you while you were in Chicago and then followed you into Cameron. What did he say to you, Tessa? What does he have on you?"

"He threatened Cillian. He told me not to interfere with your marriage, or he would kill him and put me in your place. I—I can't do that, Ronnie. I can't—" Her breath wheezes, tears springing into her eyes.

"Shhh, it's okay, Tessa." I fucking knew it. Our father is seriously a piece of shit. He doesn't care about us, he never did, all he cares about is advancing his standing in his stupid, fucked-up world. "You don't have to do anything, okay? I—I'll take care of it."

"What are you going to do?" She sniffles, dabbing at her eyes to stop the tears from streaking her makeup further.

"What I have to."

I either find a way to escape, find a way to get rid of Mikail, or I need to remove my father from the picture. With him gone, the reins would be thrown to Tessa by blood since he doesn't have any sons. Some may contest her position, other families or even cousins coming forth to try and overthrow her. They could do it, but Tessa might end up just giving away the power just so she doesn't have to be dragged back into this world. How would she explain that to Cillian? How does *anyone* explain to their significant other that they're a legacy? A fucking heir to the mafia throne.

I failed at telling Reese and look at where that got me. Trapped and sold off to the highest bidder. Fated to be some mute housewife that pushes out babies for a man I know nothing about and will never love. A guillotine hovering over the only person I've felt comfortable being myself around. I would rather die.

I don't *want* to die.

CHAPTER FIFTY-ONE

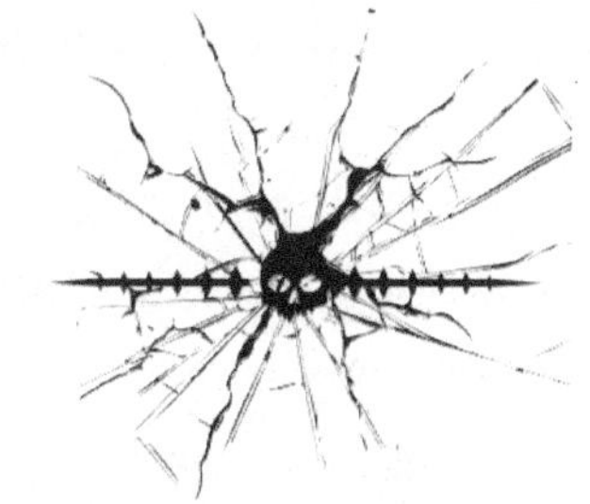

REESE

"What happened?"

Eden breezes past me, locking onto Kaine who is coming out of the bedroom dressed in some of my clothes. He's rubbing a towel against his hair, pausing when he sees her. "You called her?" He murmurs, glaring at me now while Eden fusses over him.

"Of course I did."

"Kaine, are you okay?"

"I'm fine," he huffs. "What did he tell you?"

"Everything. Why would you do something so stupid!" She turns and glares at me, stomping towards me and poking me in the chest. "How could you let him go with you?"

"I'm sorry, Eden." I mean it. I really *am* sorry that I dragged Kaine into that mess and almost got him killed. No. I *did* get him killed, and now I'll have to live with that guilt, knowing that my friend lost his life today because of me.

Her eyes soften at my sincerity and the guilt oozing out of me like toxic sludge. I flinch when she reaches her hand towards me, but she just places her palm against my cheek. "Are you okay?"

"No."

I let out a shuddering breath and try to pull away from her, but she slides her arms around my waist and hugs me tightly. I look over at Kaine, expecting anger from him, but there's pity in his eyes and a sad smile on his lips. I watch him as I wrap my arms around her, choking back a sob when she squeezes me tighter.

"We'll get her back," she whispers.

I pull away from her, shaking my head. "There is no we. I'm not letting anything like what happened today happen again. You're both going to stay safely tucked away at home until this is all over, Eden. I can handle this on my own."

"But you don't have to. When are you going to realize that?"

"Yes, I do."

"You've helped us—"

"It's not the same and you know it. I know what's waiting for me at the other end of this and I won't continue to put you or Kaine in harm's way when I *know* how dangerous this is."

"Reese—"

"This is not up for discussion." She snaps her mouth closed at that, turning to look at Kaine as he makes his way over to us. I don't like that look on his face, a look that tells me he wants to argue with me or punch me, I'm not sure which yet. "Don't."

"Don't what? Don't tell you you're being an idiot for doing this alone? Don't tell you it's okay to ask for help? Don't tell you that this is so beyond fucked up that only an insane person would try to go up against and entire Russian mob all because of a girl?" He grips Eden's arm and pulls her into him, draping his arm across her shoulders. "All of it is true, Reese. If what you still have to face is even a quarter worse compared to what we just dealt with, you won't make it out of there."

"Do you think I don't know that? I can't leave her, Kaine. I can't let them take her away from me like this."

"Coming from the guy who had to be guilted into telling the girl he loved her," he snaps.

"She didn't guilt me! I've loved her for a while, but every time I feel anything for anyone, something bad always happens. Look what happened, Kaine. I told her how I felt and now she's gone. I'm fucking cursed and fucked up and seriously losing my god damn mind."

"You're not cursed."

"Aren't I?" I laugh. "What part of my life makes you think otherwise? I almost lost you today, Kaine. For good."

He pulls away from Eden to stand in front of me, brows furrowed as he tips his chin up. "But you didn't. I'm the one who wanted to go with you. It was my decision, not yours. You didn't drag me into shit, and I knew it could get bad, but I don't care, Reese. All I care about is making sure *you're* okay."

"I don't need you." He blinks at that. I know it's harsh to say that, but I don't. Letting him and Eden come with me will only be a distraction at this point. Neither of them are cut out for this lifestyle, and I can't risk something happening to them.

"You don't mean that," he whispers.

"I do. I'm going alone, end of story."

"It's a suicide mission, Reese. At least call your uncle for help."

"No."

"You're going to get yourself killed." I shrug and his eyes widen. "You're not...planning to come out of this, are you?"

"All that matters is getting Ronnie out of there and killing every last one of them so they don't try to go after her again. She deserves to live a normal life, Kaine. She's like me. She's been trying to get away from that life and got dragged back into it. I know what she feels and what she's going through, and I won't let her end up like me."

"What do you mean?"

"Fucked up and broken. She's *good*, Kaine."

He shoves me so hard I go stumbling back, catching myself on the edge of the coffee table. My ass smacks off the ground hard, and I swallow back my protest when Kaine looms over me, glaring so hard it feels like a physical blow.

"So are you! You're a fucking idiot if you think you're not, and I won't just stand here and let you talk shit about yourself or go off to get yourself killed. If you won't call your uncle, I will." He turns quickly and I scramble to my feet, grabbing his arm and throwing him on the couch. "What the fuck." He grunts in surprise when he attempts to get up but I shove him back down.

The fucker kicks me square in the gut, launching me back. Wood splinters when I crash down on the table and Eden screams in surprise. "Stop!" She yells, trying and failing to stop Kaine coming towards me. "Kaine, Stop!"

He rips out of her grip and drops on top of me, fist colliding with my jaw. Stars scatter across my vision, my mind hazing over with the urge to fight back. I don't want to hurt him, but he'll keep pummeling into me if I don't *do* anything.

"Get off!" My head snaps to the side on the next blow, my ear ringing from the force of it.

"Kaine, stop!" Eden screams again, but he doesn't. Blow after blow lands no matter how many times I try to grab at him. He just keeps ripping out of my grip, fury overtaking his features.

"Kaine!" I snap, bucking my hips and sending him toppling over me to land on the floor. I scramble over him, gripping into the back of his neck to pin him to the ground. He's breathing heavily and still struggling under me to try and get away. "Fucking stop!"

He stills when the lights in the apartment flicker, and I swear I can *smell* the fear coming off of him. I wipe my mouth, wincing at the cut there and the liquid warmth of blood oozing out of it. He got some decent hits in, but I wasn't fighting back. He's angry and has every right to be, and if he needed to do that to get rid of some of his frustration at my actions, then so be it.

"I'm not just going to let you go off and die," he pants. "You can't do this. You can't leave me."

Guilt settles into my gut when tears spring to his eyes, turning the green into glistening emeralds. That single eye staring back at me is enough to break me, and I slowly release his neck, settling back onto his legs. My own breaths are ragged, tearing through my lungs as I try to calm myself down and not react to his baiting. That's what it was. He was baiting me into fighting back so that he could try to take me down in the hope of hurting me enough to not be able to go after Ronnie.

"Kaine, you need to calm down."

"I can't!" He thrashes again, nearly knocking me off him. "You can't do this!"

"I have to. What would you do if it were Eden and you were in my position? Would you just sit by and watch it happen? Would you not try to do everything you could to save her, even if it meant risking your life and possibly dying for good? If you can tell me that you would let Eden go so easily, I'll stay behind with you, but if not, you need to let me go."

He props himself onto his elbows, head falling between his shoulders. 'I can't," he sobs. "I can't just be okay with this, Reese. It's not the same as just sneaking up on someone like Stephen and getting rid of them. They're going to know you're coming once they find out what happened at the warehouse. I can't let you do this."

"You have to."

"I—I can't!"

I pull him up into me, wrapping my arms around him. He curls his hands into my arms and fucking breaks. Eden steps up behind us, resting her hand on my shoulder while her own sobs echo and mingle with Kaine's. I didn't want this. They deserve a normal and happy life after everything they've been through, and here I am, dragging them down with me into the pit of my past.

Eden drops to her knees behind me, trying to hug the both of us in her tiny embrace. "Kaine," she sniffles. "You need to let him go."

Bless her huge heart and being able to understand what I'm going through. I know she doesn't want me to do this either, but she knows that if I don't, I won't be the same. Ronnie is her friend and she wants her home, too, even though she doesn't understand the full gravity of the situation.

"Fine," Kaine sniffles, dropping his hands where the fall limply at his sides. "Promise me something though."

"What's that?"

"Promise you'll do everything you can to not die."

My heart tightens painfully in my chest when he turns his head to look at me. It's been a long time since I've seen Kaine this broken, the last time being when Eden tried to kill herself. I hate that look; the look of a man on the edge of completely breaking into a million pieces. He tries to be strong and pretends to have his shit together, but I see through that just like glass. The thing about glass is no matter how strong it seems, it's easy to shatter it into nothing with the right force.

"I promise."

I have no choice but to make that promise, letting my own resolve settle into me and give me strength. Kaine might not realize what he's done for me by fighting me and breaking in front of me, but he's given me another reason to fight to survive. I will prove to my uncle and to myself that I'm more dangerous than they realize, and I'll take what belongs to me by force if I have to. I'll tear down the whole system if that's what it takes.

Kaine clears his throat, shuffling awkwardly away from me on his knees before lurching to his feet. He stumbles slightly, wiping his eyes quickly before turning to face me. Eden is still hanging onto me, crying quietly into my back while her fingers dig into my chest. I don't deserve friends like them. Friends that care about me to this level and that know every dark secret about me.

I pat her hand, lacing my fingers through hers and giving them a squeeze. "Eden."

"Sorry," she says, quickly pulling away from me. I get up first, bending down to help her back up to her feet.

"Please don't cry," I murmur, wiping the stray tears off her cheeks, but new ones just keep following the wet tracks already formed there.

"I can't help it," she hiccups.

"I know, but you don't need to cry for me. I'm right here." She nods, scrubbing at her own eyes while she pulls in a shaky breath. I turn to face Kaine, hating how dejected he looks. He won't even meet my eyes, keeping his trained on the ground in front of him. "Are you good?"

"No," he huffs. "But it doesn't matter, does it?"

"Your feelings matter, Kaine. I'm not trying to brush off your concerns, but I need you to understand that this isn't something that I can just let go. You don't understand why I can't ask my uncle for help. You don't understand the leverage he would have over me if I got him involved in this. I would never be able to have a normal life ever again. I would be dragged back into the underworld and I'd be stuck there. I'd never be able talk to you or see you like I do now because I can't risk them using you against me. I'm not doing this to prove a point, I'm doing it so when this is all over, I have something to come back to. I can't lose you either, and this is why not only can I not allow you to come with me, but I also can't involve my family."

It's that bad?"

"Yes, Kaine, it's that bad." I cup the back of his neck and yank him into me, hating that he's still avoiding looking at me. "I'm not pushing you away because I want to, it's because I need to. I shouldn't have let you go with me to the warehouse and that's something I'm going to regret for the rest of my life."

"Is it true that Kaine is on his last life?" Eden asks quietly.

"I'll fix it, Eden. You both should have more time."

"How can you fix it? The only ones who can control death are the reapers, Reese, and they take life, they can't give it away."

"Avery and I are going to have a little chat. The deception behind all of it is pissing me off and I don't like that there was no warning at all for that. If I wasn't able to see the reapers, I wouldn't have known what was about to happen."

"Why now? Why are you able to see them now?"

"About that." I realize I'm still hugging Kaine against my body, but he's not fighting me or trying to pull away. He must really be upset if he's allowing such intimate contact for so long from me, but I'm not going to chirp him for that since I know how hard all of this has been for him. "I've been able to see the reapers for a little bit, but I didn't realize it was them until I saw one take Julia's soul. They were at the funeral, too and had a more solid form, and the ones today stayed in shadow form until I grabbed the one."

"Wait, you physically pulled a reaper into our world without a body?"

"Yeah, why?"

"That shouldn't have been possible. If it were, Luther and Avery wouldn't have needed to possess bodies."

"It's possible, it just takes a lot of energy."

She quirks a brow at that, a smile pulling at her lips when she catches me lightly petting Kaine like a child. I swear his body melts into mine at the contact, and it's seriously so adorable.

"How do you know that?" Eden asks, pulling my attention from Kaine back to her.

"Avery told me. I'm sure he won't appreciate me telling you anything, but I seriously don't care anymore. He's pissing me the fuck off."

"Oh, I'm definitely pissed off with you right now, Reese."

"I don't fucking care. You're a fucking prick and you tried to take my friend away from me after pushing me to fucking save him."

"It's not that simple."

"Save it. We'll talk about this later."

"So, you just talk to Avery whenever you want now?"

Kaine tries to pull away and I let him go, glad that he seems calmer now and his tears have dried up. The poor bastard has really had it rough today. "He's in my head, Eden. I can't get rid of him, but at least now it's less of a haunting and more like an annoying roommate."

"That's fucking rude."

"Get used to it, you freeloader."

I guide Kaine back over to the couch since he still seems out of it and sort of locked in his own head, and Eden takes up the seat next to him, rubbing at his back. They're seriously adorable together. I love how vulnerable he gets with her and how he leans into her touch. Seeing them like that makes me miss Ronnie even more, pushing my desperation and need to go after her right now.

I know it's not the smartest move and I need to plan better and wait to attack. By now, Misha knows something happened at the warehouse, but I made sure to call Holland on the way home to clear out all the surveillance footage, leaving them with no way of knowing what happened or who attacked them. They'll know it was an attack once they pull out the bodies and they see that most of them still have bullets riddled through them. My goal is to take advantage of their confusion and attack them right away. From what Holland told me, Mikail is already in the city and he's staying at the Petrov home. Not ideal, especially since if I find out he tries to touch Ronnie, I have no choice but to eliminate him as well.

He's not my target. None of the Ivanov family are my targets, and as long as they slink back to their territory when this is over, I won't have any need to get rid of them. I don't know what will happen once I wipe the Petrov family from this world. Misha doesn't have any male heirs, only two daughters. I know nothing about Theresa outside of what Ronnie has already told me, but I wonder if she'll step up and take over once her father is out of the picture.

Ronnie should get some satisfaction from the fact that Dimitry has been taken care of. Though, she might be upset with me because she didn't get to deal with him herself. I'm sure she would have loved to make him suffer for what he did to her, but she might shut down a bit once she realizes that I know those details. Not the nitty gritty, but enough to feel vengeful and rip him to shreds. I'm sure none of it was good in any way, and the more I think about it, the more I wish I could bring him back to life just so I could kill him all over again.

"When are you going to do this?" She asks, slowly running her fingers through Kaine's hair until his eyes flutter closed.

"Tomorrow. I need to rest and get myself mentally prepared for it."

"Are you just going in there, guns blazing?"

"I'm not sure yet. I don't want to risk hurting Ronnie by doing that, so it needs to be a bit more strategic. I'm waiting for the layout of the house from my contact, but once I have that, I'll have a better idea. I think they have a security system as well, so my hope is that we can hack into that and get a look inside to see what I'm dealing with."

"Are you sure we can't help you?"

"You've both done enough for me already. If you guys want to stay the night, you can. You can take the bed, and I'll just stay on the couch."

She glances down at Kaine, who has now curled himself on the couch with his head on her lap. Her gaze softens as she stares at him, the loving look shooting a pang of jealousy through me. "That would be great. I don't think he'll make it home."

He's completely wiped out, not stirring or fighting me as I pick him up in my arms and carry him to the bedroom. Any other time I would chirp him for carrying him like this, but I just don't have the heart to make fun of him when he's like this. Eden follows behind me quietly, watching me as I set Kaine down on the bed and cover him with the blankets.

"If you want to take a shower, I can grab some clean clothes. I'm sure Ronnie wouldn't mind you borrowing her stuff so you're comfortable."

She shakes her head and rests her hand on my shoulder. "I'm okay, Reese."

The look she gives me makes it seem like she's refusing the offer for a different reason. My eyes widen when she moves to Ronnie's side of the bed, pulls the pillow away and sets it down on the chair in the corner, leaving her with the thin under-pillow.

"What are you doing?"

She pauses when she pulls the covers back and lets out a sigh. "I don't want my smell on her stuff, like her clothes or her pillow. I know how comforting someone's smell can be when you're feeling down." She moves back towards the pillow, picking it up carefully, and walks back towards me with it. "You should take this with you. It'll help you sleep better."

I take it from her, staring at it like it might hold all the answers I'm looking for. Before I can stop myself, I bring it up to my nose, inhaling deeply. It smells like her. Soft lilac, vanilla, citrus, and honey. I don't realize Eden is watching me until I open my eyes, not registering I had closed them when Ronnie's scent hit me like a truck.

She smiles and tucks herself into bed behind Kaine. "Goodnight, Reese."

"Goodnight, Eden," I whisper, turning off the light on the way out, holding the pillow tightly against my chest.

Something so small and meaningless to many and she caught onto it right away. We're similar in a lot of ways, it's probably why I got along with her so easily. That and the fact she's sort of fucked in the head as well and has her own traumas. There's almost an unspoken bond between people who have experienced some form of hardship in their lives, a strange pull that draws us together so we can seek comfort in one another. Comfort we were never granted when going through those moments that threatened to break us.

The pillow shouldn't be something I want to treasure, but now that it's in my hands and her smell wafts towards me as I walk, I don't want to let it go. I can't have her here right now, but at least there's still a small piece of her I can hold onto until I do what I need to do and get her back. When I get her back, I'm never letting her go again. I'll never doubt our relationship or be fearful of the emotions that are trying to consume me. *When* I get her back, not *if*. There is no room for mistakes. There can't be any hesitation in my actions or remorse in my heart. Tomorrow, she'll be back in my arms, and I will make it back to my family.

Family.

Kaine and Eden are my *family*. They're all I have aside from Ronnie, and I refuse to lose any of them.

I settle onto the couch, not wanting to deal with the mess of a table at the moment. Fuck, Kaine really went feral on me, destroying my fucking property. I should be surprised that I don't have a single wound on me, my lip already healed from the beating he laid into me, but I'm not. I know it isn't Avery this time. Something is fundamentally different about me, more so now since accepting the lurking power beneath the surface.

I curl against Ronnie's pillow, staring at my faint reflection in the blacked-out television screen. It morphs right in front of me, shifting until the fractured edges of Avery's form comes more into focus.

"What do you want?"

"You're pushing it, kid."

"Pushing it? What part exactly?"

"Why don't we start with the fact you've bypassed your mortal body and have tapped into my power without my permission."

"Hmm, sucks when you get used, doesn't it?"

"This isn't even close to the same," he snarls, and I swear his form seems like it wants to come out right through the glass and strangle me. His anger is palpable, but I don't give a shit.

"It might not be the same to you, but I think it's only fair. Now, you're going to give Kaine his Lazarus back or we're going to have a problem. Also, I want to know how much time Eden has, and I want you to fix that, too. They're both going to live to a ripe old age like you promised. No more of this bullshit."

"You don't get it. You're the reason he lost his Lazarus to begin with. I've been trying to set everything right and you went ahead and fucked everything up."

"What do you mean? I saw the reapers there. They were sent to collect the souls of those people I killed."

"I didn't send them; you fucking summoned them."

Well, fuck me. I did *not* expect that at all. How the fuck did I summon reapers; it makes no sense at all. "How—"

"Because you're tapping into the power of someone who controls them, Reese. As I said, this is serious. They didn't have proper instruction, they just knew they needed to be there, but they didn't know why. This is where Kaine's Lazarus comes in. You're changing people's planned deaths, Reese. The last time I had a reaper going off on his own like that, I sent him to the pits."

"I'm not a reaper."

"You're sure acting like one."

"I never collected any souls. If anything, I'm death itself."

"What the fuck do you think death is? Death is a reaper, Reese. He's THE reaper. He's the one that oversees everything and makes sure the souls go where they're supposed to go. I might be a leader, but I'm still a soldier."

"Fine, whatever. Call it whatever you want, but you're going to fix this. I gave you a soul in Kaine's place so now you're going to take those souls that I supposedly claimed before they were meant to be taken, take those lives, and give them to Kaine and Eden. Even out their death dates."

"It doesn't work like that."

"Make it work like that. A life for a life. Take those lives and give it to them."

"You're a pain in the ass, you know that?"

I smile, snuggling further into the pillow. "Get used to it. You'll fix his Lazarus?"

He sighs, looking so fucking done with my shit. *"Fine, but I need to figure out what I'm going to do with you. You're not supposed to be able to tap into any of my abilities the way you are. It's dangerous."*

"Good. I need to be dangerous for what I'm about to do. Tell me, Avery. Are any of the people I'm going after tomorrow on your little list?" He doesn't answer right away, and I wonder if he'll respond at all. He just stares at me, a muted being reflecting in the glass. "Fine. Don't tell me then."

"There's only one person in that house that's meant to die tomorrow."

"Yeah? Who's that? I'll make sure they'll suffer the longest."

"I can't tell you that."

"Can't or won't."

Goodnight, Reese."

His form shimmers, merging into the darkness until my own image reflects back at me. "Fuck you, Avery."

CHAPTER FIFTY-TWO

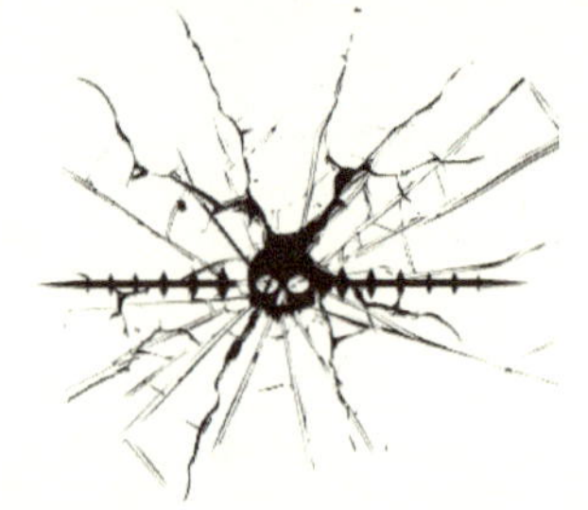

RONNIE

The day starts off the same as it did yesterday, minus my body feeling like absolute ass from being drugged. A knock at the door and another staff member dropping off food without so much as a glance in my direction, and once again, me being bored out of my mind. Seriously, is it so hard for them to drag in a TV or bring me a tablet so I can keep myself entertained? Scratch that. They wouldn't risk bringing me a tablet and giving me access to the outside world—to Reese.

I don't feel like eating. Definitely not the shit they keep bringing me. With all his staff it's sort of insulting that they keep bringing me food that I won't eat. Tray after tray they've taken back with nearly full plates where I've only picked off things I deemed edible. It's like my father doesn't even know me. Who am I kidding, he doesn't. Either that, or he just doesn't give a shit, and this is his way of telling me to shut the fuck up and be grateful. My stomach growls, but staring at the shitty slop oatmeal, just tightens my gut, a threat that it's about to upheave its lackluster contents.

I push the food aside, deciding to just let myself soak in the bath for a little while. It's not like I have anything else to do until they decide to let me out of here, and I want nothing more than to find something to distract myself. It's wishful thinking. There's nothing I could do to stray my thoughts away from how fucked up all of this is, my wandering thoughts always back on him—on Reese. I just want to talk to him. Just one more time so I can hear his voice and commit it to memory. It's only been a day, and it already feels like I'm forgetting certain things about him, his scent being the most devastating one.

I always found comfort in his smell, and I swear there are moments where I still catch whiffs of it in the air, certain things that remind me of him. It's like my brain is clawing at anything to remember him and what I had and lost.

The bathroom is just as pathetic as my bedroom, not a hint of anything I would ever have for myself in it. It's so plain and sparce, lacking any touch of home or familiarity. The only thing here that reminds me of the me I used to be is the fact there's still a lineup of the bath oils and salts I used to use, something my father didn't clear out once I left this house. Now that I think about it, he's probably never come here since I left. Whether that's from not wanting to or finding it too difficult, I'm not sure. My heart still hopes that he might have thought it too difficult to see any of my things, even if there weren't many of them. It's still a shrine of the girl I was, the pathetic attempt at trying to make this house a home.

It's not that my father didn't get me things I needed or wanted, it's just he didn't put the effort into even asking me. I rarely had the courage to *ask* him for anything, saving my requests for things I felt would be useful. He wasn't a dad to me in the slightest, my memories of him being cold and distant, the only ones that come to the forefront of my mind. Maybe in the past—when I was younger—they were different, but I can't ask him any of that, and Tessa doesn't remember any kind words or gestures either.

The bath quickly steams up the room, the smell of lilac and lavender curling against my sinuses. I shudder as I lower myself into the water and settle my head back on the edge. I smile up at the ceiling, the one cool thing about this room. The skylight shows a beautiful day outside, the sun shining and making me jealous of its chipper mood. I half expected the weather to reflect how I'm feeling inside, gloomy and dark, but maybe I should take it as some glimmer of hope instead.

The heat of the water helps relax me a bit, but it does nothing for my wandering thoughts. I knew it wouldn't. I knew it would just be a temporary reprieve and nothing more. The thoughts of my future and the fact I'm going to be forced to marry Mikail next week is like a heavy boulder crushing my chest, threatening to end my life before I even got the chance to *have* a life.

I know my father probably believes I've lived as much as I need to, what with my disobedience and galivanting with school and going off with some random man. He's not random though, is he? Reese is anything but ordinary in more ways than one. Even if I were to disregard the fact he has a tie to the supernatural world, he's not a normal man. He's a member of the mafia. Not directly, but his uncle must have enough leverage over him to call on him if he needs to.

I laugh to myself, slightly horrified that I ended up falling for a mafia man when my goal was to get as far away from this world as possible. He's nothing like them. He's not like my father or Mikail, and he doesn't impose rules on me or expectations. Reese has allowed me to be me—*encouraged* it. I still kept myself pretty guarded around him, but I know that was my subconscious fear bleeding into my voice and actions.

I vow to never hide anything from him ever again if I just get the chance to be with him in the end. I'll tell him the truth about everything myself and tell him I love him every single day. I can just imagine the lightness I would feel before the worry settles into me at knowing that he knows everything about me. He might already know who I am. He knew about Dimitry, and with his connections, he would easily be able to find what he needs to. I buried my identity, deep enough that at surface level no one would be able to find anything. But him? If he wanted to dig deeper, he would find every dirty secret from my past.

Oh, God. He would be able to fine *everything*, including my attempt at making a sexual harassment complaint against Dimitry which got squashed blindingly fast by my father. He wasn't happy that I went to the police, even more furious that I got in contact with someone that wasn't on his payroll. Because of me, an innocent man lost his job because he was willing to help me and it wasn't what the bratva wanted.

At the end of the day, Reese might not even want me if he knows the truth. Not only did I lie to him, but I'm also a rival mafia princess that has been in an underground war with his own house. Like Romeo and Juliet, but I hoped our ending wouldn't end in tragedy. I'm such a hypocrite for ever getting mad at him for hiding things from me. Haven't I been doing the same thing the entire time I've been with him?

I've been in the water too long, letting the heat dissipate until there's nothing left but cold water and the reduced scent of my bath oils. It wasn't as satisfying as I hoped it would be, only a temporary escape from the shackled confines of my prison. My fingertips are wrinkled, hair slightly damp because I didn't bother to put it up in my usual bun before getting into the water. I don't care about looking my best at this point. I'll let my weird, swamp-thing personality fly in the wind just to disgust Mikail. Maybe if I weird him out enough, he'll reject me and papa will have no choice but to release me.

He only gets what he wants because of threats and deadly promises. Doesn't he know he would get so much more compliance if he actually acted like a dad and not some sperm donor playing dress up?

I hate the fact I don't have any of my stuff with me, having been forced to leave everything behind when Dimitry showed up. Half the clothes that are here are still things from when I was younger, some still fitting since I loved baggy clothes that could wrap around me. Even then, I was desperate to feel some form of comfort, even if it came in the form of material things that could cradle me like I wished so many times before would come from someone and not *something*. It's at least one small joy and comfort, pulling out a thick sweater, loose fitting t-shirt, and baggy sweatpants, I set everything down on the bed and quickly change into them.

They're comfortable, but tears spring to my eyes when I bring the collar of the sweater up to my nose and I don't find Reese's smell there. I miss wearing his things, knowing that they touched his skin. I think he secretly liked it when I would steal his sweaters, and he definitely made it a point of wearing one a few times before not-so-subtly leaving it out for me to claim for myself.

The click of the lock on the door has my back stiffening and my eyes darting to the clock on the wall. It's still too early for lunch. My skin prickles with fear, and I slowly turn around to face the door, but it doesn't open. I frown, waiting a few long, excruciating minutes, but the door never opens.

As quietly as I can, I sneak my way towards it, grip the handle, and slowly turn it. I almost sob at the fact I'm not met with resistance, the door creaking open enough for me to peek out into the hallway. There's no one there and it's eerily quiet.

Someone is letting me out, and I don't know whether to be wary of that or thrilled, but I don't question it. I open the door enough to sneak out into the hall, being as careful as I can with my steps on the hardwood floors. It's been a while, but past moments of sneaking around have ingrained the louder panels into my brain. It's still a long way to the exit, but if I can make it outside, I can run. I can get as far away from this place and find shelter somewhere with a phone. A typical person would call the police for what happened, but that's fucking useless for me. The police can't help me, and there's only one person I want to call.

I hear voices trailing from my father's office as I head down the stairs, his door partially open. They sound angry, and I swear I hear bits and pieces about the warehouse again. Whatever happened there has diverted my father's attention temporarily, giving me the time I need to get the fuck out of here. If I ever find out who helped me today, I'll have to thank them over and over again. Running might not do much, but it'll at least give me some time to come up with a plan.

The fact I haven't run into anyone yet makes me believe that luck is finally on my side. The entrance door is right there, just a few feet away with the promise of freedom. I bolt for it, flipping the lock on the door and swinging it open.

Pain sears through my scalp as I'm wrenched back by my hair, the sudden jerk sending screaming pain through my neck. I cry out in surprise when I'm thrown to the floor, sliding against the tile. Mikail looms over me, a look of fury overtaking his features. I scramble back, trying to get away from him, but he's right fucking there, right over me, gripping my throat in his hand.

"Where do you think you're going?" He whispers harshly. "You just don't get it, do you? You're my golden ticket, Mushka. There is no escape for you."

He pulls me up, my feet scrambling for purchase on the floor to try and ease some of the pressure on my neck. My hands claw and grip into his wrist to try and get him to release me, but his grip tightens further. I can't breathe; I can barely swallow. This hold is only meant to inflict pain and illicit fear, and he's succeeding on both counts. Gone is the fake sweetness from last night. Now, his true, venomous colours are glaringly bright.

"Let me go," I choke out, trying to fight off the darkness creeping into my vision.

"Give her an inch and she takes a mile. You failed your test. I thought you were more obedient than this, dear, sweet, Veronica, but you took that kindness and decided to run."

My eyes widen. Is Mikail the one who unlocked my door? I'm so fucking stupid. No one here is on my side, but I had that one small shred of hope that one of the staff was taking pity on me and giving me the opportunity to run. Of course he set me up. Of course he laid a trap for me, giving me the option to listen to my father or suffer the consequences.

"Mikail." My father's voice sounds beyond bored, no anger or reprimand in it at all. "You've been proven wrong as I said you would be."

The mother fucker was in on this. What am I, some kind of bet? At least my father knows me a bit better than I gave him credit for, knowing full well I would run if the opportunity presented itself. The fact he's letting Mikail manhandle me in this way tells me that he's allowed this treatment if he were to be proved wrong, as he put it.

It's the final nail in my coffin. There is no salvation here, only pain and misery from both my father and the man I'm now forced to marry. This is just the beginning, and I hate being proved right in the fact he's just like his cousin, if not worse.

I choke and gasp down air when he finally releases me, my legs wanting to give out from the sudden jolt of oxygen struggling into my system. "I hate being proved wrong," Mikail sighs, and then pain explodes across my face. My lip splits open and my temple throbs from the blow to my head, matched only by the pain on the opposite side where my skull cracks against the tile floor.

He's vicious and brutal and didn't hold back on that hit. I struggle to lift my head to look up at him, at the monster now in control of my life. What's worse is the fact my father laughs—actually laughs at the treatment of his own daughter. No. I was never a daughter to him. All I am is a pawn in his wicked game, a piece to move around the board with only one purpose, to sacrifice itself for the king.

CHAPTER FIFTY-THREE

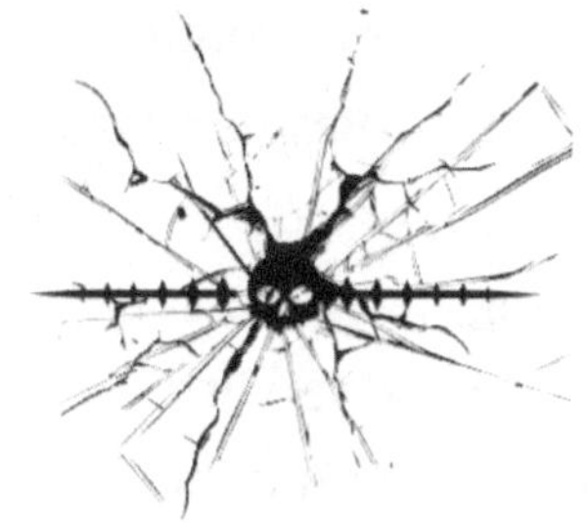

REESE

"I've removed all trace of you on any of their systems and wiped the hard drives of all video footage. Your uncle isn't happy about the fact you made such a mess of things," Holland murmurs.

"It could have been worse. If I didn't have you wiping everything out, everyone would have known what really happened there, including the bratva. It's better for all of us if they think it was some type of issue on their end. Dimitry was an idiot for setting off that explosion, but at least it covered my tracks a bit."

"Who's the kid that was with you?" I stiffen at that, not having thought that Holland would actually go through the footage before erasing it. The last thing I need is him digging into who Kaine is in general, but even less in connection to me. I can't exactly explain it away because why would I take some random person in there with me.

I say the first thing I can think of that makes sense but won't draw suspicion. "Hired help. I told you I didn't want Declan to get involved so I outsourced to a mercenary."

"A mercenary that wears a Batman mask and doesn't seem to know how to use a gun properly?"

God damn that fucking mask. Of *course* he noticed that. "He wanted to keep his identity hidden. It's sort of his thing...different hero masks for different assignments. You don't need to worry about him."

"Hmm, it's kind of cool if you ask me."

I shake my head, dragging my hand down my face. It's already later in the day than I would like, but I need to make sure I have every aspect of this planned out before I get moving. Kaine and Eden left about an hour ago, not without arguing once more for good measure. Kaine couldn't even look at me properly, his eyes puffy and red from fucking crying because of me. He's more worried about me dying than I am, but he did give me a thankful smile when I told him he still had Lazarus.

I put my own conditions there under the guise that it came from Avery, telling him he couldn't be reckless with his actions again and if he wants to hang onto his Lazarus like he was meant to. He's no longer allowed to go with me on any of my extracurricular adventures. It was a small lie, but coming from a reaper made it have a bit more weight to the threat. I'll take advantage of Avery and his pull for as long as I can, even if that means lying to Kaine to protect him.

"Did you get the blueprints on the Petrov house?" I ask, changing the subject before he decides to dig deeper on Kaine.

"I did, and I did you one better. I'll send over everything to your email right now." I open it the second it comes in, smiling at the lengths Holland went to. "Did you get it?"

"I did."

"Okay, so, you've got the general layout of the property plus any renovations that have been made over the last five years just to be sure. I've pulled video surveillance from the last month as well. I can't get information on what's exactly in each room, but I've sent a drone over with thermal reconnaissance to see what you're dealing with."

I pull up the feed on the drone, noticing all the heat signatures popping up. At least fourteen people are on property at this very minute, three at the entrance, a few in a larger room where another heat signature registers. I can only assume it's the kitchen by the details showing.

My attention goes back to the ones at the entrance, where there looks like there might be some sort of altercation going on. One of the signatures is sprawled on the floor while the other stands above them, the third one standing at a distance. Of course, Misha has problems within his household, and he doesn't hesitate to deal with those problems as quickly as possible. I scan the other rooms, trying to find any sign of Ronnie, but they all look like blobs of colour.

I cross reference the signatures with the blueprints to the house and none of them are actually in anything that would be labeled a bedroom. Where the fuck is she? I wouldn't think her father would give her such free range of the house, not with the way I know Ronnie functions. Knowing her, she'll try and do whatever she can to get out of there if she has the chance. She won't just take what's happening to her lying down. Unless they drugged her. Unless they have her confined somewhere that even thermal imaging can't see.

"Is there a basement or any form of shelter on property?"

"Not that I can see. It's more of a raised ranch style home, two levels, most of the bedrooms on the upper level with the kitchen, living room, and entertainment areas on the main level. There's a security booth set up at the end of the drive and the property is gated off. It's just outside the city so there's more ground to cover. Are you sure you can handle this on your own? You won't know who's an innocent employee and who's actually part of the bratva circle, Reese."

"You say that like it should matter."

"Doesn't it? You're the one who has always had the moral compass, so it's not like you to want to take out people who really have nothing to do with the dark undertakings."

"They knew who they were getting involved with the moment they took the job."

"Sure, but what's to say they weren't threatened or coerced? It could be something they feel they have to do because their family is being threatened or something."

I hate that he's right. I don't *want* him to be right because I want to go in there and not worry about people getting in the way and trying to protect them or prevent them from getting killed. Can I handle killing innocent people just because they got involved with the wrong people and ended up getting in the way of my vengeance? I need to decide what I'll do quickly because one way or another, I need to do this today.

"I'll figure it out."

"This isn't something you can just decide on the fly. You need to go in there with a proper plan, or you won't be making it out of there unscathed."

That's one thing I don't think I have to worry about. As long as I'm able to tap into Avery's power, I should be able to handle getting shot a few times without dying. It'll hurt like a mother fucker, but the feeling of being slightly invincible is giving me a lot more confidence in this situation. Well, as long as the fucker doesn't decide to rip the cord on me and leave me vulnerable just to prove a point. That's if he even *can*. He would have surely done it by now, right?

"Is there any video feed within the home?"

"There's a little bit, but it seems to focus mainly on where the staff is stationed and then at the entrance."

"Send me the feed."

The link pops up in my email and I quickly open in, six different cameras popping up. My eyes narrow on the one at the entrance and I quickly enlarge it. My blood runs cold through my veins as anger pulses through me.

Ronnie.

It's Ronnie lying on the floor with Mikail hovering over her and her father standing by like he doesn't give a shit that his daughter is passed out on the floor. No, not passed out. There's blood trickling from her lips and neither of them seem to care.

"Is there sound on this?" I whisper harshly.

"There is."

Their voices carry through the speaker on my laptop, pushing my fury higher. "I told you she was difficult to control, but you didn't believe me," Misha chuckles. *Chuckles*. The fucker is laughing after the fact that Mikail hit his daughter. What the fuck is wrong with these people?

How could he possibly despise his daughter to this extent that he allows some random man to hit her? No man should hit her. No one should be laying hands on what is fucking mine. I shouldn't be surprised, knowing that he allowed Dimitry to defile his daughter and abuse her from a young age. Someone that was supposed to be her bodyguard but ended up being her fucking keeper. She was treated like a pet, not a family member that is meant to be loved and cherished.

Watching and hearing them makes me physically ill. I want to turn away, but I don't want to stop watching her, afraid that if I do, she'll disappear again. My poor girl lying limp on the floor while these two assholes speak like she's nothing but a nuisance. I touch the screen with shaking fingertips, my rage and sadness at war with one another inside my body. She's right there—right *fucking* there. I wish I could just reach through this screen and pull her to me, cradling her against my body while I comfort her and tell her it'll be okay. Tears blur my vision and I know I need to stop and cut the feed before I completely lose every ounce of composure I've struggled to hold onto. With shaking hands and a rattling breath, I close the laptop, feeling the instant regret and pain clawing at my chest. There's nothing I can do from here. I need to get there and take care of this before more happens to her.

"Are you okay?" Holland asks quietly.

"Not even close," I admit. "They hurt her. I'm going to fucking enjoy killing them."

"You know that by now they probably know who you are, Reese. They're going to take this as an act of territory war."

"It won't matter because they'll all be dead. Tell Declan he can reap the rewards once I'm done with this and that it's my official resignation from the family. He needs to leave me alone completely because I'm done. I'm not fucking doing this anymore. I'm not working for him on the side because he feels like I still owe him. This is my payment in full."

"He can't exactly take over the Russian territory when there's still heirs, Reese. He's going to think that your precious Veronica is a threat."

"She's not and she won't be. She ran away from that life, Holland. That's a sign that she wants nothing to do with it."

"And the other sister?"

"She's getting married, so I doubt she wants to be involved in it either. I'm sure she'll step away when there's a threat to her life and what she's trying to make of herself."

"When are you planning to do this?"

"In a few hours. I want to make sure I have everything in order before I even head out there, and I want to scope out the property a few times. I'll have to keep an eye on who's coming in and out of the place within that time as well and adjust my plans if I end up having more people to deal with. First step is taking out the outer guards without drawing attention to them."

"I don't do this often because I prefer staying behind a computer if I can help it, but if you want someone with you out there..."

"I appreciate the offer, Holland, I really do, but you don't *do* field work. I don't want you going and getting hurt or becoming a liability for me."

He laughs. "Fair enough. I know I'm not cut out for the shit you and your family do, and the only thing I'm good for is sticking to my nerdy tendencies."

"That's not what I mean, Holland."

"It's fine. Just be careful and call me if you need help with anything," he says before ending the call.

It's bad enough that I know he'll be watching the whole time, leaving less room for error and a lot more questions on his end if he ends up seeing anything weird. The last thing I need is him witnessing something like what happened at the warehouse. I got lucky that he didn't there and that was only because the explosion cut off the camera feed he would have had access to. The smoke, flames, and debris covered my tracks better than I could have hoped for, and that's one of the reasons I'm planning to take some safety measures with me just in case.

I hate the idea of blowing up Ronnie's childhood home, but if it means getting in and out without being discovered as a vessel for a supernatural being, I'll do what I have to.

CHAPTER FIFTY-FOUR

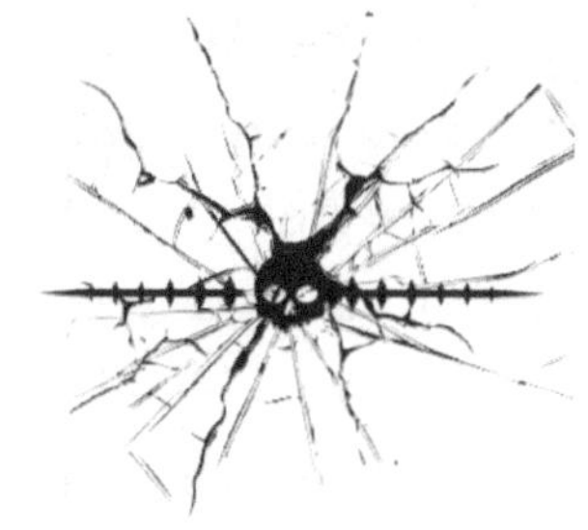

RONNIE

The feel of a hand brushing down my head has me jolting upright in bed and scrambling back. The panic inside me claws at my chest and every instinct is telling me to shy away and run. I take in my surroundings, realizing I'm back in my room and the person sitting on the edge of my bed is my sister.

I hate that look on her face. The look of pity and eyes that glisten with tears. She tries to reach out to me, but I pull my legs away, curling them up against my chest. "Don't touch me."

"Ronnie, I'm not going to hurt you."

"You already did. You left me. You fucking left me when I needed you the most. You *abandoned* me to that monster and now look what happened."

She frowns, slowly pulling her hand back to settle on her thigh. "You know I couldn't stay here, Ronnie. You were a child. I couldn't take you with me."

"No. You didn't *want* to take me with you. You didn't want the responsibility of having to care for anyone but yourself. I needed you and you weren't there!"

I don't mean to bring up the past this way, but after what happened this morning, the dam on my emotions has broken. It's a weird feeling, divulging everything I've kept bottled inside for years. Through the regret of saying the words, I feel a sense of relief as well. I need to say it. I can't let it keep eating away at me, and it's time my sister feels the guilt of her actions.

"I know how bad it was for you—"

"You know nothing!" I snarl. "You don't know what I had to go through, what I had to endure, Tessa. I was used and abused and fucking violated, and you know what papa did? Nothing. He did *nothing*, Tessa. Nothing to stop the abuse, but why would he when he was vicious all on his own."

"What are you talking about?" She says quietly, her face going paler with each word I speak.

"Dmitry..."

Her eyes widen. "Did he..." I nod. "Oh, god. I'm so sorry, Ronnie."

"Don't. I don't need your useless apology. I needed you then and you weren't there. I don't fucking need your pity now."

"Ronnie, I'm trying here. It's why I reached out to you and told you I was moving back to Cameron. I want to be in your life."

"Why are you here?"

"I told you last night."

I shake my head. “I mean *here*. In my room.”

“One of the maids told me what happened to you earlier and I wanted to check on you and make sure you’re okay. I doubt papa knows I’m in here.”

“Well, you better go before he takes the preferential treatment towards you and throws it out the window.”

“Ronnie, he’s not exactly happy about the situation or the fact I’m marrying someone outside the family.”

“Sure, but he’s leaving you alone because he feels like he has more control over me. I have someone, too, Tessa. I’m with someone I want to spend the rest of my life with.”

“I don’t know what to do to help you, Ronnie.”

“Help me get out of here! Help me escape this fucking prison before I get killed. I can’t be what they want me to be, and I won’t just stand by and let papa marry me off to someone that only plans to abuse me. I want to get back to Reese. I love him so much, Tessa, and I rather die than marry Mikail.”

“Have you spoken to Reese since you’ve been here?”

I shake my head. “No. They took my phone from me when Dimitry brought me here. I don’t know if he’s okay or not because Dimitry forced me to break up with him while he had a sniper rifle trained on him. It was one of the hardest things I’ve had to do, and I can’t get the look on his face out of my head. I crushed him, Tessa. I had no choice because I wouldn’t be the reason he got killed right in front of me.”

She doesn’t look at me at that. I’m sure she’s wondering if her fiancé will be in the same position. He’s already been threatened in secret, but I don’t think they’ve gone the physical route like they did with Reese.

"I'll try and find a way to get you out of here," she whispers. "There has to be a way."

I don't say anything because I don't think there *is* any way out of this. Not without one of us or both ending up getting hurt. The more this day goes on, the more panic I feel. I think I still had a bit of hope that I could get out of this. The small glimmer of escape today seemed like a beam of light guiding me to my freedom, but it was all false. It was a trap and I fell for it like a fucking idiot. No one here is on my side, so why would I think that someone would help me get out of here.

CHAPTER FIFTY-FIVE

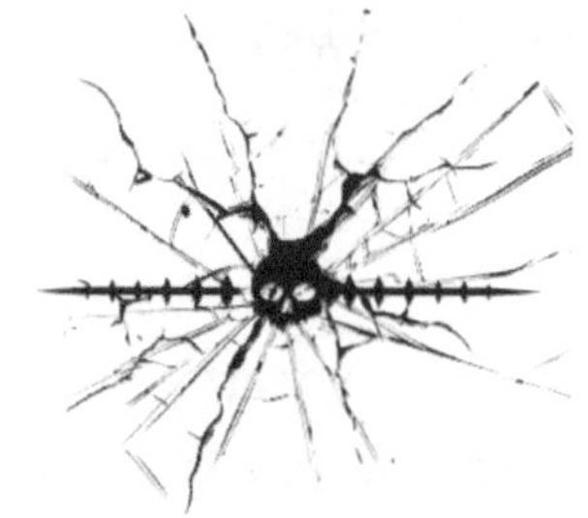

REESE

I'm seriously surprised none of my neighbours notice me walking out of the apartment loaded with weapons once again. Maybe I shouldn't be surprised. This is a good part of town, so why would they ever assume that their doctor neighbour would just be walking around with various knives and loaded guns.

I'm about to start the truck when my phone vibrates in the cup holder. I give it a glance, expecting either Holland or Kaine. I scramble to grab the phone, nearly dropping it while my heart threatens to beat right out of my chest.

"Ronnie?" Silence greets me and I pull the phone away for a second to see if the call got disconnected but she's still there. "Ronnie, are you okay?"

"This is Tessa."

My heart sinks, my entire body deflating. "Why do you have Ronnie's phone? Where is she?"

"They took her phone from her when they brought her here, but I found it and decided to call you. I—I can't get her out of here on my own. She's under full watch and when she tried to escape this morning she...they beat her and locked her back up in her room."

"Which room is it?"

"What?"

"In the house. Where is she located in the house?"

"Her bedroom is the second one to the right of the stairs."

"East or west. Your right could be my left."

"East of the stairs."

"You need to listen to me very carefully. If you're in that house right now, you need to get the fuck out of there. Don't tell anyone or do anything suspicious, just get out."

"What? Why?"

"Just do what I'm fucking telling you to do. If you value your life, get out."

"Do you want me to tell Ronnie I talked to you?"

"No. If you do that, she might try to do something stupid. All I want you to do is leave and don't look back."

"Okay. Please save her, Reese. I know you don't know me, and I don't know much about you, but I don't know what else to do for her. My hands are sort of tied."

"I hope to finally meet you on the other side of this."

"Goodbye, Reese."

I hate that Ronnie doesn't have her phone on her. It would make things so much easier if I could speak to her myself, but having Tessa talk to her might leave too much room for interpretation. The last thing I want is Ronnie does something stupid in an attempt to help me with whatever I'm doing. For Tessa to be calling me, she either knows who I am or is assuming that I'm capable enough to do what needs to be done.

I'm starting to have doubts in myself on whether or not I *can* do this, but I don't have any other options. I need to do this or my girl is fucked. I quickly set up my phone with the directions to the Petrov home and pull out of the parking lot. I'm struggling to keep myself calm while I drive, my hands clenching and unclenching on the steering wheel.

I'm playing my plan in my head, letting the city stream by in a blur. If she wasn't in the home, I would just throw everything I could at the building until it came down in a pile of rubble, but she's on the upper level which is going to make it more difficult to get her out of there safely.

I can work my way through the lower floors and get to her at the end, but if someone is on the upper level and hears what's going on, they might grab her and use her as a shield. Maybe I can get to her first, scale the wall from the outside and break into her room. I'll have to check out the layout again and see what I'm working with from the outside.

I hate that I can't park closer to the house without being flagged. I'm about two blocks away from the front of the property, pulling the laptop up to the front seat so I can pull up the blueprints. I swear under my breath when her room is the only one without an outside window, but it does have a skylight over what I assume is the bathroom. I could try going in through there if the glass is breakable enough to either break it with my body or shoot at it. The risk should be pretty low if I were to use one of my guns, but she might freak out enough that she'll scream and draw attention to herself.

Fuck, there's no easy way to do this without signaling someone in some way. The first step needs to be taking out the security at the gate without it being completely obvious. I move the feeds I have onto my phone and shove it into my pocket. Holland gave me an earpiece in case I needed him for anything, so I slip that in and get to work loading myself down with weapons. A mask of some sort would be the smartest thing to do, but that would also draw attention to me in this part of the town. It'll flag me right away if the cameras catch some weirdo walking outside the property with a mask on.

Once I have everything that I think I need on me, I throw my leather jacket on over top to cover up some of the guns. I keep my head down; hands shoved in my pockets as I make my way around the property. I want to get a feel for the fence line and everything outside the home before I go for it and scale it. There doesn't seem to be any guards on the outer edge, but I do see the security system. Some of the cameras actually follow my movements so I pull out my phone and punch in the code Holland gave me to start looping the system. He recorded sections from each camera so it's a plain old day like nothing is going on to give me time to sneak around.

By the time I make it back to the front of the house, I have a thin sheen of sweat forming on my brow, but the stage is set. I fucking hate scaling shit. I run at the fence, grabbing the upper metal bar and launching myself over it, my feet thudding against the dense grass on the other side. This definitely would have been easier in the dark, giving me more places to hide and a way to sneak up on the guard tower a bit easier. For now, the trees act as cover as I quickly make my way across the property, peeking around the tower to see the guard sitting on his phone.

Fucking useless. What's the point of all this paid muscle if they can't do their job properly. It works in my favour so I can't exactly complain, but I would be pissed if I were Misha. All this power being used for nefarious means. While one digs for oil, others drown in their own blood. There is no common ground or chance of mediation or peace, it's all about power and the rise in standing with these people. I've never been like that—never wanted it.

Keeping myself close to the ground, I grab a few rocks and toss them against the opposite wall. The guard jerks his attention up, quickly getting to his feet with his hand on the butt of his gun. The moment he steps out of the booth with his back to me, I rush him, clamping my hand over his mouth and cupping his nape at the same time I shift my grip into his jaw and twist. The snap is loud in my ears, like a gun at the start of a race. This is the beginning and there's no going back now.

I drag his limp body into the booth and snag the earpiece from him. There's a little bit of chatter but nothing that would flag me being here, which is exactly what I had hoped for. Everything is going to plan so far and easier than I anticipated. It's hard doing this all on my own and having to check the cameras and thermal imaging while moving across the property.

"Fuck," I grumble, tapping the earpiece. "Holland."

"Running into trouble already?"

I roll my eyes, leaving the guard booth to make my way up to the house. "No trouble at all but I've decided some outside eyes might be a bit helpful."

The prick laughs, but there's distinct clacking of a keyboard over the line. "You want me to be your eyes?"

I'll have to make sure to take out the cameras once inside so he doesn't catch me doing something no human should be able to do. That's the downside to bringing someone like him into this, but I couldn't exactly reach out to Kaine without prepping him. A decision I'm now beginning to regret, knowing how pissed off he was that I wouldn't let him help me with this.

"The thermal imaging should be enough. I'll have eyes on the ground, and it's not like it matters if they're armed or not. No matter what, I need to take them all down, so I won't be stopped along the way."

"But if I use the camera system in combination with the thermal, I'll be able to tell you ahead of time."

"Holland," I snap.

"Fine, fine. Don't get your panties in a twist."

"Prick."

"Don't start. You know you're acting like an asshole yourself right now. This is stupid and I shouldn't be helping you like this after you not only refused your uncle but also threatened him."

"You should feel special then since I like you and trust you more than my uncle."

He's probably blushing and flustered at the comment, and I sort of wish I could see it, but from the sudden silence, I know that I said the right thing. He mumbles something under his breath and lets out a long breath that rattles against his lips right into the earpiece.

"You're cheating," he finally says.

I grin at that, knowing how right he is. "Just admit it, Holland, I'm your favourite."

"Hardly."

"There's no one you love more than me."

"You haven't met my cat. Sir Meowskers is way more lovable than you, doesn't talk back, and doesn't ask me to do stupid shit."

"Seriously? You know cats think humans are their slaves, right? That's why they shit in a box and expect you to clean it, and you do because you're the perfect little slave boy."

"How dare you. He's a cuddler."

"He's contemplating murdering you in your sleep but thinking better of it because if he does that, he won't get fed in the morning."

We both laugh, lightening the mood enough that I feel some of the tension leaving my body. I have nothing against cats. I actually love the little fuckers and always wanted one myself, but I didn't want to take on the responsibility of taking care of an animal when I could barely manage taking care of myself. Maybe I'll get one for Ronnie after this is all over. A small gift that shows her I'm serious about us and I love her. It's not a kid and I *definitely* don't plan for one of those for a while, but she might like something that can snuggle up to her when I'm not around.

"Where'd you get the cat?" I ask as I carefully make my way across the lawn towards the house.

"Cat distribution system."

"What the fuck is that? Is that a new shop or something?"

"No," he snorts. "The cat just showed up and picked me. You shouldn't pick a cat, that never ends well. The cat needs to pick you."

"So, it's a stray?"

"Basically, yeah. Why? You want one?"

I shake my head at the clear amusement in his voice. "I think eventually, yeah. It'll humanize me a bit more, don't you think?"

"You're more human than a lot of people already and don't you ever think otherwise."

His words have a lump forming in my throat and my stomach tightening into a knot. If he only knew how wrong he was, he wouldn't be speaking to me so casually. I think I'm less human than Kaine and Eden at this point. I'm not Avery level in the non-human side of it, but I'm pretty fucking close. I haven't felt like myself for quite a while and I'm beginning to lose hope that I'll ever go back to the Reese I was before Avery made himself known.

CHAPTER FIFTY-SIX

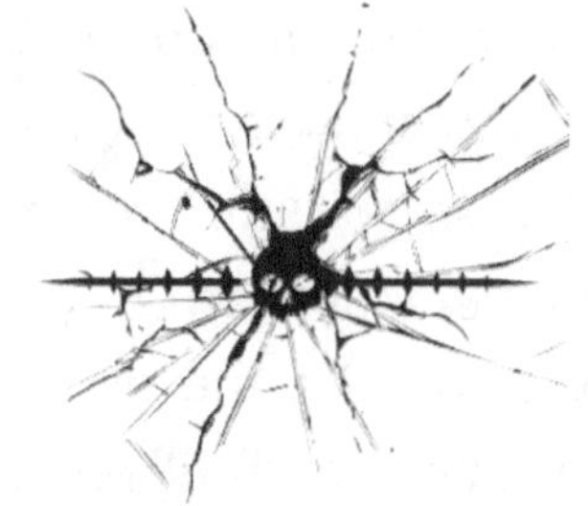

REESE

"Incoming."

I flatten myself to the wall, hearing the crunch of gravel up ahead. Carefully peeking around the corner, I see two more guards, guns poking out from their waistbands like fucking amateurs. They're laughing, puffing on their cigarettes, none the wiser that they're about to meet their maker. The moment my thoughts move to the fact I haven't seen any reapers yet is when they decide to make themselves known. Avery is going to be pissed about this but I'm not doing it on purpose. I rather they *not* be here, the distraction that they are. Their forms shimmer in the light, still not taking on any semblance of a true human form.

The guards are too far away for me to take out both of them quietly like I did with the one at the entrance. I didn't want to use my gun just yet. not wanting the risk of being too loud and drawing attention. The silencer is good, but if anyone is listening, they'll notice the noise anyways. Killing them right up front isn't ideal either, what with having two dead bodies lying around for anyone to find. I could drag them into the bushes, but then I'm risking being seen anyways and then it just blows everything up.

Wait. What if I just blow shit up. I could use the moment of panic and disarray to draw whoever I need to outside and pick everyone off as they come out the door. Misha won't come outside because he's a coward and will rely on his people to take care of the threat. Mikael doesn't actually have any loyalties to this family, so he'll be bunkered down inside as well, armed, I'm sure, but I'm okay with that.

I don't know who I would rather leave until last. Her father, who has dragged his daughter into this mess, and in turn, me since I was *trying* to get out of this lifestyle, or Mikail. I want to make them both suffer, maybe her father more than the prick who laid hands on her today. Her father was the one who allowed Dimitry to touch her in the first place, standing by and watching just like he did today. Fucking piece of shit. Just thinking about it has heat spreading through my body and my blood boiling.

"Is there anyone close to the entrance right now?" I whisper.

"There's one, everyone else seems pretty spread out with only two on the upper floor."

One of them is definitely Ronnie, but I pull out my phone and double check to make sure she's still in her room. I sigh in relief, glad that her bedroom is off the back of the house and won't feel too much of this.

"What are you doing?" I pull one of the grenades from my pocket, clamp down on the striker lever, and pull the pin. "Reese, what the fuck are you doing?"

"Fire in the hole." I throw the grenade, watching the striker spring up as it flies through the air and lands in between the two guards. Their faces are pathetically comical, wide eyes and frozen bodies before the panic sets in. It's too late, the grenade detonates, exploding the ground and littering them with metal fragments while limbs sheer off and blood spatters the surrounding area. The sound is deafening, shaking the ground beneath my feet and the foundation of the home. A few screams come from within the house and the one guard Holland saw inside comes running out, gun drawn.

My bullet hits its mark the instant he's in view, his head jerking to the side on impact before his body hits the ground. "You're insane," Holland murmurs.

"Yup." Another person comes running out, stopping right at the entrance when they notice the chaos out front. They fire their gun aimlessly into the tree line, clearly a fledgling who knows nothing about this life. I feel sort of bad watching him panic and pant until his gun is empty. He frantically tries to reload, fumbling with his mag and dropping it to the ground. "Pathetic." His fall isn't as far and less dramatic as the bullet rips through his temple.

"He was a kid."

"As am I, and yet, I know what this life is about. You either live the life properly, get out, or die trying. He shouldn't have been here, and I don't need you trying to guilt me into sparing any of these worthless humans. They made their bed; they can lie in it. No one is going to stop me from getting back what's mine."

"I get it."

"Do you?"

"Yes, I do."

"How's it looking inside?"

"You took out four of the ten within the house. The two that were upstairs have been joined by a third at the moment, and three others have run out the back."

"Those three must be the normal staff. I need to finish this before Misha has time to call in reinforcements."

I don't have time to wait around and see if they'll come outside. Knowing them, they'll try to stick to what they know and barricade themselves in one of the rooms with weapons of their own. Two of the reapers move into the house and I follow them in, striding inside like I own the place. There's no point in sneaking around now, not when I have no intention of letting the two fuckers leave this place. They won't have any chance in telling anyone who attacked their home and the bratva. It's not like I'm on some sanctioned mission anyways, but if he knows who I am, he'll assume I'm doing this for my uncle. I don't need any motivation to do this outside the fact they kidnapped Ronnie, hurt her, and threatened the life she's been trying to create.

"Come out, come out, wherever you are!" I call out, straining my ears for any sound or signs of movement.

"You're a sick fuck," Holland cackles. "You look crazy, too."

I glance up at the corner of the entrance, noticing the red light flashing from the security camera. We can't have that. I focus everything on the camera, feeling the heat rising within me as I raise my hand towards it. I can't just take out the one. I need to take out every link in this home if I have any hope of hiding the power slowly coiling inside me.

"Tread carefully," Avery murmurs into my mind.

What is there to be cautious of? This is something that needs to be done and it'll benefit him. The less people that see me using his power the better, and Holland is one of the last people I want witnessing this. I wouldn't put it past him to tell Declan. He'll be compelled to do it whether out of fear or the annoying loyalty.

"What just happened? I lost the feed on the internal cameras. Like, all of them, Reese."

"Stick to the thermal like I told you to."

"What did you just do?" I ignore the question, slowly making my way up the stairs. "You're not going to tell me, are you?"

"What gave it away?"

"You have one coming out of the first room at the top of the stairs."

He comes out alright. I guess my steps weren't as quiet as I thought they were since Mikail Ivanov comes out, gun pointed. The first shot goes wide, the second clips my shoulder, sending a burning pain through my body. I holster my own weapon and rush towards him, a move he didn't expect if his wide eyes and open mouth are any indication.

I want to tear into him with my bare hands. Make him hurt. Make him fucking suffer. My fist collides with his jaw just as he gets another shot off, clipping my hip this time. The pain isn't as bad as the first one. It could be my body getting used to it or the adrenaline pumping through my veins and burning through my nerves like liquid lightning.

He staggers to the side, somehow managing to hold onto his weapon. The psycho actually laughs, wiping at his busted lip before turning his glare on me. "Who the fuck are you?" He snorts, spitting blood onto the wooden floor.

"Your worst fucking nightmare." I hit him again, grunting when he nails me with a knee to the side, hitting where he shot me. The fucker plays dirty, another motivational marker to push me to kick his ass. "You dared lay hands on *my* fucking girl?" I snarl, tackling him to the ground and taking out a side table just inside the bedroom door.

He scrambles across the floor, kicking out at me when I try to grip into his leg to drag him closer to me. "You attacked a mafia home because of a fucking girl?" He snaps. "Are you fucking insane? You're dead!" He laughs. "You're going to die here."

"Not before you do, and she's not just some fucking girl, she's *my* girl, and she was taken from me."

He tries to kick out at me, giving me room to grab him and drag him towards me. He reaches for the gun he dropped at the same time I pull one of my blades from the holster beneath my jacket and I slam the blade through the back of his hand. He screams out in pain, jerking his arm in a desperate attempt to get free, but the blade is lodged deep into the wood. I grab his other wrist, smiling wickedly as I slam his arm down on the ground and slowly pull another blade free. He shakes his head back and forth, eyes wide and pleading.

It's too late for begging, not that it would matter. His next scream sends a shudder of satisfaction through me, blood now oozing from both his hands being impaled by my blades.

"You should have refused Misha," I whisper harshly, gripping into his jaw and grabbing another blade. His eyes dart around wildly, surely looking for something or someone that could help him. "You seem to take great pleasure in hurting others. Always laughing and smiling while inflicting pain. I think it's time to adjust your appearance to the jester you are."

A small tribute to Kaine and his obsession with Batman. Mikail freezes completely the second I hook the blade on the corner of his mouth, slowly sliding the steel in. "Please," he says carefully. "I won't touch her."

"You already did and that's the problem here." Muscle and tendon tear like butter under the sharpness of the steel, the cut slicing right up to his upper molars. He's shaking now, tears streaming down his cheeks as a pathetic sob slips through his maimed lips. I hook the blade onto the other side, giving him a small reprieve when I slice quickly. Another sob and a small scream, but it's not nearly enough. "Look at you. So pretty with that smile," I tease, relishing in the pain on his face. "I'm going to take you apart, piece by fucking piece."

I feel the reaper behind me without even looking at it, it's presence like a cold shroud curling against my body. Not yet. They can't take him yet. As long as his heart is still beating, I'll have my fun with him. I'm going to do to him what I had hoped to do to Dimitry. My sadistic vengeance was cut short with him, but not now. Now, I plan to savor every moment before his death.

"You and your cousin are the same in so many ways." I tap the tip of the knife against my lip, eyeing one of his hands and then the other. "Which one did you use to hit her?"

"What?" He gasps, but the word is muffled and wrong since his mouth no longer works properly.

"Left or right? Tell me which hand you used to strike Ronnie."

"Fuck you!" I press the blade to his index finger on the right hand, slowly putting pressure down. "Stop! No!" He screams when the reddened metal slices through tendon and scrapes against bone, blood squirting out all over the floor. I move to the next finger. "You fucking psycho!"

"We're all a little psycho with the right motivation." Another finger falls away and another scream breaks through his horrifying maw.

CHAPTER FIFTY-SEVEN

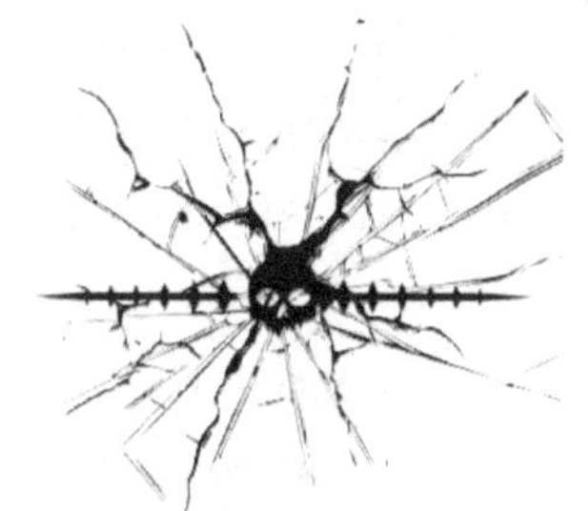

REESE

“Papa, no!”

My head jerks to the side at the sound of Ronnie’s panicked voice, quickly getting drawn back to the sound of Mikail’s gurgled laugh. “You lose,” he rasps.

“Not yet.” I slam the blade into his chest and lurch to my feet, glaring at the reaper. “Take him and make sure that wretched soul never sees the light of day.”

The reaper hesitates for a moment but does what I say, much to Avery’s dismay. *“You need to end this.”*

“Oh, I’m planning to.”

“If you keep going down this path, there’s no coming back, kid. You’re letting my power in too deep. It’s going to change you.”

"Fuck you, it already has. If you didn't want to risk this happening, you should have never possessed me in the first place. You're *my* fucking bitch now."

The scene unfolding in front of me as I come out of the room and look down the stairs doesn't make any sense. Anger surges through me with each methodical step I take, my hand finding my gun and slowly pulling it out of the holster. My eyes flick between Ronnie and her father behind her.

"Don't move," Misha snarls, shoving the muzzle of the gun against Ronnie's temple. "I said don't fucking move!"

He backs away slowly towards the entrance, dragging his daughter with him. She claws at his arm wrapped around her chest and my heart breaks for her. Her left eye is bloodshot, the skin around it purple and blue, and her lip is crusted and scabbed over with a vicious cut. Her eyes widen when she realizes it's me, tears springing into her eyes.

"Looks like you've been snared, little rabbit," I whisper, and she chokes out a sob.

"Reese."

Hearing her voice tightens my chest. It feels like it's been too long since I heard her voice and seen her beautiful face. I don't like seeing her like this, weak and vulnerable. This isn't the Ronnie I know, but she's still the one I love. All her trauma has been brought back to the surface just by being here, only to be made worse with continued abuse.

"Not another step or I kill her," Misha says harshly.

I stop, shifting my gaze from her to him. There's no stopping the rage and venom I have coiling inside of me from leaching out towards him as I glare at him. "That is your *daughter*. How can you show no love towards her? How can you be so cruel? You should cherish her and protect her, not continue to throw her to the wolves in the hopes of benefitting your goals."

"You're right, she's my daughter, and as my daughter, she should do as she's told. It's her responsibility to marry and benefit our organization. She's a princess who should be queen."

"That's where you're wrong. She's already a queen, just not to you."

"Irish scum like you has no place here. Your existence has been a plague on this city, and with this union, we plan to eradicate you."

I grin at that. "What union?" I ask, my brow lifting in question. "If you mean that sack of meat upstairs, he won't be giving you shit unless it's a shallow grave and maggots feasting on your corpse." He pales at that, eyes darting around frantically. "There's no one left. All your guards are dead, and the rest of your staff ran at the first sign of trouble. It's just us, Misha, and I doubt your reinforcements will show up before I kill you."

He cocks the gun against Ronnie's temple, the sound radiating through the room. "Drop your gun or I shoot her."

Can I get to him before he's able to get off a shot? There's a reaper hanging behind him, watching like a sentient spectre, and showing no signs of how this event will play out. There's only one so that should be decent odds that it's Misha. I take another step, jolting to a halt when another reaper phases through the wall to stand next to the other. No. This can't be right. It's one thing if I'm the one meant to die with Misha, but what if it's here for Ronnie? It's not a risk I'm willing to take, but I don't know how to get to her without her getting caught in the crossfire.

"Fine," I murmur, tossing the gun towards him and lifting my hands to show him I don't plan to attack.

"What the fuck are you doing?" Holland hisses in my ear. I ignore him, keeping my eyes trained on the two of them.

"Pick it up," Misha murmurs, releasing Ronnie and shoving her forward while he keeps the gun pointed at her back. She's shaking, eyes locked on mine. "I said pick it up!" He yells. She flinches, blinking rapidly as she slowly bends down and picks the gun up, holding it at her side. "Kill him."

Her back stiffens and her jaw begins to tremble. "Papa—"

"I said shoot him! Kill him or I kill you. It's your choice, milaya."

She shakes her head back and forth, taking a tentative step towards me. "I—I can't."

"Do it!"

"I can't kill him!" She screams, tears streaming down her cheeks.

This is a horrible situation, one that Misha should have never put her in. Not only is he forcing her to kill someone, but she's also having to kill someone she cares about. I hold my hands out to my sides and give her a sad smile. "It's okay, Ronnie," I whisper. "You need to live."

"I don't want to live without you!" She sobs, shaking her head and sending her tears scattering. "I rather die than kill you."

She gasps when Misha presses the muzzle of his gun to the back of her head, giving her a shove for good measure. "The only one dying here today is him."

I know he's wrong for the simple fact the reaper count tells me that two of us will die. The longer I watch them, the heavier the dread settles into the pit of my stomach. I still have one gun tucked against my back, but can I get to it quickly enough to shoot Misha before Ronnie shoots me or he shoots her? It's the only logical outcome. Ronnie will live—she *has* to. If this is where I die, I'm okay with it, as long as she survives this. She'll be okay. She'll still have her sister and Eden and Kaine.

Fuck.

Thinking about Kaine just spirals me further. I won't get to say goodbye to him or that I'm sorry for being such a fucking idiot. It doesn't matter anymore. I did what I had to for him and got him the life he deserves.

"Shoot me," she whispers.

"Excuse me?"

"Shoot me! I won't fucking kill him, so you'll have to kill me, you coward!"

"Useless," he snarls, shoving her out of the way. She stumbles to the side, falling to the ground as Misha points the gun towards me. I reach for my own gun at the same moment he squeezes the trigger, both our shots ringing out at the same time.

Misha falls to the ground, gasping and gurgling around the gunshot through his neck. I don't feel pain, but what I do feel is arms wrapped around me. Arms that are slowly falling away.

No.

Ronnie stares up at me; eyes bowed in sadness as blood trickles from the corner of her mouth.

"No!" I catch her before she can fall to the ground on her own, easing her down. My hand is shaking as I pull it away from her back, the skin covered in her blood. "Ronnie, why would you do that?"

Her hand trembles as she reaches up to touch my cheek, her fingers gentle and the touch loving. This was not how I wanted things to happen. This was not how I expected to hold her. "I couldn't...let you...die," she whispers. "You've been through so much, Reese." She coughs, the sound wet as blood escapes her lips. "I'm so sorry I...hurt you. I—I didn't mean it. Any of it."

"I know, baby." I can't stop my own tears from falling, my hand brushing through her hair in gentle strokes. "It'll be okay. You'll be okay."

She smiles, eyes closing on a choked sob. Her breathing is ragged and raw, each inhale a struggle to chase the oxygen she needs. "I love you."

"I love you, too, Ronnie." A dark shadow crosses over our bodies, pulling my attention upward to the reaper hovering next to us. "You can't have her," I grit out. It tips its head, slowly lifting its wispy hand out. "No!"

"Reese," Avery whispers into my mind.

"Take me, not her. You can't have her!"

"That's not how this works and you know that. You've already interfered enough."

"Fuck you, Avery! This isn't over. Not like this."

Think, Reese, think. There has to be something I can do to save her. She's too far gone to get her to the hospital in time, and with the reaper literally about to rip out her soul, I'm running out of options here. I can *feel* her soul beginning to untether as the reaper reaches for her again.

I'm up in an instant, my hand wrapping around the reapers throat hard enough its shadows fragment from the force of it. I slam it down into the ground, forcing its corporeal form into existence. It's a man this time, glowing green eyes staring widely up at me as he claws at my wrist. "Don't touch her!" I snarl.

"Reese, let him go," Avery murmurs.

"No! You will not take her."

"She's already dead. Her soul is coming undone and she needs to be collected before she wanders."

"She's not dead yet." I release the reaper, looming over him as heat boils in my blood. "Don't move."

Shadows erupt from the ground, gripping and clawing at his body until he's wrapped in a cocoon of black smoke. I move back towards Ronnie and kneel down beside her, propping her up in my arms. Her eyes are closed now, the faint beating of her heart getting slower and quieter. I need to think. Avery healed Eden and Kaine. He has the power to mend wounds so I should be able to do the same thing. I don't know what I'm doing or what will happen to me if I succeed, but I don't care. It should have been me. I'm the one who should have been shot today. I'm the one who should be dying, not her. Never her.

"It'll be okay," I whisper, placing my hand against the wound on her back where her blood is still pouring out and her skin is beginning to turn cold. "I love you, Ronnie." I close my eyes, picturing the hole in her back closing and pushing out the bullet still lodged there. Pain rips through me, skull crushing agony that has me gasping and crying out.

"You need to stop."

"Fuck you," I grit out. "I'm going to save her, even if it means giving up my own life to do it. That bullet was meant for me, not her, Avery."

"The bullet was always meant for her. This isn't your fault, Reese. Ronnie was meant to die here."

"I refuse to accept that. If you want a soul, you take mine in her place but let me save her first."

"You don't even know what you're doing."

"Then help me! Help me save her. Please," I sob. "I'm fucking begging you. I can't lose anyone else. I refuse to lose another person that I love. I can't—" A shock of electricity rips through me, forcing my body to curl in around hers. "I *won't* let her die."

The longer I stay tethered to her like this, the more it feels like my life is slipping through my fingers. I don't care. If this is what it takes, I'll do it. I'll pour all I am into her if it means she gets to see another day. She'll have the opportunity to live the dream I had for us, the future I dreamed for the both of us. She'll get to see another sunrise and sunset, even if I'm not the one sitting next to her on that porch. She'll be happy. She'll smile and become a wonderful mother to beautiful children and live to a ripe old age.

I have nothing left. My body is weakening, falling, slumping against her until we're both lying on the floor. I think I hear Holland saying something in my ear, but I can't make it out. My vision blurs on Ronnie's face. She looks like she's sleeping, the tears on her cheek drying out against the blood coating her skin. I feel weak, struggling to lift my hand one more time to brush against her pale cheek. The darkness is creeping in, shadows dancing across my vision and blurring the reality around me. I tried. I tried so fucking hard to give her what she deserves, but I think it's too late. I don't want to be here. I don't want to live, knowing that I failed her in every way that mattered.

“I’m sorry.”

CHAPTER FIFTY-EIGHT

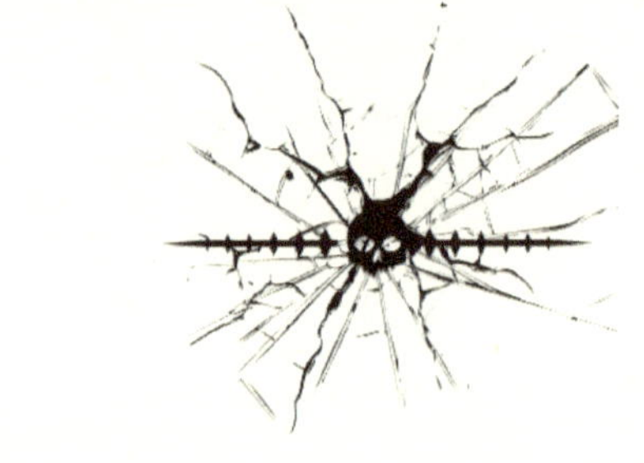

RONNIE

Beep. Beep. Beep.

Everything feels like lead weights. My mind, my eyelids, my entire body. The beeping sounds distant, echoing like sound in a well, and there's a strange hissing sound like wind through a tunnel. Am I dead? I don't feel dead, not with the pain coursing through my body. I thought death would be peaceful and full of light at the end, but all I feel is pain and sadness.

The look on Reese's face when he realized what I had done is burned into my memory. The look of pain and betrayal. The look of regret and love. He loved me in the end and was angry at me for doing something out of that love. I couldn't watch him die. I couldn't let it happen after I fought so hard to save him from Dimitry.

I feel cold, but there's warmth in my hand, my fingers twitching to cling to it. Pressure wraps around that hand before more warmth caresses my forehead and cheek.

"Ronnie?"

I fight against the weight pressing into me, prying my eyes open and flinching at the burning light pouring into my retinas. It's hard to focus. Hard to solidify the form in front of me, but I recognize that voice.

"Eden?" I croak out, my throat feeling like sandpaper. Slowly she comes into focus. She looks tired. Eyes puffy and red like she's been crying for hours, hair a disheveled mess, and trembling lips.

"You're awake," she laughs through tears. "Don't try to sit up." She gently pushes me back down and grabs a corded button next to my bed. "I'll get one of the nurses in here to check you over so just sit tight."

"Reese?" Her throat bobs on a swallow and she turns away from me. What does that mean? Why isn't she answering me? "Where's Reese?" I thought I saved him. I thought he would be okay, but did I fuck it up? Did he get shot anyways? Was my father not dead in the end? How the fuck am I still alive?

"He's—"

"Oh, you're awake." A nurse walks in, interrupting whatever Eden was about to tell me. I curse under my breath, wanting nothing more than to tell this asshole off because I need to know if he's okay. "How are you feeling, Miss. Halladay?"

Another tick to the shit list. Miss. Halladay, like I'm not a fucking doctor myself. I glare at him until his stupid smile falters. He panics when I rip out the IV in my arm, rushing forward to stop me.

"Back off."

"You shouldn't be doing that. You've lost a lot of blood and you're dehydrated. We need to keep you monitored."

I ignore him, shoving him away when he tries to push the IV back in. "Eden, where the fuck is Reese? How did I even get here?"

"He's in a room down the hall. Kaine is with him waiting to see if he'll wake up."

"What happened?" She glances at the nurse and gnaws on her lip. "Get out." He looks like I just slapped him across the face, offended not even covering the look of horror crossing his features. "I'm fine or have you forgotten I'm a doctor as well. I don't need you to tell me what to do when I know what my body feels like. Get out. I won't ask again." He doesn't though, he hovers awkwardly next to the bed, shifting his eyes from me to Eden.

"She'll be fine," Eden says, motioning for him to leave. I can feel her glaring at me as I throw the itchy blanket off my body and shift my legs to the side. My feet touch the ground, but they don't stay under me, forcing me to grab the edge of the bed to steady myself. "You shouldn't be walking around. As a doctor, you know better."

"I need to see him."

"He's not even awake."

"Tell me what happened."

"You and Reese were brought in last night. Some guy named Holland showed up with both of you in the emergency bay. You were both covered in blood and unconscious, but neither of you had any injuries."

My hand instinctively moves to my back. I know I got shot. I felt the burning fire of the bullet ripping through me and the blood pouring out of me with no end in sight. "That's not possible. I got shot."

She moves towards me, shifting the gown to the side to check out my back. "Oh my god."

"What? What is it?"

"You—there's—fuck. Did Reese tell you about Avery?"

"Yes." My anxiety spikes at the name of the reaper being mentioned.

"You've been healed. You're marked like me and Kaine and now Reese, too."

"What? What does that mean? I don't understand any of this."

"I don't know how it happened, but a reaper must have stepped in to help you. I don't know what's happened with Reese though. I don't think he has any new marks on him but I'm not sure. It's hard to know what's happened when he isn't awake and Holland didn't say anything."

"Wait. How did you two end up here?"

"Reese has us as his emergency contacts when you're not available."

"I need to see him."

"Fine." She moves to one of the cabinets and pulls out a robe, helping me into it. She wraps her arm around my shoulders, letting me lean into her as she leads me out of the room and down the hallway towards Reese's room. She knocks before opening the door, but it doesn't give Kaine enough time to wipe the tears completely from his face. "Hey," she says, leading me over to the bed.

His eyes shift to me, his brows dipping into a frown. "What are you doing here? You should be resting."

"How is he?" I ask, hating seeing Reese lying on the bed like that, motionless and hooked up to monitors.

Kaine's gaze shifts back to him, my heart tightening at the concern on his face as he grips Reese's hand and reaches up to brush his hair back from his face. I can see how much he cares about Reese, always treating him well and doing everything he can for him. Kaine is the type of person that would defend him until his last dying breath, and it's obvious how careful he is with him right now.

"He still hasn't woken up," he says quietly. "The doctors don't know what's wrong with him or why he's still like this. It's just like he's sleeping. I should have been there."

"There's nothing you could have done."

He shakes his head and pulls in a deep breath that rattles in his chest. "I still should have been there."

Eden walks towards him and settles her hand on his shoulder, giving it a gentle squeeze. "Let's go home for a little bit. I think you need to get some proper sleep and take a hot shower."

"I don't want to leave him," he whispers. "If it were me, he wouldn't leave me."

"You know he wouldn't want you running yourself thin either. Just a few hours, Kaine. I'm sure Ronnie will call if anything comes up."

He looks at me then, eyes filled with sadness and showing an insane level of exhaustion. "He loves you," he says quietly. "He knew what he was going into and he didn't care, Ronnie. He only had one thing on his mind and that was getting you out of that situation, even if it meant he didn't come out of it himself. Reese has always been like that. He's always been reckless and willing to do the hard shit that no one else would ever think of doing. I'm...glad you're okay."

"I'm okay because of him. I don't know how, but I know he did something to help me." He frowns, eyes burning into me. I can't look back. Everything in me screams to turn away, so I do. "Eden said I have marks on my back...where I got shot."

"You were shot?" I nod. "I don't understand—"

"Reaper," Eden sighs. "I don't know if it was Avery or not, but if he's still possessing Reese, it would make sense."

"That doesn't sound like him. Avery is a stickler for rules and isn't easily swayed like that. Unless Reese promised him something..." He shakes his head like he's trying to get rid of whatever though just went through his mind.

"What? What did he promise?"

"I don't know, but it could be why he's not waking up."

I don't want to think about that. I can't handle it if in the end Reese ended up sacrificing himself to save me. It was *my* responsibility to save him because of the shit storm I dragged him into. We both lied, but his lies didn't end up putting me in any dangerous situations. If I could go back and change things, I would. First, I would have told him the truth about me right from the beginning and given him the choice on whether he could handle being with someone that had mafia ties. At least then, everything would have been on the table, and he could have made an informed decision when it came to our relationship.

Instead of doing that, I basically tricked him into falling for someone that wasn't even real, just a shell of my true self, a fucking mask. I feel like a piece of shit for hiding things from him, and in a way, manipulating him. Does he feel the same way? Does he wish he would have been honest with me about who he is as well? I don't think my opinion of him would have changed just for knowing that side of him. I don't care who he is by name, all I care about is who he is as a person.

Reese is sweet and kind and so fucking giving, but under all of that is a deadly man who won't hesitate to remove anyone he feels is in his way. I should have seen it simmering beneath the surface. All his moments of anger and frustration still flexed so much control while the monster beneath clawed and scraped at him to be set free.

It's not just a birthright; it's a way of life. Something that is ingrained in us from a young age. I know it's far worse for males born into the family. I know what I've been put through and what I've experienced and had to endure. I'm trained as well, but nowhere near the level Reese has been. He's a finely honed weapon waiting to be used, but he's tried to take away the power his family has had over him.

His mother got him out. The one person that was with him through all of it and stuck by his side, trying to give him a life he deserved outside of the one he was born into.

“Who’s Holland?” I ask. I know the change of subject is weird but I’m trying to make sense of it all. Some things just aren’t adding up, like why he was alone through all of that. If he had the power of the Irish mob behind him, they wouldn’t just give up the chance to take down one of the bratva branches and the ability to overthrow and take over the territory. Fuck, that territory should fall to Tessa now unless someone does decide to overthrow her and take it for themselves. All of this has put a target on her back as well, putting her life in danger.

“Holland is one of his contacts. He must have had an open line of communication with Reese, and when he didn’t respond, he went in.”

“You mean an Irish mob contact?” Kaine’s eyes widen. “I know who he is, Kaine. My father found everything on him, and he tried to use that information against me.”

“And…you’re okay with this?”

I shrug. “It doesn’t make me love him any less. If anything, I think I love him more, if that’s humanly possible. He obviously knew who I was and he still came for me. He risked his life for me and took out people I never thought would ever leave me. I hated my father and the man he wanted me to marry, and there’s another…Dimitry.”

“He took care of him the other day.”

“The warehouse?” Kaine nods. “He came for me right away.” I don’t even know what to say. The day after I left him and broke his heart, he put his plan into motion.

“Kaine,” Eden says, squeezing his shoulder again.

“Fine, but only for a few hours.” He lifts to his feet, knees popping as he stands. “Promise you’ll call.”

“I will. I won’t leave him until you come back.” Even after they return, I won’t leave his side until he wakes. *If* he wakes. No, I can’t think like that. Reese is going to wake up—he has to—and if he doesn’t…I don’t know what I’ll do.

CHAPTER FIFTY-NINE

REESE

"You just don't listen, do you?" My eyes spring open, expecting blinding light to greet me, but all I see is darkness. Very familiar darkness. Light footsteps get closer to me, followed by a heavy sigh. "I tried to warn you, kid. Your body can't handle that level of power when it's being used like that. It's one thing when I'm the one wielding it through you, your body a simple vessel, but the power never flows through you directly. You just had to fucking siphon to that extent."

"Shut the fuck up, Avery," I grumble, staring up into the empty darkness.

His face pops into view above me, his features clear as day, like his skin holds some weird internal light. "I will not shut the fuck up. You're stuck here until I fucking deal with you." He rolls his eyes, backing up once again to give me space. "I don't even know how to deal with you. This isn't something that's ever happened before and I feel as though it's partially my fault."

"Partially?" I snort. "When it comes to seeing reapers and souls and the fucked-up powers, I'm pretty sure that's completely your fault."

He waves his hand in front of his face and rolls his eyes, dismissing my comment like it's irrelevant. "Semantics."

"You're a dick."

"That mouth of yours is going to get you into more trouble than you're worth."

"Pretty sure my mouth has gotten me out of trouble plenty of times. I'm quite good with my mouth."

He grins at that and shakes his head as a deep, booming laugh bubbles out of his throat. "You're ridiculous. Making jokes when your life is on the line is not a very smart defense mechanism. This is serious."

I slowly prop myself up on my elbows, trying to take in my surroundings, but everything is as black as it was the last time. No flicker of light, no hint of life as far as the abyss spreads out around us. There's no rhyme or reason to this space, a feeling of existing but not at the same time. I feel untethered, even though there's a gentle tug in my chest, right behind my ribs.

"I knew what could happen when I went to save Ronnie and I'll live with the consequences. Or die, depending on how you look at it. I've already told you I don't care what happens to me as long as the people I love are safe. All I want is for them to live out their lives the way they deserve, even if it's without me."

"You're willing to do that? You're willing to let Ronnie go and know that she'll find someone else to take your place and give her the life she's been desperate for? After everything you've done for Kaine, the sacrifices you've made, you're okay to never see him again?"

A lump forms in my throat, thick and restricting, no matter how hard I try to swallow around it. Air seems nonexistent in my lungs, but I nod my head, resigning myself to what he's implying. "If my death is what needs to happen for them to be happy, yes, I would give it all up for them."

"You're an idiot, you know that?"

"Why do you say that?"

"You humans and your love. Do you not understand the stupidity behind it? You all do unimaginable things in the name of love like it's some sort of cure all or protection, even going as far as to do unspeakable things because of it. Look at you. You went off on a rampage and killed countless people in just a few short days because of this love. Do you not think that's excessive?"

"Not at all. I've done far worse in the past for lesser reasons."

"You didn't have a choice."

"Didn't I? I could have ended my life then and saved everyone I killed. I could have spared their lives if I weren't a selfish person trying to survive."

Avery crouches down beside me, brows furrowed and lips pressed into a hard line. "Wanting to survive doesn't make you selfish. Wanting a life for yourself doesn't make you selfish, Reese. Your mother did everything she could to provide for you and raise you into the man you are today. She didn't sacrifice herself, she lived and cared for you as a mother should."

"She still left me. She was still taken from me in the end."

"And how did that make you feel? How do you think the people who love you would feel if you were to leave them like she left you?"

I hate to admit it but he's right. If they feel even a fraction of what I felt when I lost my mother, it would crush them. Am I that important to them? Will my memory live on within them and haunt them when anything reminds them of me? Ronnie was willing to die for me as well, throwing herself in front of a fucking bullet so that I could live. That love is dangerous. The love we feel for each other could end up destroying us. Leaving her will still put her at risk if my uncle decides to overtake her family's territory. She could get caught up in that war anyways, making my death worthless.

"Aren't I already dead," I murmur. "It felt like I was dying while I tried to help her. I don't even know if she made it out or if we're now both destined to be wandering through the abyss." I look at him then, pleading with my eyes. "Please don't keep us separated. If my soul can be with hers, I want at least that much from you."

"She's alive. You were able to manipulate my power and healed her wound before it completely took her life. She's currently in the hospital as we speak."

A mixture of relief and sadness wells up inside of me. I drop my head, trying to hide the tears that are threatening to break through. "Good. That's good then." My chest rattles on my next inhale, shoulders slumping in defeat. "I'm ready."

"Ready for what?"

"You're here to collect me, so just get it over with already. I know I deserve it. I've done terrible things and ended up using you the same way you've used me. I've broken your laws and threatened your reapers. Just fucking get it over with, Avery."

"Technically, those rules only apply to the reapers under my order. You're not a reaper, Reese. I can't exactly punish you for your actions. Anyone else might classify you as a rogue like I did with Luther, but he went against direct orders. When have you ever listened to anything I've told you to do? There is no compulsion there for you to fall in line, and my words to you were more a warning and a recommendation." He pats my shoulder and lurches to his feet, holding out his hand to me. "Come on."

My throat feels like it's closing in on itself as I settle my hand in his, letting him pull me to my feet. "Will it hurt?"

"Maybe. It's hard to know what'll happen...when you wake up."

CHAPTER SIXTY

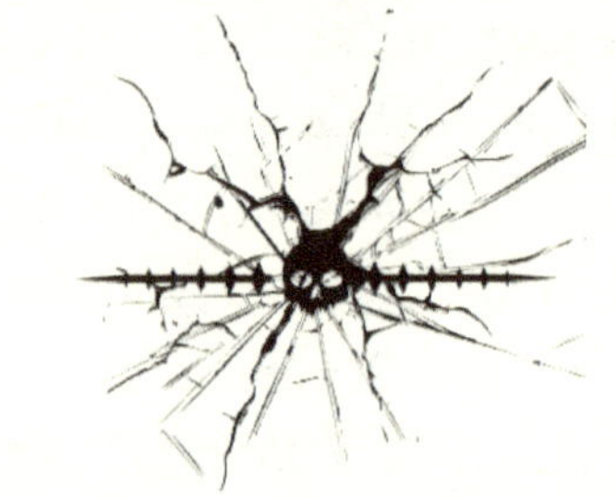

REESE

Maybe? *Maybe?* I feel like I got hit by a bus. Not the pain I was expecting when I asked him and I'm still a bit confused, but I don't feel dead.

When I wake up.

That can only mean one thing, right? I'm alive. Avery didn't claim my soul like I expected him to, instead, shoving me back into my body to suffer through what I've done to myself.

"Fuck," I groan, trying and failing to lift my hand to touch my throbbing head.

"Reese?" A broken voice asks. I strain to open my eyes, blinking away the haze settled into my vision. "Reese!" Ronnie comes into focus, hair disheveled and eyes red from crying. She still has the bruise marring her face and the cut on her lip, but she's here. She's really here and alive and walking around. She's dressed in a hospital gown with a thin robe thrown over her frame, but she's fucking here. Her fingers tremble as they carefully touch my cheek, like she's checking to make sure I'm real, too.

"Ronnie," I whisper, my tongue feeling two sizes too big for my mouth. It's dry and thick and a struggle to use it properly. My breath wheezes out of me when she throws herself over me, squeezing me in a death grip. She sobs into my neck, nuzzling her face against my skin. "Are you okay?"

"I am now," she sniffles. I grip into her, lifting her body up on top of mine. "Reese," she huffs. "You're still healing."

She squeals when I wrap my arms around her, crushing her against my chest. "Let me enjoy this. I missed you so much."

Her eyes meet mine as she props her chin on my chest, eyes filled with sadness and longing. "I'm sorry I was cruel to you. I—I didn't want to leave you."

"You were trying to protect me." I press my lips to her forehead. "I'm glad I didn't scare you away."

She smiles at that, hiding her face in my neck again. "So, you'll forgive me?"

"Hmm, I think you might have to work for some of that forgiveness, but yes, Ronnie, I forgive you."

Her fingers trail soft circles along my collarbone, the sensation creating goosebumps on my skin. "I'm sorry I lied to you about who I am."

"I lied to you, too."

"We're both so fucked up," she laughs, the sound not holding much humour.

"Fucked up but two broken pieces that fit well together. I don't know what'll happen now, but I'm not going anywhere, Ronnie, and I hope you stick around, too."

"Of course I will. There isn't anywhere else I want to be, Reese. Do you think your family will step in now?"

"Maybe. I don't know what my uncle plans to do, but there's still the threat that Mikail's family will try to retaliate. I wasn't trying to cause a war between the different groups, that's why I did all of this on my own, but they may take it as an act of war against them."

"My sister is the oldest. It'll fall to her since she's the next in line to succeed."

"I spoke with her—your sister. She called me from your phone and told me where you were. She helped quite a bit with just the information she had available to her."

"I didn't know that."

"I told her not to tell you. I didn't want you to do something to try and help me get you out and end up getting hurt in the process. I guess it didn't really matter in the end. You still got hurt. You still got fucking shot."

"I wasn't going to let my father kill you."

"Are you upset with me for killing him?"

"No. If you didn't do it, I would have done it myself. He never loved me. He never saw me as a daughter, just someone he could use to help him gain more power."

"I took care of Dimitry and I made Mikail suffer. No one has a right to put hands on you and make you hurt. No one who harms you deserves to live."

"My own guardian angel," she giggles.

"More like your own reaper on a leash."

Is the joke in bad taste? Probably. Do I fucking care? Nope, not at all. Avery caged himself within me, but I no longer hold animosity towards him. He's given me what I asked of him and has allowed me to live when I've done everything to deserve his wrath. He protected me, not as a vessel, but as a person. He healed me again, the gunshots I suffered aching but not painful, and when I glance down, I notice the new threads of darkness inked into my skin at the shoulder. I'm sure the one on my hip is the same; tattoos that paint me as other and no longer fully human. I may not be as invincible as Kaine or Eden, but I have a bit of an edge now in comparison to someone like Ronnie. She's still human. She's still vulnerable.

"How did we get to the hospital?" The thought registers late and a slight panic begins to pulse in my chest. If we were found in the home, I'll more than likely be visited by the police soon enough. Her home was left in ruins with bodies everywhere. I'm not left with much room to spin the story in my favour at this point, and I highly doubt my uncle will try to get me out of this situation when it risks his standing and the hooks he already has within the police force.

"Your friend Holland brought us in, according to Eden."

"Wait, Eden was here? Was Kaine?" She nods. "Holland brought us in?" She nods again.

That idiot. I told him not to get involved. Him interfering like that is going to bring Declan's wrath down on him. It was one thing to use him and have him help me from a distance, but he threw himself right into the fire and got us out before the attention was drawn to us. I don't know whether to thank him or kick his ass, both needs battling it out inside of me for dominance.

"I want to go home," I murmur, hugging her again.

"Me, too. I'm sure the doctors will want to check you over first and I'll make the call to Eden to see if they'll drive us." She moves to pull away but I don't let her go, not wanting this to end just yet. "Reese?"

"Just a little longer." She laughs at that, curling herself into me again and letting me enjoy the feel of her body against mine and the warmth radiating out from her.

CHAPTER SIXTY-ONE

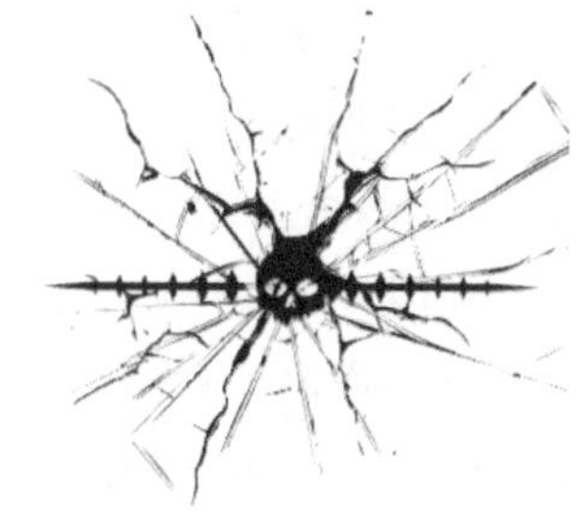

REESE

"How are you feeling?"

Kaine holds out a bottle of beer to me and flops down on the couch next to me. The girls are busy in the kitchen, insisting on cooking us dinner. Ronnie and I were both released with a clean bill of health and no explanation as to why we were unconscious in the first place. They wouldn't know what happened to either of us anyways. Ronnie made sense. She lost a lot of blood and needed to be looked after, but as for my own unexplained reason for not waking up, it definitely had a supernatural reason.

I used power that was never mine to use. I tapped into a force that doesn't exist in this world. It was one thing when Avery used my body as a vessel to do what he needed to do because my body was just that, a physical form for him to use his power. When I did it, it wasn't the same. I used his abilities, but I was using my weak human body to power everything. It took a toll on me, and I shouldn't have woken up.

I still don't understand why Avery took pity on me and helped me in the end. I didn't do anything to warrant that from him, turning my back on him at every turn and going as far as to rip into him every chance I had. I know I got lippy with him on more than one occasion, but he never retaliated in a way that would harm me. He could have said no to my request about Kaine and his Lazarus, he had every reason to, and I couldn't exactly blame him for trying to find the balance once again.

I owe him more now than I did before, something that should bother me more than it does. I hate owing people anything, never wanting to be dragged into something I don't want to do of my own free will, but with him, I don't feel as hesitant now to help him.

Because of him, I still have my best friend and the girl I love. Because of him, I'm still alive and breathing fresh air. I still need to call Holland and make sure he's okay after everything. I thought I heard him speaking to me in the end, but I couldn't focus on anything, my own heart pounding in my ears, overtaking anything else that was going on around me.

Kaine bumps into my shoulder, pulling me away from my thoughts and back to the present. "Seriously, are you okay? You had us worried there."

"I feel okay. As for whether I am or not, only time will tell. I don't know what's going to happen now or if I'm going to keep experiencing the things I have been. I think Avery is still with me, but he's been quiet since I left the hospital."

"I can't believe he saved Ronnie."

"He didn't. I'm the one that did it. I just—I couldn't let her die, man. I just put all my will into helping her—into fucking fixing her. I guess it was too much for me and that's why I passed out."

"Your buddy Holland really came through for you in the end there." Kaine sounds a bit disappoint. I'm sure he wishes it were him there and not Holland, but Holland wasn't supposed to be anywhere near the property anyways. He clearly has the same bad habits as Kaine and doesn't listen to what's good for him. They would probably get along really well if they were to ever meet. Not that I want to let that happen because it's bad enough that Kaine is even a small blip on their radar at this point. The last thing I want is my family finding out the type of tie that Kaine has to me. They already know I did a huge favour for him when they spied on the farmhouse, but I don't think they got a proper look at Kaine. The property was dark and we were careful.

"He's not my buddy, he's an employee, and he did something he wasn't supposed to, Kaine."

"I'm glad he did. If he hadn't, you'd both be in handcuffs right now."

"Ronnie wouldn't. She had nothing to do with it, and she was a victim of everything that happened. I—" A hand on my shoulder stops me mid-sentence. Ronnie smiles down at me, slowly moving around the side of the couch until she's standing in front of me. "All done?" I ask.

"The lasagna is in the oven, so we just have to wait." I smile when she climbs on top of me, straddling my hips and sitting into my lap. I love it when she runs her fingers up and down my nape, my skin pebbling at the gentle contact. "I hope you have an appetite."

"Hmm, I could definitely eat."

"Are you planning to do anything later?"

I grip into her hips and lift my own slightly into hers, loving the way she pins her bottom lip between her teeth. "Am I supposed to be doing something later?" She shrugs. "Hmm, not something, unless you want to be my toy so I can use you."

Her cheeks redden and her mouth pops open in surprise. "I—"

"Do you want to be my toy, Ronnie?" I whisper, leaning in close enough to nip at her ear. "Do you want me to use you?"

"We—we have company." Her eyes drift to Kaine, who I'll admit, I sort of forgot he was even sitting there. His eyes are wide, darting between the both of us. "Sorry," Ronnie murmurs.

"Don't apologize. If Kaine didn't want to see this he would leave. Wouldn't you?" I pin him with a glare and he swallows, startling when Eden walks up beside him.

"I—well, it's not like you two are going to fuck in front of us, right?" He laughs. "Right?" He says again when I don't respond.

I grin. "I'm not shy and I feel a bit...pent up. It's been a while since I've had my girl."

"Eden, we should go."

"But I just put dinner in the oven," she whines.

He turns his head slowly, staring at her with wide eyes. I can't quite pinpoint the look on Eden's face. Her cheeks are flushed and she's fidgeting awkwardly, her eyes darting between Kaine and us tangled together. What is she up to? I'm nothing like

Kaine. Where he wants to hide most of his relations with Eden, keeping his PDA to a minimum because he doesn't want anyone to see her, I just don't give a shit. At the end of the day, Ronnie is mine and no one else's. If they're embarrassed for us, I don't give a shit. If I want to kiss her, pin her, or fuck her, no one is going to stop me.

Eden's eyes widen when I dip my fingers under Ronnie's shirt and slowly start to lift it up her body. "Reese," Ronnie whispers, her voice trembling.

"Do you trust me?" Her throat bobs, but her head nods imperceptivity. "Good girl."

"Fucking hell," Kaine murmurs, lifting to his feet and moving away from us. Eden grabs his arm, stopping him from stomping out of the room. "Eden, come on."

"But...I want to watch."

The poor guy's jaw practically unhinges. It's sort of comical and I can't keep the smile from my face. This is a fight waiting to happen, a topic we've covered once before. "Eden—"

"Please."

Fuck, he's in trouble now. Eden begging him is like kryptonite to him. It's hard for him to say no to her when she does that, and she doesn't do it often. She knows how to play him, but I'm honestly surprised she's pushing him with this. Kaine was adamant with her about not wanting her to be involved with other guys or even looking at others. It took him a long time to be okay with me fucking touching her, so this is a very fine boundary.

"Eden."

"Please, Kaine. I—I want to watch them."

Ronnie sucks in a sharp breath. Whether it's from the fact Eden just said that or the fact my cock just hardened in my pants, I'm not sure. The idea that Eden wants to watch me fuck Ronnie is turning me on. I don't think of Eden in that way, but I'll admit, the idea of being watched is sort of doing it for me.

"Come on, Kaine," I tease. "You might learn something. You can just sit down over there and watch. No touching, no interaction." I motion to the single couch next to us and I swear if looks could kill, his glare would turn me into a withered husk.

He shoves his hand in his pocket, rips out his wallet and paws through it. "One time," he hisses, shaking a piece of paper in front of Eden. Well, fuck me, the girl's eyes actually light up when she sees the paper, which I now realize is one of the vouchers from Eden's little coupon book. "Fuck, I can't believe we're doing this," he murmurs.

"Do you just carry that shit around with you everywhere?" I laugh.

"Of course I do. I never know when I might need something." He's probably regretting that decision now.

"Reese, I don't know about this," Ronnie whispers. Her entire body is trembling against mine and I sort of feel like an asshole for not even thinking about how she would feel about this. Usually, she's pretty open to anything and not shy about her body. That's one thing I love about her, too. Even though she has her own insecurities, she still pushes through them and has confidence in herself.

"If you don't want to, you don't have to, but neither of them will judge you and I love you."

She presses her forehead against mine, her body relaxing into me. "You love me?"

"More than anything," I whisper.

"Okay."

CHAPTER SIXTY-TWO

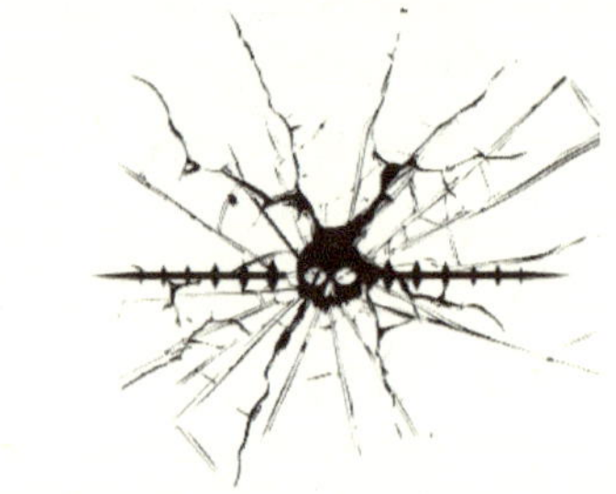

REESE

She pushes away from me and I let her, watching her as she pulls her shirt off the rest of the way. She shimmies her pants down her legs, leaving her in nothing but her bra and underwear. I see Kaine and Eden moving from the corner of my eye, shifting themselves to the chair I pointed to earlier. Kaine settles in first, tugging Eden down between his thighs, facing us. He wraps a possessive arm around her torso, pulling her back against his chest while he watches Ronnie kneeling down in front of me.

Seeing her staring up at me from the ground just about sends me over the edge. That seductive look, the way her eyes glisten behind those thick lashes. The sensual way she pins her lip between her teeth while her fingers curl into the edge of my pants to coax everything down my legs. I lift my hips, giving her an easier time to do so, and my cock bobs, smacking against my stomach. Eden gasps and I glance over at her, seeing Kaine watching us with his chin resting on her shoulder.

He moves his hand across her chest, teasing her nipples through her shirt while his tongue lashes out against the skin on her neck. Her eyes flutter closed, and I'm sort of in shock. I didn't expect him to play himself, knowing that I can see them clearly sitting there. They're both fully clothed, something I know Kaine won't rectify because it's Kaine after all.

"Fuck," I groan, tipping my head back on the couch when Ronnie's lips curl around the crown of my cock, her tongue swirling and licking in hot, sensual strokes. My hand drops shakily on her head, following the motion as she bobs up and down on my length. "That's it. Take it all."

"Kaine," Eden whimpers, pulling me to look over at them again. Kaine has one hand up under her shirt while his other one is buried in her pants. She leans back heavily against him, her hand reaching up to dig her fingers into his hair. His eyes lock on mine while his mouth moves, licking and sucking at her skin.

Ronnie chokes around my cock, taking me deep into her throat. Fuck, I'm so god damn hard and turned on by everything going on. My fingers curl into her hair, tangling into her strands and shoving her down deeper onto my dick. My back tingles, balls tightening as I completely unload down her throat.

She gasps, coming up for air with cum dribbling down the corner of her mouth. I quickly swipe my thumb against it and shove into her mouth. Her eyes widen. "Suck." She swirls her tongue around the digit, sucking against it hard enough that my half hard cock stiffens further.

Her hands move up my stomach, under my shirt, slowly pushing it up my chest. I grip the edge of it, tearing it off my body and tossing it to the floor to land amongst the other discarded clothes. She watches me through it all, eyes hooded and filled with lust. How could I have been so blind all this time. I can see it in those eyes; how much she cares for me and trusts me. She wouldn't be doing this if she didn't believe that I would take care of her and keep her safe. I'm an idiot for ever putting up that wall between us in a pathetic attempt to keep her at arm's length. If I learned anything from my mother, it's that I need to feel things with my whole heart for it to have true meaning. How can anyone live a full life when you're only putting half of yourself into it?

All my actions and decisions have been made with hesitation and fear at the back of my mind when I should have just been honest right from the beginning. I know that fear of judgement is what held me back. The terror I felt in knowing that if I fucked any of it up, it wasn't just a broken heart I was risking, it was a loss of life. I'm stronger than that. When did I lose confidence in myself? When did I start to allow others to dictate my life and the people in it?

"Come here," I murmur, holding my hand out to Ronnie.

She gives me a questioning look, her hesitation clear in the way her hand trembles as she places it in mine. She's adorable. She's always had this slight shyness about her, a barrier to the badass girl buried underneath. I knew from when I first met her that she wasn't what she seemed. Anyone with true fear wouldn't have stood up for Eden the way she did. She didn't even want any form of acknowledgement. She did it because it was the right thing to do for someone that was nothing but sweet and kind to her. That's what makes her special, and that's what pushed me to give her a chance.

She climbs on top of me, her wet panties dragging against the length of my cock before she settles into me. Gripping the back of her neck, I hold her still, forcing her to look right at me. "You're perfect," I whisper.

"Don't."

"Don't what? Tell you you're perfect?" She nods. "Why not?"

"Because I'm not."

I lean towards her, my lips hovering a breath away from hers. "You're perfect for *me*." My lips crash against hers, devouring her whimper as she parts her mouth for me. Our tongues clash and roll against each other's, her body pressing into mine. She grinds against me, my hand shifting down her back to guide her hips, pulling her down harder. "Fuck, I love you."

It's crazy how easy it is to say those words now. There's no hesitation, no doubt, nothing stopping me from allowing my buried feelings to rise to the surface. I love her. How could I ever be cruel to her and not say it back. It was painful to turn away from her, like a dull, rusted blade was slowly being pushed into my heart, tearing away at the fragile flesh until it was a mutilated organ.

I grip into her underwear, tearing it away from her body. I smirk at the huff of frustration she lets out, a deep chuckle rumbling in my chest. "You love it," I snort.

"Barbarian." She grips into my hair, tugging back hard enough that my mouth pops open in surprise. Fucking hell, that's hot. Her aggression has my cock straining to be inside her. My fingers slide up her back, gripping the clasp of her bra. The sound of it snapping away resonates in the room. "I'm surprised you didn't rip that off, too."

"Did you want me to?"

"When has me telling you no ever stopped you?"

She hums low in her throat when I pull one of her nipples into my mouth, sucking on it and swirling my tongue. I love the way her body presses into me, the way she seeks out the contact, desperate for more. She gasps when I clamp my teeth onto it and tug, a shudder tearing through her body.

"Reese," she whimpers.

Fuck, I love hearing my name falling from her lips. I risk a glance at Kaine and Eden. She's lost in whatever Kaine is doing to her while he's the one watching us. Well, that's an interesting turn of events. For someone who was so against any type of exhibitionism, cuckolding, or voyeurism, he's sort of getting into this. I can't disappoint him now, can I?

I grip into Ronnie's hips, forcing her onto her knees. She's shaking, slowly lowering herself back down onto the head of my cock. Fuck, she's so tight and warm and fucking perfect. "That's a good girl," I huff, holding myself back from driving up into her. Inch by inch she takes me into her, and each inch feels like pure bliss. "Fuck, Ronnie."

She was made for me, her pussy moulding to my cock and taking it perfectly. A harsh breath escapes my lips at the feel of it tensing and fluttering around me, sucking me in deeper and deeper until her hips are flush against mine. She wiggles her hips, pushing her ass against my balls, and the sensation ripples through my body, pushing heat down my spine.

"Are you going to be a good girl and show Kaine and Eden how good I can make you feel?"

She nods her head, resting her forearms on my shoulders. Her fingers move up and down the nape of my neck, tangling through the hair there and sending another shiver through my body. The slow slide of her cunt up my shaft has a long breath wheezing through my lungs and a soft moan escaping my lips when she sits back into me.

"Again," I groan, loving that she doesn't hesitate, doing it again and again until she sets a sensual rhythm, riding my cock like the good fucking girl that she is. Her soft whimpers and heavy breaths push my own arousal higher, mixing with Eden's soft panting breaths. I grip Ronnie's hair, tugging her head to the side and exposing her neck. My eyes lock on Kaine's as my tongue slides against her smooth skin and my teeth graze the delicate tendon in her neck. "You feel so good," I whisper, nipping at her ear.

"You—you feel good, too," she mewls.

My cock thickens at her words, the praise wrapping around my ego. I can't hold back any longer. My fingers dig into her hips, puckering the skin as I grind her down and drive up into her at the same time. She cries out, walls tightening around me.

"Not yet. You're not allowed to come yet, little rabbit."

"Please," she whispers.

I stop, forcing her body still while my cock pulses and throbs. I grit my teeth at the feel of her walls still tensing around me and the way she tries to fight my hold. "Not. Yet," I say again.

She's shaking now, full body tremors while her breath actually wheezes through her chest. She's so fucking close already, but I want to take her as high as possible before letting her fall over the edge.

"I thought you didn't like edging," Kaine chuckles.

"I don't like *being* edged. There's a difference." I pull back so I can look at Ronnie fully, at her flushed cheeks, hooded eyes, and parted pouty lips. "I like doing it though, don't I?" I swear I can hear her thick swallow, but she nods her head, trying her best to keep still, even though I know she wants to grind against me and ride out her own pleasure. I brush her hair behind her ear and cup her jaw, trailing my thumb against those perfect lips. "Beautiful."

She's being so good, not just with doing as I ask, but by being confident enough in herself to do this in front of them. Kaine is probably painfully hard at this point, only putting his focus on Eden and pleasing her while his own cock is straining against his jeans. The sick fuck might even like that little bit of torture, but his self-control is definitely higher than mine. I couldn't do it. I would have bent her over the edge of the chair and railed into her by now, claimed her completely while watching the show.

"How's your dick?" I chuckle.

"You're an asshole."

"You scared to get naked in front of me. I know you've got a nice ass, Kaine. Nice and perky."

"You're making this weird."

"Hmm, weird would be saying I'd fuck that ass." He breaks eye contact at that, cheeks turning an embarrassing shade of pink. "If it helps, you can call me bubba."

"He's already been claimed by Tiny," Eden giggles, making me laugh as well.

He makes it way too easy to chirp him, but he's not as volatile as regular people would be with gay comments or being hit on. I think he likes it. I think he enjoys the idea that he's attractive to everyone, including the opposite sex.

"Keep up the jabs and I'll fuck your mouth," he murmurs against her ear.

"You say that like it's a punishment." She pushes through his hold on her, turns around, and drops to her knees in front of him. His eyes widen, darting to me with panic on his face. I just smirk at him, finding it hilarious how flustered he is from the fact Eden isn't this shy little thing he thought she was. There's no reason to be. We're as close to each other as people can get without being family, and there's no judgment from anyone in this room.

He tries to stop her, the little shit, but his attempt is weak at best. He groans loudly when she finally works his zipper down and pulls out his cock, the head already glistening with precum. He was so close to coming already that his body jerks when she licks his length and wraps her lips around him.

"Fuck," he grunts, digging his fingers into her hair. His lust-filled gaze grows heavy, eyes hooded and shifting from her to me.

"Make me come, Ronnie," I murmur, loosening my grip on her. She doesn't hesitate to start moving again, her hips shifting harder and more erratic as she pants and moans. Her fingers dig into my shoulders hard enough to make me hiss at the sting of it.

Fuck, this has to be one of the hottest things I've ever experienced. I've never entertained the idea of doing something like this, but curiosity always made me wonder what it would be like. Ever since Eden made Kaine that little booklet, I looked into everything I saw scribbled on those vouchers. I didn't expect it to be this good—to feel this raw.

"Reese, I'm so close," Ronnie pants. "Please. Please let me come."

"Not yet. Keep going, Ronnie."

The poor girl is shaking, a thin sheen of sweat coating her body as she forces herself to keep riding me. If Kaine's garbled grunt is any indication, he's already there, spilling into Eden's mouth without reservation.

I grip Ronnie's hips, thrusting into her hard enough that she gasps and falls towards me, circling her arms around my neck and burying her face into the crook of it. She's panting so hard I can feel the heat of her breath cradling against my skin.

"Come for me," I groan, tensing around her when her teeth sink into the flesh on my neck to muffle her scream. "That's it. Fuck, Ronnie. Fuck, you're so good." My balls tighten so hard it takes my breath away, my cum exploding into her until it's dribbling out of her onto my thighs. I kiss her shoulder and her neck, tugging on her hair to pull her away from me. I kiss her lips, delving my tongue through her open mouth and loving the taste of her with each aggressive clash of tongues and teeth. I'm still deep inside of her, my cock twitching its final release.

I curl my arm around her back, reaching down to grab my t-shirt from the floor. She blinks at me slowly, weakly lifting her arms for me to slip it on over her body.

"Go get cleaned up," I whisper, kissing her lips one more time and steadying her as she slowly slides off of me. Her legs tremble, body swaying as she walks towards our bedroom in a haze, not saying a word while walking past Eden and Kaine.

Kaine grips Eden's jaw, dragging her up towards him to press his lips to hers, a soft hum vibrating in her throat. She seems satisfied with this turn of events, pleased that Kaine finally gave in and did something completely out of their normal routine. The guy can barely move, his chest heaving with harsh breaths while Eden tucks away his dick back into his pants. She glances at me, quickly turning away before lifting to her feet and fixing her disheveled hair.

I pull on my pants and make my way over to them, Eden almost seeming embarrassed now that it's all over. Kaine tips his head in my direction, eyes still glazed over and half closed. "You look satisfied," I snort.

"The girl sucks a mean dick," he huffs.

"Did you enjoy yourself or do you regret it?"

"It wasn't as bad as I thought it would be." His eyes widen when I grip his jaw and lean in closer to him, Eden letting out a small gasp. "What—" I press my lips to his, just a light touch, and he doesn't fight it.

Interesting.

When I finally pull back his eyes are like saucers and his jaw is dropped in shock. "No regrets," I murmur.

"What the fuck was that?" He says shakily.

"That was sort of hot," Eden whispers.

I smile, patting her on the head as I walk past her to check the food. "Don't get used to it. It was a one-time deal just to say it happened, nothing more. May as well push the boundary while we're all still in the *'what the fuck just happened'* phase."

I risk a glance back at Kaine, smirking when he touches his fingers to his lips. It was probably his first kiss from a dude, but better me than Bubba or Tiny or whoever. I'd break him out of prison anyways. A guy like him wouldn't last a day in a place like that, not that I would ever tell him that to his face. Kaine likes to believe that he's a tough guy, and he is, don't get me wrong, but in certain situations, he would definitely turn into someone's bitch.

Ronnie pads her way back down the hall, looking chipper and refreshed. Her smile is contagious, eyes locked on me until she notices the stunned Eden and still slightly freaking out Kaine. "What's wrong?" She asks, stopping next to Eden and touching her arm gentle.

Eden turns to look at me, a smile fighting to stay off her face. "Reese kissed Kaine."

"What?" Ronnie screams. "What the fuck? I missed it?"

I frown, tilting my head in confusion. "Did you want to see me kissing him?"

She throws her hands up in frustration and walks towards me with the most adorable pout on her face. "I mean, it would have been fun to watch Kaine's reaction to that."

"He didn't do much. He sort of just sat there in stunned silence."

"Lame."

"Why don't you get kissed by a girl and tell me if you wouldn't just stand there." Kaine finally snaps out of his stupefied state, turning into the sass pot we all know and love. Ronnie rolls her eyes, turning away from me and walking over to Eden. She grabs her, cups her cheeks, and slams her lips against Eden's.

To be fair, I think my own shock mimics Kaine's at this point. Definitely didn't expect that to just happen out of the blue, and Eden's reaction is pretty much the same as Kaine's. No, wait. She's actually kissing her back, leaning into her and closing her eyes like she's actually enjoying it. Kaine's face is going to be permanently stuck in a shocked state if we keep up these shenanigans. I half expected him to rip Ronnie away from her, but I think he's too floored by the whole thing, maybe even a bit turned on. Eden was right, it's sort of hot.

Ronnie pulls away with a huge grin on her face, wiping her thumb across her lips. "You're a good kisser," she says.

Kaine gasps dramatically, looping his arm around Eden's waist and tugging her back. Eden squeals, tripping over his feet and falling back into his lap. "She's mine," he grumbles. "You can't have her."

Ronnie laughs at that, shaking her head. "Don't worry, I don't plan to try and steal your girl." She walks back towards me, loops her arm through mine, and smiles up at me. "I have everything I need right here."

She looks so happy, an expression I plan to keep on her face for the foreseeable future. I cup her jaw, loving the way she leans into my touch and parts her lips when my thumb brushes against them. "Can I keep you," I whisper.

Her brows knit together, a look of sadness crossing her features. "For as long as you want to, Reese."

"Forever. I want to keep you forever."

CHAPTER SIXTY-THREE

RONNIE

ONE MONTH LATER

"I can't believe the wedding is tomorrow."

Eden looks nervous to all hell, pacing the length of the apartment back and forth. The boys are out for the night, Reese promising they'll get home at a respectable hour. Eden didn't want to go out, opting for movie night, junk food, and just a chill night in. So much for chill. The girl looks about ready to pass out with nerves.

I pour her another glass of mojitos, motioning her over. "Come on, settle down. There's no reason for you to be nervous."

She flops down on the couch, grabs the glass, and chugs it back. She holds the now empty glass out to me, smacking her lips. "I need more liquid courage."

I shake my head, filling her glass again, which thankfully she sips this time. "Why are you so on edge? You two love each other and everything is planned to perfection."

"I don't know. What if something goes wrong? What if Kaine changes his mind and decides this is stupid and leaves me at the alter?"

"Eden, that would never happen. He's beyond obsessed with you. Why would you ever think that?"

"People change their mind, Ronnie."

"Kaine isn't a person, he's a freak of nature. I don't think I've ever met anyone as obsessed with someone as him."

"Reese."

"Reese is different."

"He sure is. He went on a literal murder spree to get you back. Pretty sure that tops Kaine's level of obsession."

"Sure, but you have Kaine locked down, where Reese and I are sort of still in the aftermath phase."

"He wants to spend his life with you. He wants forever with you, Ronnie."

"Yeah."

I really don't want to be on this topic. I shouldn't feel jealous about Eden and Kaine's relationship, but I do. It's selfish of me to want what they have, right? I mean, I know it's normal to want to settle down and get married, maybe have a few kids, but having that as a goal just feels sort of...wrong.

"What are we watching?" Eden asks, grabbing the bowl of popcorn and propping it on her crossed legs.

"Whatever you want. Tonight is your night."

"Hmm, maybe something funny? Oh! Let's watch Bridesmaids!"

"Sure," I laugh, searching for the movie and putting it on.

It feels like I haven't gotten to hang out with Eden like this in a while. Kaine is usually lurking around or randomly shows up whenever we're having get-togethers. Not that I really mind, but I do miss hanging out with her. It's easy to blame him, even though I know I'm partially to blame as well. Our schedules have been a bit chaotic. I see Kaine more than I do Eden just because I work with him. I hope the separation doesn't get worse once they're married. They'll be gone for about two weeks, an all-inclusive vacation to Hawaii for their honeymoon. I would love to go away for a little while and just forget the world I live in, letting myself enjoy the days, soaking up the sun without a care in the world.

I wonder if that would be something Reese would want to do. We both deserve it. We need to find real time for ourselves so we can finally heal from everything we've had to endure.

Eden laughing rips me from my thoughts and I quickly mimic her, so she doesn't realize that I've been completely zoning out. She doesn't deserve my distracted thoughts. She's having a hard time as it is, stressing over the wedding and hoping everything goes perfectly tomorrow. I'm glad she didn't want to go out tonight. I don't think I could handle having to socialize and fake it with other people around. The apartment is quiet, a lot quieter than mine and Reese's. We're not in a bad part of town or anything, but our home is a lot smaller and older than the one Eden and Kaine have. It's nice.

"What is that?" Eden murmurs, glancing over the couch behind us towards the patio.

"I don't hear anything."

She grabs the remote, pausing the movie. "It sounds like music coming from outside. That's weird." She sets the popcorn down on the table and walks towards the patio. I prop myself on my knees, facing the backing, watching her as she opens the door.

The sound of Bad Omens filters through the now open doorway mixed with the sound of people talking. "What's going on?"

She steps out onto the patio, glances over the edge of the balcony, and freezes. "What the fuck!" She screams. "You're not supposed to be here!"

"Eden!"

Fucking hell. Kaine's voice vibrates through the air, followed by the sound of Reese cackling like a hyena. "You said you were going out and then staying at Reese's. Go away, Kaine!"

"Ronnie!" Reese calls out. Eden glances back at me, rolling her eyes. I sigh, getting up from the couch to see what the fuck the two idiots are doing. "Ronnie!" He says again when I come into view. "I—I have something to say—say to you!"

"Are you drunk?"

"Maybe!"

"Reese, I'm going to call you two a cab, just stay down there." I back up to him still yelling for me, and step back into the warmth of the apartment. "Fucking idiots," I grumble. "I'm going to go down there and wait with them until the cab comes. The last thing we need is two drunken idiots wandering off before the wedding."

"Why would they come here? They were supposed to go out to a club near your place."

"No idea, but they must have taken a cab here."

"I'm coming with you."

"Eden—"

"I want to make sure Kaine isn't completely obliterated. I'll be pissed if he sleeps through the wedding."

We both grab some sweaters and head downstairs, the sound of the music growing louder as we make it through the lobby. Kaine is swaying to the music, belting out the lyrics in a surprisingly good voice, while Reese paces back and forth, staring up at the balcony we vacated minutes ago.

"Reese, what the fuck?" He startles at the sound of my voice, but he grins widely and runs towards me, picking me up in his arms. I scream in surprise when he spins us, my legs flopping around like a dead fish from the momentum. "Put me down."

"I missed you," he sighs, cupping my cheeks the second he sets me back down on my feet.

"It's been like four hours. You're drunk and you need to go home. Turn that down," I snap at Kaine. "You're going to piss off the neighbours."

Eden scurries towards him, wrestling with him to get his phone out of his hands. He gives it up eventually and she quickly turns off the music, leaving us in a sudden silence that feels thick and heavy for some reason.

I try to back away from Reese, but he grips my hands in his, keeping me tethered to him. "Reese," I sigh.

"There's something I want to say to you," he murmurs, sounding a bit more sober than he did when he called out to me on the balcony. His eyes are a bit glassy, pupils blown out and darkening the natural hue of his irises trying to burn through. "I need to do this now."

"Can't it wait until the morning? You two promised you wouldn't come around tonight. Kaine isn't supposed to see Eden until tomorrow."

He shakes his head. "No. It can't wait. I need to do this now." He releases one of my hands and digs into his pocket, stumbling back a step when he finally pulls whatever he's digging for, loose. "Ronnie," he says shakily. "I know I've been an asshole to you and have lied to you and I've hurt you in so many ways, but I want you to know how much I love you. How much your very existence means to me. I didn't want to believe that I deserved someone kind and gentle in my life, that it could be for me—what I've always wanted. I never thought I would find someone who would see every dark part of me and still stick around because they cared about me with their whole heart. Words don't seem like enough to express any of these things, and my actions are lackluster at best, but I love you so fucking much."

He sounds completely sober, though his sudden outburst seems a little insane. I don't know how to handle him when he's like this. It's one thing when he's shut down or the complete opposite and emotional in a way that breaks my heart. This is raw and real and so not like him.

He takes a deep breath, the sound rattling in his chest as he slowly lowers himself down to the ground in front of me. "Ronnie." My eyes widen, hands flying up to my mouth when he holds a small black box within his grip. "I don't know what the future holds, but I don't want a future that doesn't have you in it. I want to see you laugh and smile every single day. I want to hold you and cherish every precious moment we're granted. I want to *be* with you, mind, body, and soul. I want you to be mine...forever. Will you do me the honor of becoming my wife."

I'm in shock. It sounds like Eden is too from the small gasp and squeal of joy coming from behind me. Kaine doesn't say a word. The fucker probably already knew about this psychotic plan and actually kept this secret to himself. Eden is totally going to kick his ass for that. I want to say something meaningful and wholesome. Something that would hold as much weight as every word he just spoke to me in earnest. I don't know what to say though. His declaration has left me speechless, and his actions have left me frozen in shock.

How long has he been planning this? How hard was it for him to say all those words? Words that I know he means with his whole heart. That heart is huge beyond measure. A heart that's open and filled with so much love for those he claims as his own.

I take a tentative step closer to him, my hands shaking as I slowly lower them down from my face. I can't stop the tears from falling down my cheeks at the look on his face, the desperation and love in his eyes. He wants this. He wants *me*.

"I've always been yours, Reese. Forever."

"Is—is that a yes?"

"Yes," I whisper.

The smile that spreads across his face has heat spreading through my chest, warming me from the inside out. I feel the flame of that happiness consuming me—igniting my soul. He quickly wipes his own eyes, shakily pulling the ring from the box and carefully sliding it up my finger. It's gorgeous. Something too extravagant for someone like me, but I know he picked it with his heart. Small little details that others wouldn't notice, but seeing the ring up close has my heart almost bursting through my ribcage.

The band is made of etched wings, the center diamond princess cut with gorgeous sapphires on either side of it. It was my mother's birthstone, a small detail I let slip when we finally opened up to each other about our lives before, our full past, and the two women that raised us to be the people we are today.

"It's beautiful," I whisper, staring at the gorgeous ring gleaming against my skin.

He slowly lifts to his feet, grips my hips, and tugs me closer to him. My hands settle gently against his chest as I look up at him, trying to find better words to express how happy I am. I didn't see this coming. I had no clue he had thought about any of this, but this isn't a ring you can just walk into any jewelry store and buy. This is something that had a lot of thought and intention behind it, something he would have had to have specifically made.

"The ring is nothing compared to you," he says, bending down close enough I feel his breath ghost across my lips. The heat of him radiates into my body, sending my own temperature skyrocketing. "You're the only person that I need in my life, Ronnie. I love you so much."

I close the distance between us, snaking my hand up his chest to grip into the back of his neck. He groans into my mouth, parting his lips for me to kiss him deeper. Our tongue clash, our bodies melting into each other until I no longer know where mine ends and his begins. Everything else blurs out of focus. All my doubts, my pain, my regrets. Everything that has been holding me back breaks away. The chains of my past unshackling from my body have me gasping into his mouth, the sensation of true freedom foreign and new.

I don't want to let him go. I want to cling to him. I want him to stay with me, but I know he needs to go. They can't stay here when they promised to stay away until the wedding. He pulls away too soon, forehead pressed to mine and panting breaths skating across my skin. I don't think I've ever been as happy as I am at this moment in my entire life.

"I love you, Ronnie," he murmurs, his voice breathless and shaking.

"I love you, too, Reese. I love you so much it hurts."

"I don't want to hurt you anymore. I never want you to feel pain or sadness when you're with me. I don't want to ever be the cause of your heart breaking ever again."

I pull back enough that I can stare up into his eyes, giving my head a small shake. "This hurt is good. This hurt makes me feel alive. You know I would do anything for you—*be* anything you need me to be, whether that's a friend or a lover, someone you can open up to or just sit quietly with. Whatever you need, Reese."

"I just want *you*, just as you are. I don't need you to be anyone else, Ronnie. You're perfect."

"I don't know whether to gag or cry," Kaine mumbles, and I roll my eyes.

"You were pretty sappy when you proposed. I have it on video," I snap back.

Little shit really knows how to ruin the moment. I spin around to face him, but Reese wraps his arms around my waist, stopping me from stepping towards him. I can't help leaning back into him, especially when he kisses my neck and rests his chin on my shoulder. I can just imagine the glare he's giving Kaine, but now that my mind is settling back into reality, I can smell the alcohol on him.

Kaine is holding Eden the same way Reese is holding me. He smirks at me, gently rocking Eden back and forth in his grip. "Yeah, you were pretty quick to get that camera out. Makes me wonder what else you record."

Reese's hold on me tightens. "You've already watched us fuck, but if you want a souvenir, just let me know."

That shuts him up. I don't think he expected me to snap back with that at all, probably waiting for me to cower or shy away from the implication. He clearly doesn't know me.

"Ronnie, I'll understand if you want to go home with Reese. I can just lock Kaine up in the she-den if I have to until the morning."

"I'm sorry I ruined your night," Reese says quietly.

Guilt settles into me at his comment. I've let my own happiness overshadow Eden's big day, and Reese is feeling the weight of his actions now. The need to do this was probably nagging at him, pushing him to tell me what he needed to, even if that ended up requiring some liquid courage to do it. The fact

Kaine *let* him do it eases my negative emotions a bit, but I don't want to disappoint Eden.

"No, Reese. You didn't ruin anything at all. I'm so happy for both of you, that's why I'm saying it's okay if you two want to go home together."

Eden is too good for this world. Someone as sweet as her never deserved the pain and hardships she's had to endure. As much as I would love to go home and snuggle up with Reese, this weekend is about Eden. "I—I want to stay with you, Eden."

Reese hugs me tighter, his warm breath tickling my ear. "I'll see you in the morning."

"You're not mad?" I say quietly.

"I have forever with you, and I plan to lock you up for a while and take care of you. Every single inch of you, over and over again. I'm going to worship you like the goddess you are."

"Upgrading me from rabbit to goddess?" I laugh.

"Hmm, you'll always be my little rabbit, wild and free."

The cab pulls up a few minutes later and we say our goodbyes, both of us lingering with our significant others. This is real. Reese is my fiancé—my future husband. I can't keep the smile from my face as I watch him and Kaine getting into the car, both of them laughing and waving at us like children.

Eden drapes her arm across my shoulders, hugging me against her side. "Congratulations," she says happily. "I'm so fucking happy for you. I knew this would happen."

"Did you?"

"I mean, I didn't *know*. Reese never said anything to me, and I'm not sure if he mentioned it to Kaine or not, but I could tell that it was bound to happen. He really loves you, Ronnie, and after everything that happened, after the fear of losing you forever, it just makes sense that he would want to give you all of himself and show you what he wants for your future."

She turns us, guiding us back into the apartment complex. "I'm scared." It's weird to admit that. I don't think I've ever said anything so vulnerable to her, but I can't shake this feeling curling around inside of me. It's like an itch I can't scratch. A phantom sensation writhing beneath the skin and making me feel on edge about all of it.

"Don't be scared. Isn't this what you wanted? To be with him?"

"Of course it is, I just didn't think he would want to get married, and I resolved myself to that. Reese never seemed like the type."

"I don't think you're the only one that's scared, Ronnie. I'm sure it was difficult for him to work up the courage to say everything he said to you tonight and to ask you to spend your life with him. He's an amazing person and you're really lucky to have someone who cares that much about you. He's proved himself over and over again, risked his life to get you back because he knew how much you deserved to be free. If anyone is going to understand you and what you've been through, it's him. You're both very similar in a lot of ways, which should bring you two closer to one another."

"It's still crazy to think how alike we are. I never expected to find out that he was raised with mafia ties like I was. It sucks that we're on two different sides of a secret war, but I'm hoping now, with my father out of the picture, it'll make it a bit more difficult for the bratva to move around freely. They took a heavy hit with his death and with Mikail's, since he was set to inherit his father's position as well."

"It's time you live, Ronnie. It's time you stop hiding from who you were and embrace the badass that you are. You have someone that can match your energy, and that should be exciting, not difficult."

"Come on. Let's go stuff our faces and have a fun night." I don't know what's going to happen now. My focus needs to be on Eden and making tomorrow as special as possible for her. Hopefully, Reese remembers what he did tonight and wasn't so far gone that he did something out of desperation when he wasn't completely of sound mind. I won't know until tomorrow comes, and I won't get to really speak to him until after the ceremony.

CHAPTER SIXTY-FOUR

REESE

"Fuck, I'm so nervous," Kaine murmurs, fixing his hair for the millionth time in the mirror.

We both woke up hungover, heads pounding and mouths like cotton. Drinking to that level probably wasn't the best idea, but the shots just kept coming and words spilled out uninhibited. At least we were in a good enough headspace to realize we needed to leave the bar before we started talking about sensitive shit in mixed company. It was just the two of us, Kaine having removed most of his so-called friends from his life. He's invited a few of his co-workers to the wedding, but he's not close enough to them to have wanted to invite them out for a random night of partying.

I proposed to Ronnie. I fucking went to her like an absolute psycho in the middle of the night and got down on my knees for her. It was fucking pathetic. She deserved something so much more—something better. It should have been done in some far away land surrounded by beauty, not some dark fucking parking lot outside my best friend's apartment. What the fuck was I thinking?

I bought the ring a week after everything that had happened with her father, knowing that I wanted to marry her and spend the rest of my life with her, but I couldn't think of the best time to do it. With wanting it to be special, I knew that I needed to book some elaborate trip, but if I did that, she would have suspected something. We don't *do* vacations, at least, not in that sense. We've gone off to some cabins in the past, but even that seemed so small in comparison to what I wanted to do for her. Meanwhile, I was a fucking lowlife that got wasted and proposed to her in the most uncool way possible.

She probably hates me for that or is second guessing saying yes to me. I *did* put her on the spot last night, but I would hope that she wouldn't say yes just to be nice. I want to see her—I *need* to fucking see her and apologize to her.

Kaine drags his hands through his hair, pausing with wide eyes. "Fuck!" He frantically tries to fix his hair again and I've finally had enough.

"Will you calm the fuck down," I grumble, grabbing his hands to stop him from tearing his hair out. "This is what you wanted. It's a special day, you look great, and Eden will be waiting for you. What the fuck are you so nervous about?"

"I don't know. What if I fuck this up somehow?"

"You literally had rehearsals. If you fuck this up, you're an idiot."

He shakes his head, dropping his eyes to the ground between us. "Not the wedding, Reese. What if I fuck this up with Eden? What if I'm a shitty husband to her."

I grip the back of his neck and lean my forehead against his. "You're not going to fuck that up. Being married is no different than the way you two have been living already and you've been amazing to her. She loves you and you love her. You would both do anything for each other, Kaine. You're freaking out for no reason, okay?"

"What if—"

"No. No what ifs. I'm going to take you to the ceremony and you're going to get married, grab your new wife and kiss her, and you're going to live happily ever after. Period."

His arms wrap around me tightly, a shattered breath escaping his lungs. "I don't think you'll ever know how thankful I am to have you as a friend, Reese."

"I *do* know, Kaine. We're brothers." He pulls away and wipes his eyes, clearing his throat awkwardly. "Don't smear your mascara."

"Shut up," he laughs, shoving me.

"Let's go. We can't be late to your own wedding."

He follows quietly behind me, staying silent the entire elevator ride down. He's still fidgeting, fixing his hair, and constantly straightening out his suit. He looks good; cleans up nicely, too. He's not one to get dressed up often, so when he does, he has a presence about him that shows the sophistication and wealth he grew up in.

The limo should be picking the girls up shortly, and I'm excited to see Ronnie in a dress. I'm sure she'll look amazing in it, and from the colour scheme Eden chose, it'll look great against her complexion. Kaine lags behind once we get to the lobby, but I don't say anything, walking in front of him and holding the door open for him to walk through. He gives me a weak smile, his eyes still lost and distant in whatever is going on in his head. I don't understand why he feels like he can screw this up. Marriage for them isn't going to change anything except proving to the world that they love each other enough to be tied together legally.

I don't like how quiet he's being. It's not like him at all. He's one of the most talkative people I know, throwing comments out left and right about the most mundane things. The silence is starting to get to me once we hit the road, Kaine's gaze focused on the window and the city streaming by. I pick a song from one of my playlists and let it stream through the cabin of the truck, peeking at him from the corner of my eye. I notice his body perk up a bit at the song, one that I picked specifically for him. It's a bit on the older side, but still a classic and one I know he can't resist singing along to. All The Small Things by blink-182 fills the space, and I can hear him already humming along to it. I grin when the chorus hits and he just can't help himself anymore, screaming out the lyrics and turning to me with happiness on his face.

When he's like this, it's hard to be trapped in the past and darkness, falling into the contagious good mood he exudes. He's easy like that. When he's like this, it's impossible not to get along with him and want to be a part of his fun. I chime in on the song, making him laugh and sing a bit louder as we drive to the venue.

They didn't want it in a church, both of them no longer believing in that side of religion, but I can't blame them after they've experienced as much as they have. They went with a local officiant that they met by chance, and they agreed to marry them at a beautiful gallery that Eden had connections to.

The reception is a bit later, after we head over to the park to get some photos, and they went all out with the catering. Kaine wanted anything and everything he could pack into the menu, giving Eden as many options as possible, even though she argued that the menu didn't have to be that extensive. That was something he wasn't budging on though. When it comes to food and Eden, he's not holding back.

"They're not here yet," Kaine murmurs when I pull up in front of the gallery.

"Usually, they're not. They'll be here soon though. Ronnie texted me earlier and said the limo was picking them up ten." He pulls his phone from his pocket and starts typing on the screen. "What are you doing?"

"Texting Eden," he mumbles.

"What? Why?" When he doesn't answer me, I reach over and grab his phone from his hand, palming his face when he tries to grab it back.

"Reese! Come on!"

"Why are you texting her, Kaine?" He struggles against my grip, smacking my arm and chest, reaching towards his phone. I hold it as far away from him as possible and read the message he hadn't sent yet.

Kaine: Eden. I love you and I can't wait to see you. I can't wait to spend the rest of my life with you. See you soon, Vixen.

Fuck, it's adorable. I don't know why he didn't just tell me what he was sending, unless he feels embarrassed for his sappy little message. I press send and hand it back to him, laughing at the look of panic on his face.

"Why did you send it?"

"Why did you type it out if you weren't going to send it?"

"You're such a dick. I—" His head snaps down when the phone pings, his gaze softening.

"What did she say?"

"She called me her soulmate."

"Do you feel better now?" He nods. "Do I get a thank you?"

He sighs, rolling his eyes and shoving his phone back into his pants. "Thank you, Reese."

CHAPTER SIXTY-FIVE

RONNIE

"I feel like I'm forgetting something!"

Eden is darting around like a sociopath, shoving things she doesn't even need into a small bag. "You're going to wrinkle your dress," I sigh, watching the death grip she has on the bunched-up material at her hip. "Seriously, Eden, you have everything you need. You just need yourself and your phone and your keys to the apartment. That's it. Nothing else matters because you're ready."

Her phone pings on the table and I move to grab it for her, but she's a tornado whipping past me, ripping it from my hands. "It could be Kaine cancelling the wedding. Oh, god. What if he doesn't want to get married."

Fucking hell, she's losing it. I knew she had a few screws loose, but I didn't think she was actually delusional. "Kaine is so beyond obsessed with you. The only way this wedding wouldn't happen would be if he died, and even then, he would find a way to come to you in ghost form just to make sure he's tied to you."

Her entire body relaxes when she reads the message, a small smile pulling at her lips. Her eyes dart back and forth over and over as she reads the message again and again before finally texting back.

"Who was it?"

"Kaine."

"Is everything okay?" She nods, taking a deep breath and tucking her phone into her bag before holding it out to me. "You seem to be in a better mood and more calm all of a sudden."

"I swear he knows when I'm having a meltdown, and he always knows what to say to bring me back." She closes her eyes, shakes her arms out and pulls in a long breath. It sputters out of her mouth, making her lips flap comically. "Okay, I think I'm ready."

I rub my hands up and down her bare arms, trying to relax her further. "You're more than ready. You look beautiful, and Kaine is going to lose it when he sees you."

The sweetest smile graces her lips and a cute blush creeps across her cheeks. "So, I look okay?"

"Stunning."

She really does look beautiful. The dress has beautiful tapered straps, the bodice forms to her chest and waist beautifully, accentuating her curves, and the skirt itself has a bit of a flair to it. She didn't want a ton of tulle, and it was a good decision, letting the skirt fall seamlessly over her hips to still show off her frame without a ton of exaggeration. The train is cute, too, with the ability to pin it up later so she can dance freely. The hem of the dress matches my own dress, a gorgeous lace in a deep purple tone. It'll look stunning later when it gets pinned up, framing her waist in a bit of colour. The dress is perfect and matches her personality.

"We should head downstairs. The limo will be here soon."

"Do you think it was stupid to not have more bridesmaids?"

"I don't think so. You want people that mean something to you, not just people to stand with you when they haven't been by your side through everything. I would do the same thing and only have you with me."

"Do you have an idea of when you want to get married?"

I shake my head. "I want to leave it up to Reese. I don't want him to feel any type of pressure when it comes to it, so if he wants to wait or has a specific date in mind that works better for him, then that's what we'll do."

"I'm sure he'll go with whatever you want though."

"Is it wrong of me to want to do anything he wants?"

"What do you mean?"

I shrug. "I just—I don't know. I feel like sometimes I should fight back on certain things, but I don't *want* to. I want to do whatever I can for him because I want to make him happy."

"Ronnie, you shouldn't change who you are just because of him. He fell for who you were, and that includes all your dark little details."

"That's the thing, he didn't *know* my dark details until recently. I know I've been hard on him, and knowing everything about him now, I feel like I've been unfair with my behaviour."

"He won't ever hold that against you. He wouldn't have gone to the lengths he did. He would have saved you and walked away after because he's a good person and wouldn't have left you to the fate you were thrown into."

I hate that she's right. I still hate the fact that Reese risked his life for me like that. I don't say anything else about it because I just don't know *what* to say. There's no point in trying to argue when she's right. Everything she's said is completely on point, and I both love and hate how observant she is. I grab her jacket off the back of the couch, a beautiful faux fur cropped jacket that goes well with the dress. I can feel her eyes on me as I walk towards her with it, but I don't look at her—I can't. I help her into it and clear my throat, grabbing her bag and heading for the door.

She follows, giving me a small smile as I let her through and lock it behind us. She struggles a bit with the train of her dress, and I quickly take up my maid of honor duties, holding it up while we walk towards the elevator.

The limo is already waiting for us up front, the driver standing outside the back door, dressed to impress with a smile on his face. "Good morning, ladies. You both look lovely today."

"Thank you. I'm getting married." He blinks, giving Eden an awkward smile now as he opens the door for us. "I should just not talk for the rest of the day," she grumbles when I slide in next to her.

"You're fine," I laugh. "You're nervous and that's normal."

She smooths her dress over her legs, looking out the window at her apartment. “I’m getting married.”

CHAPTER SIXTY-SIX

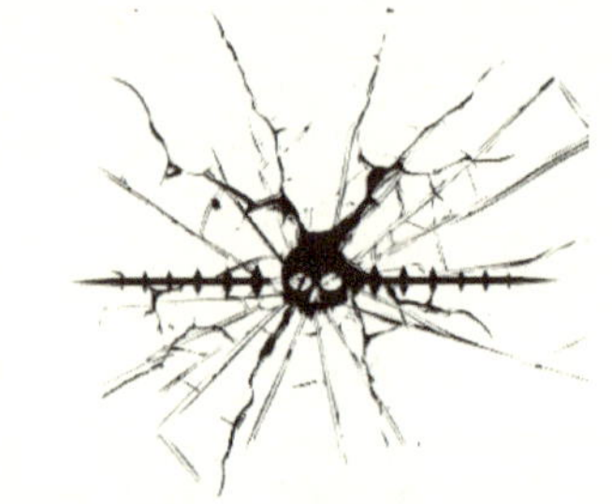

REESE

Kaine looks about ready to pass out, watching the small number of guests filing into the main gallery area. I have to admit, the setup is pretty nice, surrounded by different art pieces and sculptures. I'm surprised Kaine was able to swing something like this, what with the risk of any of the pieces being damaged. I did half expect Eden to want the ceremony in some bookstore or library since she has a big enough obsession with books to rival Ronnie's obsession.

The number of times we've walked in on those two whispering about some of the shit they've read is sort of insane. One of their latest reads was about three guys and one girl, and something about a sort of club with special keys where they're assigned to a room with strangers to do what they want. The cover was pretty sick, with a guy and girl on the front, their faces painted like skeletons. I'm not sure what it was called now, but they did an immersive read of it, following along with the audiobook, and admittedly, the dudes sounded sort of hot, so I get it.

The poor guy can't figure out what to do with his hands, shifting them from behind his back to in his pockets and switching to being clasped in front of him, just to start the cycle all over again. He's sweating, too. Glistening sections along his temples and nape where his hair is beginning to curl from it.

Jackson and Lisa walk in, coming up to me and Kaine. Kaine stiffens when Lisa pats his arm, trying to ignore her. He still doesn't like her or trust her, hating her for what she put Eden through growing up and then when she moved to Cameron.

"The limo just pulled up," Jackson says, and Kaine lets out a heavy breath, his hands trembling as he rakes his fingers through his hair. "I'm going to go meet up with Eden now."

"Okay. Thanks, dad."

I'm glad his relationship with him has gotten a bit better and Eden asked if he would walk her down the aisle. Jackson cried from what Kaine told me, overwhelmed with emotion at the fact she wanted him to do something so meaningful. With Eden's dad dead, she didn't have many options. Kaine suggested she walk alone, which ended up in an argument that never should have happened.

I had offered to do it myself if she needed someone by her side, and Ronnie offered as well, but she felt it was the right thing to do in asking Jackson. He's technically her father now, and her father-in-law. It's weird to think about it like that, but they honestly should never have been worried about it. They didn't grow up together and never had a relationship as siblings, and anyone who dares to belittle them for their relationship will get my wrath.

"Your dad's a good guy."

"Yeah," Kaine sighs. "He's been really good lately, and he's respected the boundaries I've put down. He knows I don't like Lisa, and he hasn't pushed us to hang out with her more than necessary. She better not fucking start today with the whole dinner thing."

"If I have to escort her out, I will."

He smiles at that. "My hero," he snorts.

The music changes and hushed whispers go through the room as everyone turns their heads towards the entrance. My heart stops beating when I see Ronnie walking in, the beautiful dark purple gown clinging to her frame and accentuating every curve on her body. Fuck, she's gorgeous and I want to rip that fucking dress off of her.

No, Reese. She'll fucking kill you if you destroyed her fucking bridesmaid dress.

It's so tempting though. She knows how much I love tearing clothes off her body, and this is just a sensual tease, begging for me to tear it at the seams. She still hasn't looked at me, her eyes locked on Kaine, but his attention is fixed on the door she came through. He's practically vibrating with anticipation.

Her gaze finally shifts to me, eyes widening slightly as they roam over my body. Damn, that look tells me she's eating me up, practically stripping me where I stand. I puff my chest out, making the suit stretch across my chest, the motion pushing her gaze up to meet mine again. She moves into her spot, smoothing out her dress like it isn't already perfect falling against her body.

"I love you," I whisper.

Her eyes dart up to me again, her cheeks reddening. "I love you, too."

I wish I could say more to her, the desperate need to talk to her after everything that happened last night clawing at my insides. My skin itches with that need and I want to touch her. I want to pull her into me and kiss her; tell her I love her again and again until my voice is hoarse.

Kaine's sharp intake of breath has me ripping my eyes away from Ronnie, back towards the door. He sways on the spot and I'm not sure if it's him stopping himself from going to her or if he's about to pass out on seeing her. She looks absolutely stunning. The dress complimenting every curve of her body. Jackson looks a bit nervous as he walks with her, his fingers lightly tapping against her hand that's gripping into the crook of his elbow. Her eyes dart around, taking in everyone in attendance before she finally finds Kaine at the front of the crowd. Her steps stutter, Jackson steadying her quickly and urging her on.

Her mouth hangs open slightly, the shock on her face adorable. I don't think she's seen Kaine in a full suit, like *ever*. Jackson stops in front of Kaine, quirking a brow when he doesn't move, standing there like a fucking statue. I give him a little shove, and he snaps out of his daze, swallowing hard enough that I can hear his throat click.

"You okay?" Jackson asks quietly, gripping Eden's hand and lifting it towards Kaine.

Kaine finally realizes what he needs to do and takes Eden's hand, guiding her closer to him. "Thank you," Eden murmurs, leaning towards Jackson and giving him a quick kiss on the cheek before handing her flowers over to Ronnie. "Hi," she says when she finally faces Kaine fully.

"Hi. Fuck, you look beautiful."

She stifles a laugh, but he's spoken loud enough that quite a few people in the first few rows hear him, soft laughter echoing around us. "You don't look too bad yourself," she smiles.

Kaine shakes his head, stepping closer to her. "You're breathtaking. You don't even look real."

Her cheeks turn a brighter shade of red at that. The minister, or whatever he is, clears his throat, trying to get them to pay attention, and I just glare at him. "Give them a minute," I growl out, my hands clenching at my sides to stop myself from throttling the idiot. This is *their* fucking day. How dare he try to ruin this moment. Whatever he sees when he looks at me has his face going sheet-white and he takes a step back from me.

When I face Ronnie again her eyes are wide and she's pointing at them, mouthing *'control yourself'*. Fuck, I must have slipped up and let a little Avery bleed through me. Can I even say it's Avery anymore? I feel like I've somehow made this power my own since he doesn't seem to have any control over what I'm doing with it. It's like, with him possessing me, he accidentally left behind a small fragment of what he is inside of me. I don't think he ever expected that to happen, or for me to know how to use it.

Kaine finally looks towards the dickhead and gives him a nod. The asshole looks to me for confirmation and I grin, even *if* it's bordering on sinister. I sort of like it, the fear I can put into people without having to physically become violent.

"Let's begin. Thank you to everyone for joining us today in celebrating the union of Kaine Montgomery and Eden Taylor."

CHAPTER SIXTY-SEVEN

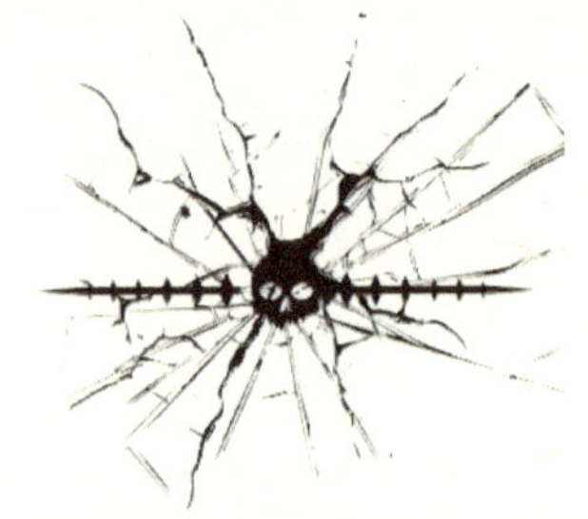

REESE

I'm actually crying because everyone else is crying. Fuck, when did I turn into such a sap? I clap along with everyone else while Kaine kisses Eden outside the gallery. Ronnie bumps into me, glancing up at me through her lashes.

"You look really good in a suit," she whispers, leaning close enough that I feel her body heat radiating into me.

"And you look phenomenal in a dress." I lean back a bit and she quirks a brow. "That ass."

She smacks my arm and laughs. "You're ridiculous."

I catch her hand before she can pull it away, rubbing my thumb over the engagement ring. She's still wearing it. This girl wants to marry me for real. "I meant every word last night. You're everything to me, Ronnie."

She props up on her toes to kiss my lips, the smile on her face making me chase her for a little bit more. She giggles against my lips before pulling away and leaning into my arm. "I know you meant it all. I'm really happy, Reese. For the first time in my life, I feel...free."

"Come on you two! Let's get some pictures taken!" Eden yells out, waving her bouquet around as she hangs out of the sunroof on the limo. "We'll see everyone later on!"

Lisa lets out a small sob next to me, wiping her eyes while Jackson drapes an arm over her shoulders. Eden didn't pay too much attention to her today, not wanting something being said between them that would ruin the moment. I don't think Kaine would have allowed it even *if* she tried talking to Eden, and Jackson didn't argue with their request. Kaine was adamant about skipping over the part that asks if anyone objects and I can't blame him.

The lady is sort of a bitch. Those tears could mean a number of things. I hope that she's actually happy for her daughter and those are tears of joy and not tears of disappointment like she tends to do with everything else that involves Eden. Am I being too harsh? Maybe, but I don't trust anyone that could hurt someone as kind as Eden.

I take Ronnie's hand, making sure she stays by my side as we walk towards the limo and slide inside. Kaine and Eden are both smiling, grins so wide Kaine's dimples kick in. "Congratulations to you both. How does it feel being Mr. and Mrs. Montgomery?"

"Surreal," Eden sighs. "I still can't believe it's over."

She squeals when Kaine pulls her onto his lap, a look of peace and happiness on his face. "It's just beginning, Mrs. Montgomery."

"Hmm, I guess you're right."

"I'm always right, vixen."

Ronnie crawls onto my lap, the sexy dress stretching and bunching against her lips. Her fingers trail the nape of my neck, and I settle back into the seat, smiling up at her. "What do you think, future Mrs. Mitchel? Is our story just beginning, too?"

"It is. I was so focused on running away from my past, that I didn't give myself time to look forward to the future. You're my future, Reese."

"You're my everything."

"Stop that," she huffs.

"Hmm, why should I? I thought you didn't want me to lie to you anymore. I thought you wanted me to be myself and to be honest."

"Yeah, but—"

"This is me, Ronnie. The *real* me. I'm broken and chaotic, but I love with all my heart."

She presses her lips to mine, stopping me from saying anything else. I won't complain about that. I love it when she shows me what she wants and isn't afraid to take it for herself. If it were up to me, I would go home with her so we can officially celebrate our engagement. She doesn't seem upset with how it happened, but the thought is still nagging me. I pull back, smirking at the pout of disapproval on her face.

"I'm sorry I didn't make last night more special. I had all these thoughts and plans, but at the same time, I wanted to do it as soon as possible. I promise to take you somewhere nice so we can celebrate."

She shakes her head. "It was you, Reese, that's all that matters. I don't need anything extravagant or grandiose, just you and our friends are plenty. Kaine proposed to Eden in front of us."

"Not by choice," Kaine mumbles. "I sort of had to do it since I couldn't exactly explain away the random jewelry box that fell out of my jacket."

"I know you. You could have easily made something up, but you're like Reese. You wanted to do it as soon as you could, didn't you?"

"I would have married her while we were still in school if it were up to me."

"That's my point. It doesn't matter how it's done. You still made it special in your own way, just like Reese did. It's something I'll always remember."

"I fucking love you," I chuckle, dragging my hands up and down her back, loving the peek of skin along her spine. "Today marks the day where everything starts."

CHAPTER SIXTY-EIGHT

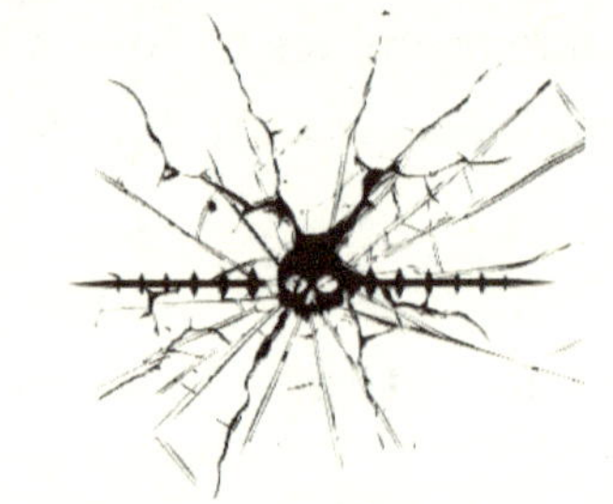

REESE

I clink my spoon against the glass until everyone in the hall goes silent. Kaine frowns up at me while Eden smiles and brushes her fingers through his hair. We never officially said we would be making speeches or anything like that, but the expectation is there, and I don't want to disappoint him or anyone else.

I clear my throat, lightly gripping my glass in my fingers as I shift my gaze from him to everyone staring at me intently. "I just want to say thank you to everyone for coming out and celebrating Kaine and Eden's official union. I think most of you know me. I'm Reese, Kaine's best friend and his voice of reason. I met Kaine when we were kids, a friendship written in the stars, if you can believe it." Most don't get the joke, but Kaine and Eden hide their awkward laughs. "From the moment I saw Kaine, I knew I needed to know him. He felt like a brother I never knew I had, and he was an amazing friend that I didn't realize I needed. He's been through so much on his own, and more with me in his company. I honestly don't know where I would be without him."

I swallow down the lump forming in my throat, my emotions threatening to break through. I wasn't planning to get completely sappy, but it's hard not to when everything I'm saying is true. He's been there for me without even realizing it. He's been my anchor through the turbulent storms of my past and present colliding, and he's held me together like magical glue while I shattered into pieces. Without him, my mind and soul would be divided, broken apart because of the darkness threatening to drag me under. Not even because of Avery, but because I have my own darkness that I'm still trying to work through.

"I've always been very protective of Kaine, so when he showed interest in Eden—one of the sweetest girls I've ever met—I felt like I needed to protect her, too. They both went through a lot last year, which was one of the hardest school years we had. Kaine had his ribs broken and she was adorable, doing everything she could for him, even though he fought her every step of the way. He's so stubborn sometimes. When they decided to get a place together and were packing up to move—"

"Don't!" Kaine gasps.

I laugh, shifting away from him while Eden tries to hold him back. I grin. "He kept arguing with me that he could pack all his shit up himself, which was the farthest thing from the truth, so I ended up having to toss him over my shoulder to get him to listen." His face is beet red now and Eden is smiling from ear to ear, shifting her eyes from Kaine to me. "But that's what friends do, we take care of each other, no matter what."

"Fucking hell," Kaine grumbles, dragging his hands down his face while everyone in the room laughs.

I lean towards him, dropping my voice into a whisper. "I warned you," I say in a sing-song voice.

"You're a dick."

"My little bride," I laugh, stepping back before he gets the chance to take a swing at me. "Anyways, I couldn't be happier for the two of them because they're absolutely perfect for each other. When you find your other half—your *better* half—you hang onto that person no matter what. You do everything for them and love them with all your heart and hope that you're good enough for them in the end."

I look down at Ronnie, at her gorgeous eyes staring up at me with love and admiration.

"It took me a while to figure that out and apply it to myself, but Kaine and Eden have been an inspiration for me, showing me a path that I didn't think I deserved. I don't think I would be where I am today without them both." I raise my glass up, tipping my head up to the ceiling, where the lights flicker. "And to Avery, I know you're listening, you came through for me in the end. Thank you."

I drink, chugging back the burning liquor with everyone's eye fixed on me. *"A little theatrical, but I appreciate it none the less,"* Avery muses.

I smirk, ignoring his comment, and sit back down. Kaine glares daggers at me and Eden laughs. "Is that the story?" She snorts. "You carried him like a fucking bride?"

"I did. He was such a cute bride, too."

"I hate you," Kaine huffs.

"You'd be lost without me." Everyone starts clinking against their plates, cheering for the happy couple. "Looks like you're up."

He rolls his eyes and stands up, holding his hand out to Eden. She looks radiant with her bride's glow, the happiness on her face contagious. He pulls her up against his chest and she just has enough time to place her hands there to stop him from crushing her before he slams his lips against hers. Ronnie sighs next to me and I glance over, noticing the dreamy look on her face.

"That'll be you soon," I whisper, kissing her cheek.

"Yeah? When do you want to get married?"

"Whenever you want to. I'm not in a rush because I want it to be perfect for you in every way. Whatever you want to do, we'll do it."

"Hmm, I think I'd like a spring wedding. I like the flowers coming into bloom."

"Spring it is."

"I don't want a big wedding either. Something small like this would be nice."

"Whatever you want, Ronnie."

She reaches up to cup my cheek, her thumb moving rhythmically across my jaw. "You're too good to me, you know that?"

"Not good enough, but I promise to be better."

"Hmm. Tessa is getting married in November, so you'll have to be my plus one."

"How is Tessa handling everything?"

"She's doing okay. The family hasn't tried to push anything on her quite yet, and Cillian is being pretty supportive with all of it, especially with being thrown into that world without knowing."

"She's got a lot to deal with to try and keep control of it all. Is she willing to go that far?"

"I think so. She doesn't want to run away from this and have someone take over that will start doing the same thing that was done to us. We don't have any immediate family that would try to take it from her, but the families that had fallen in line under my father might try to mutiny."

"Between that and trying to plan a wedding, she's got her hands full."

"When are you going to go with me to meet them? Tessa has asked about you a few times, and even Cillian is curious."

"Why? I'm nothing special."

"Aren't you? You saved my life, Reese. Of course, my sister wants to meet the man that means everything to me. Cillian will be my brother-in-law soon, too, so we need to be nice."

"Is he not nice?"

"I mean, he got a bit friendly with my dad, but I'm not sure if he was just trying to make a good impression on him. I haven't gotten a full read on him yet, but I haven't spent enough time with them to get a proper feel for him."

"Fine, I'll meet your sister."

"She's having a dinner in a few weeks that she invited us to. Will you go?"

"Sure."

Her thumb moves to my lips, gently tugging the bottom one down. I dart my tongue out to lick her and she smiles, humming low in her throat. "I love you."

"I love you, too."

Music starts playing through the speakers and the DJ calls Eden and Kaine out for their first dance. Poor Eden looks nervous with all the attention on her, eyes darting around and her cheeks flaming at the sound of clapping and cheers. Kaine looks like he's in his element, grinning like an idiot as he drags Eden out there.

She squeals in surprise when he spins her around and pulls her into his body to sway to the music. My heart clenches at the enamored look on his face as he stares down at her—at his new bride. At the person who is willing to love him through all the darkness and spend the rest of their life with him.

Ronnie sniffling draws my attention to her, tears welling along her lashes and threatening to break free and smear her pretty makeup. "Are you okay?" I whisper.

She nods, letting out a choked laugh. "Yeah, I'm just...happy for them."

"Are you just happy or...?"

"Maybe a little bit jealous." I don't know why that comment hurts as much as it does, but it's like I just got pricked with a sharp blade. "I'm jealous at how easily Eden shows Kaine how much he cares. It's like she doesn't have to try and there's no secrets there to ruin their relationship."

Now I feel like an asshole.

Her reasoning isn't even close to what I thought it was going to be, and now I sort of feel bad for her and a bit of guilt at the whole thing. I'm in the same boat as her, growing up not trusting anyone around me or showing anyone how much I care about them. It's not like I *didn't* care; I just didn't want to show anyone that side of me and have it been taken as a weakness.

My family would definitely use anyone I care about against me to try and get me to do what they want. I hope they don't think they can pull that shit now, especially after I just wiped out an entire family in a single day and two assholes from another.

If anything, what I've done has still benefited them, and they should take that as my payment to officially be done with the family business. I want out and I refuse to be dragged into more of their bullshit.

"You're trying your best, Ronnie. You've gotten better and I feel like you're slowly opening up to me and letting me into your heart. I'm trying to do the same, too, because I don't want you to ever feel like you can't trust me. I don't want to hide things from you anymore."

"That could be us?"

"That *will* be us."

A small smile tugs at her lips, but I can still see the edge of sadness tugging at her eyes. "I'm...going to use the restroom," she says, carefully pushing back her chair and smoothing her dress down her body.

My eyes follow her the entire way, watching the way her hips sway and the way she tries to keep her shoulders back to show more confidence than she's feeling. Before I realize it, my own chair is scraping back, louder than I expected it to be, and drawing the attention of Kaine.

He quirks a brow, drifting his eyes towards the doorway where Ronnie is slipping through. A huge grin spreads across his face and he nods, jerking his head towards the door. A subtle acknowledgement of where my head is at. It's not like I need his permission to slip away for a little bit, but it's still nice to know that he agrees with my actions and supports me, even on his wedding day.

I roll my eyes, a smirk sliding onto my face as I strip off the jacket of my suit and head for the doors. I can feel a few people watching me, but I don't give a fuck. They can think what they want of me, but to their eyes, it should just look like I'm going to comfort my fiancé when she's crying.

I *plan* to comfort her.

I have every intention of making her happy and feeling better than how she's feeling now. She doesn't need to feel guilty for her emotions because they're natural, especially after everything we've been through.

A few people linger in the hallways, heading back into the main area. My eyes scan every corner as I make my way towards the bathrooms to wait for my little rabbit to come out.

I watch, waiting patiently until she finally steps out, brushing loose strands of hair behind her ear. Her eyes meet mine and she freezes, a small line forming between her brows.

"Reese, what are you—"

"Run, little rabbit," I purr, undoing the top button on my shirt.

Her eyes widen, mouth popping open in surprise. Her throat bobs on a swallow, her gaze drifting around in slight panic. "Reese—"

"Ten."

"Reese, we can't."

"Nine." Another button; another step towards her. "Eight."

"You're insane," she whispers shakily, her body coiling on instinct, ready to flee.

"For you I am. Seven."

A bigger step towards her has her finally reacting, a squeal ripping through her lungs, followed by a cackle of laughter at the sound of her heels scrambling against the tile floor in her attempt at escaping me.

She's not really trying, but it's an effort at least. The rabbit likes the chase, but she loves getting caught more. At least when it's *her* monster chasing her.

"Six!" I call out, smiling at the fact she went down the hall I expected her to. I know for a fact it's a dead end, so my prey is most definitely caught at this point. I walk into the opening, seeing her further down, stopping when she reaches the wall. "Five."

She wheels around, eyes wide and chest heaving when she realizes the trouble she's in now. It's sort of adorable seeing her vulnerable like this, mainly because we both know she's safe. A game like this shouldn't bring fear, only excitement.

"There's nowhere for you to go, Ronnie," I croon, slowly unbuttoning the rest of my shirt. Her eyes drift down to my chest, her eyes bowing slightly when they land on the new marks marring my skin. Her shoulders slump, making me pause my steps.

I swallow the lump forming in my throat at the look of sadness on her face. These marks are a reminder of one of our darker times, one I want us both to move on from. I don't want her to feel guilt or sadness when she looks at me in general, but least of all when she looks at my body.

This body is no longer just mine, it's hers as well. I want her to find comfort in my embrace and to feel confident in telling me everything she wants out of life, especially if it includes me.

"Don't," I say, the one word snapping her attention from my chest, back up to my face. "I know that look, Ronnie. This was never your fault." I close the distance between us, tucking her into the dark corridor. Her fingers reach out towards me, tentatively touching the swirling darkness marking my skin. "Do they bother you?"

She shakes her head. "No," she whispers. "I think they suit you, but it still makes me sad to know that I almost lost you that night."

"I'm right here. I'm not going anywhere, Ronnie." Her hand splays over my heart, head tipping back to look at me. I step into her, trailing both my hands up the side of her neck to cup her cheeks, forcing her eyes to stay locked on me. "I love you. I'll always love you, whether that's in this lifetime or the next, that'll never change. You own every piece of me, including my soul."

"Reese," she whimpers, lip trembling as her eyes begin to glisten.

I press my lips to hers, tentatively at first. She parts her mouth, teasing her tongue against the seam of my mouth until I give her access. We both moan into each other, her hands drifting down my chest to scramble with the belt still wrapped around my waist.

I moan when she bites down on my lip, tugging it hard enough to make it sting. A small sigh slips out of me when she finally gets my pants undone, freeing my aching cock from the confines of the material.

My fingers drag down her sides while my mouth moves along her jaw. I love the way she tips her head, giving me access to her throat like a needy please. Bunching the material of her dress along her thighs, I grip into her ass and hoist her up onto my hips, driving into her with one brutal thrust.

Her head thumps against the wall, mouth parting on a small moan as she takes me completely. Fuck, she feels so good. So fucking warm and tight and a perfect fit for me. She's amazing in every single way, her body made for me.

Her body trembles against mine as I stay still, giving her a few seconds to adjust and catch her breath while my own heart is thumping wildly. It feels like it'll burst out of my chest from the simple pleasure of being buried inside of her.

I could die right now, and I would be the happiest I've ever been. All my life I thought I was broken beyond repair, incapable of being loved and loving in return. This girl changed me, opened her heart and soul to me, and showed me that I was more than I was made to believe.

"I love you," I groan, nipping at her neck as I slowly draw out of her and slam back in, reveling in the way her body tenses and relaxes against me. Her legs curl around my hips, heels digging into my ass to draw me closer.

"I—I love you, too. I love you so fucking much, Reese. Fuck, harder."

"Yeah? You want harder?" I pant, snapping my hips into her and driving into her deeper. A gurgled cry crawls up her throat, her nails digging into my shoulders. Her skin is hot against mine, dampening with every thrust into her. “How’s that, rabbit? How does it feel to be trapped by me? Pinned and fucked until you’re crying out my name.”

“Oh, god.”

I stop. “*My* name.”

“Reese,” she whispers.

“Louder.”

“Reese!”

Long gone is the worry that we’ll be seen or heard, her voice now trembling and breathy as she chants my name, over and over. I’m such a needy shit, wanting such petty things just to boost my ego, but I love that she doesn’t question it or argue, giving into my demands like the good fucking girl that she is.

“Fuck, Reese, I’m coming.”

“That’s it, baby. Come all over my cock. Fucking strangle it.”

She does just that, ripping a grunt of surprise at just how vicious her orgasm hits me. Even if I wanted this to last, to drag on for hours, I couldn’t with the way she’s clamping around me like a vice. I come, spilling into her in hot waves until we’re both spent and panting, clinging to each other. My own legs are trembling as my body presses into hers, pinning her to the wall. She’s trying so hard to stay wrapped around me, her arms resting limply against my shoulders.

“Would you ever want kids?”

I cringe internally at the fact I just fucking asked that. It was never on my mind before, something I actually wanted to stay as far away from because I didn’t think I would ever be capable of being a good father to anyone. How am I supposed to take care of someone who relies on me when I can barely take care of myself. Her body stiffening against mine makes me think that the question should have stayed buried, never to see the light of day.

"Do you?" She asks, surprising me enough to pull back at look at her. There isn't anger or sadness on her face, more like mild curiosity.

"I—I don't think I did before, but now...I don't know. I think if it's something you want in the future, then I would be okay with it now. I don't know if I would be a good dad though."

A smile pulls at her lips, and she lifts her hand to cup my cheek. "You're an idiot if you think you wouldn't be the best dad ever. If you want kids in the future, then we'll have kids. I want a life with you, Reese, and whatever that life includes, I'm okay with it. If you decide you don't want any, then we won't have any. All that matters to me is you."

"You mean that?"

"Of course I do. I'm in this forever, Reese."

She laughs when I press my lips against hers and curls her arms around my neck, locking me to her. This kiss feels different, like a true binding between us. I didn't think it was possible to love someone more, but she keeps surprising me. I think she'll *keep* surprising me, and the love between us will be endless, something we'll never be able to put a limit on.

I'm not complaining in the slightest. It's nice to know that I have something to look forward to. Multiple somethings by the sound of it. I feel fucking giddy. For the first time in my life, I feel beyond happy. Happy enough that I could literally swing this girl around to show her just how happy I am.

"Nice ass!"

"God fucking damn it," I grumble, turning my head to glare at Kaine. He's standing at the end of the hall, a massive grin on his face and a blushing Eden next to him. She's clinging to his arm, trying and failing to avoid looking at us. "I thought you didn't like her checking out other guys!"

"Meh, it's her wedding day. If she wants to see your ass, I'll let her just this once."

"Oh my god," Ronnie laughs, burying her face in my chest.

"He knew I was coming to find you. The little fucker probably stalked us out here."

"Come on you two! We're doing cake!"

Eden squeals ahead of the sound of Kaine's feet thumping against the tile as he chases after her, both their laughter echoing in the hall. "They're ridiculous," Ronnie laughs.

"They're either going to keep us young or age us well before out time." I slowly lower her to the ground, helping her straighten out her dress and her hair before putting myself back together. She smiles when I hold out my hand to her. Every time she places her hand in mine without hesitation, it sends a flutter of joy through me. "Come on, future Mrs. Mitchel."

EPILOGUE

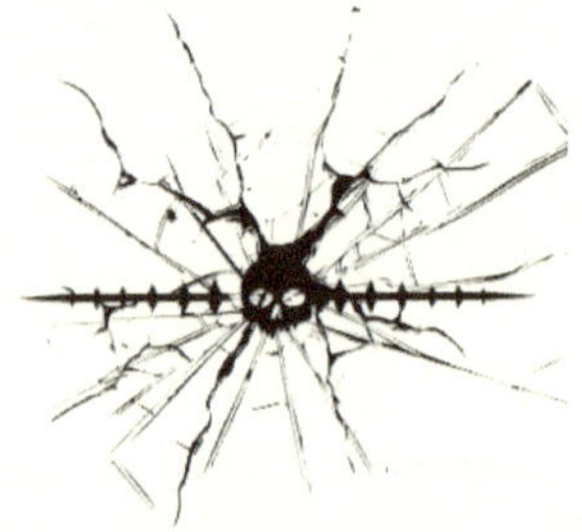

REESE

TWO WEEKS LATER

"We need to go or we're going to be late!" I walk into the bedroom to find Ronnie on the floor playing with the kitten I got her. The little demon darts around her, following the stupid string toy she's obsessed with. The moment she sees me, she jumps towards me with her hackles up, trying to make herself look tough. "Ronnie," I sigh.

"She wanted to play!"

"She always wants to play. Come on. Get up and get dressed. We need to be at your sister's house in like twenty minutes."

Her eyes widen. "Oh, fuck. It's already that late?"

"Yes," I laugh, plopping down on the floor and snagging the kitten so Ronnie can get ready without the distraction.

I ended up caving and got a cat. Well, I didn't *get* a cat, the cat found me. It was by one of the dumpsters outside my gym, and just like Holland said, the cat distribution system worked its magic. She was a pathetic little thing and looked rough. I thought that Ronnie might be mad that I brought a stray home, but she squealed like a child and snagged her from me before I even got the chance to explain what happened. She was out the door with my credit card ten minutes later, on her way to buy our new baby some supplies.

Little Mia is adorable when she's not being a terror. She gets into everything and runs around at the ass crack of dawn, bursting into our room and yowling until I either get up and feed her or lock her up in the bathroom to get a bit more sleep. She's a little shit, but I do love her, and she makes Ronnie extremely happy.

"Eden and Kaine are coming home tomorrow, right?" Ronnie asks as she jogs towards the bathroom.

"Yeah. I'm picking them up from the airport at one."

She peeks back around the corner, her hands in her hair as she frantically tries to put it up into some weird messy bun on her head. The look always makes me laugh because of how it flops around, making her look like the rabbit I claim her to be.

"Can I come with you?"

"Don't you have to work?"

She shakes her head, regretting it when half her hair slips through her fingers. She huffs, grabbing the strands to try again.

"I took tomorrow off. I wanted to hang out with Eden to see how her trip was."

"Yeah, you can come." Her lip twitches. "Don't start," I snort. "We don't have time for that."

"Maybe if you weren't a marathon man, you'd be better at quickies."

"I thought you liked how thorough I am."

"Oh, I do, but it also sucks when I want it and we have to go somewhere."

"Hmm, I guess we'll have to start practicing." The poor girl's eyes actually light up, a smile spreading across her face. "Just not right now." I feel bad when her face falls and those perfect lips pout out.

"Fine, but when we get home—"

"When we get home, I'm going to fuck you until your legs are shaking and your voice is hoarse from screaming my name. I might even push it far enough that you'll pass the fuck out, Ronnie. Don't test me. If I have time to eat a meal and fuck you senseless, I'm going to do just that."

She gulps, the sound loud enough that it reaches my ears and her entire neck and face begin to turn red. She doesn't say anything, snapping her gaping mouth closed and slipping back into the bathroom.

I grin like an idiot, playing with Mia and letting her attack my fingers with her little needle teeth and claws. It's way too entertaining to rile her up like that. She'll be thinking about it all night, especially if I keep teasing her through the night with seductive words and gentle touches. She'll be a puddle before we even get back home. Nice and wet and pliable, just how I like her.

By the time Ronnie emerges from the bathroom, Mia is tuckered out, passed out on her back with her tiny eyes closed and her mouth slightly open. We're late already, and I'm surprised Tessa hasn't messaged her to see where the fuck we are. Tessa might even think that I'm not planning to go, having avoided the last few dinner invites and get-togethers over the last month. I've had no desire to meet her or hang out with her and her weird fiancé.

The fact he didn't feel threatened by Misha in the slightest when he met him puts me on edge. No one with a brain wouldn't feel some form of apprehension with the way he spoke of his daughters and how he was treating Ronnie.

He's already on my shit list and I haven't even met the guy. Ronnie says he seems okay, just a bit closed off at times, but he tries to be friendly for the most part. I'm curious what he actually thinks of the whole situation that Tessa has been thrown into. I know Ronnie would have been able to handle it, the queen that she is, but I don't know anything about Tessa other than what Ronnie told me. Those stories weren't all good either.

The fact she left her sister to fend for herself with a monster like Misha as her father makes me sick to my stomach. I understand the impulsive need she had to get out of there, but why wouldn't she just take Ronnie with her? Why couldn't she muster up the courage to save her sister instead of leaving her to survive the monsters that didn't think anything good of her.

If I have to protect Ronnie from her own sister, I will. I don't give a fuck about any of it. No one is going to threaten what

Ronnie is trying to accomplish and the life we're trying to create for ourselves. We have a child now for fuck's sake. Sure, she's furry and has four legs, but she's still our baby and we love her.

"Okay, I'm ready to go."

"Damn." My eyes skate across her entire body, drinking in every inch of her gorgeous body. The dark jeans cling to her legs, showing off that perfect ass of hers. The tank top is low cut, revealing plenty of cleavage. She grabs a jacket from the closet, and I bounce to my feet, grabbing her arm to stop her.

"What's wrong?"

I lean down and kiss the swell of her breasts, trailing my mouth and tongue across her collar bone and up the column of her neck. She shudders against me, her fingers digging into my biceps as she leans into me. "Hmm, that's better," I murmur, nipping at her jaw and pulling her earlobe into my mouth. She sways towards me when I pull back, her face flush just from that small encounter. That's what I like to see. Those are the reactions that keep me begging for more. "Now we can go."

"That's—that's not fair."

"You only get a taste, Ronnie."

"Bye, Mia." She crouches down beside the cat, petting her gently between her eyes with her finger. Mia chokes out a little meow and starts purring, flopping onto her side. "She's so cute."

"She really is. The perfect child that shits in a box."

She mumbles something under her breath and pushes herself back to her feet, turning and punching me lightly in the gut. "Ladies don't shit."

I arch a brow. "Really? I think the toilet bowl after you've had Taco Bell would disagree."

She gasps. "How dare you."

"Poo-Pourri is staying in business because of you."

"You're an asshole."

"Everybody poops, Ronnie," I laugh. She stomps out of the room, shoving her arms into the jacket. I follow her out into the main area, watching her collect her things and shoving everything into her purse. She pauses at the door and turns her head to look at me. "What?" I snort.

"Let's go," she says, shaking her head.

She heads towards the elevator while I lock the door. It pings open pretty quickly and I have to rush to it because the little shit doesn't try to hold it open for me. I slam my palm into the door, pushing it back open while I glare at her. I catch the small twitch of her lips before she turns to stare at the corner. I step into the box, turn and push the button to the lobby.

"Keep up the shenanigans and you're going to get punished later," I murmur, facing the doors. I still catch her blurred reflection in the steel, her head turning to look at me. Even if I couldn't see her turn my way, I can *feel* her. I've always been able to feel her, but it seems to be more obvious now, like whatever Avery's touch has done to me is somehow heightening my senses.

She stays quiet the whole ride down, not even responding to my comment. Her lagging behind me is pissing me off a bit, so I drop into step with her and drape my arm across her shoulders. Her warmth radiates into me and her body stiffens slightly, as though anticipating me actually doing something to her. She can't still be mad about the poop comment, right?

I walk her right up to the passenger door, gripping into her when she tries to pull away from me. "Are you mad?" I finally ask.

"No," she whispers.

"Then why are you being so quiet?"

"I don't know. I guess I just find it weird sometimes when you can talk freely about stuff like that. Girls tend to just keep things like that to themselves. You know, keep the illusion that we're these perfect beings that always smell like roses."

"You're perfect no matter what. You could be sick, puking all over the place with snot and crusty boogers in your nose, and I would still love you and take care of you. You're human, Ronnie. You don't need to pretend with me, and any guy that's squeamish about shit like that doesn't deserve to own a dick and call themselves a man. Your perfect whether you look perfect or show all your imperfections."

"Why do you have to say shit like that," she groans.

"Because it's true. Because I want you to stop being so guarded about what you say or do around me. I want all of you. All your joys and happiness and all your flaws and darkness." I spin her around and pin her between my body and the truck, sliding my leg between her thighs. Her entire body trembles and sinks down, her head thunking against the glass on the door. "Don't ever hide from me." She tries to turn away but I grip her jaw, forcing her gaze to stay locked on mine. "Do not look away from me."

"I—I won't."

"Promise me."

"I promise, Reese."

I tease her a bit more, rubbing my knee into the seam of her jeans and pulling a whimper from her lips. I don't think it would take much to get her there, but we really don't have time and I feel bad. I hate edging her and not following through. Fuck it.

She gasps when I shove my hand down her pants, curling my fingers into her. She's soaked; her panties and her pussy, my fingers gliding right into her. "Look at you, primed for me, aren't you?" A small moan slips from her lips. "Do you want me to make you come?"

"Reese," she pants when I shove into her.

"That's it, baby. I love it when you say my name like that."

"Oh, god."

"Who's finger fucking you?"

"What—"

"Is it god?"

"No," she whimpers. "Reese!"

I don't care that we're out in public. I don't fucking care that anyone could walk by right now and see us. Her legs tremble and a whimpering moan slips from her lips. I press my mouth to hers, stifling her voice. I can taste my name on her lips, the muffled word caressing my tongue as she comes undone on my fingers.

She's panting, barely keeping herself up against the side of the truck. "Get in the truck."

She swallows, gripping into the hood of the truck now to give me room to open the door for her. I still hold her, hanging onto her so she doesn't collapse on her unsteady legs. Once she's settled into her seat, I pull my fingers into my mouth, tasting her. A moan rumbles in my throat, pulling her attention to me. Her eyes widen and I hold her gaze, licking each finger clean while she stares at me.

She jumps slightly when I close the door on her. The walk around the front of the truck is beyond uncomfortable, and I try and fail to adjust my cock into a more comfortable position. I basically edged myself while trying to not do that to her. It's going to be a very uncomfortable car ride.

The moment I pull out onto the street, she's reaching over to take my hand in hers, pulling it onto her lap. Stealing a glance at her, I can't help but smile at the look of peace on her face while she watches the buildings flash by. She cradles my hand in both of hers, her soft skin radiating warmth into me. Her thumbs gently graze the back of my hand and I give her a little squeeze. She turns to me, eyes soft and loving, and a beautiful smile spreads across her face.

"Are you in a better mood now?" She bites her lower lip and nods her head. "Good. I'm glad I satisfied you then."

"You always do," she muses. "You're *very* good at satisfying me."

The way she says it has heat spreading through my body, her tone seductive and desperate for more. Fuck, I really wish I could just pull the car over, drag her onto my lap, and fuck the need out of her. If she had gotten ready when I asked her to originally, we would have had more time to play. Now I'm stuck with a raging boner while we drive to her sister's house for a dinner I don't even want to go to. Hopefully, she doesn't want to stay too long, and we can go home and pick up where we left off.

The drive is short enough, a decent sized home on the outer edge of the city. Ronnie still gawks at it like it's the most amazing thing ever, even though she grew up in a home four times the size of this one. Is it the architecture? It has a bit more of a historical feel to it without seeming ostentatious, but I thought Ronnie preferred more modern feel to buildings. Huh, learning something new about her every day.

"It's pretty," she says when I open the door for her and hold out my hand to help her out.

"It looks…weathered."

She shakes her head with a smirk. "It has character," she snorts.

She slides her hand into the crook of my elbow as we walk up to the home. "Is this the sort of home you like? To live in I mean."

"I wouldn't say no to a place like this, but old houses sort of creep me out a bit, too. What if they're haunted?"

I laugh, playfully digging my fingers into her ribs. "I'll protect you from the ghosts."

She tries to squirm away, but I pin her to me, grabbing her arm before she can make it too far. She quickly brushes her hand over her hair and outfit and pulls in a deep breath before knocking at the door.

"Why are you nervous? You've been here before so none of this should be surprising."

"I'm nervous for *you*. Please behave yourself. I know you're not a huge fan of Tessa, but I want you to at least give her a chance."

"No promises."

"Reese—"

Her argument is cut short when the door opens, revealing who I assume is Tessa. She sort of looks like Ronnie, lighter brown hair, same shaped eyes as her, but her other features seem harsher—more uninviting. She looks like her father, which just ticks her up on the shit list for me.

She's smiling as she looks at Ronnie, but the smile falls slightly when she glances up at me. She swallows, holding out her hand to me. "You must be Reese. Ronnie has told me so much about you."

I stare at her hand until it begins to shake and she lowers it awkwardly. Ronnie elbows me in the gut but I ignore it. I said I would be civil, not nice. Tessa needs to earn my kindness at this point because she hasn't done enough good in my eyes to warrant forgetting the bad.

Tessa steps out of the way and motions us inside. "I can take your coats."

"I'm good," I murmur as Ronnie hands hers over. She full on glares at me, mouthing for me to be nice. I ignore her, glancing around the entrance to get a feel for the girl and what she's like.

The place doesn't feel as inviting as I expected, generic décor littering the place. The walls have some ugly ass paintings on them, and useless knickknacks that seem extremely out of place.

Tessa notices me staring at the so-called art and smiles, pointing at it. "Do you like them? I did them myself."

I snap my mouth closed on the comment I was about to make, choking down the insult. "They're...different," I say, settling for something less vicious.

There's no emotion behind the paintings at all. Even with abstract art there should be...something. I should *feel* something. This is just a jumbled mess of depression with no rhyme or reason to the strokes or colours. They don't even mesh well together or complement each other in any way. I'm not an artist by any means, but I think I could do something better with my eyes closed and mashed up fruits.

"I want to say thank you for saving Ronnie. I didn't know what to do to get her out of there myself."

"Hmm, at least you were finally useful for something."

"Reese!" Ronnie snaps, but Tessa holds up her hand to stop her.

"It's fine. I'm assuming you told him everything, and I can't expect him to forgive me as easily as you have, Ronnie." She motions for us to follow her down the hall, the smell of food already wafting through the home. "Hopefully you get along better with my fiancé than you do me," she laughs. He's in the kitchen when we walk in, busying himself at the stove, which I'll admit surprises me. "Reese, this is my fiancé, Cillian Grant. Cillian, this is Ronnie's..." She glances back at Ronnie and gives her a smile. "Her fiancé, Reese Mitchel."

He doesn't turn right away, but I notice his back stiffen and the muscles flexing with pent up tension. A prickling sensation skitters up my spine, making the fine hairs on the back of my neck stand on end. Something is wrong. I don't know what it is but there's a warning bell going off in my head. Is it a reaper? Is this Avery's way of telling me that the man in front of me is possessed by one of his own?

Cillian sets down a spoon on the counter and slowly turns around. The blood in my veins turns to ice when he faces me fully, his eyes locking on mine, sinister, with the fake promise of kindness. He smiles, but I see it for what it is and it's not warm and inviting, it's smug. This little fuck. This is so much worse than a reaper.

"Nice to see you, Reese," he says, giving his head a small bob in acknowledgement. See me, not meet me. Mother fucker. "Ronnie, it's so good to see you again. How have you been?" Every instinct in me is screaming to step in front of her, to stop her from moving towards him to shake his hand. "Aw, come here." He pulls her into him, wrapping his arms around her. I just stare at the exchange, trying my best not to tear through this room towards him and rip his fucking arms from his body.

"Cillian," I say through gritted teeth. Without knowing what he's playing at, I can't say or do anything. If I do, I could be putting Ronnie at risk. Why is Tessa with him? How the fuck did these two meet? I *know* Cillian and none of this makes sense. I grab Ronnie when he finally lets her go and pull her into me, wanting nothing more than to fucking leave now and take her *and* Tessa with me.

"I hope you're hungry," he says, feigning that smile again. "I can't wait to chat with you and get to know you."

This is beyond fucked. I can feel Ronnie staring at me, trying to figure out why my body is in full fight-mode, but I can't tell her until I figure this out for myself. I can't tell her and risk her saying something which could create a snowball of problems. Cillian Grant. Cillian, with eyes so familiar they're burned into my soul. Using a false name to not draw attention to who and what he is, something I'm sure my uncle told him would work. Cillian Brennan...is my cousin, and the heir to Declan's empire.

Fuck me, this isn't over. Not even close.

AUTHOR NOTE

I hope you enjoyed SHATTER, book 2 in the Souls Collide Trilogy.

Book 3 will be available soon for pre-order.

You can stay up to date on all my new releases and upcoming books by following me on socials and joining my newsletter. You can access everything through my linktree.

https://linktr.ee/authormelissasilva

If you enjoyed this book, I would love it if you left a review. You can dive into my other books as well, all linked in my linktree.

The Hunting Saga (4 books)

The Forgotten Gods Series

The Forbidden Powers Series (8 books)

Confession

Fated Flames

www.ingramcontent.com/pod-product-compliance
Lightning Source LLC
LaVergne TN
LVHW041051080826
845145LV00007B/1529

* 9 7 8 1 9 9 8 5 0 0 3 1 4 *